STIFFS AND SWINE

This Large Print Book carries the
Seal of Approval of N.A.V.H.

A SUPPER CLUB MYSTERY

STIFFS AND SWINE

J. B. STANLEY

WHEELER PUBLISHING
A part of Gale, Cengage Learning

GALE
CENGAGE Learning·

Detroit • New York • San Francisco • New Haven, Conn • Waterville, Maine • London

GALE
CENGAGE Learning

LIBRARY OF CONGRESS CATALOGING-IN-PUBLICATION DATA

Stanley, J. B.
    Stiffs and swine / by J.B. Stanley.
        p. cm. — (A supper club mystery series) (Wheeler
    Publishing large print cozy mystery)
    ISBN-13: 978-1-59722-887-9 (pbk. : alk. paper)
    ISBN-10: 1-59722-887-7 (pbk. : alk. paper)
    1. Henry, James (Fictitious character)—Fiction.
    2. Librarians—Fiction. 3. Overweight men—Fiction.
    4. Shenandoah River Valley (Va. and W. Va.)—Fiction.
    5. Dieters—Fiction. 6. Clubs—Fiction. 7. Large type books.
    I. Title.
    PS3619.T3655S75 2009
    813'.6—dc22   2008046323

Published in 2009 by arrangement with Midnight Ink, an imprint of Llewellyn Publications Woodbury, MN 55125-2989, USA.

Printed in the United States of America
1 2 3 4 5 6 7 13 12 11 10 09

For my brothers, Mead and John

(and to Porkfest —
may it live on in infamy)

The only time to eat diet food is while you're waiting for the steak to cook.

— JULIA CHILD

ONE:
TUNA CASSEROLE

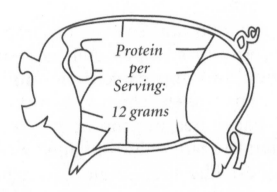

James Henry, head librarian of the Shenandoah County Library system, counted out five quarters. He hoped to use the vacuum at the self-service car wash to rid his aged white Bronco of the sand that had accumulated on the floor mats during his vacation at Virginia Beach. There had been a thunderstorm on the last afternoon of his trip, and the sand that had been dampened and clumped into the mats' grids had the consistency of a bowl of grits.

As he grumbled over the exorbitant cost

of five minutes' worth of vacuuming time, James removed the snakelike hose from the tin base, slid the quarters into the slot, and expectantly waited for the vacuum to roar to life. When it remained silent, he jammed his index finger on the return change button and was given nothing for his effort. He assaulted the button, pushing vigorously, but the machine refused to relinquish a single quarter.

Now, irritated and sweaty, he draped the vacuum hose in a sloppy coil back onto its steel hook and approached the dollar-bill changer. His wallet, which was stuffed with slips of paper bearing the names of books he wanted to read, only contained a ten and two singles. The first single had a fleabite on its top left-hand corner that was approximately three millimeters in size, and the machine spit it out like a child rejecting a forkful of Brussels sprouts.

The second single must have passed through the hands of an origami artist. It appeared to have been folded horizontally and vertically, balled into a monetary knot, and stained by coin dust and dirty fingers before James received it in change from a gas station outside of Norfolk. In addition to the worn paper, the bill had been decorated with a woman's name written in bubbly letters, a drawing of cartoon lips, and a series of *x*'s and *o*'s. The bill changer began refusing the dollar the second James placed its edge inside the machine. He tried again. The machine ejected the bill so rapidly that it fluttered to the ground before James could catch it.

"Look here, you!" He pointed a threatening finger at the machine and made one last attempt to straighten out the dollar's kinks against the lip of the bill changer. Taking a deep breath, he whispered, "Just take it. Take the damn dollar." He pushed the bill in. The machine pushed it out. In. Out. In. Out.

"Damn it!" James hit the bill changer with the palm of his hand and then stuffed the dollar back inside his wallet.

"You don't look very relaxed for a man fresh back from a week at the beach," an amused voice said from the interior of a sheriff's department cruiser. "Am I going to have to run you in for property damage?"

James smiled, delighted to see the lovely face of his friend, Lucy Hanover. As usual, her beautiful skin radiated good health, and her large, cornflower-blue eyes sparkled with good humor. Her caramel hair was pulled into a tight French twist, and the sophisticated hairstyle allowed James to gape over how thin Lucy's face had become since the beginning of the summer.

"Have you lost more weight?" he asked her. "Your face . . ."

She nodded. "I'm doing a protein diet right now. It's really helped me get toned, and I'm not hungry on it. Maybe the rest of the supper club should give it a try." She examined herself in the rearview mirror. "I think gorging on all that Mexican food over the winter may not have been the best idea for a dieting group. Between the enchiladas and the donuts at the station all spring, this summer has been all about being disciplined."

"Those enchiladas tasted good going down," James said as he eyed her uniform, which consisted of beige pants and a chocolate-brown shirt bearing the embroidered shield just below the shoulder. He took a step closer to the brown cruiser, noting how bright the yellow star painted on the driver's door appeared against the dark background, and peered into the window at the gun belt strapped around Lucy's waist.

"Wow!" He looked her over, unaware that his blatant observation of her trimmer figure could be perceived as too forward or even downright rude. Luckily for James, Lucy was too flattered by his attention to be offended.

"It's been awhile since we've all been together," she said, clearly pleased to be the source of James's admiration. She turned off the car engine and relaxed in her seat. "I'm excited about getting back to our regular dinner meetings tomorrow night."

"Me too," James replied. "I can't believe how busy we've all been. I guess we all needed a change of scenery. Every one of us has been out of town — just on different weekends."

"Speaking of gettin' out of Dodge, how *was* the beach?" Lucy's tone was purely conversational, but the brief blaze that entered her eyes warned James that a full interrogation was imminent. When he hesitated, she quickly added, "Did Murphy go with you?"

Here it was: the moment James had dreaded for over five months. He was finally going to have to tell Lucy that Murphy Alistair, editor and reporter of the *Shenandoah Star Ledger,* was officially his girlfriend. The supper club members knew that they had been dating, but James had never made it clear that they were serious enough a couple to take a vacation together.

In truth, James had had a wonderful

spring with Murphy. They went to the movies, local plays, music shows, and a slew of events all over the Valley so that Murphy could glean material for her articles. When they weren't hiding away in a mountain inn or browsing antique shops or farmers' markets, they were at work. They rarely spoke on the phone during the day, but after James left the library, he often went straight to Murphy's. In her neat and tasteful apartment, they shared delicious meals and then made love with the windows open. Soft music swirled through her bedroom, and the stars perched so low in the summer sky that James felt as though they were in danger of being blown away by the fan rotating on the sill.

The only odd thing about their time together was that Murphy preferred that James not spend the entire night with her. She was working on a book, she had told him enigmatically, and did her best writing late at night. When he asked what it was about, she told him it was a work of fiction and that she'd tell him all about it once it was finished. James knew that many people had aspirations to write a book but found that their dreams never materialized into reality, so he didn't take Murphy's claim about being a novelist too seriously. Still, he respected her desire to give it a shot, and so he sneaked back home before midnight, feeling much younger than his years as he crept up the squeaky stairs to his bedroom.

All in all, James and Murphy had shared five blissful months together. And to James, the best part was that they never, ever argued.

That is, until Murphy arrived at the beach to spend the Fourth of July weekend with him.

James had been alone for the first four days of his vacation week. Because of the multitude of responsibilities required to operate a daily newspaper, Murphy could only take a few days off work. And though James happily anticipated her appearance on Friday, he was utterly content at the beach without company. He slept late, took leisurely strolls, and let the days slip by as he read book after book and drank giant cups of iced coffee.

Though he hadn't been aware of it until he left Quincy's Gap behind, James had desperately felt in need of some downtime. After all, he and his supper club friends had become embroiled in yet another murder case over the winter, and his relationship with Lucy Hanover had not taken the romantic turn he had once hoped it would.

Instead, Lucy had fallen head over heels for a hunky aspiring sheriff's deputy and dropped James like a rock. And even though Lucy later regretted her decision to chase after the handsome deputy, James rejected her appeals to give their relationship another try. It was too late anyway, as James was already involved with Murphy.

In addition to hunting down a murderer and coping with romantic upheaval, James's home had undergone a major kitchen and bathroom makeover. The house and yard had been a mess, and Jackson Henry, James's father, had hired an assistant. Together, the pair of them had banged and clattered well before six each morning. Exhausted, James was almost grateful that Jackson had reverted to his hermitlike life-style in order to produce new paintings to be sold from a famed D.C. gallery. His temperamental parent locked himself in his shed for hours every day, only surfacing for meals or to receive visits from Milla, the owner of Fix 'n Freeze, a company revolving around cooking classes and small-scale catering.

Milla had become such a regular fixture in the Henry home that James often wondered if she would close her business in New Market and conduct her classes from the Henry's cozy kitchen instead. Not that James was complaining, but after an entire spring of Milla's fantastic cooking, he had packed on at least ten of the twenty-plus pounds he had lost the year before.

Still, Murphy didn't seem to mind the expansion of doughy flesh that had appeared around James's middle, and he was grateful that she didn't complain about his preference to make love with the lights off. Recently, however, it seemed to be the only thing she didn't complain about. During their three days together at the beach, Murphy had been bossy and sulky, and had displayed an irrational jealousy every time a pretty girl walked by them on the beach.

"Are you done staring at that girl?" Murphy had barked when an attractive young woman wearing a pink bikini and matching pink headband sauntered past them during the first afternoon of Murphy's arrival.

"I was just looking at her tattoo," James had responded honestly. "She just seemed too preppy to have the lyrics of one of those gangster rap songs tattooed across her shoulder blade."

Murphy had scowled. "You checked her out long enough to see whether the tattoo artist had spelled everything correctly, that's for sure!"

"Isn't people-watching part of the beach experience?" James had said, trying to placate his girlfriend. "You know, making comments on people's suits, their sunburns, tattoos, cute kids?"

Ignoring him, Murphy had strode down to the water and, garnering plenty of stares for her own trim body and sun-streaked hair, dove into the Atlantic and begun to swim away from the shore with such confident strokes that it seemed as though she never planned to return.

After their tiff at the beach, Murphy had nagged James for allowing his hotel room to become untidy and demanded that he reduce the level of air conditioning. Once he had straightened the room and set the temperature gauge to her satisfaction, she insisted on sitting on the balcony and planning every second of their next two days.

"Can't we just relax and do things as we feel like it?" James didn't like to follow a schedule when he was on vacation. "If we run around and check off everything you've got listed here, we'll be exhausted!"

"Well, I want to visit the lighthouse *and* rent jet skis." Murphy had tossed some brochures onto the table. "And I haven't been to the battleship *Wisconsin* in years. I'm going to write a couple of travel articles

18

on the Norfolk area while I'm here. I've been so busy editing my manu—" She had halted abruptly and then pointed at him. "You're a guy, you should like military history."

James had bristled. He liked all kinds of history, but would rather read about it on the beach than traipse around a battleship beneath a blazing August sun alongside hundreds of other perspiring tourists. Eventually, Murphy wore him down and he agreed to spend Saturday and Sunday as she saw fit, but he didn't enjoy himself, and there had been nothing romantic about their time together.

"Guess we're not quite ready to buy a house with a picket fence and have an army of kids," Murphy had joked at the end of their weekend, but James saw no humor in their situation. They had bickered and snapped at one another too many times in such a short interval, and James spent the entire drive home wondering whether he and Murphy were as compatible as he had once believed. She had suddenly become jealous, controlling, and insecure, but he had no idea why.

When he had asked her about her atypical behavior, Murphy had brushed him off and claimed he was exaggerating the situation.

However, since they had returned to Quincy's Gap, her demeanor had remained crotchety at best. James was worried that she was keeping something from him, but Murphy had insisted that he was overreacting and being paranoid. Still, they had not spent the night together since their botched holiday weekend, and that said a lot to him about Murphy's sudden desire for space.

"Yoo-hoo!" Lucy waved her hand at James, forcing him back to the present moment. "Planet Earth calling. You ready to land your rocket and answer my question?"

James started. "Yes," he answered, more tersely than he intended. "Murphy came for the last few days. It's just that things didn't turn out as I had hoped they would."

A glimmer appeared in Lucy's blue eyes. "That's too bad," she said without a trace of sincerity, and then her expression grew cloudy. "Guess things rarely end up how we hope they will."

The pair fell silent, and just as James searched for an excuse to continue abusing the change machine, Lucy suddenly seemed to remember something. Digging through a pile of papers, empty plastic soda bottles, and other assorted trash, she pulled out an envelope. After examining the return address, she brushed some crumbs from the business-sized envelope and held it out for James to see. "Have you gotten a letter from the Hudsonville Chamber of Commerce?"

"I haven't gone through all of my mail yet. Why, should I be expecting one?"

"Yep, but since you haven't read it, I wanna watch your face while you do! Here." She passed the letter to him. "Apparently we're celebrities now. Well, at least in Hudsonville anyhow."

"Hudsonville?" James asked. "Where is that?"

"Way south off of I-81. Close to the North Carolina border. I hear it hosts the region's biggest barbecue festival." Lucy smiled mischievously. "But don't let me spoil the surprise. Read on."

James briefly examined the town seal, which showed a drawing of an anxious-looking Native American handing a suckling pig to a complacent pilgrim. Pine trees grew in abundance on a hillside behind the two figures and the text INCORPORATED 1885 was written in block letters above the tallest tree. The letter read:

Dear Ms. Hanover,
First of all, congratulations on becoming a deputy for the Shenandoah County Sheriff's Department. I am confident

that the citizens of Quincy's Gap and its environs will benefit from your past experience in apprehending criminals.

The officers here at the Hudsonville Chamber of Commerce have followed the endeavors of you and your friends in our local newspaper, the *Hudsonville Herald.* We are very impressed by the fact that your group ensured the capture of several extremely dangerous felons. For the most part, media has granted the credit for each of these arrests exclusively to members of the law enforcement. We have friends in Quincy's Gap, however, and know the whole story, as do most of the fine citizens of our county. The *Herald* has run a very popular series on your supper club.

In short, you and your friends are celebrities here in Hudsonville, and we would be honored if your group would consider spending the week with us at our forty-seventh annual Hudsonville Hog Festival as guest judges. We would like you to judge the Queen Sow Contest as well as award the cash prize and trophy to the winner of the Blueberry Pie-Eating Contest.

Of course, the town of Hudsonville will gladly pay for your lodgings at our town's nationally rated bed and break-fast, and our local sponsors will provide you with plenty of free meals and merchandise during your stay.

The festival begins in two weeks and, while we apologize for the short notice, we truly hope that you will join us for this fun, family-oriented, and finger-licking-good festival.

If you have any questions, feel free to call me anytime.

A Mr. R. C. Richter signed the letter. Several titles, including President of the Hudsonville Chamber of Commerce, as well as four different telephone numbers were listed below his name.

"Is this for real?" James folded the letter and slid it back into the envelope.

Lucy nodded. "Sure is. The word is, their *original* celebrity judge cancelled at the last minute, so they're scramblin' to find a replacement."

"They must be desperate if all they can come up with is the Flab Five!" James laughed and then stopped smiling. "You know, we're going to need a different name, considering how incredibly *not* flabby you are."

Lucy shrugged, ignoring James's last comment. "Come on, James. We're celebrities, too. I think Murphy's coverage of our activities has given us press in more papers than just the *Star* and the *Hudsonville Herald.* We're big news in these parts. The deputies on our bowling team tease me about us being household names all the time."

James blinked in surprise. "Are you on the team? I thought *Deputy* Keith Donovan was adamant about keeping it an all-male endeavor." James grimaced as he spoke Keith's name. He and Donovan hadn't gotten along since high school.

"I'm not *on* the team." Lucy frowned. "I just go to the games. That jerk Donovan hands out all the duty assignments, and he's given me desk jobs whenever he can, while he and Glenn handle all the larceny and A&B cases. The most exciting thing I've done all summer was transfer someone from jail to the courthouse!"

"A&B?" James inquired, hoping to keep Lucy from sulking.

"Assault and battery." Lucy's radio crackled. A dispatcher announced a stream of unintelligible code, and Lucy sat up in her seat and reached for the keys, her eyes twinkling. "Gotta go, James. We've got a case of possession of a firearm by a convicted felon. See you at Gillian's tomorrow night."

Gillian, owner of the Yuppie Puppy dog salon as well as Pet Palaces — custom-made homes for pampered pooches, felines, and birds — had prepared a creamy tuna casserole loaded with cheese, green peas, and fried onions for the supper club meeting. She had layered the surface of the casserole with cheese crackers, which had been baked to a golden crust.

Lindy Perez, high school art teacher at Blue Ridge High, had brought a tossed salad, while mail carrier Bennett Marshall had purchased a peach pie from the local bakery, the Sweet Tooth. Lucy arrived with a basket brimming with fresh blackberries in case her friends preferred a lower calorie dessert to peach pie, and James had followed one of Milla's easier recipes and had thrown together a cucumber, tomato, and dill salad.

"So, did everyone get the same letter from Hudsonville?" Lindy asked, helping herself to greens.

Gillian poured her friends glasses of chilled mint tea. "*I* for one cannot imagine surrounding myself by meat for four days! It would be inconceivable for me to be stuck there, visualizing how many pigs, chickens, cows, and who knows what other animals have given up their spirits for such an inhumane contest."

"Woman, this is barbecue!" Bennett threw his hands into the air. "What do you think cavemen were doing back in the day? They weren't planting organic soybeans or huntin' for tofu. This festival is about food the way it's meant to be." Bennett's dark eyes gleamed. "Racks of beef ribs wrapped in foil, cooking over a slow-burnin' fire — yes-sir! Peel back the foil and brush on a thick layer of spicy sauce and then rip the butter-soft meat off the bone with your teeth. Hmmm. Yes, ma'am. That's the way man was meant to eat!"

James took a bite of the tuna casserole, which had the consistency of lumpy pudding, and silently agreed with Bennett. "We don't have to judge the food, Gillian, so you don't have to eat any meat. And just think: whichever pig we choose as the queen of the Hudsonville Hog Festival gets to live out the rest of her days at a local farm. Some lady keeps every winning queen sow. The school kids take field trips to go see all those sows living high on the . . ." He didn't finish his absurd sentence. "Anyway, I thought the fact that she'd be spared from the ax would be right up your alley."

"How do you know all this, James?" Lucy inquired.

"I went to the Hog Fest website." James reached for the salt and pepper and sprinkled a generous amount of both on the remains of his casserole. "I think being a guest judge would be fun. Besides, we've seen each other so little lately that it would be a good way to reconnect." He jerked his finger at Lucy. "And since Lucy here has turned into Deputy Skinny, we could use our time together to come up with a new name for our supper club."

Bennett stopped pushing food around on his plate and clapped Lindy on the back. "I agree. Okay, that's two of us who wanna go, Lindy. Think you can tear yourself away from that handsome principal of yours and head south for a little trip with your friends?"

Lindy blushed. "Luis and I haven't been together *that* much, though he's taken me out to enough late dinners that I've gained back a dress size." Frowning, she crossed her arms across her chest. "Besides, y'all have been just as busy as I have. Why, we've only gotten together once since Lucy's become a deputy. And I've missed you all," she said, thumping the table, "so I'm in." She turned to Lucy. "How about you? Will

27

Sheriff Huckabee let you off for a few days?"

Lucy helped herself to a few blackberries. "I think so. Their big bowling tournament is the week before Hog Fest and I've got to pull double shifts so that a bunch of the boys can practice. They're going to owe me some time off."

Gillian pulled at a strand of orange hair, which had been recently streaked with strands of bright blonde. "Oh! Am I the only one who *feels* this won't be a *valuable* bonding experience?" She pouted. "I really don't think this trip will serve a *higher* purpose."

James put a hand on his friend's shoulder. "They're having dog agility trials, Gillian. The festival won't entirely be about barbecue. It actually might be the perfect place to distribute your Pet Palace brochures. If these folks can spend ten thousand bucks on a grill, they can ante up for a custom doghouse for their fancy RVs. You should have seen the photos of some of those campers on the Hog Fest website."

Even though Gillian was best known in Quincy's Gap for behaving and dressing like a middle-aged hippie, she was also a shrewd and successful businesswoman. She digested James's suggestion for a moment and then nodded. "I could expand our line to include doggie travel homes," she mused and then gazed at her friends. "Fine, I'll go, but I'm bringing incense and healing candles for my hotel room. I don't want the *aura* of animal flesh to *pollute* my living space in Hudsonville."

"Then you'd better get your own room," Lindy interjected. "No offense, Gillian, but patchouli just isn't one of my favorite scents."

"All right, my friends and fellow pig pickers," Bennett said happily, raising his glass of tea in a toast. "I'm ready for cold beer, a plate piled high with pulled pork, and a whole mess of hush puppies!"

"We're going to have to start another diet as soon as we get back," Lindy sighed and then cut herself a generous slice of peach pie.

TWO:
BANANA BREAD

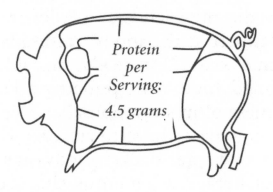

Protein per Serving:

4.5 grams

At the library the next day, James was busy completing the weekend's hold requests. After reviewing the requests sent in via email as well as those written on index cards, he printed the patrons' names in block letters on sheets of paper and wrapped the paper around the requested books with rubber bands. The books were then arranged by patrons' last names behind the circulation desk.

James liked to begin every week fulfilling

this task. He liked the orderliness of it, but he also enjoyed having the books ready and waiting for his patrons to collect. Week after week, there seemed to be more and more requests. Sometimes it was merely the addition of one name, but with every new request and each new library card printed and laminated, James's heart swelled with pride.

Even now, as he gazed at a group of mothers reading aloud to their young children in the Reading Corner, he thought about how the number of library patrons of all ages had grown since he had reluctantly accepted the position of head librarian a few years back. Even though most of the townsfolk still called him Professor Henry out of respect for his former position as an English professor at William & Mary, James wouldn't trade his current vocation for anything.

James finished the requests and then spent a moment observing the Fitzgerald twins, Francis and Scott. The twenty-something brothers were busy conducting a seminar in the library's new Technology Corner, which was yet another satisfying improvement that James and his devoted staff had brought about. The twins, unaware that their boss was watching them with something akin to paternal fondness, were absorbed in instructing a group of elderly patrons on the nuances of the Internet. Suddenly, one of the old women let out a bloodcurdling shriek.

"What's wrong, Mrs. Hastings?" Scott asked, going quickly to the woman's side.

Speechless, her wrinkled lips agape, the woman pointed a trembling finger at the computer screen.

"I typed in Pussycat Girls!" the woman finally squawked once she could catch her breath. "My granddaughter talks about their music all the time and I wanted to see what they looked like." She put a hand over her heart and filled her lungs with air. "But sweet Lord! *These* girls are stark naked!"

Both of the male patrons flanking Mrs. Hastings craned their necks in order to stare at the nude and gyrating bodies of two young women that had appeared on the screen. The name of the website, which bore a similar title to that of the pop band, was illuminated in electric pink letters and surrounded by pornographic images and videos.

"Sorry about that," Scott said, his cheeks ablaze in embarrassment as he returned the screen to the library home page. "I believe they're called The Pussycat *Dolls,* Mrs. Hastings," he murmured close to her ear.

"Hey!" one of the old men protested as the sexy women disappeared. "I didn't get a chance to look." He cast an imploring look at Mrs. Hastings. "What'd you type, Doris?"

Mrs. Hastings shrugged. "I put in p-u-s —"

"Okay, folks!" Scott raised his voice above his customary whisper and ran an agitated hand through his unruly hair. "Let's move ahead and we'll show you how to find news and weather reports."

"Oh goodie. Weather!" One of the patrons clapped. "I hear we're gonna have record-breakin' heat for the next few weeks."

"Well, then, I'm not goin' outside," another replied, cackling. "I'm gonna buy a computer and *surf* 'round for those cutie-pie *dolls* Doris found."

Once the brothers had successfully redirected the attention of their small class, Francis pulled his brother aside. He pushed his thick glasses farther up the bridge of his nose. "Someone's been messing with our filters again," he said, concerned.

"I think it's those high school kids who have been coming in here every Friday. Things are always out of whack with the computers after they leave."

Francis frowned. "And they never check

out any books. Mrs. Waxman says they just mess up all the magazines and make a lot of noise. I've felt bad leaving her to deal with them alone. I know she's a battle-axe and can hold her own, but she shouldn't have to play maid to a bunch of rude kids."

"You're right. And battle-axe or not, she's not getting any younger. Guess we should tell Professor Henry what's been going on," Scott suggested. "He'll know what to do."

As the twins wrapped up their seminar, Wendell Singer entered the library. The retired school-bus driver was the library's sole bookmobile operator. He was a whiz with engines and had kept the aged bookmobile, which he had fondly named Lena Horne after the jazz sensation, up and running at minimal cost. Lena was greatly prized by many patrons throughout Shenandoah County as she and Wendell brought library materials to day care centers and hospitals, nursing homes, to the jail, and to rural patrons who preferred not to leave their farms during busy harvest times. Lena also provided services for the handicapped, the housebound, and homeschool families. Unfortunately, the stress of traveling up and down mountain roads had taken their toll on the fifteen-year-old bookmobile. Wendell had repeatedly warned James that it wouldn't be too long before his beloved Lena would have to be put to rest. She was already operating on what Wendell referred to as "duct tape and a prayer."

When James saw Wendell's solemn face that Monday morning, he feared that Lena's end had finally arrived. He was right.

"What happened, Wendell?"

The older man removed his Stihl baseball hat and scratched the bald spot in the middle of his head. "She's done broke down again, Professor." He worried the hat in his hands. "I don't think anyone's gonna bring her back from this one. She's finally crossed over to the other side, sir."

James placed a comforting hand on Wendell's shoulder. "You know you don't need to call me 'sir.' Come on back with me." He led Wendell into the break room. "Let me get you a cup of coffee and a slice of banana bread. Mrs. Hastings baked it for us just this morning."

After he had served the dependable driver a piece of the rich, moist bread, James peered out the window in search of the bookmobile.

"You won't find her out thata way," Wendell said, chewing. "She's sittin' like a dead duck in the lot of one of them tourist view spots on Skyline Drive. Transmission's shot, and I done think her timin' belt's given up the ghost, too." He barely glanced at James as he mumbled morosely. "She's gonna have to get towed outta there, sir. Ain't no way she's movin' on her own steam."

James sat down opposite Wendell and sighed. "It's that bad?"

Wendell nodded. With a trembling voice he said, "She's given this county her best. Got nothin' left in her to give. We've done taken it all."

Afraid that Wendell might begin to cry, James poured the older man another cup of coffee. "We don't have the budget for a new bookmobile," James stated matter-of-factly. "I sure wish we did, but that Technology Corner emptied our coffers pretty thoroughly. I'm not sure what we'll do without Lena."

"Well," Wendell stood and carried his cup to the sink, "it's gonna take more than winnin' the Halloween float contest to get this here library a new bookmobile." He put his hat back on and pulled the rim down low on his brow. "I'll have Lena towed to my place. I've already got two ole buses there so she'll have some company." He stood and gave James an imploring look. "We've got to find ourselves some new wheels, Professor. I gotta have a job and, 'sides me, there's a whole mess of folks that's gonna have to go without books, and they ain't gonna like that none."

"No, they won't," James replied ruefully. "After all, a life without books is an unfulfilled one at best."

"Huh?" Wendell stared in confusion.

James walked him to the door. "I was just agreeing with you, Wendell. I'll find a temporary vehicle for you to use until I can figure out a more permanent solution. You need your job and people need their library materials. I'll figure something out."

"This here's why I didn't ever wanna to be the boss of nothin'," Wendell said sympathetically. "Too many headaches. I'll drive whatever you git me to drive, Professor. Shoot, it could be an ice cream truck and I'll bring folks books with it. Good huntin', sir."

"Thanks." James sighed again and watched Wendell exit the library.

He returned to his chair behind the circulation desk and began to mull over how he could get his hands on the funds to replace the bookmobile. He knew from previous research that the cost of a new bookmobile would require a minimum of $150,000. James planned on holding another lucrative Spring Fling to benefit the library come

May, but his patrons dependent on the bookmobile couldn't wait nine months for service to resume.

Where on earth am I going to get that much money? he thought, and he stared at the image of Lena on the library's homepage. *Why did you have to leave us now, Lena?*

"Professor," Scott broke into James's grim musings, "Francis and I are concerned about the activities going on here on Friday evenings."

"It's the high school kids," Francis chimed in. "I think we might need to stay later so we can help Mrs. Waxman keep an eye on them."

James reflected on the unusualness of having a bevy of high schoolers in the library on a Friday evening during summer vacation. "Mrs. Waxman told me that every week there have been more and more teenagers hanging out here. But why? Is it the computers?"

"That's what we thought at first," Scott answered. "They do fill up all the seats in the Tech Corner as soon as they can, but mostly they just sit around reading magazines."

"The thing is," Francis said hesitantly, "I was a bit late leaving work last week, so I got a taste of what's going on and I think they're up to no good. There's this one kid, Harris — he's always been into fantasy novels. But now, whenever I try to talk to him about the newest Steven Erikson or Jim Butcher books, he acts like he doesn't care. It's totally weird."

"Some people grow out of certain genres though, bro," Scott tried to comfort Francis.

"Not this kid. You look inside any of his school notebooks and you'll see drawings of all kinds of fantasy characters, from wizards to trolls to beautiful fairies. For some reason, Harris has begun to hide his interest in books when he comes here on Friday. I only see his artwork when he's here during the week, studying by himself."

"Some things about high school never change," James muttered. "Is Harris trying to impress one of the other kids?"

Scott and Francis exchanged looks. "I'd say it's a rising senior named Martin Trotman," Scott said. "They all seem to gather around him when he comes in, but we don't know why. And honestly," he admitted with a doleful expression, "we haven't stuck around to find out. Though we will now!" he added fervently.

Francis nodded. "Yeah, Scott's right. We usually just head straight to Blockbuster before all the good stuff gets checked out, but we've heard enough about this crew from Mrs. Waxman to know that there's no way Martin is here to check out books. According to her, he's got a foul mouth and more piercings than the whole High Hills Harley Gang put together."

"And half the brain cells," Scott chortled.

"Why don't you two take this Friday off?" James suggested. "I'm going to miss the following Thursday and Friday to be a guest judge at the Hudsonville Hog Festival, so I'll work alongside Mrs. Waxman this time and see what these kids are getting into. Have you changed the computer passwords recently?"

"Just a few days ago, Professor," Scott replied. "If they can break through our firewalls, they're smarter than we thought."

"Harris is the only one with enough computer savvy to do that," Francis said. "He and I have talked shop more than once."

James looked up and saw a line forming at the reference desk. Patting Francis on his back, he said with more assurance than he felt, "We'll get to the bottom of all this. Why don't you help those patrons while Scott handles shelving? I've got to make some phone calls to fellow Virginian librarians."

"Is there a conference coming up?" Scott inquired.

"No." James rubbed his temples, which had begun to throb. "I'm hoping one of them knows of a nice, fat grant that's just sitting around waiting to be claimed. Lena's run her last trip, men, and I can't do another thing until I figure out a way to get us a new bookmobile."

After work, James forced himself to visit the YMCA, where he spent forty minutes on the elliptical reading the latest Barry Eisler thriller.

"You know, you'd burn twenty percent more calories if you'd close that book," Bennett remarked as he stepped onto the machine next to James's.

"No, I'd burn one hundred percent less, because I wouldn't be here," James replied breathlessly. "Everyone thinks librarians just sit around and read all day, but this is one of the few chances I have to catch up on my To Be Read pile."

Bennett brandished a copy of *The Big Book of American Trivia* and set it on top of his elliptical with a thump. He then used a potato chip bag clip to keep the pages from closing and programmed the machine. Smoothing his toothbrush mustache, he climbed onto the elliptical and began to pump his arms and legs. "I hear you, man. If I'm going to make it onto *Jeopardy!* I've gotta read every free second of the day." He chuckled. "Maybe I'll get lucky and there'll be a barbecue category when I get to the tryouts in Philly in August." His face grew stormy. "If only I was ready when the contestant search was in D.C. last March. I couldn't pass that damned online test, so I knew there was no sense in goin' and makin' a fool out of myself. Shoot, *Alex* might've been there."

"Don't be too hard on yourself," James panted. "You said it was nearly impossible to pass the written test, right?"

Nodding, Bennett puffed, "Most folks fail. You gotta pass the test and then play a mock game. I've been practicing every night for years, so I'm not frettin' over that bit, and I've passed the online test a mess of times this summer, so I feel like I'm gettin' close to my goal."

"Well, I've seen you push buttons on your TV remote like you were an actual contestant. You've got a lightning fast trigger finger," James complimented his friend. "I know you're going to make it on the show, Bennett. And when you do, maybe you can win enough money to buy our library a new bookmobile."

Bennett rolled his eyes. "I'm sure you'll dream up some crazy scheme to get your hands on some greenbacks. You've done it before, my man." He snorted. "Shoot, just get your girlfriend to put an ad in her paper saying the person who gives the most loot gets the new book bus named after them."

James considered Bennett's idea for a moment. "That's not half bad. I think I will ask Murphy to run an ad on behalf of the library."

"Things still goin' strong with you two, then?" Bennett asked, and James wondered whether his friends approved of his relationship with the feisty reporter. Even though Murphy had helped the Flab Five solve a murder case last winter, James suspected that his friends were leery of trusting her. After all, she had run several stories containing intimate and sometimes embarrassing details regarding their weight battles. And while none of the supper club members minded seeing their names in print, they didn't enjoy seeing their current weight or body mass index listed in black and white.

James pumped his arms and legs rapidly for a few moments and then answered Bennett's question. "Murphy and I are doing fine, thanks."

"She comin' to Hog Fest with you?"

"No," James replied quickly. "She'll be busy covering a wine festival, some equestrian event, and a yodeling contest while we're gone. No time for pork," he joked and then realized that he was relieved that he would be spending time alone with his friends during their jaunt to Hudsonville. Guilt turned his feet leaden and he had trouble moving the elliptical forward. He pressed the red STOP button, waited for the machine's momentum to ease to a crawl, and stepped down from the pedals.

"Maybe I'll take her out for barbecue this week, since she's going to miss all the fun," James told Bennett and then gathered his towel, water bottle, and book.

"A woman who will tear meat off a rib bone and get sauce all over her face is a keeper. Now go on home so I can finish this chapter on seventies sitcoms," Bennett said, wiping sweat from the dark brown skin of his brow.

Driving home, James prayed that today was one of the days Milla had come to call on his father. If the Henrys were lucky, she wouldn't have booked a cooking class or a catering gig and would be filling their kitchen with tantalizing aromas as pots boiled on the stovetop and dishes bubbled in the oven.

When James saw her minivan parked alongside his father's old pickup truck, he smiled in expectation.

"Hello, James!" Milla trilled as he walked in the back door. The aroma of garlic immediately assaulted him — a favorable sign that Milla was fixing something scrumptious for dinner. The diminutive woman, who was in her midsixties but had the energy of a young girl, pushed back a clump of pale curls from her forehead and grinned at James.

"You look like a hungry man," she observed, and she removed a bottle of white wine from the fridge.

James kissed her cheek in greeting and then peered under the lid of a large skillet on the stove's back burner. "How's Pop?" he asked.

Milla frowned and shooed James away from the stove. "He's neckdeep in paint. I swear, he's gonna start sleepin' in that shed pretty soon."

James sat at the kitchen table and ripped the heel off a loaf of crusty homemade bread. Without bothering to butter it, he popped the warm bread in his mouth as he watched Milla move about the kitchen. It struck him that she looked as though she had always been there, cooking for the Henry men, but it was James's mother who had once filled the room with a similar air of warmth and vitality. James knew that Milla's ease within his mother's domain was no cause for sadness and that his mother would be pleased that such a kind-spirited person now cared for the two people she had loved most during her lifetime.

As if sensing the direction of James's thoughts, Milla turned from the stove and said, "Is this okay with you, James? Me being here and all but takin' over this kitchen?"

"It's more than okay," he replied, pouring out glasses of wine for them both. "You're a blessing, Milla. To me and to Pop."

Milla blushed. "Oh thank you, dear." She sipped her wine, her cheeks pink from her culinary exertions. "I sure do love comin' here, but it's gettin' harder and harder to commute to Quincy's Gap, take care of my Fix 'n Freeze clients, and make sure Prince Charles is gettin' enough attention."

James paused for a moment and then remembered that Prince Charles was the name of Milla's Corgi. "Pop still doesn't want to drive to New Market? Even if it means seeing you?" James asked.

"Lord, James. I've barely convinced him to run into town for groceries. That's as much progress as I've made. He says he's gotta paint. Says that he's got plans and these paintings are the key to those plans. He wants them to sell out real bad, James."

"I haven't seen any of the latest ones."

Milla jumped up. "The veal's gotta simmer a bit anyhow, so come out and look at the piece he finished yesterday. It's so incredible, you won't believe your eyes."

James hesitated. "He's not fond of me entering his domain while he's working."

"Pffah!" Milla grabbed his arm. "He's just an old dog with a sharp bark. He's not gonna bite anyone, though he sure likes to pretend he could."

Trailing after Milla's small form, James approached his father's shed. Jackson had told his son time after time not to bother him while he was working, and for the most part, James had been respectful of his wishes. Jackson tended to be impatient and cross whenever Milla wasn't present, so James avoided antagonizing him whenever possible.

As Milla called out a hello and rapped on the shed door, James gazed at her in admiration. Milla's companionship had softened Jackson's sharp edges so much that he had truly begun to emerge from the reclusive behavior that had gripped him for years.

James had heard his father laugh more this summer than he had since the time he moved back into his boyhood room following his mother's death. James was glad to hear Jackson's laughter, for it was a rich sound, deep and rumbling like a peal of thunder or a train's echo inside a long tunnel. The three of them filled the house with pleasant noise the way a family should, and James wished for their present state of harmony to last indefinitely.

Jackson growled upon seeing two people in his shed, but Milla playfully swatted at his shoulder with the potholder she had absentmindedly carried outside with her. "Don't curl your lip, Jackson. I forced James to come out here against his will. Show him that wonderful diner painting and then we'll eat."

When Jackson hesitated, Milla put her hands on her narrow hips. "I made veal with shallots and garlic, and it'll be tough as your work boots if you don't show the boy that picture right this second."

Wordlessly, Jackson gestured to a large canvas hidden beneath a tarp. Grumbling, he ordered, "Cover it up 'fore you leave, ya hear?" Jackson then prodded Milla back out of the shed, but with a lightheartedness that made James grin.

"Lemme sink my teeth into some of that delicious veal," Jackson pleaded once he and Milla were outside. "I'm starvin'."

" 'Course you are!" Milla chided in return. "You're turnin' into a bag of bones. Lord knows what would happen to you if I didn't show up at your door every now and then."

"Nothin' good, Milla." James could hear the smile in his father's voice. He tried to ignore the rumblings of his own belly as he reached forward to remove the tarp. When the painting was revealed, it took James several moments to soak in all the details set forth on the canvas.

Jackson had painted a diner scene, but it was different from what James had expected. Instead of a painting depicting the faces of the patrons seated at the counter, Jackson had only portrayed their hands and the breakfasts they had ordered. The row of hands gripped forks, knives, and coffee cups or sprinkled salt or Tabasco sauce on scrambled eggs and hash browns. The hands belonged to workmen. James could guess that much without taking note of the flannel shirt cuffs bordering their wrists or the enormous breakfasts each man had ordered so that he might be fueled for a long morning of physical labor.

The hands drew James's eye and demanded attention. Each one varied in size and shape. Some had dirt-encrusted nails, others had nicked knuckles, while another had grease stains revealed in a glimpse of palm. The waitress's hands were more slender than the men's, but they bore their own scars, lines, burns, and brown age spots acquired from a life of service. One of her hands held a glass coffee carafe while the other was frozen in time, placing several paper napkins next to a plate bearing a tall stack of flapjacks.

James studied the painting a few moments longer, marveling over how Jackson had cleverly manipulated shades of blue and yellow in order to create a feeling of movement in his piece. The two colors, highlighted by touches of black or white, were filled with wonderful contrasts of light and shadow.

Look out, Norman Rockwell, here comes Jackson Henry, James thought, and he was once again awestruck by his father's God-given talent.

"It's fantastic, Pop," James said when he re-entered the kitchen. "What diner did you go to? I mean . . . when did you have the chance to study those people and their hands?"

Jackson smirked and tapped his temple.

"It's all right up here, boy. That's an old memory." He buttered a piece of bread on both sides and took a bite. "Shoot. That diner's long gone now. I heard it's some kind of spa. You can pay a hundred bucks to have someone slop mud on your bare ass." He chortled. "I'd toss some of 'em in a pigsty for half the price!"

James admired Milla's beautifully arranged platter of veal cutlets in silent reverence as she chattered away. She brought dish after dish to the table, setting things just so, while Jackson kept his eyes fastened on his son.

As Milla searched in the fridge for some Parmesan cheese, Jackson dumped a heaping spoonful of tortellini on his plate and, finally blinking, said, "All things change, son."

Not knowing what to make of his father's cryptic statement, James ignored it, relished every bite of Milla's dinner, and then excused himself. He wanted to call Murphy from the privacy of his room and ask her out for a dinner date. She cheerfully accepted, and James was certain she was pleased that he seemed interested in keeping their relationship on track despite their rocky weekend at the beach. They small-talked about their day for a bit and then

James asked Murphy if she would run an ad on behalf of the library in order to raise funds for the bookmobile.

"I don't think I can, James," Murphy surprised him by answering. "People know we're dating. If I give you the ad pro bono, they'll think you're getting special treatment."

"But it's for the library, not me," he protested.

Murphy sighed. "I know, but it's all about perceptions."

James felt his ire rise. "And who is the *they* that will *perceive* that I've been granted favors?"

"Other local governmental agencies, charitable organizations, et cetera. The *Star* has pretty extensive coverage in our county, you know." Murphy's voice grew tense. "Don't get angry. I'm just trying to separate my personal and professional lives."

"You didn't seem to care about them blending when you wrote that piece on activities for couples visiting Virginia Beach," James argued.

"Oh, *please*," Murphy huffed. "I didn't mention *us!*"

"That's true," James argued unkindly, "because you left out the part about dragging your partner around until his feet bled when all he wanted to do was relax!"

Murphy was silent and James instantly regretted having picked a fight. His intention had been to smooth things over with her, not to dredge up fresh doubts about their relationship.

"I've got to go, James. I've got a deadline," Murphy said tersely and hung up.

James flounced back onto his bed and covered his eyes with his hands. As darkness fell outside his window, he thought about what his father had said at dinner. "All things change."

They sure do, James thought miserably. *And I hate change.*

THREE:
COLE SLAW

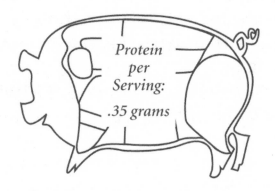

Protein per Serving:

.35 grams

A few days later, James and Murphy spoke to one another with stiff politeness over dinner at Blue's Barbecue House less than a week before James was meant to leave for Hudsonville. Most of their conversation centered on work, and while James agonized over the broken bookmobile and shared his puzzlement over the presence of the teenagers at the library on Friday evenings, Murphy relayed how pleased she was with the creativity and ambition illustrated by her newest reporter, Lottie Brontë.

"Scott still has a huge crush on her, but he's afraid to ask her on a date. They seem made for each other, too. I mean, how many people are named after authors?" James said as he cut into his barbecued chicken breast. Without waiting for Murphy to answer, he continued by asking, "Did she ever mention that *Battlestar Galactica* birdhouse he made for her?"

Smiling for the first time since James had picked her up, Murphy laughed. "Are you kidding? That thing's not doing the world's sparrows or finches any good. Lottie says it's a work of art and can't be exposed to the elements. Instead, it holds a place of honor on her desk next to her computer. You know," her hazel eyes twinkled, "I think she may even take it on the road with her when she covers stories outside the county."

Murphy took a bite of her own chicken and grimaced. Lowering her voice, she said, "I've never been a big fan of this place. This sauce is way too sweet and the meat isn't exactly fall-off-the-bone tender. Maybe you can bring back some new recipes from Hudsonville and give them to Blue."

James glanced at the ancient proprietor of the restaurant, who had his head resting on his fist and was noisily snoozing behind the register. Murphy, James, and a young man waiting for a takeout order were the only other occupants of the small room. Wiping his hands on a paper napkin, James eyed the greasy pool oozing from beneath his chicken breast. The red-tinged grease had infiltrated his pile of cole slaw, so James shoveled the slaw into his mouth to avoid further contamination.

"The slaw's good," he said, his mouth stuffed. "But I agree about the sauce."

"Should you even be eating this kind of food?" Murphy gestured at their meals. "I thought you were on a salt restriction."

James pulled more napkins loose from the napkin holder on the table. The contraption, whose stainless-steel surfaces were marred with scores of greasy fingerprints, sprung open like a trap and dozens of napkins fluttered across the table and onto the floor. Several fell right onto James's chicken and were immediately saturated in barbecue sauce. Murphy sniggered, which annoyed the already embarrassed James.

"I just saw Doc Spratt the day before yesterday," he replied defensively. "My blood pressure's back to normal levels again. Doc told me to be careful not to eat too much salt, and I'll watch my intake, but I'm not going to pass up all foods containing sodium forever." He closed the napkin holder and placed the pile of unused napkins on top. "Besides," he shrugged, trying to get the last strands of slaw on his plastic fork, "something's going to kill me one of these days. Might as well be food that tastes good. I'm not going to live my whole life eating lettuce, turkey breast, and multigrain cereal. I want to actually *live* life, instead of living just to avoid dying."

"Wow." Murphy mocked him with her wide eyes. "*That* was deep. Have you been checking out books from the self-help section again?"

Despite the fact that James knew Murphy was only teasing, he felt a wave of annoyance wash over him. "We can't *all* have naturally speedy metabolisms or blood pressure so low that it borders on being categorized as the walking dead."

Murphy sighed. "I admit, it's tough to be perfect." She then poked James playfully with her fork. The tines left four pinpricks of grease on the back of his hand. "Come on," she said, grinning. "If your blood pressure can get back to normal, then so can we. I liked us the way we were, James. So we had a lousy weekend. It happens to the best of couples. Sometimes, for a lot of different reasons, people just get out of sync.

Can we forget it and move on?"

The warmth and sincerity in her voice made James feel ashamed of his churlishness. He rubbed at the spots on his hand with a napkin and then took her hand in his own and squeezed it. "Yes, we can move on. That's what this dinner was supposed to be about. Thanks for reminding me of that."

"That's settled, then!" Murphy pushed her plate away with her free hand, her eyes twinkling with delight. "Oh, I wish we could do something fun together this weekend, but I've got to go to the historical society's benefit dinner on Friday and the cat show on Saturday. Feel like hanging out with me at either one of those fun-filled events?"

James shook his head. "I'm giving the twins a day off Friday so I can spy on the high school kids, and on Saturday, I promised to drive Pop to New Market so he can watch one of Milla's cooking classes. He wants to do a painting of the students making pastry dough, so he'd like to covertly study them while they work." James slurped the remains of his painfully sweet tea. "This is a big step for him — visiting Milla instead of her coming to our place."

Draining her unsweetened tea, Murphy sat back in her chair. "What a cute couple. Do you think they'll get married?"

Having wondered the same thing recently, James nodded. "I think they will. It's the way folks their age do things. They date for a bit and then they get married. They don't really dither around."

"That's the way things are *supposed* to go for couples of all ages," Murphy grumbled.

James sensed that they were entering a risky conversation topic, so he steered the discussion back to his father and Milla. "If they decide to wed, I'll be really happy for them both. They're both widowers and they seem really comfortable with one another."

Murphy stood and tossed a wad of soiled napkins on the vinyl tablecloth. James sensed that the subject of marriage had soured Murphy's mood, but he didn't feel inclined to find out why. Glancing at Blue, who had a trickle of drool running out the side of his mouth, Murphy shook her head. "You might be happy for them," she said, "but it'd be a big change for you."

"Why?" James said, holding open the door for Murphy.

Looking at him as though he were a complete simpleton, Murphy blurted, "Because you'd finally have to move out of your boyhood room!"

On Friday, temperatures soared into the

nineties and the humidity pressed down on the Shenandoah Valley like a heavy hand. The library overflowed with patrons all day, but especially during the hours of eleven and two, when the temperature peaked and the sun threatened to scorch the hair right off of people's scalps.

James was aware that almost half of the patrons reading in upholstered chairs or waiting for an opportunity to use one of the computers for the forty-five minute maximum were at the library because it was air-conditioned. The elderly were especially susceptible to the hot weather and had arrived at the library in droves, blatantly disregarding the *No Food or Drink* sign posted on the front door. Bearing thermoses of sun tea or homemade lemonade and plastic baggies of sandwiches, potato chips, and cookies, they gathered in groups at the wooden tables and played bridge or chatted over stories in the newspaper.

James didn't have the heart to remonstrate them, even when they scattered crumbs on the carpet or raised their voices above the expected whisper. Besides, all of the older patrons adored the Fitzgerald twins and plied them with baked goods and hard candies until the boys swore that they had more adoptive grandparents than they could keep track of. And even though the twins devoured every morsel of food that crossed their paths, they remained as thin and lanky as ever. In their absence that Friday, James found himself laden with fresh oatmeal cookies, cranberry scones, and cheese biscuits.

"Well, I *am* going to be here until nine," he said, happily examining the pile of unhealthy goodies on his desk.

The oatmeal cookies proved the perfect accompaniment to James's afternoon coffee. As soon as he had washed out his *Forget Google, Ask a Librarian* mug and returned to the circulation desk, the high school students began to drift in.

By the time retired middle school teacher Mrs. Waxman arrived at five thirty, there were at least six teenagers seated at computers or leafing through magazines. By six thirty, the number had doubled, and by seven thirty, it had tripled.

James and Mrs. Waxman took turns hushing the boisterous group and asking them if they needed help finding any materials. They all refused, stating that they were meeting friends or waiting to use one of the computers. One teen even pretended that she was a member of a book club and that she was waiting for her group to decide on which novel to read next. When James offered to provide recommendations, she shook her head vehemently and quickly said, "Oh, that's okay. We only read the *It Girl* books." She then turned her back on him and began to type a text message on her cell phone.

Deciding to approach the kids on an individual basis, James strolled up to a young girl in a denim miniskirt that barely covered her rump and asked, "Can I help you find something, Miss?"

The girl hastily closed a folder and stuffed it, along with what appeared to be a pen-sized X-Acto knife, into her canvas purse and giggled nervously. "No thanks. I'm waiting for a computer to open up."

"And what might you be utilizing our fine new computers for?" James asked, his voice betraying his suspicion. "Just out of curiosity."

A boy sitting too close to the girl with the short skirt sneered. "Dude, she doesn't have to tell you anything. There's, like, privacy laws against that. What she does on the computer is her business. You're a public *servant*," he said as his lip curled, "so be careful or you could get sued."

Though James felt like grabbing the surly teenager by the throat and squeezing hard, he smiled patiently instead. He wanted to use this opportunity to guess what had driven the motley assembly of kids into the library, and he felt that he had a pretty clear idea of what their goal was, having glimpsed the small knife.

Forcing his eyes to turn steely, he whispered, "That's right, son. I am a proud servant of the public. Our town is filled with a host of public servants. Let's see, we have mail carriers, the folks working at the DMV, and the fine men and women of our sheriff's department. I have one friend in particular, a Deputy Hanover, who feels *very* strongly about preventing young drivers from driving while under the influence." The boy turned his eyes away from James and did his best to appear bored.

James looked at the girl and allowed his gaze to soften slightly. His tone conversational, he continued. "This officer is also devoted to tracking down each and every fake license in the county. She truly wants to keep all of the drivers within our county safe, and those possessing false licenses are often some of the worst drivers, due to their inexperience."

The girl blanched. James had struck a nerve by mentioning fake licenses. Silently apologizing to Lucy for taking such liberties in her name, he plowed on. "You know, I believe you could spend six months in jail for carrying one of those licenses." James flicked his eyes back to the boy, who continued to act disinterested, but his fidgety hands belied his agitation.

"A person could face a fine *and* a year's time in jail for making and distributing fake IDs," James concluded.

At this opportune moment, a hulking young man wearing a thin leather coat and walking with a cowboylike swagger entered the library. His hair was dark, long, and greasy, his skin shone with oil, and he was clean-shaven except for a straight line of hair growing down the center of his chin. The hair had been dyed orange. In addition to the odd facial hair, the imposing young man had a row of small silver hoops protruding from his right eyebrow and a barbed-wire tattoo encircling his wrist.

This must be Martin Trotman, James thought, recalling how the twins had described the leader of the teenage assemblage. James casually approached Mrs. Waxman and pretended to consult her about a damaged book. As they talked, he asked her to watch Martin without being obvious. Mrs. Waxman patted her bouffant hair as she reported in hushed tones that Martin had usurped the chair of the girl in the miniskirt. The girl then whispered into Martin's ear and the mature-looking young man scowled.

"He's staring this way," Mrs. Waxman murmured. "At the back of your head. He doesn't seem too pleased, either."

"I think he's the ringleader and that some of these kids have been dealing in fake IDs." James puffed out his chest, quite pleased that he had solved the mystery of the teenagers so quickly. "I doubt Martin does any of the labor himself. I'd guess the girl in the short skirt is one of his assistants. He must be in charge of fulfilling orders and collecting money."

Mrs. Waxman mulled over his theory. "It's possible. But how many of these IDs can one kid need? These teens are here week after week."

James frowned. "I'm not sure. I guess they're using the licenses to try to buy alcohol or get served at bars. Not around here though," he snorted. "Sammy down at Wilson's Tavern would throw them out on their ears and *then* call their parents."

"On the other hand, this could be quite an entrepreneurial group we're looking at here." Mrs. Waxman eyed Martin again. "Perhaps they're selling the IDs to other delinquents around the Valley. There are a lot of kids who would like to try to pull one over on the liquor stores or less observant barkeeps."

Rubbing his temple, which had begun to throb with the beginnings of a headache, James glanced at the door in time to see a scrawny teen with glasses and acne enter the library. The boy furtively slipped a book in the return slot and then edged his way to where Martin sat. James hustled behind the circulation desk and removed the eight-hundred-page fantasy book that the teen had returned.

I believe Harris has entered the picture, James thought. Scott had mentioned that Harris liked fantasy novels but had recently displayed some odd behavior when the other teens were present on Friday evenings. Curious about the conflicted young man, James watched as the anxious-looking boy settled himself at a wooden table by the magazines and absurdly pretended to read a copy of *Dog Fancy.*

James kept one eye on Martin and the other on the rest of his patrons, but as the evening wore on, he found that he could only find cause to reprimand the teens for raising their voices or putting their feet up on top of the wooden tables.

Martin seemed restless for the entirety of the two hours he spent in the library. He often disappeared into the lobby, and although James immediately trotted into his office and looked out the window whenever the young man ventured out, he never saw Martin in the parking lot.

"Where's he going if not to his car?" James murmured to the darkening sky.

By the time the library closed at nine, most of the high school kids had dispersed. Martin had left first and then slowly, usually in groups of two or three, the rest followed.

"They were calmer tonight than on other nights, James," Mrs. Waxman said after the last patron had left. She began to straighten the magazine area with swift, efficient movements. Mrs. Waxman was one of the few townsfolk who didn't call James 'Professor.' After all, he had once sat in the back of her classroom, praying that her eagle eyes would pass him over whenever he forgot his grammar worksheets, and he still felt like a child in her formidable presence.

James assisted the retired schoolteacher in tidying up the library. Mrs. Waxman was moving more slowly than she had in the past. She had recently been diagnosed with rheumatoid arthritis, and he worried that the evenings and one weekend day she worked were too hard on her inflamed hip.

Opening the front door for her, he asked how her medication was working.

"I won't be dancing the polka anytime soon, but it's keeping the aches at bay." She gave James a maternal pat on the back. "Don't worry, I've got plenty of years left in me yet, and I'm going to work in this library until I can't walk anymore." She smiled. "I'm at home here."

James nodded. "Me too," he said, gazing happily at the vibrant row of fairy-tale character drawings done by the students in a local second-grade class, which Scott and Francis had posted around the lobby. "And now that those high school kids know we're onto them, we can go back to having our peaceful branch again."

Mrs. Waxman shrugged. "I don't know. I rather enjoyed being in the midst of a mystery for once."

James walked the older woman to her car. "The best thing about mysteries is solving them. *This* one is definitely solved," he said brightly and wished Mrs. Waxman good night.

Four:
Warm Chicken
Salad Sandwiches

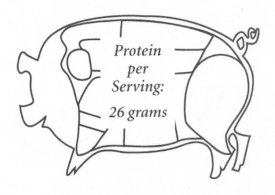

Protein per Serving:

26 grams

James and Bennett drove through the town of Hudsonville in search of Fox Hall Lane. The bustling town was bigger than James had imagined, and it was utterly charming. Wooden barrels stuffed with red geraniums, yellow strawflowers, and purple salvia lined the sidewalks. The spotless glass windows of the storefronts glinted in the midday sun and colorful flags depicting a crowned pig seated in a field dappled by dandelions and thistle hung from every streetlamp. Pink balloons floated from the backs of green park benches and there wasn't a parking space in sight. James couldn't help but note the variety of the vehicles. They ranged from expensive sedans to family-oriented minivans to rusty pickup trucks, and the cars bore local license plates as well as those from states as far off as Arkansas and Kansas.

Bennett rolled down his window and the sound of a jaunty fiddle tune floated into the Bronco. Shopkeepers wearing pink and black baseball caps had set tables with special Hog Fest wares onto the sidewalk. Families browsed the tables or hurriedly tried to finish ice cream cones before the summer heat reduced them to sugary puddles.

The energy of the street fair was contagious, and James was eager to check in at their bed and breakfast so that he and his friends could wander around Hudsonville before the festival's opening ceremony later that afternoon.

"There's your turn." Bennett pointed ahead at a signpost partially obscured by a mammoth oak tree. He examined the sheet containing their driving directions for the tenth time and then gestured at the odometer. "After 2.7 miles, we'll see the sign for the inn. We turn left, and then proceed .7

miles to the gravel parking lot." He swiveled in his seat. "The girls are still right behind us. I'm sure glad everyone was able to get a couple days off."

"Did you bring any homework?" James asked, keeping an eye out for the sign.

Bennett nodded. "Man, I sure did. I've got a book on world culture trivia, a book on bird trivia, and a book on sports trivia." He snorted. "Shoot, my bag was so heavy you'd think I was a woman gettin' ready to fly to Paris instead of a bachelor headin' out for a weekend of barbecue."

James spotted a modest wooden plaque bearing the name *The Inn at Fox Hall.* He turned into a narrow lane lined with tulip poplars. Though the large, mature trees were not in bloom, James could visualize how magnificent they must look in May. He pictured the tulip-shaped flowers, which were green and had a band of orange on each of the five petals. James had always thought that the blooms resembled a fox's face, and he couldn't think of a more appropriate tree to grace the entryway of an inn called Fox Hall.

As the house came into view, Bennett whistled. "Man, we've got some nice digs for a bunch of small-town celebs here to decide who's the fairest piggy of them all."

"It's certainly picturesque," James commented as they drew closer to the nineteenth-century house, which was painted white with black shutters and had a long front porch lined with potted ferns. "But I hope it's been updated. If we don't have any air conditioning, I'll be checking into the Comfort Inn instead. I can drown out the sounds of the highway by cranking the fan to its highest setting."

"Hog Fest is pretty huge in these parts, my man. I don't think you could find room in a shed if you wanted to." Bennett examined his printouts again. "According to the inn's website, it was renovated five years ago. All the rooms have A/C, Jacuzzi tubs, and digital cable. And if the A/C doesn't do it for you, there's a big ole swimming pool out back."

Thinking of how his enlarged belly would look in a swimsuit, James shook his head. "I'll stick with the Jacuzzi tub, thanks."

James parked his white Bronco in the gravel lot and waited as Lucy pulled her Jeep into the adjacent spot.

"This is a *paradise!*" Gillian exclaimed as she alit from the car, twirling around with her arms spread à la Julie Andrews in *The Sound of Music.* "I am *so* glad I decided to *release* my misgivings and join you, my friends." She pointed at a rustic wooden sign to the right of the parking area. "Look! Nature trails! An indigenous garden walk! The pond and gazebo! You'll *never* get me back in the car."

Bennett glanced at his watch. "There's also a welcome lunch today bein' served on the back porch. I'm more interested in food than in some mosquito-infested pond right now. If we hurry, we can just make it."

"I'm ready to eat, too." Lindy dragged an enormous suitcase onto the flagstone path leading up to the main house. "I wonder if we're staying in the house or in one of those darling cabins over there."

James glanced at the miniature log cabins in the distance, which were almost entirely obscured by trees. His eyes then returned to Lindy's bag. "We're only here for four days, Lindy. What on earth have you got in there? A small child? Or did you decided to bring your boyfriend with you after all?"

Bennett sniggered as Lindy stuck her tongue out at James. "Hey, they invited us here because we're kind of heroes to them. I consider it my responsibility to look the part."

Lucy grabbed Lindy's suitcase and shoved the handle of her much smaller wheeled bag into Lindy's hand. "I see you've got a new

French manicure, too. You'd better let me carry this or you could chip the polish." Lucy pulled the suitcase effortlessly up the path.

"Wow, you're really strong," Gillian said as Lucy easily lifted the bulging bag up the front steps. "Are you *channeling* some kind of *inner* power?"

Smiling indulgently at her friend, Lucy replied, "Nothing complicated like that. I've been eating a lot of lean proteins and doing strength-training workouts."

"A protein diet?" Bennett immediately perked up. "That means a whole lotta meat, right?"

Opening the wide front door, Lucy stepped inside the inn's main hall and waited for her friends to join her. "It's not a diet. You don't count calories or anything. It's just a way of eating. It makes me feel good and I have a lot of energy." She patted her nearly flat stomach. "I've been trying to work on my balance by strengthening my core."

"Forget about that. I'm not gonna be on a balance beam anytime soon. What about the meat part?" Bennett persisted, but before Lucy could continue, the proprietress of the inn appeared in the hall and welcomed them with a professional smile.

"Y'all must be my celebrity guests," the slim, elegant woman gushed. "I'm Eleanor Fiennes and I am *so* honored to have you staying here." James found her warmth a bit forced, and as he gazed at her shiny brown hair and narrow, darting eyes, he couldn't help comparing the lithe woman to a ferret. Pulling two sets of keys from the top drawer of an antique desk, Eleanor handed one key to James and one to Lindy. "I've got you two gentlemen in the Hunt Room and you ladies in the Equestrian Suite."

James stared at the weighty brass tag stamped with the image of a fox head and then met Bennett's eyes.

"Hope you don't mind the light bein' on 'til real late." Bennett grinned. "I can't take time off from my studies."

"Um, excuse me." Lindy cleared her throat as she held out her key. "Are all three of us sharing one bathroom?"

Eleanor Fiennes nodded. "That's the best I could do, I'm afraid. Why, this inn's been booked for Hog Fest weekend since last year! I had to push a whole family into one of my older cabins simply to accommodate you five on such incredibly short notice." She grinned humorlessly. "Fortunately, a few tickets to the festival stopped them from being dissatisfied."

Sensing that she had offended their hostess, Lindy immediately backpedaled. "Oh, we really appreciate that, Mrs. Fiennes, and we are grateful to be staying at your beautiful inn. Thank you so much for your trouble."

Eleanor eyed the suitcase on the floor next to Lucy. "Can you manage your luggage?" When Lucy nodded, the proprietress looked relieved. "Good, good. Well, your rooms are on the second floor and lunch is being served as we speak, so shake out the wrinkles in your clothes and come on down for some of our famous hot chicken salad sandwiches."

James was quite hungry, and the idea of lunch was more appealing than spending more than a few minutes examining his room. As it turned out, there wasn't much to see in any case. The room was masculine and had a set of twin beds covered by ivory quilts stitched with maroon stars. The walls were a forest green and held three oil paintings depicting fox hunts. James had never been fond of the idea of a pack of dogs and a group of armed horsemen tracking down and cornering a terrified fox. He viewed foxes as beautiful and clever animals and wished that the tradition of shooting them for sport had become illegal years before it actually did.

As James hung up his favorite jeans and two pairs of khaki pants, Bennett dumped a pile of books on the single nightstand and poked his head into the bathroom.

"Kinda feels like home," he said, pleased with their cozy room.

Without wasting any more time, the two friends hustled downstairs and out the back door where the wooden porch was crowded with glass-top tables, white metal chairs, and dozens of guests, all chewing contentedly or drinking tea from tall, clear glasses.

Several children frolicked in the pool and a young woman in a minuscule black bikini sunned herself on a lounge chair on the emerald lawn adjacent to the porch.

Eleanor appeared alongside James and Bennett but didn't speak to them right away. Instead, she cast a brief and disapproving stare in the direction of the gorgeous girl and then, with a slightly clenched jaw, gestured at a laden buffet table. "Please help yourself to our lunch buffet. We've got a watercress and mint salad with walnuts, our delicious warm chicken salad on toasted croissants, fresh berries, and Key lime or lemon tartlets for dessert. Pitchers of tea, ice water, or limeade are on the sideboard. Enjoy your lunch, now."

The two men watched her march off in the direction of the sunbather in the bikini.

After James had dished food onto a china plate decorated with a rim of running foxes and settled himself at the only available table, he realized that he had forgotten to get himself something to drink. As he headed back to his table with a glass of limeade, he noticed Eleanor berating the young woman in the bikini. The girl stood and, draping her yellow and white striped towel over one shoulder, slid her feet into flip-flops and sauntered past the diners. The conversation on the porch ceased momentarily as all eyes perused the bronzed form of the young woman. Flirtatiously tossing her mane of lustrous dark-blonde hair, the girl cast a dazzling smile at one of the male guests. James could see that the young lady was clearly Eleanor's daughter and a great beauty as well.

As the girl reached the end of the porch, Lindy and Lucy seated themselves at the table, looking perplexed.

"Why did everyone suddenly stop talking?" Lindy asked.

Bennett pointed at Eleanor's daughter, who had stopped to chat with a woman in an apron. "That lovely little vision walked on by and everybody's brains just shut right down."

"Well, she certainly looks like a healthy American girl," Lindy said flatly. "But I'd hate to be her skin in twenty years."

"You can see right off who her mama is, too. Eleanor's thin and handsome. She must've been a real looker in her day," Lucy offered. "I guess they've been blessed by good genes. The rest of us have to work every day just to fit into our uniforms."

"Hey. Where's Gillian?" James inquired.

"You know Gillian." Lucy squeezed lemon into a glass of ice water. "She wants to cleanse our room before she comes down to lunch."

"I must have been in the bathroom for that announcement." Lindy rolled her eyes. "Please tell me she's not using patchouli incense. I hate that smell."

Shaking her head, Lucy smirked. "I thought I saw a package of Egyptian Kush Musk sticking out of her purse. Who knows? It could smell even worse than patchouli."

Before either of the men could respond to Lucy's remark, a heavy man wearing a Hawaiian shirt stepped onto the porch. He cast a complacent glance around and then his bloodshot eyes fell on the figure of Eleanor's daughter. Strutting over to the attrac-

79

tive young woman, the man shook his head and made bubbling noises with his lips. As he did so, his pink and fleshy cheeks shook and his enormous stomach wobbled beneath his shirt's pattern of dancing hula girls. Sweat stained the chest area of his shirt and dripped down his puffy face and neck.

"Lord Almighty, girlie!" he bellowed hoarsely as he neared his prey. "You're hot enough to fry an egg on! Mercy me! I've seen napkins that are bigger than that there bikini." He smiled, displaying a row of yellow teeth. "Allow me to introduce myself." He bowed as low as he could until the pouch of his belly prevented him from bending over any further. "*I* am the world-famous Jimmy Lang, winner of more first-place bar-b-cue trophies than I can count and the future champion of Hudsonville Hog Fest." He nudged the young lady in the side with his meaty elbow. "You come on down to my pit anytime, you fine thang! Then you'll find out why they *really* call me The Pitmaster. I know I'm a bit on the big side — seems I gained a whole 'nother person this year — but I've got skills other men just don't have. These hands like a nice piece of tender meat, and you're about as tender as they come, girlie."

Several of the inn's guests frowned in distaste, but the majority viewed Jimmy with amusement. Eleanor made her way to her daughter's side at the same moment that Jimmy uttered his lewd invitation. After attempting to shoo her daughter inside the house, she gave Jimmy Lang an icy smile and whispered, "Francesca, please!"

Francesca slowly wound the towel around her waist as she struck a coquettish pose for Jimmy's benefit. "Do barbecue contestants make a lot of money?" she asked coyly.

Jimmy roared with laughter. "You get right to the marrow of it, don't ya? You're my type of gal, missy!" His face puffed up with pride. "We get a nice pile of cash for becomin' champion, but winnin' the money's nothin' compared to gettin' a big-time sponsor. This year's sponsor is Heartland Foods, and they wanna expand their line to include barbecue. I win this one and I'm all but guaranteed my own line of sauces and rubs along with my very own TV show on the Outdoor Livin' channel." He rubbed his tummy as he visually devoured Francesca. "Lots of money there, darlin', and I'd be more than happy to spend some on you. Folks would see you as the gal lucky enough to be with Jimmy Lang, champion pitmaster and the face of barbecue." He held up his hands as though reading a banner upon which his new title had already been written.

"Uh, thank you, Mr. Lang." Eleanor stepped in front of her daughter. "Francesca needs to get ready for tonight's opening ceremonies." She took a firm hold of her daughter's arm and smiled at an elderly guest. "She's the Hudsonville Festival Princess." Eleanor beamed. "She gets to drive the Queen Sow in the victory parade and her photograph will be in *all* the area papers."

"Francesca's or the pig's?" Jimmy asked and then guffawed.

Eleanor looked irritated. "Why, my daughter's, of course. She's won so many local pageants over the last five years that she's a shoo-in for the top five at the state competition." She pushed a lock of Francesca's hair off of her smooth cheek. "You might just be talking to the next Miss Virginia and after that, maybe even Miss America."

Now it was Francesca's turn to be annoyed. Breaking away from her mother's grasp, she sneered. "I'm going to get scholarship money based on my brains, Ma! Not my boobs!" And with that declaration, Francesca stormed into the house.

Jimmy laughed heartily and began to sing

"There she is, Miss America" as he kissed the hands of the ladies seated nearby, who giggled and twittered among themselves in response.

Visibly trying to conceal her displeasure, Eleanor asked Jimmy if there was something she could assist him with. Jimmy announced that he wanted to meet the contest judges and the representative for Heartland Foods.

"Word around the campfire is that they're all staying up here at Fox Hall," he said, winking at Eleanor. "I'm just gonna help myself to some free lunch and start my campaign for the championship!" Rudely turning his back on Eleanor, Jimmy filled his plate with three sandwiches and six tartlets, singing the Miss America theme song all the while.

Except for Lucy, the supper club members exchanged panicked stares as they realized that the only available seat was at their table. James swallowed his Key lime tartlet in two bites and gestured frantically at Lucy to finish her meal.

"It's not good to shovel food in," she said defensively and then took a deliberate bite of watercress salad. However, as soon as Jimmy Lang pulled out the empty chair next to her and asked, "This seat ain't taken, is it?" Lucy obviously changed her mind and began to eat as though it were her last meal.

As she chewed, Lucy scooted her chair close enough to James for him to be able to smell her almond-scented body lotion. Swallowing hurriedly, she said to Jimmy, "We're just about done, so if anyone's planning on joining you . . ."

"Don't rush away on my account." Jimmy shoved half a sandwich into his mouth and continued talking. James noticed that the skin of his face was dry and flaky and that overall, the man appeared swollen, as though his body tissue was retaining large amounts of water. Wiping sweat from his forehead with the back of his arm, Jimmy raised a thick pair of eyebrows and asked, "Y'all judges?"

"Yes. We're judging the sow contest," Lindy replied importantly, turning her face away as Jimmy began to noisily lick chicken salad from his fat fingers.

"Aha!" He pointed at Bennett. "Y'all are those crime-solvin' folks, ain't ya?" He surveyed the group while pushing an entire tartlet in his mouth. "These things don't taste like nothin'," he said, but he ate the dessert anyway. After several chews he declared, "I don't mean offense, but y'all don't look like no detectives."

Wiping her mouth with her napkin, Lindy stared down Jimmy. "Lucy here is the only *trained* member of law enforcement, but the rest of us contribute to crime solving by using our natural gifts and abilities. It's important to all of us that right triumphs over wrong in our community." She fluffed her chin-length black hair self-importantly.

Jimmy's mouth hung open, exposing a partially decimated Key lime tartlet. He closed his lips, which were also flaky with dried skin, and looked at James. "What are you talkin' about, girl?"

"She's just saying that we help one another," James answered, forcing himself to meet Jimmy's eyes, which seemed to shift between blue and gray depending on the light. Jimmy had crumbs stuck in the sparse hairs of his salt-and-pepper beard, and as he ran his hand over his shaved head, he left behind a trail of Key lime filling.

"I help folks, too. I'm a tow-truck driver by trade." He wiggled his hairy eyebrows. "But not for long, folks. Whether I get that contract or not, my ship is comin' into port this weekend. When I get back to Waxahachie — that's south of Dallas, Texas, for those of y'all that don't know God's country well enough — I'm gonna tell my boss he can take that rusty truck and them hours from hell and them whiny customers and shove them all where the sun ain't never shone."

Lindy placed her napkin on the table with forceful deliberation and stood up. "I think I'm going to unpack and then go over my clothes with my travel iron. Nice meeting you and good luck with your . . . grilling."

Lucy also jumped to her feet, followed by James and Bennett.

Jimmy slurped his tea and looked at his watch. "Make sure y'all ain't late for the openin' of the party. I'm gonna be samplin' some mouth-waterin' 'cue, so stop on by my trailer, ya hear?"

" 'Cue?" James inquired of Bennett when they were out of Jimmy's earshot.

"Slang for barbecue," Bennett answered immediately. "I imagine Jimmy knows every barbecue term known to man. I'm gonna make it a point to try his cooking."

"You are?" James was astonished.

"Man with that big a belly and that much swagger knows his food," Bennett reasoned. "And you heard him. He's won a whole mess of competitions already. He must have figured out some tricks of the grill, simply by eating all his own mistakes. Look, here comes Gillian. She doesn't know what she missed." He poked James in the ribs.

"Maybe *you* should've cleansed our room, James."

Back in their room, the men finished unpacking and James flipped through Bennett's trivia books.

"How's your cache of barbecue trivia?" he asked his friend.

Bennett shrugged. "Pretty poor, my man. I hope to store away a hundred facts or so by the time this festival is done." He held up a mini recorder. "I'm going to carry this with me wherever we go so I can think of questions to research later on. About all I know now is that barbecue is different 'round the country and that everybody thinks *theirs* is the best."

"All I've had recently is Blue's, and his was definitely *not* the best."

"Poor Blue." Bennett frowned. "How he's eked out a livin' on that dry meat is beyond me. And his weird sauce doesn't fit into *any* of the popular categories. Texas and the western states like a feisty tomato-based sauce, the Kansas City folks favor sweet over spicy, North Carolina likes a vinegar sauce with lots of black pepper, and I believe South Carolina and parts of Georgia make a white vinegar sauce mixed with sweet mustard. Kentucky adds Worcestershire to theirs." He paused. "I read that Florida actually makes a white barbecue sauce using mayo in the tomato base." Bennett shivered in distaste. "Doesn't sound too appealing if you ask me, but I'll try it if they've got it here at the festival."

Once again, James was impressed by the random bits of knowledge stored in his friend's keen brain. "I can't wait to watch you on *Jeopardy!*"

Bennett, who had gathered his trivia books and sunglasses, hesitated at the door to their room and wiggled his index finger at James. "Don't go jinxin' me now. I'm goin' down by the pool to read. You comin'?"

Grabbing a book on the history of barbecue from his duffel bag, James flopped onto the bed. "I was going to check out the town, but I think I'll stay in the room for a bit longer. That Jimmy Lang fellow might not have gone back to his RV yet, and I think we're going to have more than our fill of that guy by the end of this festival."

Bennett grinned. "Our fill? Nice culinary pun, Professor. I hope you get through that book fast so you can educate the rest of us on regular contest categories before we eat a piece of barbecued possum."

"You're kidding, right?" James was alarmed.

"No, man." Bennett shook his head.

"They've got a category called 'Anything Butt.' And if there's already categories for chicken, pork, and beef, then what meats do you think are left?"

James rifled through his book until he located the table of contents. "I don't know, but I'm going to find out before I end up with a piece of rattlesnake *'cue* on the end of my fork!"

INN AT FOX HALL'S
WARM CHICKEN SALAD

3 cups cooked chicken, cubed
1 cup green seedless grapes, halved
1 cup sliced celery (optional)
1 cup mayonnaise
1/2 cup toasted slivered almonds
2 tablespoons lemon juice
2 tablespoons onion, finely chopped
1/2 teaspoon salt
1/2 cup grated Parmesan cheese
1/2 cup bread crumbs

Preheat the oven to 325 degrees and lightly grease a 2-quart baking dish. In a large bowl, mix all of the ingredients except for the grated cheese and the bread crumbs. Spoon mixture into the baking dish. Mix the cheese and bread crumbs together and sprinkle them over the chicken mixture. Bake in the preheated oven until warm and the cheese is melted, approximately 20 minutes. Serve on croissants or toasted buns.

FIVE:
ROAST CORN
ON A STICK

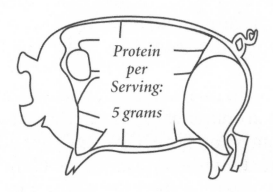

Protein per Serving: 5 grams

When James and the rest of the supper club members made their way to the Hudsonville town park, the number of people awaiting the kickoff of Hog Fest astounded them. Swarms of men, women, and children of all ages stood beyond the park entrance, talking animatedly and glancing excitedly at their watches.

The park had been divided into quadrants, the largest of which was further partitioned by the main road. Flanking the road, which led to the recreation center on one end and the tent where the barbecue entries would be judged on the other, were vendors selling fried food. These booths offered up all types of batter-dipped foods from sweet potatoes to fried okra to fried bananas to fried peanut butter cups. Behind their napkin-stacked counters, multiple vats of grease bubbled in anticipation. Perspiring merchants wearing a spectrum of colored aprons and matching visors prepared their booths for the imminent crush of hungry customers.

The Flab Five were allowed to enter the festival grounds early as R. C. Richter, the head judge of Hog Fest and president of the Hudsonville Chamber of Commerce, needed to review the rules of the sow beauty queen contest with them. Strolling down the park's main road in search of the indoor recreation center, the group gazed wide-eyed at the assortment of merchandise being positioned for sale. The fragrant line of food vendors was separated from the dry goods merchants by an area of picnic tables surrounded by garbage cans. James and his friends walked by booths of plush pigs dressed in jean jackets and straw hats, personalized leather key chains, handmade pottery, carved wooden walking sticks, necklaces made from crystallized grains of rice, water colors of the Blue Ridge Mountains, neon windsocks, Hog Fest T-shirts, and much more.

James's vision began to blur by the time they reached the end row of the tradesmen, but his eyes were assailed by a fresh variety of primary colors as they viewed the area where caricaturists, clowns selling pig-shaped balloons, temporary-tattoo artists, and face painters were tucking dollar bills into aprons or stirring paint as they occasionally checked the time. In less than thirty minutes, the festival would open. The feeling of anticipation among the vendors was palpable.

Inside the recreation center, a modern building made of glass and steel, men and women bustled about with determined strides, holding clipboards and walkie-talkies. A slim man in a blue button-down shirt waved at James and his friends as they approached a reception desk stacked with park maps, contest times and locations, and schedules for the entertainment events.

"Welcome!" The man shook hands all around. "I'm R. C. Richter, president of the Hudsonville Chamber of Commerce and head judge here at Hog Fest. Thank you kindly for agreeing to be our celebrity judges this weekend." He smiled at them, though it was clear that he wanted to dispense with the formalities and get down to business. "I trust you're finding the Inn at Fox Hall satisfactory? Eleanor Fiennes works very hard to please all of her guests."

"It's simply divine!" Gillian gushed. "Why, I saw so many species of birds on the nature walk I took after lunch that I felt as though I were truly in a *sanctuary.*"

As Gillian took a breath in order to describe Fox Hall's flora and fauna in complete detail, James put a hand on his friend's shoulder to distract her. In answer to R. C.'s question, James replied, "The inn is great, thank you. But I'm sure you're very busy and would like to give us the lay of the land before the festival begins."

R. C. nodded gratefully. "Yes. Please follow me, folks. I've got name badges for you to wear this weekend. Kindly display them in a visible location on your person at all times. These are how you'll gain entry to restricted areas around the festival. They will also grant you discounts at the majority of the vendor booths. Of course, any entertainment venues you'd be interested in attending are free of charge. Just show the ticket takers your name badges and they'll let you right in."

"Wow. We *are* getting the red-carpet treatment. I'd better look over which singers are performing. Maybe some of my favorite country bands are here." Lindy grabbed several schedules from the reception desk and glanced at them as the group hastened down a long hall to a conference room.

R. C. directed them to each take a seat in one of the maroon leather chairs. "Please make yourselves comfortable. The Hog Queen Contest will take place later this evening after a series of opening ceremony events. At eight p.m., the contestants will be paraded down a length of purple carpet. The name and weight of each contestant will be announced and your duty will be to judge each female on her size, personality, grace, and costume." He grinned. "Unlike most beauty contests, the more a contestant weighs, the higher her score. But it's not always the biggest sow that wins. Some of their owners can get quite creative with their costumes."

Lucy cleared her throat. "So we have four categories?"

"And each category should be given a score of one to ten?" James sought clarification as he didn't want to make any errors on his scorecard.

R. C. gave an affirmative nod to both

questions. "Yes. And I must emphasize an important point. The owners, regardless of their appearance *or* behavior, are not to be considered in your judgment of the contestants. I'm sorry to say that some have even tried to bribe judges in the past. I know that you five will remain unfazed by such attempts, but I thought I should warn you all the same."

"Do some of the owners dress up like their pigs?" Bennett peered at R. C. in disbelief.

"Indeed, Mr. Marshall." R. C. reddened slightly. "And some of them barely dress at all." He coughed slightly in embarrassment. "Allow me to show you a slide from last year's contest."

R. C. reached over to the wall to turn off the lights and James noticed that the armpits of his shirt were stained with sweat.

I wouldn't want to be the one to run this show, James thought, but he decided to pay close attention to the popular venues at the festival in case he could replicate any of them for the library's next Spring Fling.

As the room fell dark, an image appeared on the white screen at the end of the room. It showed an enormous and rather hairy-looking black sow wearing a pink tutu. A pink ribbon had been tied around its ear. The photo had been taken directly in front of the judges' table and the owner, a rather large woman stuffed into a matching tutu, was caught in time making an awkward attempt at a plié. The impression she achieved, however, was of possessing a severe case of constipation.

"My, my," Gillian uttered.

"Is this last year's winner?" Lucy asked, her blue eyes crinkling with amusement.

R. C. turned the lights back on. "No. I believe this contestant was one of the larger entries, but she didn't win. I just wanted you to get a sense of what you'll be seeing tonight. Of course, there's no way to illustrate an individual's personality on screen."

"What kind of personality can a pig have?" Bennett muttered, but R. C. overheard.

"You'd be surprised, Mr. Marshall. Some of these ladies will trot as proudly up the carpet as a thoroughbred racehorse. Some will give you flirty snorts or roll their eyes at you. There's plenty of ways the contestants can stand out from the field."

"I appreciate the *respectful* manner in which you refer to these contestants," Gillian said, beaming at R. C. "I was initially afraid that this contest might belittle these lovely and intelligent animals, but I can see that you truly approach this pageant with a high degree of dignity. I applaud you!" Gillian clapped her hands as R. C. blushed.

Luckily, his walkie-talkie began to crackle and he excused himself to answer what sounded like an urgent stream of babble. As the supper club members watched, the veil of sweat on his forehead began to drip down his temple. He dug a red bandana from his pocket and dabbed at his face. "Are you sure?" he tersely asked the person on the other end and then hurriedly added, "Over."

"I'm sure, boss."

R. C. replaced the walkie-talkie into its case on his belt. "It seems as though I may need to beg a favor. Four of our judges, who happen to be family members, have contracted pinkeye. Due to the fact that they are contagious over the next twenty-four hours until their antibiotics take effect, they have withdrawn from judging the Brisket category. Could I count on four of you to temporarily step into their shoes?"

Gillian put her hand to her breast. "I simply cannot come face-to-face with that much meat. I'm sorry, but I *must* refuse."

James exchanged glances with the rest of his friends. They issued him subtle nods. "We four would be glad to help," he offered.

R. C. exhaled in relief. "I do thank you. We'll be reviewing the judging policies for the food contests in the morning." He distributed schedules and a baggie filled with red tickets to all of them. "These tickets are for the food vendors around the festival. Each ticket is good for a single item. Should you need any more, just show the receptionist your name badge and she'll refill your baggie. We have a small token of our appreciation for each of you as well, which we will present tonight at the Hog Queen contest."

The head judge led them back to the main doors of the recreation center and then marched off to solve a dispute between two barbecue contestants who were both claiming the same parking spot for their campers.

"That guy's gonna need a stiff drink before this day is done," Bennett commented.

"I'm kind of parched myself," Lucy said, shaking her bag of red tickets. "Let's go spend some of these!"

"This is so much fun!" Lindy squealed as they approached the food vendors. "I feel like a kid who's just gotten birthday money from rich grandparents."

Suddenly, a deep voice boomed over a loudspeaker, welcoming all visitors to the town of Hudsonville and the commencement of the sixteenth Hudsonville Hog Fest, sponsored by the Hudsonville Chamber of Commerce and Richter's RV Sales & Rentals.

"As soon as the mayor cuts the pink ribbon at the entrance gates," the male voice pronounced, "Hog Fest will officially be under way! Don't forget to visit Richter's RVs for the best motor homes this side of the Appalachians!"

James and his friends ceased paying attention as the announcer listed locations for maps, ticket sales, and restrooms and then began to warn visitors about which items were prohibited around the festival grounds.

"I'm getting some hot sausages with onions and peppers before the mob gets in," Bennett said, pointing at a booth selling Italian sausages and all-beef hot dogs.

"Me too," Lindy agreed. "But without the peppers and onions."

Gillian twisted a strand of orange hair on her finger. "What am I going to eat at this place? I'm either going to have survive on a diet of greasy fries or starve!"

"Come on." James steered her toward a nearby vendor. "It's not all pig or fried foods. Just smell the aroma of roast corn on the cob." James held out two tickets to a woman wearing a green apron. "Your corn smells delicious."

"Thanks, hon. It's roasted with enough butter to stop your heart from beatin'."

James smiled at her. "Perfect. We'll take two."

The five friends had filled their empty bellies with sausage and corn and shared two elephant ears among themselves. After they dusted confectioners' and cinnamon sugar from their pants, they decided to check out the area where the barbecue contests would take place.

The judging area consisted of a large white tent erected on a section of grass that would normally serve as part of the park's soccer field. The two tent openings were cordoned off using thick pink twine. A sign taped to the twine warned that admittance was granted to contest officials only and that should contestants enter without permission, they would be instantly disqualified.

"This barbecue contest is so serious!" Lindy exclaimed. "I had no idea." She shifted through the schedules in her hand. "Does it say what the prizes are anywhere?"

James pointed at an orange sheet of paper as he tried to suck fragments of corn from between his back molars. "The festival champion gets the biggest prize. Anyone who wins that title gets five thousand dollars, a new commercial trailer cooker — valued at almost nine thousand — and a contract with Heartland Foods. You heard Jimmy at lunch. That contract's worth a lot of money."

"Who's Jimmy?" Gillian frowned, poking at a piece of corn caught in her lower teeth with her fingernail. "Did you have lunch with a barbecue aficionado?"

"You could say that." Bennett sniffed. "Mostly we watched as he inhaled enough food for three people."

"That's because half of it ended up on his shirt, the tablecloth, and his beard," Lindy scoffed.

"He's one of the contestants," James explained to Gillian. "He has, ah, a rather *large* personality. Calls himself The Pitmaster."

"According to this schedule, everyone competes in teams." Lindy studied the orange paper. "Jimmy's team is called the Pitmasters, but there are five other teams competing." She grinned. "You guys are gonna love these names. The other teams are the the Thigh and Mighties, an all-female team called Adam's Ribbers, the Marrow Men, the Tenderizers, and the

Finger Lickers. Each team has a leader, or spokesperson, and theirs is the only name listed in the program. They're the ones who'll be turning in their team's food to the judges."

The group climbed a small hill leading to the cooking area. "I guess it makes sense to cook as a part of a team," Bennett said. "Then you can enter every category and have a better chance at winning. Besides, according to this rule sheet, most of these guys will have to take turns staying up all night. Some of these entries, like barbecued brisket, take more than a day to cook."

"Looks like they've already started." Lucy gestured at the campground area spread out in front of them.

The five friends paused, taking in the view of hundreds upon hundreds of RVs parked alongside one another in remarkably straight rows for what seemed like miles. Striped awnings had been unfurled, and lawn chairs and folding tables had been unfolded and decorated with cloths and cushions. Boom boxes competed with one another, though most played country music, while American flags or banners representing favorite sports teams flew from camper roofs. Some of the travelers had even spread out rolls of out-door carpet in order to make their temporary parcels homier.

But above all the other pieces of equipment, there was one outdoor fixture that formed the centerpiece of each campsite: the grill. There were grills of all shapes and sizes. James spotted tiny camping grills; full-sized backyard grills with propane tanks; space-age, egg-shaped cookers; and enormous, cylinder-shaped cookers that required their own trailers and were no doubt used by the professional barbecue teams.

"Those things are so big they've gotta be towed behind the RVs," Bennett stated, looking at the closest professional cooker. "Shoot, I've seen European cars smaller than them. You could hide two grown men in one of those grills." He inhaled blissfully. "Ah, yeah! Folks are cooking some meat, all right."

"You just ate," Gillian pointed out. "How can you sound so enticed?"

"Doesn't mean I couldn't eat some more later, woman," Bennett replied pleasantly. "You know, they're gonna have chicken barbecue here, too. You don't have to eat corn and hush puppies the whole time, unless you're goin' full-scale vegetarian on us this weekend."

Gillian stared at the grills and curtains of smoke suspiciously. "That is *certainly* my preference."

"Hey! Let's go check out what the teams look like," Lucy suggested, hoping to divert Gillian. "I'd like to see what the all-female team is up to."

James hesitated. "Are we supposed to fraternize with the contestants?"

Lucy shrugged. "We haven't been given the food-judging guidelines yet. As of now, we're just tourists and, I've got to admit, I find this all pretty fascinating."

Gillian put her hands on her hips and gave her toes inside her Birkenstock sandals an agitated wiggle. "*I* would prefer to view the sand-drawing event." She held a map in front of her face. "It's in Area C. I find the combination of flowing sand and graceful motion very soothing. Would anyone care to join me?"

Receiving no offers, Gillian told her friends that she would see them later on at the Hog Fest beauty contest.

"Poor Gillian." Lindy watched their friend stride away in a flowing skirt of lavender with tiny brass bells stitched on the hem. "I hope she can have a good time at this festival."

"Sure she can." Bennett waved off Lindy's concern. "Did you get a load of all those hippie vendors? And what about the trained dog performances? And she loves our hotel. She can take nature walks for the rest of the festival once we're done pickin' out the piggy princess."

As the foursome strolled by RVs the size of commercial buses, they heard the familiar voice of Jimmy Lang. He had his arm slung around a familiar-looking young woman. As the supper club members slowed in order to witness their exchange, Jimmy whispered something into the girl's ear, gave her a light swat on the bottom, and laughed as she waved goodbye.

"Wasn't that Eleanor's daughter?" Lindy asked, appalled.

Just then, the side door of a mid-sized RV opened, and a wide-hipped, thick-thighed woman with blonde hair and black roots stepped down onto the trampled grass, eyeing Jimmy warily. "Who you talkin' to, Jimmy?"

"No one, sugar lips," Jimmy replied in a hoarse bark. "Your Big Daddy's sure thirsty, though." Once again, Jimmy was sweating profusely. "Can you be my baby doll and get me a cold one?"

The woman pulled her tank top down over a roll of exposed flesh protruding from her tight jean shorts. "Sure, hon."

At that moment, Jimmy looked up and

saw the supper club members staring at him.

"Why, if it ain't the beauty judges!" he bellowed with a smile, displaying his repulsive flaky lips and mouth filled with yellow teeth. "I'm sure glad you popped by. I've got some ribs that are just 'bout ready to eat. Gotta wait 'til the bark's just right."

"The bark?" Bennett asked, curiosity sparkling in his brown eyes.

"Yessir. That's the crust of rub that forms on the outside of the meat when it's been cooking loooong and sloooow. It's so good you'd think you'd died and gone to heaven." He swung around as the woman reappeared with his beer. "Thanks, darlin'. Y'all, this is my old lady, Hailey."

James and his friends shook hands with Jimmy's girlfriend. James figured Jimmy was about fifty years old, but Hailey was easily ten years Jimmy's junior. A tattoo of a dove flew across the round hump of her left breast, and James couldn't help but stare at the revealed flesh. Noting his gaze, Hailey pulled down the tank top, revealing a fuchsia lace bra and the rest of the dove's body.

"Isn't she purty?" She smiled at James. "I did some time in juvey. Had a drug problem until I found Jesus. Now, I'm clean and free as a dove, so that's why I got this tattoo.

Those were the only good things that came out of all my days as a user. This tattoo and my Jimmy Bear. 'Course, he's clean now, too."

"That's right, baby." Jimmy looked less than pleased at Hailey's confession. Wiping his puffy face with a dishcloth, he said, "Why don't you fetch these fine folks some brewskis? They's judgin' the pig contest in a bit and are gonna need a bit of a buzz." He took a pull of his beer and frowned. "Just doesn't taste like it used to," he mumbled.

"That's okay, thanks," Lucy quickly said to Hailey to prevent her from getting more beer from inside the RV. "We're really full. We just finished dinner, actually."

James made a show of looking at his watch. "And we'd better head over to the contest area."

As he and his friends moved to turn away, a woman dragging several small dogs behind her passed by Jimmy's cooking area. She stopped abruptly when she saw Jimmy and Hailey. Her eyes narrowed and her lips curled in anger and disgust. To James's surprise, the trim and petite woman then marched over and spit on the closed lid of Jimmy's cooker.

"I hope your meat rots on the bone!" she hissed acidly. "I hope your sauce tastes like mashed maggots! I hope that you lose every single contest you enter for the rest of your life!" She spit on the cooker again as Jimmy stood in amused silence, his meaty arms crossed over his mammoth gut. The small smile playing around the corners of his mouth only incensed the woman further. "You redneck bastard! I hope you drown in beer and barbecue sauce and bad luck! I hope you get *exactly* what you deserve in this life!" She looked at Hailey. "You're with a *bad* man. He's going to bring you down. Mark my words."

With a jerk on the leash, she stormed off.

As Hailey issued Jimmy a bewildered look, Jimmy shrugged and saluted the woman's back with his beer. Craning his neck in order to view her retreating form, he shouted, "Everybody hates a winner!" His tone was both mocking and filled with a merry laughter. "Yessir. That's me! There's losers all over this here festival, but I ain't one of 'em!" he shouted louder, attracting the attention of the competing teams, who broke off conversations in order to listen to the ravings of the leader of the Pitmasters.

"That's right!" Jimmy called out to them. "You can count on nothin' but second place, suckers! I've got the secret to perfect 'cue and you ain't got it! I'm the winner!

I'm the champion! I'm the future face of Heartland's barbecue line. Y'all can go on and pack up now. Save yourselves the trouble. Jimmy's here and Jimmy's as good as won! Y'all hearin' me?" He guffawed. "Y'alls' entry fees are goin' straight into my pocket. So this Bud's for you! Thanks for givin' me a little more spendin' money!" He drank deeply from his beer.

Most of the men and women standing around their cookers scowled angrily at Jimmy, but no one responded directly to his taunts. Several flipped him the bird, and one of the women from Adam's Ribbers called him a fat pig, but the majority of the other competitors elected to ignore his boasts.

Jimmy walked back to his cooker, lifted the lid, and began to remove foil-wrapped meat from within using a pair of metal tongs. He whistled as he worked, as though his behavior was both expected and perfectly acceptable. On the other hand, James couldn't help but notice Hailey's face as she stood on the steps leading inside the RV. Her gaze was fixed somewhere behind James and her eyes were wide with fear.

Before James could investigate the possible source of Hailey's dread, Lucy grabbed him by the arm and pulled him away.

"Come on, James. We can't keep the future Queen of Hog Fest waiting."

Six:
Pig-Shaped
Strawberry
Cupcakes

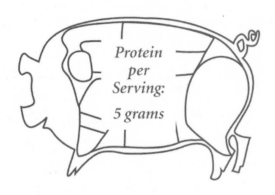

Protein per Serving:

5 grams

Hundreds of onlookers were gathered around the park's outdoor track in order to view the Queen of Hog Fest Beauty Contest. Gillian, who already was seated in a high-back chair at the judges' table, broke off her animated conversation with R. C. Richter to wave her friends over.

"Look!" she exclaimed, gesturing at their table. "Isn't this elegant? I *feel* so celebrated by these touches of finery."

Indeed, the setup was impressive. Their

table had been draped with a pink linen cloth and lush buntings in a darker shade of pink encased the perimeter. Crystal water goblets with matching pitchers had been set before each judge's seat. Saucers containing slices of fresh lemons and limes were positioned next to the pitchers of ice water. Gillian poured water into her own glass and motioned for her friends to follow her lead.

"We're going to need this *pure* and *refreshing* spring water, my friends. The local baker, Mrs. Phelps, has made us a special treat." She smiled, her good humor returned in the face of such royal treatment. "R. C. told me that Mrs. Phelps is bringing us strawberry cupcakes so famous that people have been known to drive down here from D.C. just to buy a dozen."

"Yes indeed." R. C. nodded proudly. "Mrs. Phelps uses real pieces of strawberry in the icing, and she frosts all the cupcakes upside-down so there's more buttercream per square inch." He looked up as a woman in her early seventies carrying a covered tray approached the table. "And here she comes now."

"Welcome, folks!" Mrs. Phelps gave them a hearty smile as she placed the tray on the table. With a flourish, she removed the domed top and waited for a reaction.

All of the supper club members murmured appreciative *oohs* and *ahs* when they saw the confections Mrs. Phelps had created for them. A pink cupcake rested in the exact center of a china plate drizzled with strawberry glaze. Each cupcake bore a unique pig's face, complete with candy eyes, a cookie nose, and strawberry wafer ears. However, Mrs. Phelps had given each cupcake its own look by adding rainbow sprinkle eye shadow, licorice lace eyelashes, a chocolate-chip beauty mark, pursed lips made from Red Hots, or powdered cheeks created with white gumdrops.

"Enjoy!" she told the judges and then winked at R. C. "I've got one for you, too, Mr. Richter. I left it in your office 'cause I figured the frostin' might get too gooey before you had a chance to sink your teeth into it, you bein' so busy and all."

"Thank you, Mrs. Phelps. I hope you've got plenty of extra help this weekend, because after I mention your shop in this evening's announcements, folks are going to be lined up elbow to elbow, wanting to buy some of your delicious homemade goodies."

"Oh, I've got plenty of help, sir. This weekend's my bread and butter. This here festival keeps me goin' durin' the leaner months. That's why all of us in Hudsonville are right thankful for all of your hard work." Mrs. Phelps beamed.

"It's my pleasure, Mrs. Phelps." R. C. colored, embarrassed by the compliment.

The baker appeared to be in no hurry to move away. " 'Course, I'm sure it's the same thing for you and your RV business," she said. "I bet you get plenty of sales after folks feast their eyes on the fancy trailers they've got down there in the barbecue cookin' area." Noting the time on her digital watch, Mrs. Phelps wiped her hands on her shirt and seemed surprised to discover that she wasn't wearing an apron. "Well, good luck, y'all!" she told the judges, took one last look at her baked handiwork, and then disappeared into the crowd.

"I guess this festival generates good revenue for the majority of the local businesses," James said to R. C.

"Our coffers would certainly be emptier without it," R. C. agreed. "And Hog Fest grows bigger and bigger every year. I'm very proud of its success. Why, Hudsonville has been featured in fifteen national magazines as a result of our little barbecue party."

"Have you always lived here?" Lindy asked.

R. C. nodded. "My whole life." He then

paused and let his eyes pass over the faces in the crowd. "Everyone I love is here. My business is here. My roots are here. The woman I love is here. Yes indeed, this town is *everything* to me," he added passionately and then cleared his throat. "Excuse me, but it's time for the contest to get underway. I'm going to make a few announcements and then we'll get started. Are you all ready?"

"I can't wait to check out the sexy sows!" Bennett exclaimed and Gillian shot him a dirty look.

"We're all set," Lucy replied more sedately and then took a delicate bite of her cupcake. "Wow," she breathed. "Wow!" She took another, heartier bite. "I'm going to come back and judge every year if they give us these."

"What about your protein diet?" James teased.

"Forget it," Lucy said lightheartedly. "I'm on vacation with my best friends! I'm going to eat whatever I want." She hesitated. "Well, at least for tonight anyway."

"Here, here!" Lindy clinked forks with Lucy as R. C. stepped up to the microphone. After plugging his own business and then encouraging the audience to patronize the Main Street Bakery, R. C. introduced each of the supper club members by name and embellished upon their wisdom and courage in solving crimes in the Shenandoah Valley.

As the audience clapped for them, the judges blushed in embarrassment. With the exception of Lindy, who waved at the crowd as though she were a state dignitary, they were all relieved when R. C. invited the first contestant to step out onto the strip of purple carpet that emerged from a large tent where the beauty queen hopefuls waited. The carpet passed by the judges' table and then ended in a small pen where the contestants and their owners were required to wait while the judges came to their final decisions.

"Our first contestant is Little Miss Twinkletoes!" R. C. hollered out.

The crowd roared as a massive pink pig stepped onto the carpet. She wore a silver skirt and had a wreath of silver stars set upon the bristled hairs of her forehead. Her ears were longer than James had expected, and they flopped up and down as Little Miss Twinkletoes did her best to dance down the carpet. As she came closer to the table, James noticed that her leathery skin was covered by silver glitter. Her owner was dressed in a silver evening gown that revealed a large portion of her cleavage, and her eyelids sparkled with the same silver glitter that adorned her pig.

Stopping in front of the table, the woman turned Little Miss Twinkletoes in a circle before the judges and then said, "Dance, Twinkletoes!"

The sow lifted up her front hooves one at a time and then snorted. Pleased, her owner blew some glitter in the judges' direction and then led her pig to the holding pen.

"Damn that woman," Bennett grumbled after the owner was out of earshot. "She got fairy dust in my cupcake." Scowling, he pushed his plate away and made fierce marks on his score sheet.

"Remember," Gillian chided. "You cannot judge the *contestant* based on the behavior of its *handler.* Don't pout. Here, have some of mine." She cut off a portion of her cupcake and placed it on Bennett's napkin.

The next pig was named Ms. Harley, and she was appropriately dressed in a leather skirt and a metal-spiked collar. Harley seemed bored by the entire event and had to be dragged down the carpet by her owner, a fearsome-looking bodybuilder wearing leather pants that appeared painted on her bulbous limbs. Her white ribbed tank top was stretched so tightly over her muscu-

118

lar torso that the judges could see the shadow of a black bra beneath the thin cotton top.

After Harley labored off to the pen, the judges were introduced to Jasmine, an enormous black pig dressed as a hula dancer; Cherub, a brown-spotted pig wearing wings and a halo; Candy, who wore the trademark Playboy bunny ears and tail; and Annie, a spunky sow wearing a cowboy hat and a red bandana.

Bennett's eyes grew into round moons as a pig named Hot Stuff strutted onto the carpet clothed in a gold sequined bikini and a sunbonnet. It wasn't the pig that caught Bennett's attention, however. Her owner, who led her animal using a silk ribbon instead of a piece of rope, wore a matching string bikini that barely covered either her bosom or her rump. Smiling at the barrage of whistles and catcalls from the male members of the audience, the curvaceous woman wiggled her derriere. As she did so, Hot Stuff wiggled hers, and the crowd broke into raucous laughter, followed by some lewd commentary from a handful of men.

"Where is that woman's dignity?" Gillian huffed, and she jabbed at her score sheet.

"Remember," Bennett said, poking Gillian in the ribs with his pencil. "You can't judge the owner, just the pig!"

James's favorite contestant was a pig so large that her belly almost swept the ground as she waddled down the carpet. Her name was Barbie Eden, and she wore filmy pantaloons and a veil like the original *I Dream of Jeannie.* Barbie's walk was deliberate and graceful, and when she reached the judges' table, she dipped her head, blinked her eyes, and wriggled her wide snout.

The delighted audience chanted Barbie's name.

Finally, all of the contestants were contained in the holding pen to await the announcement of the victor. The queen would then be crowned with a golden wreath, and a sash indicating that she ruled Hog Fest would be placed around her neck. To the immense relief of the supper club members, who had little experience with large swine, R. C. had volunteered to handle these tasks. Once she was crowned, the queen would take a final walk on the purple carpet and then head home for a good night's sleep. The next day, she would ride in the back seat of a convertible from the recreation center to the barbecue contest area. Her arrival would symbolize the official beginning of the cook-off portion of the festival as well as the first day of her new life as a local celebrity.

James had no trouble tabulating his scorecard. He voted for Barbie Eden to win. Bennett, who sat on his left, did not bother to hide that he had chosen Hot Stuff. Gillian had shielded her clipboard as though it contained the blueprints to a new weapon of mass destruction, but as R. C. held out his hand for her score sheet, James could see that she had picked Twinkletoes. R. C. collected scorecards from Lindy and Lucy, glanced over all five of them, and smiled.

"We have a winner," he said to the judges, thanked them, and approached the microphone.

"Ladies and gentlemen, we have seen some lovely females here tonight. Let's give them all a hearty congratulations." He paused while the crowd whooped, whistled, and applauded for the pigs and their owners. "We've seen talent, creativity, and the beauty of a few extra pounds this evening. However, only one contestant can be named the Queen of Hudsonville Hog Fest. That lucky lady will enjoy a life of fame and leisure on a local Hudsonville farm and her owner and a guest will be treated to a wonderful, all-expense-paid trip to Jamaica along with five hundred dollars in spending money. Sounds like the *royal* treatment to me."

He waited, allowing the dramatic moment to build. "Is everyone ready to hear the winning name?" The crowd cheered and R. C. grinned indulgently. "All right folks, I won't make you wait a second longer. I am proud to announce that the winner of this year's pageant, weighing in at four hundred and forty-four pounds, goes to none other than Miss Barbie Eden."

Barbie's owner shrieked in delight and then gave her pig a big kiss on the snout. Barbie grunted in return and calmly accepted her crown and sash. As Barbie took another walk on the purple carpet, flash-bulbs clicked and the theme song for Miss America played on the loudspeakers. As James watched the new queen walk past, the music couldn't help but make him think of Jimmy Lang and how the loud-mouthed barbecue expert had sung the same song during lunch at Fox Hall.

Once Barbie reached the end of the carpet, R. C. removed an envelope from his coat, handed it to Barbie's owner, and then spoke into the microphone, thanking the judges once again for their time. As the spectators began to disperse, R. C. returned to the judges' table and indicated that gift bags for all five of them were being held behind the reception desk in the recreation center.

"I didn't want them to sit out here during the contest," he explained. "There's a box of truffles in each one, and I didn't want to chance them going soft." He gazed up at the star-pocked sky. "Mind you, it's been quite pleasant tonight, but it's going to be a scorcher tomorrow, so make sure you have your water bottles filled to the brim."

R. C. wished them all a pleasant evening and reminded James, Lindy, Bennett, and Lucy to appear for the mandatory food-judging meeting at ten a.m. sharp.

"How long's that gonna take?" Bennett asked. "Don't we just say whether we like the food or not?"

"Mr. Marshall." R. C.'s pleasant demeanor turned firm. "This contest is quite serious. There are a multitude of facets to being a fair and just barbecue judge."

Abashed, Bennett nodded. "Sure, sure. Don't worry, I'll follow every rule to the letter. I'm really lookin' forward to gettin' the inside view on this whole thing."

R. C. seemed satisfied by Bennett's answer. He was about to turn away, undoubtedly to tend to another festival duty when he seemed to suddenly remember something. "You'll also find a red raffle ticket in your gift bags. Most folks pay ten dollars apiece for these, but if you're lucky enough, you could be returning to Quincy's Gap towing a brand new RV trailer behind your vehicle, courtesy of Richter's RV Sales & Rentals."

"That would get me half a bookmobile," James muttered to his friends as R. C. melted into the crowd.

"What are you using for one in the meantime?" Lucy asked.

"Oh, Wendell rigged up one of the retired school buses in his yard. He's basically toting books around in big, plastic bins strapped to the decrepit seats with bungee cords, but it's better than nothing."

Lindy pulled one of the festival schedules out of her purse. "Okay, fellow celebrities, what do y'all want to do now? I'd like to check out the rockabilly concert. It just started a few minutes ago. And we've got free entry to all of the events everyone *else* has to pay for!"

Gillian glanced at her watch. "I'd normally be meditating in order to clear my head before sleep about now, but I'll go with you. I do like the *unique* tones of rockabilly music."

Lucy shrugged. "I'm in, too. Besides, you need me to come, seeing as I'm your chauffeur." She turned to James, her eyes hopeful. "What about you guys?"

"I've gotta hit the trivia books," Bennett answered immediately. "But if you wanna stay, James, I can hike back to the inn from here. It's only a few miles."

James shook his head. "No need. This heat's made me kind of sluggish. We'll pick up the gift bags and take them back to Fox Hall," James told the ladies, trying not to let the disappointment in Lucy's face affect him. He wondered if Lucy planned to cozy up to him over the next few days, as Murphy was over a hundred miles away. He watched her and his other two female friends walk away, stopping to chat with the owners of the pig beauty contestants. Again, he couldn't prevent himself from staring at Lucy's streamlined body or notice how her caramel-colored hair glimmered beneath the strings of white lights forming a canopy over the animal pen. He had always thought she was beautiful, and nothing about their roller-coaster relationship would ever change that fact.

"Hey, man!" Bennett waved his hand in front of James's eyes. "You comin' or what?"

"Yeah, sure." James looked away from Lucy just as she turned back to see if he was still standing there.

125

James and Bennett collected five Hog Fest tote bags stuffed with goodies from the recreation center and then headed toward the parking lot. The car lot was adjacent to the camper area, and James noticed that more and more people were gathered around their barbecue cookers. Crescents of smoke drifted into the night and the glow of lit cigarettes made the cooking area seem as though it had been overrun by a swarm of fireflies. Raucous laughter filled the air, and James guessed that bottles of beer and whiskey were being passed around among the cooking teams.

"They've got to stay up all night tonight, right?" he asked Bennett.

"At least one of them will. They wanna cook those briskets just as slow as they can to make the meat as tender as filet mignon." He smacked his lips together. "Always been a favorite of mine, brisket. I can hardly wait to sample all the entries tomorrow. That's what I call a first-class Southern-style lunch. A big pile of meat and not much else. Yessir."

As James gazed down the aisles between campers, he noticed the familiar bulk of Jimmy Lang behind one of the larger RVs. He was speaking to a taller man wearing a white T-shirt and cargo shorts. James was too far away to hear their conversation, but both men appeared agitated. The taller man's profile was hidden from James behind a baseball cap worn at an angle. The cap was black and had some kind of silver symbol on the front, which was unfamiliar to James. The brim of the hat dipped up and down as the man nodded his head, trying to drive his point home.

As James watched, the taller man suddenly took a threatening step toward Jimmy, raising his voice to an angry shout. Jimmy wore what James assumed was his typical expression of amusement, but when the man finished yelling and stomped off, Jimmy's smile immediately faded away.

Unaware that James's attention was elsewhere, Bennett chatted about the festival events that he planned to attend the next day.

"You'd better read that barbecue book of yours tonight," Bennett suggested, but James didn't reply. He was too fixated on Jimmy's posture, for the large man had slumped back against the rear of the trailer and had bowed his head so that he could hide his face in his hands. This Jimmy bore little resemblance to the boisterous and cocksure man James had seen earlier in the day, the man who claimed he would be the festival's champion and be well on his way to a life of fame and fortune. Instead, he seemed tired. In fact, though the barbecue contest had yet to begin, Jimmy Lang already looked defeated.

Seven:
Blue Ribbon
Brisket

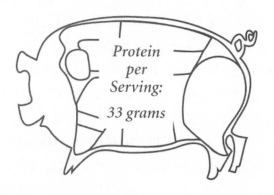

James had never slept in the same room with Bennett before, and he was unsure whether he could survive a second night as his roommate. Bennett studied his trivia books until after midnight and then fell asleep with the table lamp on. Lying flat on his back with his arms stretched out to the side, Bennett's mouth hung open and the sounds that erupted from his throat sounded like the contented growls of a hibernating grizzly bear.

By quarter after six in the morning, James gave up any further attempt at sleep. Removing the pillows he had piled over his head, he pulled on a pair of jeans and his favorite William & Mary sweatshirt, slid his bare feet into a pair of worn loafers, grabbed his book on the history of barbecue, and crept downstairs.

The stairs creaked as though protesting his early arrival. No one else seemed to be awake. The entire first floor of the inn was silent, but James remembered that the note to guests placed in their rooms indicated that there was a self-service coffee urn located in the main hall and that coffee would be ready each morning by six thirty.

Ten minutes, James thought. He hoped Eleanor would be punctual in setting out the coffee urn. In the meantime, he decided to settle himself in a rocker on the front porch. The morning was gray and a low mist hovered over the tired-looking summer grass. Robins poked around for worms in the lawn as jays pecked through the sprinkler-moistened soil of the garden beds. There was a refreshing coolness to the early air that carried a faint hint of autumn.

James inhaled deeply and caught a whiff of rain. His mother always claimed that she could tell when rain was imminent by stepping outside her back door first thing in the morning and taking a deep breath. In the days before the Weather Channel, she had been the family meteorologist and had never once been wrong. James had often grumbled about taking a golf umbrella to school when none of the other children carried one, but he also remembered sharing its shelter with a few of the other kids as they waited at the bus stop.

"Rain can't be good for the festival," James said into the stillness and then opened his book to a section entitled "Presidential Barbecues." As he read about Lyndon Johnson's diplomatic dinners, which were conducted as family-style barbecues, James heard noises coming from the room behind him. Swiveling in his chair, he noticed that it was positioned in front of the kitchen window and that the window had been left open a crack.

"Coffee time," James murmured contentedly, glancing at his watch. He decided to finish the section on Johnson before claiming the first cup when he heard Eleanor's voice from inside the kitchen.

"Francesca Fiennes! Where on God's green earth have you been?" she asked angrily.

There was no response from Eleanor's

daughter.

"I told you to be home by midnight, which I thought was a mighty generous curfew for a person of your tender years, and how do you thank me? By keeping me up all night, worrying that you'd been abducted or . . . something worse!" Eleanor paused and then cried, "I even called the sheriff, Francesca! I was *that* worried!"

"I was *going* to call you." Francesca finally spoke, though there was no remorse in her voice. "But my cell battery died and then it got later and later at night and I . . . just fell asleep. I was hanging out at the festival with a bunch of my friends and we crashed in someone's tent."

"Someone's *tent?*" Eleanor sounded horrified. "*Whose* tent?"

Francesca didn't answer. Instead, James heard the rattle of silverware.

"I asked you a question, young lady." Eleanor's tone was strained. "In case you've forgotten, you are still living under *my* roof. I work my fingers to the bone each and every day, and the money from *this* inn pays for your clothes, your cell phone with the *dead battery,* and your contest entry fees. So when I tell you to be home by midnight, you'd better be home by eleven fifty-nine!"

"I don't want you to pay for those stupid

132

contests! I've never *once* asked you to spend money on them!" Francesca snapped. "I *told* you. I want to spend my free time tutoring disadvantaged kids. I want to be a teacher — not win a stupid makeup or modeling contract."

"We've been over this a *thousand* times." Eleanor was exasperated. "You can *be* a teacher *after* you've entered the Miss America contest. The judges will love your passion to help those little needy —" She broke off and then whispered fearfully, "Sweet Jesus! Are those love bites on your neck, Francesca?"

"They're called hickies, Ma. Get with the program, will you?"

James heard the crash of dishes. "That's just great, Francesca! Are you trying to drive me to an early grave? So you were out all night with some boy, doing God knows what, and now your neck is full of blemishes, your eyes are red, and you've got purple bags beneath them. You're *supposed* to be a princess today! Not some roll-me-in-the-hay teenage tramp!" Eleanor drew in a ragged breath. "Oh, that's right. You weren't in *hay* with a boy, you were in some filthy, mildewed *tent*."

There was a moment of silence and then Francesca calmly replied, "Who said I was with a boy? It could have been a *man.* An *older* man."

"Good Lord." James could almost visualize Eleanor grabbing onto the counter for support. "Please tell me that it wasn't that disgusting barbecue man, Jimmy Lang."

"I can't kiss and tell." Francesca goaded her mother.

"I'll *kill* him!" Eleanor raged. "So help me, I will! I've got plenty of pesticides and poisons to rid this world of *that* fat, nasty pest! Oh, the thought of him touching my beautiful girl! Franny, how could you?" Eleanor wailed, and then the sound was cut off as she covered her mouth.

"Don't worry, Ma. I'll still be ready for my enviable car ride with a *pig,* but I'm not going to follow *your* life plan for me much longer. I mean it!"

Seconds later, the front door slammed and Francesca appeared on the porch. She looked at James, keenly aware that he had listened in on the entire exchange with her mother.

"Coffee's ready," she told him nonchalantly and then headed off toward one of the nature trails.

From inside the kitchen, James could hear the muffled yet pained sounds of Eleanor weeping.

■ ■ ■ ■

Over a breakfast of sausage rolls, strawberries, and hunks of aged cheddar cheese, James told his friends about the altercation he had overheard.

"Francesca and Jimmy Lang?" Lindy asked and then gave an involuntary shiver. Glancing around to make sure that none of the other guests were listening, she lowered her voice. "That's too gross to picture."

Gillian examined the dregs of tea at the bottom of her china cup and frowned. "Do you think Eleanor was serious about having poison around the inn? I'd have thought she'd use harmless, *natural* pesticides. Maybe I shouldn't accept any more of her herbal tea blend recommendations."

"Just 'cause the woman has a nature trail doesn't mean she's down with all that goin' green mumbo jumbo," Bennett informed Gillian.

"Mumbo jumbo?" Scowling, Gillian regarded Bennett with disdain. "We only have *one* planet to call home, and if *we* don't take care of it —"

"If there's such a thing as global warming," Bennett cut her off, "then why is there a wintry chill in the air on an August morning in Virginia? Tell me that!"

"Because a cool front has come in from the mountains. It's supposed to rain all afternoon and into the evening," Lucy informed her friends. "I watched the local news while Lindy was curling her hair."

"Poor R. C.," Lindy sympathized while checking to make sure that her thick, black hair was still held captive in its invisible coating of hairspray. "And all of the vendors counting on nice weather. Rain must really cut into their profits."

James swallowed the last of his coffee and set the mug back onto the table with a firm thud. "I hope it *does* rain. I can come back here and take a nap. My *roommate* makes sounds that a freighter crashing into a cliff couldn't match."

"Must've been lyin' on my back," Bennett said with a smirk. "Just gimme a push so I roll to the side. Won't make a peep then."

"You could've advised me about that little detail *before* last night," James replied sulkily as his friends laughed.

"Come on, sunshine." Bennett nudged James in the side. "We don't want to keep R. C. waitin'."

Lucy checked her watch. "Gillian, are you going to hang out here for a bit or do you want a ride to the festival grounds now?"

Then, before Gillian could answer, she said, "Or I could just leave you my car, and Lindy and I can ride over with James." She quickly added, "And Bennett."

Gillian folded her hands in her lap and closed her eyes. "I've already been on a most *restorative* walk through the woods this morning. My soul has been so *refreshed* by the wise spirits of those old pines. Can you imagine all they must have witnessed?" Spreading her arms out as though embracing the air, she opened her eyes and cast a serene glance at Lucy. "I think I'll join you at Hog Fest. I'm going to watch the dog show. Mr. Richter agreed to allow me to hand out Pet Palace brochures to the audience members. What a *gracious* spirit he has."

"Well, since we'll all be eating barbecue for lunch, you can meet us after we're done judging." Lindy held out a map to Gillian upon which she had drawn a circle. "I checked out the vendor list and there's a Greek food booth near our judging area. You could get a salad and a few falafels and then join us for the announcement of the winner."

Gillian clapped with delight. "Oh, thank you, Lindy! I've never met a chickpea I didn't like!"

Bennett grimaced. "Let's get out of here, James. All this talk of vegetables is gonna put me off my meat!"

R. C. paced inside the tent where the judges would assess all the food entries in each barbecue category. A series of industrial floor fans spun noisily in all four corners and the tent felt refreshingly cool. Despite the temperate weather both inside and outside the tent, R. C.'s cheeks were flushed. As the four supper club members settled themselves at the table set in the center of the room, R. C. pulled back the nearest tent flap and examined the gray sky.

"He must be worried sick over the chance of rain," Lindy whispered to her friends.

"The festival grounds are packed, too." Lucy shot R. C. a troubled look. "Maybe the rain will hold off."

As the foursome exchanged weather predictions, a couple in their late sixties entered the tent and greeted R. C. He shook their hands and then led them to the two available seats at the judges' table. Next, he cleared his throat and straightened his pink bow tie by a millimeter.

"Welcome, judges, and thank you for coming. I see you're all wearing your name badges. That's good." R. C. proceeded with introductions. "Mr. and Mrs. Connelly are seated on Mr. Henry's right. The Connellys own a four-star steak restaurant in Blacksburg. They've judged for us for the past five years."

"We like to break free of the daily grind and come over here for some down-home 'cue." Mr. Connelly grinned at James. "This your first time judgin'?"

When James nodded in affirmation, Mrs. Connelly reached over and patted his hand. "Oh! Y'all are in for a treat! And the brisket competition is my personal favorite."

R. C. peeked out at the thick clouds again and then coughed into his hands. "If I may . . ." The six judges gave him their full attention. Consulting an index card, he began his lecture. "I would like to review the judging guidelines. First of all, please do not consume any alcohol prior to or during the judging session."

"Guess I'd better hand over my flask, then!" Mr. Connelly kidded.

Ignoring the playful outburst, R. C. continued. "Please do not socialize with the contestants prior to the judging. As of this moment, kindly refrain from entering the cooking area *at all.* All entries will be placed before you and marked by a number. You will taste the item — in this case, brisket —

and score the entry."

"How much can we eat?" Bennett asked eagerly.

"That is an excellent question, Mr. Marshall." R. C. looked thoughtful. "Eat enough to be able to score the food, but you should pace yourself. You will be consuming a fair amount of brisket this morning and as you know, brisket isn't exactly a light meat."

James raised his hand.

For the first time since their arrival at the tent, R. C. cracked a smile. "Yes, Mr. Henry?"

"Can we talk to each other while we're eating?"

R. C. shook his head. "No. There must be absolute silence during the tasting. We wouldn't want you to influence one another's decisions. You may talk only *after* you've written down the scores for each entry. Now, here are the scorecards. You'll see that you'll be judging the meat based on a scale of one to ten. One being the worst meat you've ever tasted and ten being . . . well, a bite of pure heaven."

"It says here that we're scoring based on appearance, tenderness, and taste." Lucy looked confused. "I don't get how we can judge appearance."

"Think of it this way," R. C. said. "If the

140

entry is placed before you and it really looks like something you'd like to dig right into, then the presentation should be given a high score. Here is a list of illegal garnishes." He handed each of them a sheet of paper. "If any of the entries are served with these garnishes, they will be disqualified."

James consulted the list of banned garnishes, which included endive, radish, cabbage, kale, red leaf lettuce, or any other vegetables. The only acceptable garnishes were parsley, green lettuce, and cilantro.

"What the heck does kale look like?" Bennett mumbled in James's ear. When James shrugged, Bennett pulled nervously at his toothbrush mustache. "Where's Gillian when we need her?"

"If the meat's on something green and leafy, then it's probably a legal garnish," James replied, but he was beginning to feel anxious about the level of detail required in being a food judge.

"Let's continue." R. C. consulted another index card. "If there are no further questions on garnishes, I would like you to recite the judges' pledge located on the bottom of your scorecard. Please read it aloud with me now."

James located the pledge and then recited the words: "I, James Henry, pledge to judge today's food with objectivity and integrity. I will abide by all of the judging guidelines and will do my utmost to ensure a fair and just contest."

"Goodness!" Lindy exclaimed with a nervous giggle. "I feel like I'm under oath in a court of law or am being filmed for Judge Judy."

R. C. took a step toward her. "You have a very important role in the success of our festival, Ms. Perez," he told her. "I'd like to remind you all just how significant the barbecue contests are to the public's general impression of Hog Fest. Hudsonville depends heavily on this festival and, therefore, our town is depending on you to do your best as a judge."

Lindy's mouth hung open and Bennett mopped his brow with a paper napkin from the pile stacked in front of each of their seats.

Relaxing his tense stance, R. C. checked his watch again. "Why don't you all chitchat for a few minutes? The first entry should be arriving any moment now."

James was still anxious and turned to the Connellys for reassurance. They promised him that there was nothing difficult about being a food judge, as the scoring was all based on personal preference. They added that the blue-ribbon winner was usually the entry that the majority of judges awarded the highest scores. It always outshone all the other entries.

"The hardest part is scorin' the first entry," Mr. Connelly explained. " 'Cause you've got no comparison. That's why none of the barbecue teams ever wanna go first. It's just the luck of the draw if your team gets picked to go to the head of the line." His face brightened. "And here comes the first brisket now."

James turned in time to see a pair of attractive young women wearing red and white checked aprons place a Styrofoam takeout container in front of each judge. The container was filled with slices of glistening brisket. James pulled the meat closer, inspected the bed of shredded lettuce, and noted that some of the edges of the garnish had turned an unappealing brown. The bark of the meat was covered in globs of sauce, some of which had dripped onto the lettuce. James felt that the presentation could have been stronger and gave the entry a five in the appearance category.

After cutting away a piece with his fork, James popped the brisket in his mouth. The initial taste was that of an overly sweet tomato sauce. In fact, James sensed that there was too much brown sugar or molasses in this particular sauce, though the meat itself was incredibly tender. He wrote down a nine for the tenderness category and a six for taste.

Deciding not to eat another bite, James swallowed some water and then watched as the Connellys and his friends completed their scorecards. After everyone scored the first entries, Bennett sat back in his chair and exhaled in relief. "Whew! That wasn't as tough as I thought it'd be."

"Yeah," Lindy agreed. "I guess that's because we all love food, so we're naturals for this kind of thing."

Lucy dabbed at her mouth with a paper napkin. "Maybe we should start a business. Food Judges for Hire. We could judge barbecue contests, pie bake-offs, decide who makes the best fried chicken, chocolate cake, peanut brittle, casserole, food using maple syrup, sweet potatoes, strawberries . . ." She grinned. "Can you tell I'm feeling a bit burned out on my protein diet?"

James returned her grin and was about to compliment her again on her weight loss success when the second entry was set before the judges and the room instantly fell silent.

The entry was average overall and James

wrote down sixes for all three categories. The third entry was far superior to the first two. The brisket was nicely presented in a fanlike pattern over large lettuce leaves, was extremely tender, and was covered by a delicious smoky glaze that hinted of black pepper, garlic, and soy sauce.

"That one was really good," Lucy said after their scorecards had been collected. "I ate three pieces of that brisket."

"Definitely the best so far," Bennett concurred. "Don't you kinda wonder which entry is Jimmy's?"

"If he's as good as he claims, it might have been that last one," Lindy stated and then made a zipping motion across her mouth as the fourth entry was brought it. The moment it was placed in front of the judges, Mr. Connelly held out his hand and shouted, "Stop!"

Concerned, R. C. scurried over to the table. "What is it, Mr. Connelly?"

"Well, I hate to say it, but this brisket is sittin' pretty on a bed of endive. That's on the list of illegal garnishes, right?"

R. C. examined the entry and sighed. "You're correct, sir." He gestured to the two girls in the checkered aprons. "Ladies, please remove this entry and bring in the next." Disappointed that he hadn't even had the opportunity to sample the disqualified entry, James anticipated the fifth entry's arrival. When it was set before him, he immediately smelled something spicy. As he inhaled deeply, he realized that the brisket had been arranged on a bed of fragrant cilantro. The garnish was a suitable accompaniment for the tender meat, as its flavor was distinctly spicier than the previous entries. James chewed a bite and then took another, savoring hints of paprika, cayenne pepper, and onions. It reminded him slightly of chili and was certainly a distinct entry. He gave it high scores.

After the score sheets were turned in, Mrs. Connelly drank her entire glass of water and then waved at one of the girls to refill her glass. "I think I got a piece of jalapeño in mine!" She gasped, her eyes watering. "My mouth is on fire!"

R. C. offered her a package of saltines. "Bread is better than water if your tongue is burning," he suggested, and he waited until she had eaten all of the crackers and seemed to have regained some feeling back in her tongue. "Are you able to continue?" he asked her.

Wiping tears from her cheeks, she nodded. "I'm fine. I just think my piece had some *extra* spice. I'm afraid that mistake is gonna cost somebody."

The next entry tasted particularly fruity, but James couldn't pinpoint which fruit he was eating. The blend of the fruit flavors in combination with the meat was interesting, but James wouldn't have ordered the brisket in a restaurant. Like the first entry, it was simply too sweet. Even though he sensed the fruit and added sugars were made less intense by the addition of ginger and a salty flavoring that he couldn't identify, James didn't enjoy the combination.

"What was the fruit used in that sauce?" he asked the other judges once the entry had been whisked away.

"Mango," Lindy answered. "I'd know that taste in a heartbeat. My Brazilian mama is wild about mangoes. I *really* liked that entry."

Bennett snorted. "Why would you go ruining a perfectly fine piece of meat with a mango? Would someone explain that to me? Bet it was that women's team, those Adam's Ribbers."

"That's mighty sexist of you, Bennett!" Lucy's blue eyes flashed. "I think —"

Their debate was instantly interrupted by the arrival of the final entry.

James instantly approved of the entry's appearance. The brisket had been sliced thin and laid out on a bed of emerald green, curly leaf parsley. The ruffled leaves of the garnish set off the two-toned meat. Having read up on the entire process of barbecuing meat the night before, James now knew that the reddish-pink shade showing on the meat was caused by the smoke ring — the chemical reaction that occurred when the nitrates in the smoke blended with the protein in the meat. These brisket slices had a more dramatic smoke ring than any of the previous entries. James scored it a nine out of ten for appearance.

Pulling the meat from the fork with his front teeth, James was shocked at its tenderness. It practically disintegrated with each movement of his jaw. And then there was the taste! James tried to chew slowly, but he simply couldn't. He hurriedly swallowed the first piece and then popped a second into his mouth. There it was again; the perfect blend of garlic, tomato, chili sauce, mustard, and brown sugar. As he shifted the meat over his tongue, he detected a trace of nutmeg and the most delicate hint of honey. Beneath all of these flavors was an underlying layer of Worcestershire infusion along with a breath of whiskey.

This is the best barbecued brisket I've ever had, James thought. He scored the entry another nine on tenderness and a ten on taste. He then continued eating, waving away one of the girls when she came to collect his plate.

Bennett did the same. "Oh no you don't, missy! This here's my lunch," he told the young woman.

As R. C. reviewed the scorecards, he seemed to tabulate which team had won quite quickly. James assumed the champion brisket was the last entry. After all, everyone had kept their portion of the entry and seemed to still be relishing every forkful.

In the space of ten minutes, R. C. and two other men from the Hudsonville Chamber of Commerce had reviewed the scorecards and were prepared to announce the first-, second-, and third-place winners in the Best Brisket category. They asked the judges to exit the tent and join them by the podium, where the trophies and cash prizes would be awarded.

James saw Jimmy and Hailey standing expectantly in the front of the large crowd. Both Jimmy and his girlfriend wore bright red T-shirts that read, *The Pitmaster Loves a Tender Butt.* The competing teams wore color-coordinated shirts, hats, or aprons. James noticed that Jimmy's team was the smallest and that most teams consisted of three or four members.

R. C. began his announcements by declaring that the entry from the Tenderizers had been disqualified due to the use of an illegal garnish. The three men in their team, wearing orange aprons bearing a black meat tenderizer in the center, began to shout at one another. Above their discord, the sound of Jimmy's hoarse laughter could be heard.

"Dumb asses!" he shouted at them.

James thought Jimmy looked even worse than yesterday. His flesh appeared more swollen, and there were dark bags beneath his eyes. Of course, Jimmy wore his customary expression of amusement and was already muttering insults at the competition just as he had the evening before.

"Mr. Lang." R. C. leaned toward Jimmy. Though he spoke away from the microphone, the warning in his voice was clear. "If you cannot behave in a civilized manner, I will ask you to leave the contest area."

"Sure thing, boss. I'll scoot off after you hand me my trophy!" Jimmy opened his arms, displaying a complete view of his enormous belly and sweat-soaked shirt.

Ignoring Jimmy, R. C. announced that the third-place winner, who would be awarded two hundred dollars cash, was the Marrow

Men. The audience cheered as a man wearing overalls and a chef hat embroidered with flames and the name of his team accepted an envelope and a white silk ribbon. R. C. then called for a representative from the second-place team, the Thigh and Mighties. A middle-aged woman took the ribbon and the envelope from R. C.'s hand and then planted a big kiss on his cheek.

"This is our very first ribbon!" she exclaimed and waved it in the air. The crowd applauded her loudly and several people shouted congratulatory phrases such as "You go, girl!" and "Cook that 'cue!"

One of the other men from the Chamber of Commerce collected a small trophy with a blue ribbon attached to its base in order to present it to the winner. When R. C. announced that the Pitmasters had captured the first-place prize, Jimmy hollered with delight. The noise sounded strangled in his hoarse throat, but it was a triumphant howl all the same.

Pumping R. C.'s hand, Jimmy grabbed the microphone and said, "Get used to me, folks. I'm gonna be winnin' all of these this weekend." He then blew a kiss to Hailey and stepped to the side of the podium and surveyed the crowd, clearly wanting to bask in his victory a little longer. Trying his best to mask his irritation, R. C. reclaimed the microphone and began advising the audience about the time schedule for the remainder of the barbecue contests.

"I'm gonna get another blue ribbon tomorrow!" Jimmy tried to shout, but the words came out as a croak.

It was at this moment that Gillian appeared in the front row of the crowd. She waved at her friends and then her eyes fell on the figure of Jimmy Lang. As James and the other supper club members watched, Gillian stared at Jimmy, her eyes wide with shock. Slowly, as though her body found it difficult to function, Gillian walked toward Jimmy.

By this time, R. C. had completed his announcements and had switched off the microphone. The audience members had mostly dispersed, seeking lunch or their next round of entertainment. The barbecue contestants headed back toward the cooking area and Jimmy, who had been busy smiling at himself in the reflection of his trophy, finally realized that the show was over. No one except for Hailey waited to congratulate him. When he saw that Gillian was blocking his path, he paused and grinned at her. "Hey there, Red," he said as though greeting a fan. "You waitin' to shake the winner's hand, huh? Maybe get a picture, too?"

Gillian didn't answer. She kept staring at Jimmy, her face drained of all color. Her fists were clenched so tightly by her sides that her knuckles were moon-white, but her shoulders sagged as though a great weight had been placed upon her back.

"Little lady?" Jimmy cupped the trophy under one arm and scratched his shaved head in confusion. "Do I know you from somewhere?" He waited while Gillian mutely stared. "Well, if you're gonna just stand there actin' like a retard, then I'm outta here! I'm Jimmy Lang, future champion of Hog Fest, and I've got places to go!" He made a move to brush by Gillian.

Suddenly, her right arm shot out like a hammer and she hit Jimmy square in the nose with her closed fist.

"Yes, you know *me!*" Gillian shrieked as blood oozed forth from Jimmy's nose. Absently rubbing her hands, she yelled in a voice torn with pain and grief — a voice her friends had never heard before. "And I know *you!* A day doesn't go by that I don't wish *you* were rotting in the ground!"

Tears fell down her face as she screamed, "How could I *ever* forget how much I *hate* you! YOU BASTARD! YOU *SHOULD*

KNOW ME! YOU KILLED MY HUS-
BAND!"

EIGHT:
CUCUMBER TEA
SANDWICHES

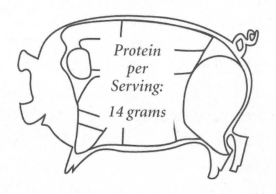

Protein per Serving: 14 grams

To say that James was stunned by Gillian's words would be an understatement. He stared at his friend, who had covered her face with her hands and was crying hard, her shoulders shaking and the bangles on her arms clinking in disharmony. James blinked hard once, then again, but the reality remained unchanged. Gillian had been married? Or had his ears deceived him? Did Gillian just accuse Jimmy Lang of killing her husband? *What* husband?

James turned toward his other friends and could tell from their expressions that they too were bowled over by Gillian's words. Even Hailey was awestruck. The only person who didn't appear the slightest bit surprised was Jimmy. Cradling his nose with his meaty hand, he backed away from Gillian, grabbed Hailey by the arm, and walked off toward the cooking area. He never said a word.

Somehow, his departure allowed James to regain power over his own limbs. He moved toward Gillian, his right arm extended with an offering of a paper napkin.

"Hey, it's okay," he spoke to her softly, as though he were comforting a scared animal or frightened child. "Gillian. It's okay. He's gone now."

Sensing that someone had spoken her name, Gillian raised a face awash in agony. Her eyes gazed unseeing at the napkin, at James, at the handful of gawking onlookers. Her closest friends stared back at her, blindsided into frozen silence. James could see that he would receive no immediate help from them, and while he stood there, desperately trying to think of some way to comfort Gillian, she suddenly turned and ran behind the tent, quickly disappearing in the mass of wandering festivalgoers.

A full thirty seconds later, Lindy whispered, "What just happened here?"

Instead of answering, Bennett walked back inside the tent where moments ago they had all been happily assessing the virtues and vices of barbecued brisket. The other supper club members watched him as he sank into one of the chairs and pulled at his mustache furiously. "Did that crazed woman actually say she had a husband?" he asked his friends as they fell into their own chairs.

"Yes," Lucy replied. She blinked several times and then poured herself a glass of water from one of the pitchers on the table. She drank down the entire glass and then wiped her lips with the back of her hand. "A husband supposedly killed by Jimmy Lang."

James shook his head. "So none of you knew she had been married?"

Lindy threw her hands wide in a gesture of helplessness. "Gillian has certainly never mentioned *that* little detail to *me* before!" She anxiously ran her hands through her black hair. "Maybe there was something in her falafel," she suggested wildly. "Maybe her breakfast tea was spiked! Maybe she hung out with some of those dog people after their show and smoked a . . . I don't know, a peace pipe! But *that* —," she pointed outside the tent as though Gillian were still standing there, "that *person* was not the Gillian I know!"

James agreed with Lindy. Gillian was passionate about many topics, but in general, she had a calm and well-balanced nature. The explosion they had just witnessed followed by the intense crying and then the mad dash into the crowd were behaviors someone else might exhibit. Gillian, their animal- and earth-loving, tree-hugging, orange-haired friend, who favored tie-dying T-shirts or creating homeopathic remedies, wasn't prone to dramatic outbursts.

"What should we do?" James asked. "Whatever's going on, she's obviously distraught. We should look for her — make sure she's okay."

Lucy nodded. "You're right, James. But where did she go?"

"I think she'd want to get away from all this bustle," Lindy said. "She may head back to the inn."

"Why don't you take the Jeep and see if you can find her?" Lucy proposed to Lindy. She then turned to Bennett and James. "We should split up. I could ask R. C. where the dog show people are staying and ask them if they saw or talked to Gillian before, well, before she came to meet us."

"Hold the phone, folks." Bennett was still

yanking on his mustache. "What if what Gillian said is true? She had a man and that man was somehow hurt by this Jimmy fellow." His dark eyes were lit with anger. "I'm gonna talk to that loudmouth SOB and see what he's got to say for himself. You notice he was mighty quiet after Gillian blasted him. He didn't deny a thing."

"Well, she *did* clock him in the nose," Lindy argued. "I think he was trying to stop the blood flow."

"Hell of a shot she gave him," Bennett said in admiration. "But I saw the big man's expression. I think that ole hillbilly recognized Gillian."

James couldn't shake the image of the pain in Gillian's voice and the anguish in her face. "I'm going with you, Bennett. Let's get to the bottom of this whole thing right now."

Lucy held up her cell phone. "Call me if you guys find out anything," she commanded.

As James and Bennett walked toward the cooking area, the sky mirrored their mood. Dark gray clouds, swollen with unshed rain, massed over their heads. A light wind foreshadowed the coming storm by pushing at flags, banners, and pinwheels. There was an urgent feeling among the crowd that hadn't existed an hour earlier. People moved more quickly, hoping to reach their next destination before the rain, and James noticed that some of the noncompeting cooks had stowed away their barbecue equipment in exchange for windbreakers and coolers of beer. They gathered into groups, settling on folding lawn chairs or the stoops of their campers, and gossiped, sharing bottle openers and bags of potato chips as they watched the sky.

For the professional teams, however, the weather made no difference. Their cookers were stoked, the smoke was rising, and the team members were huddled together holding earnest conversations. By this time, no doubt, word of the drama that occurred immediately after Jimmy won the brisket competition was spreading through the rows of RVs, folding campers, and travel trailers like a brushfire.

"I, um, don't think we can just waltz up to his door and demand an explanation," James said. He felt a surge of his customary sense of caution return as soon as Jimmy's RV came into view.

"Maybe he'll be outside." Bennett shook a festival schedule. "The chicken and rib contests are comin' up tomorrow. If he

plans to be the champion, he's likely practic-
in' different sauces and infusions and rubs
already."

"Let's just peek around the back of his
camper," James suggested.

As the two men approached the RV with
as much stealth as they could muster, it was
quite obvious that Jimmy and his girlfriend
were not holed up inside the vehicle. In fact,
Hailey was demanding to know the reason
behind Gillian's allegation and she wasn't
bothering to keep her voice lowered. James
was sure most of the neighboring campers
could hear her shrill, rapid-fire questions.

Jimmy, on the other hand, replied to the
barrage in a bored tone. "I told you, sugar
baby, that woman's soft in the head. I don't
know nothin' about her."

"But you did fifteen years, Jimmy. You told
me that when we met durin' those counsel-
ing sessions for criminals aimin' to turn
their lives around. You was just like me,
Jimmy, 'cept I was doin' time for possession
of marijuana and you *said* you were doin'
time for dealin'." She paused. "We were bat-
tlin' the same demons. Drugs. It's what
bonded us durin' group therapy. Right?"

"That's right, doll, and we're both clean
as rocks polished by the river, so can we
have a beer and get on with mixin' up the

mop for the chicken?" James could barely understand Jimmy, as his voice had grown even more hoarse.

"Forget the beer," Hailey answered testily. "Yeah, that woman seemed a little wacko, but seein' *you* is what made her come all unhinged. You'd better be straight with me, Jimmy, 'cause if I find out you're lyin' to me about why you were in jail . . ." She trailed off as though trying to come up with a solid threat.

"You'll what?" Jimmy pounced on her unfinished words. "You'll take your fat, Bible-readin' ass off elsewhere? I'd like to see *that* day! Who would want you?"

James and Bennett exchanged startled glances.

"Ouch," Bennett whispered, touching his palm to his heart.

"Man, what a charmer," James murmured.

"Lots of men would! 'Specially barbecue cooks!" Hailey spluttered angrily. "You *know* you'd never win a single contest without my help!" After Jimmy offered no comeback, she sniffed and then walked toward the camper's door. "I'll be inside readin' my *In Touch* magazine. If you want help on that chicken mop, and you know you're gonna need it, you can come get me. And when you do, it'd better be with an apology and the truth about that redhead on your lips! Otherwise, stay out there and kiss all your blue ribbons goodbye."

James and Bennett heard Hailey's heavy tread on the RV's steps followed by the muffled footsteps of her moving around within the large vehicle.

"Hush up, woman!" Jimmy made his way to the closed door and hit it with what sounded like a metal cooking tool. "You talk like that again so's folks can hear, and I'll shut your big mouth for good! I can take those blue ribbons or leave 'em. I got a whole 'nother reason for bein' here!"

Hailey didn't answer, but James could hear cupboards being opened and forcefully closed again. A few seconds later, a radio was switched on and the volume turned loud enough for James, Bennett, and half the campground to discern that Hailey was listening to church hymns.

"Sounds like Jimmy may not be the *real* Pitmaster," Bennett whispered to James. James nodded and then took a quick glance around the corner of the RV. Jimmy was standing near his cooker, his face tilted toward the sky. Muttering angrily, he rubbed his arms.

"Stupid redheaded bitch," he said, spitting on the ground in a way that reminded

James of the angry action taken by the female dog owner the day before. "Of all places for her to turn up." He rubbed the skin on his arms vigorously and then turned back to the RV.

"Hailey, baby. I'm sorry." Jimmy mounted the first step, causing the RV to keel slightly, and knocked at the locked door. "Could you please gimme my flannel shirt? It's gettin' right chilly out here. Come on, baby. You know I'm nothin' without you. Open up and let me give ya a nice backrub." He knocked harder. "Hailey!"

After a pause, the door opened and Hailey said, "You want a shirt? You want a mop for the chicken? You want lots of stuff. Then it's time to repent, Jimmy Lang. Come inside and confess your sins."

Grumbling, Jimmy hesitated for a moment and then disappeared into the camper. No more sounds were heard above the muted organ melodies blended with the harmonious voices of a large choir.

"Guess that's the end of Jimmy for a while," James said derisively.

"Is that guy nuts?" Bennett said once they had left the cooking area. "I know the sun isn't shining and there's a breeze blowin', but how can he be cold? It's August and Jimmy's got enough extra blubber on him to keep a few Arctic walruses nice and snug." He squeezed his own belly. "I know I've got plenty to spare, too, but I've got nothin' on that man."

James felt a stress headache approaching. "Jimmy's a strange one. You saw how volatile he was with Hailey. Maybe he *has* killed someone."

"Well, we're going to have to get the story from Gillian. I have a feeling Jimmy would only lie to us anyway," Bennett said. "I don't know what made me think he'd just spill the whole story to us."

"Well, Jimmy obviously knows Gillian. You heard what he mumbled to himself. And what about confessing and repenting to Hailey?" James asked cynically.

Bennett rolled his eyes. "Oh, I think Hailey is being hand-fed a serious tall tale right about now."

"Come on." James quickened his stride as they headed toward the parking lot. "I think those clouds are getting ready to dump on us."

"Looks that way," Bennett agreed. "Let's get back to the inn, get some coffee, and sit down with the ladies. I bet by now they've straightened out this whole mess and are waiting with a logical explanation for Gillian's loony behavior."

"I've got my doubts about everything being sorted out, but there should be coffee at any rate," James answered wearily.

James knocked on the door of the hotel room shared by Lindy, Lucy, and Gillian, but received no answer. Shrugging, he retraced his steps back to the first floor and dialed Lucy's cell phone number.

"James?" She sounded breathless.

"Did you find her?" he asked.

"No." The word was infused with disappointment. "We're just coming back from one of the walking trails behind the inn. Where are you?"

"Standing in the lobby," he said. "We spied on Jimmy a bit, but we didn't actually talk to him. We still have no idea what's going on."

"Me neither. The dog people weren't much help. Most of them received Gillian's brochure and have been pretty preoccupied dreaming about doggie palaces. They all told me basically the same thing — that Gillian was pleasant and *very* energetic. Sounds like she was her normal self." Lucy sighed. "Apparently she and that lady who spit on Jimmy's cooker yesterday were quite chummy, but I couldn't track that woman down."

"So there were no leads from that group at all?"

"I'm not sure of anything, but meet us on the back porch," Lucy ordered. "Eleanor is serving an afternoon tea. She said a lot of people come back from the festival to relax a bit before returning for dinner and an evening of entertainment, so you'd better claim a table for us." She paused. "I think it's going to rain any second now. Maybe Gillian will just show up when it does. We can have her favorite tea ready and waiting."

James hung up and followed Lucy's advice. He and Bennett returned to their room, scooped up their books, and hustled downstairs to the back porch where they draped pool towels over three of the empty chairs at their table. James did his best to concentrate on a chapter entitled *The Great Meat Debate,* which examined the East Coast notion that pork was the superior meat to use when barbecuing, versus the Kansas City and Texan claims that beef made a better choice. Bennett seemed absorbed by his trivia book, but when Eleanor stepped onto the long porch bearing a tray laden with sandwiches, he snapped his head around at the sound of her footfall.

"The cakes aren't quite done yet," Eleanor stated with a tired smile. "You're welcome to some sandwiches if you're feeling peckish, however."

James observed the proprietor as she fanned out a pile of cocktail napkins. He wondered if Eleanor and her daughter were on speaking terms yet. He knew that the pig parade was scheduled to begin at eight p.m. and that it would be followed by a fireworks display. Hopefully, the weather would cooperate or there'd be no pyrotechnics. The makeup covering the marks on Francesca's neck would need to be waterproof.

This day has turned out to be very unfestival-like, James thought. Between Eleanor and Francesca's fight, Gillian's eruption, the demonstration of Hailey and Jimmy's conflicted relationship, and the rain that was sure to send R. C. into a state of panic, the aura of celebration had turned rather dour.

Bennett scraped his chair back and closed his book, interrupting James's ruminations. "I can't focus," he declared and jerked his thumb at the buffet table. "Want some grub?"

"Sure," James answered gratefully. "Looks like cucumber sandwiches up there. Can you get me a couple? They seem kind of small."

In fact, each sandwich was easily consumed in two hearty bites. James wolfed down three and then licked his fingers. "These are terrific. I like how one piece of bread is rye and the other one's white. I think I taste fresh chives in the cream cheese, too."

Bennett nodded. "Nothin' like good food to take your mind off your troubles."

At that moment, Lindy and Lucy arrived. Both women were pink-cheeked from their brisk walk on the nature trail. James watched as the hopeful light in both of their faces was extinguished as they noted the three empty chairs at the table.

"She hasn't come back?" Lindy's question was rhetorical. Instead of responding, Bennett handed her a plate of sandwiches. As the group concentrated on their food, Eleanor appeared on the porch with an urn of tea, followed by a woman wearing a maid's uniform who carried a platter bearing tiny cakes and homemade oatmeal chocolate-chip cookies.

"The tea has a subtle hint of almonds," Eleanor announced to the guests gathering on the porch. "It's very refreshing."

Bennett served himself a steaming cup and a selection of desserts. Back at their table, he picked up the cup, blew on the surface of the hot tea, and then replaced it in the saucer without taking a sip. "Here we are, eating a vegetarian snack and drinkin' herbal tea, and the one person in the world who would be tickled pink by this spread isn't with us."

The supper club members exchanged glum looks and quietly ate their food. In the distance, thunder rumbled and the treetops beyond the pool shifted back and forth in the strengthening wind.

"Maybe the rain will bring her back," Lucy murmured.

But when the downpour began a few minutes later, causing excited shrieks from some of the other guests who scrambled to move their chairs farther away from the open air, there was still no sign of Gillian. Her friends stared into the curtains of rain and silently waited.

INN AT FOX HALL'S CHECKERBOARD CUCUMBER CREAM CHEESE AND CHIVE SANDWICHES

20 slices cucumber, peeled and sliced very thinly
salt
1 (3-ounce) package cream cheese, softened
1/2 teaspoon dried chives (or fresh, if available)
10 slices crustless rye bread (tea-sized)
10 slices crustless white bread (tea-sized)

Sprinkle the cucumbers with salt and set them in a colander to drain for at least 1 hour. Stir the cream cheese and chives in small bowl. For each sandwich, spread 1 slice of rye bread with the cream cheese mixture. Layer 1 slice of white bread with 2 cucumber slices. Cover with the rye bread slice, cream cheese side down. Cut in half to form two triangles.

NINE:
"FALAFEL TENT"
GYRO

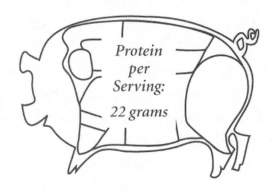

The rain pelted down all afternoon. By early evening, it slacked off and became a light drizzle, hinting at the possibility of ceasing altogether. The storm had mottled the ground with patches of muddy puddles. Leaves and dead branches dislodged from the trees by a determined wind were scattered everywhere.

James had napped for almost two hours. His lack of sleep from the previous night, combined with the steady rhythm of the rain, made it impossible to resist. At first he had gone to his room, intending to read until Gillian returned. Four sentences into the chapter describing the marinades meant to be injected into a piece of meat in order to increase the overall flavor, his lids grew heavy as anvils. It was easy to surrender to the darkened room and the absence of the sonorous noises produced by his roommate the night before.

When he woke, it was with a stab of guilt that he had slept while Gillian might have been wandering, upset and alone, in the unrelenting downpour. He hoped that she had made herself cozy in one of the town shops and that she was now safely back at the inn, ready to explain everything to her friends over dinner.

At quarter to six, just a few minutes after James sat up in bed and ran his fingers through his disheveled light brown hair, Bennett burst into the room. "We're headin' down to the festival. Gillian still hasn't come back. The girls have spent the last hour combin' through every store in town but no dice. She isn't there." He checked his reflection in the mirror and tucked his shirt further into his pants, eyeing the paunch around his waist critically.

James rubbed the sleep from his eyes and

grabbed his wallet and the room key from the nightstand. "Is it still overcast?"

Nodding, Bennett pulled a windbreaker from his leather satchel. "I thought I was packin' like a little old lady when I stuffed this in my bag. Who knew that an August evening in southern Virginia could raise goose bumps?"

Lindy and Lucy were waiting for the men by Lucy's Jeep. Lucy wore a sweatshirt bearing the crest of the Shenandoah County Sheriff's Department while Lindy was decked out in a black sweater trimmed with a faux fur collar. James pulled a face as Lucy opened the back door and indicated they should slide in. Noting his grimace, Lucy gave James a rough push on the back. "Don't worry, James. I cleaned it out before we left Quincy's Gap."

James blushed, for Lucy had known that his hesitation in entering her car was based on the fact that its interior typically resembled an overturned garbage can and often smelled just as bad. Her sloppiness had been one of the things he liked least about dating her. Her home, her yard, and her car were always in a constant state of disarray, and though James didn't care if things were a little untidy, he drew the line at rotting food or surfaces made sticky with

174

soda dregs or flattened pieces of chewing gum mottled with dog hair. Thinking of his failed relationship with Lucy reminded James that he should check in with Murphy at some point, but that could wait until Gillian was found.

The four friends rode to the fairgrounds in silence. As they approached the parking area, Lindy unfolded a piece of paper containing a listing of the evening's events. "I'm trying to figure out if Gillian would be interested in any of tonight's entertainment," she told the others. "There's the parade, of course, followed by a country music concert. Other than those two things, it's just the usual rides and carnival games and stuff."

"No animal shows?" Lucy asked.

Lindy shook her head. "No. The dog show happened this morning and there was a SpongeBob production for kids this afternoon, but I really can't see Gillian sitting through that."

"I don't get that SpongeBob cartoon one bit," Bennett mumbled. "No wonder kids today are so mixed up. How are they supposed to learn life lessons from a bunch of ugly underwater invertebrates?"

"And which cartoon do you think teaches kids anything?" Lindy raised her plucked eyebrows in curiosity.

"Me, I'm a Peanuts fan. Charlie Brown could teach us all a thing or two," Bennett replied as Lucy pulled into a parking space.

James said, "Looks like the lot is still full. I guess the rain only scared folks off for a short while." Drawing in a breath of the refreshing evening air, he listened to the cacophony of sounds rising from the festival. There was music, the expected rumble of unintelligible announcements emanating through the PA system, and the ever-present murmur of the crowd. James gazed at the rows of lights in the distance. "Where should we go first?"

"Let's find R. C. He may be able to contact his staff with his walkie-talkie and find out if anyone's seen Gillian," Lucy suggested.

"Brilliant idea." James smiled at her. "We're lucky to have a sheriff's deputy with us."

Lucy's face glowed with pleasure.

The foursome walked to the recreation center with care. The mass of humanity had clearly reformed with the break in the weather and hundreds of feet had quickly flattened the wet grass and expanded the stretches of mud. Every now and then a child would break free from his parents' grasp in order to splash in one of the numerous puddles. As the supper club members passed the petting farm area, a little boy missing both of his front teeth sprayed James's khaki pants with brown water. Eyeing his dirt-splattered pants in dismay, James wondered why he hadn't had the foresight to change into jeans before leaving the inn.

Lindy chuckled at his distress. "See? You should have brought extra outfits! You'd better hope Fox Hall has a washing machine."

By the time they had made their way to the recreation center, however, Lindy's good humor had vanished and she was quite cross. Her new wedge sandals were caked with mud and several petals from the fabric flowers that had been attached to the center of each shoe had disappeared.

"Damn it!" Lindy frowned unhappily at her footwear. As they entered the building, she did her best to wipe off the mud using the textured doormats. "These are totally ruined!" she bleated once inside.

R. C., who was seated behind the receptionist's desk, examining the document spread before him, looked up in alarm. "Did you say rain? It hasn't started again, has it?"

Lucy hastily assured the frazzled director that the sky was totally free of precipitation and then went on to ask for his assistance in locating Gillian. She briefly told him everything that had happened after the brisket competition had ended.

A crease appeared on R. C.'s brow. "Yes, I heard about what your friend said to Mr. Lang. I have to admit that I find the whole story very disturbing." He paused, rubbing the crown of his head where James imagined a strong headache must be blooming. "At one time, Jimmy was good for this festival. His, eh, larger-than-life persona used to be a draw. His cooking skills were above average, but it was the way he made such a big show of everything he did that caused people to gather around his grill." He mopped his forehead with a bandana. "Now, I fear, he's become more of a detriment to this festival, especially if he's a convicted felon."

"Um," Lindy stammered. "We're not completely sure that our friend's accusation is true. She —"

"Whether Gillian's got a screw loose or not, Jimmy Lang has been to jail," Bennett interrupted. "He and his girlfriend met in some ex-con talk-about-your-feelings session."

R. C. gave Bennett a searching look. "How do you know that?"

Bennett launched into a coughing fit while glancing at James out of the corner of his eye.

"Um, we kind of overheard Jimmy and Hailey talking outside their camper," James explained cryptically. "We all split up to look for Gillian. Bennett and I were searching the campground area," he added, stretching the truth. "And that was hours ago. There's been no sign of her since."

Picking up a pen from the desk, R. C. said, "I know your friend has light skin and a full head of reddish-orange hair, but what other details can I add to her description?"

"Her full name is Gillian O'Malley," Lucy said. "She's approximately five foot six. Forty years old. Thin legs. Barrel-chested. Wearing a long, silver skirt, lime-green T-shirt, and an armload of silver bracelets. Carrying a hemp purse stitched with butterflies." Lucy turned to her friends. "Did I leave anything out?"

Impressed, the other supper club members shook their heads as R. C. relayed her words verbatim via his walkie-talkie to the large group of workers running the festival. When most of them reported back that they hadn't seen a woman matching Gillian's description recently, R. C. requested that they all keep a sharp lookout for her and immediately report any sighting to him.

Lucy thanked R. C. profusely and then handed him her cell phone number. "Please call me if anyone spots her."

R. C. noticed the concern etched on Lucy's face and responded by squeezing her lightly on the shoulder. "Why don't you all get something to eat? By the time supper is over, I'm sure someone will run across your friend."

The four friends wandered down the mud and water-streaked road flanked by the merchant's booths and the food vendors. No one spoke up as they passed one illuminated sign after another advertising fried chicken, beef hot dogs, Angus burgers, barbecued ribs, turkey legs, seasoned cheese fries, and personal pan pizzas. They were too focused on looking at the faces in the crowd to concentrate on any particular food.

"Let's go to that stand where Gillian had lunch," Lindy suggested. "Who knows? Maybe she really liked it and will go back there for dinner."

"They better serve somethin' else besides chickpeas," Bennett muttered.

"They've got gyros or chicken souvlaki platters," Lindy assured him.

When they reached the vendor's booth, entitled the Falafel Tent, they each ordered the gyro platter and a large Coke. Lucy found an empty picnic table nearby and they settled themselves down to eat, speaking little as they kept their eyes fixed on the passersby.

"Is this meal a good choice for the protein diet?" James asked Lucy. He wasn't particularly interested, but was merely trying to jump-start a conversation.

"If you stick to just the lamb and the salad. That rice isn't necessary. I probably should have gotten the souvlaki platter, as chicken is a much leaner meat than lamb, but I've been eating lots of chicken this summer. Shoot, I'll starting clucking if I swallow another piece of poultry." She took a bite of seasoned lamb and a glob of yogurt sauce fell onto the swell of her right breast. James watched as she dabbed at her cleavage and then quickly looked away, embarrassed by an unbidden memory of running his fingers over Lucy's soft skin.

"So here we are. Friday night at the fair," Bennett mumbled, checking his watch.

"That's right, it's Friday!" James wiped his mouth with his napkin and removed his cell phone from his pocket. "I've got to check in with the Fitzgerald twins just to make sure that nonsense with the high school kids is really over. Be right back."

"If they've been making fake IDs, I'm going to be very interested in learning some of their names." Lucy issued him a dark look.

"I don't have any hard proof," James said, getting up from the table. "The IDs just seemed the most logical explanation. If I'm right about my theory, then the kids won't be hanging out at our branch anymore. I'll have scared them off."

"That doesn't mean they won't *use* the IDs they *already* made," Lucy replied judgmentally.

"Oh, I doubt they're any good." Excusing himself, James wandered into the empty judging tent and dialed the circulation desk's extension. Scott answered right away.

"I had a feeling you might check in on us, Professor." Scott greeted his boss with his customary cheerfulness.

Assuming from Scott's tone that all was peaceful at the library, James said, "So all's as it should be this evening?"

"Not quite," Scott answered with deflated enthusiasm. "The kids are back. All the ones from last week and some new ones, too."

"What!" James was shocked. "What are they doing?"

"Same thing. Paying homage to that brute Martin and messing up all the magazines." Scott paused. "And they're definitely less

182

willing to listen to Francis and me," he confessed ruefully. "We're not having much success keeping them quiet."

James looked at this watch, struggling to keep his irritation at bay. "How many non-teenage patrons are there?"

"Only two. Mr. and Mrs. Schroeder. They're picking out a pile of books to take to the beach next week."

Visualizing the teenagers creasing magazines and talking in loud voices as they chewed gum and conducted their illicit activities nearly drove James insane with frustrated anger. He wished he could teleport to Quincy's Gap and have Lucy drive to the library while wearing her uniform and a fierce scowl. He knew that she could frighten some sense into the group of teen miscreants without uttering a single word.

"Okay, this is what you're going to do," he told Scott. "First of all, go turn off the A/C. As soon as the Schroeders are finished checking out, make an announcement over the intercom system that due to technical difficulties with the air conditioning system, the library will be closing early."

"Seriously?" Scott said after a stunned pause. "Can we do that?"

"Oh, we're doing it!" James shouted and then felt guilty about taking his frustrations out on Scott. "Really, Scott. This thing with the kids is getting out of control, and I can't help you from here." James sighed. "And I want to apologize for assuming that I had the problem all figured out."

"No worries, Professor," Scott assured him. "Francis and I know that you'll get to the bottom of this mystery sooner or later."

James grinned. "Thanks for the vote of confidence. Now, close up shop and go see a movie or something. You guys deserve a treat after putting up with that group *again*."

Stuffing the phone angrily into his front pocket, James picked his way through the muddy grass to where his forlorn friends pushed food around on their plates.

"I can't stand this!" Lucy declared, standing up. "It's time to split up and search every inch of this park, from the campground area to the face-painting booths! I can't sit still for another second!"

Bennett also rose and cleared their table of their unfinished meals and drink cups. "Come on, James. We're not goin' back to that inn without Gillian."

The four friends scoured the festival grounds until almost ten at night. They interrogated anyone carrying a walkie-talkie, poked their heads into magic shows, animal pens, tents in the camping area, and port-ajohns. They questioned merchants, entertainers, and any crowd members wearing Birkenstock sandals or trailing a dog on a leash.

Finally, exhausted and dirty, they met back at Lucy's Jeep. When James and Bennett heard that Lindy and Lucy had no better luck in finding even the slightest trace of Gillian, they all grew disheartened. At a few minutes past ten, R. C. called to say that his network of festival workers had had no success either.

"I'm sure she's waiting for you at the Fox Hall," he said in an attempt to console Lucy.

But back at the inn, Gillian's bed was empty and her belongings were untouched.

"Before I go to bed," Lucy stated wearily to her friends, "I'm going to call the local sheriff."

"Let us know if there's any news," James said gloomily. Lucy promised that she would phone them and then closed the door to their suite.

Following Bennett as he shuffled off to their room, James thought it would surely be impossible to fall asleep. With his worry over Gillian and the goings-on at the library, his mind was on overdrive. However, the moment he closed his eyes, his body seemed to melt into the bed and immediately drown in dark waves of sleep.

The ringing phone jolted James from a dream in which he and Murphy were at the beach. The sun was burning his pale cheeks and forehead into a crisp red but he couldn't move a muscle. Looking at the incoming surf, he realized that Murphy had buried him neck-deep in sand and then had run off to interview a man who was screaming that his surfboard had just been bitten by a twelve-foot shark.

Blinking the dream away, James switched on the bedside lamp. Bennett answered the phone. As his friend croaked out "hello," James pulled the digital clock within inches of his nose. It was three minutes past seven.

Bennett listened to the caller for several seconds and James tried to read the mixed expressions passing rapidly across his friend's face. He sensed that whatever Bennett was hearing was completely unexpected, for Bennett's eyes widened into black pools as he nodded mechanically.

"I see," Bennett finally said in response, his voice leaden. "We'll meet you downstairs in ten minutes." He waited, listening again, and then sighed lugubriously. "Yes, of course I'll tell him."

Replacing the receiver with a gingerness

that was atypical, Bennett finally looked James in the eye. "That was Lucy. She didn't have good news, my man. Jimmy Lang was found dead this morning — inside his camper." He stood slowly, as though his body was stiff.

"Jimmy's dead?" was all James could think to say.

"Yeah. The local sheriff wants to meet us in the judges' tent in fifteen minutes. They wanna question us about yesterday." He reached out and squeezed James on the arm, as though hoping to comfort both of them with the gesture. "It gets worse, James. Gillian was there when Hailey found Jimmy's body. The law boys have got her in custody."

"Who?" James said, trying to fathom what Bennett had just told him. "Gillian or Hailey?"

"Gillian," Bennett replied as he grabbed his jeans from the closet. "They think she murdered Jimmy Lang."

Ten:
Sheriff's
Department Coffee

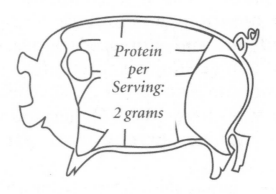

Protein per Serving:

2 grams

Though James plied Bennett with a thousand questions as he sped to the festival grounds, his friend could offer little more in the way of new information.

"I'm in the dark myself, man!" Bennett finally shouted when James demanded to hear the precise details of how Jimmy Lang had met his end.

"But it must have been a violent one or Gillian wouldn't be sitting in a holding cell right now," James persisted as though his friend had never spoken. He zoomed into an empty parking space next to Lucy's Jeep, turned off the engine, and burst open his car door with so much force that his Bronco shuddered. When he saw that Bennett's mini recorder had fallen from his friend's pants pocket, he scooped it up and shoved it into his own and then slammed the Bronco's door closed.

"Where are we supposed to go?" James looked around frantically. "To the crime scene?"

"Look, there's Lindy," Bennett said with palpable relief, pointing at a figure heading toward them. "Maybe *she* can give us some answers before we both crack apart like boiled eggs."

Lindy was jogging straight for them, her unbrushed hair forming a black tornado over her head as she ran. As she grew nearer, James could see that tracks of black mascara lined both of her cheeks and she had buttoned her blouse incorrectly so that one side was longer than the other. Stopping within three feet of her friends, Lindy paused to catch her breath. James stared at her misaligned shirt, unintentionally observing that there was a gape large enough at chest level to expose a flash of the red and white polka-dotted bra she wore underneath her rust-colored blouse.

"Lucy's talking to the sheriff right now. I'm supposed to take you straight to them," Lindy informed James and Bennett between pants and then started walking back in the direction from which she had come. "Isn't this awful?" Her brown eyes pooled with tears and she swatted them away in annoyance. "Do you think Gillian really could . . . ?" she trailed off and then shook her head fiercely. "No! She's no murderer!" Clinging to James's sleeve, she cried, "What are we going to do?"

James held out his hands in supplication. "Please, Lindy! Tell me what the hell is going on! How can I help when I don't know a damned thing?"

Struggling to regain her composure, Lindy stopped short and took several deep breaths, unknowingly pressing her hand over the puckered hole in her shirt. "Okay, here's what I know. I overheard the sheriff telling Lucy that Jimmy Lang died of propane poisoning. He went to sleep last night with a portable heater turned on high and the window vents fully open. Apparently, someone taped over the window vents, the plumbing pipes, and even climbed onto the roof and covered the roof ventilators with several layers of duct tape. Jimmy couldn't get a lick of fresh air if he wanted to and over the course of the night, he just slipped away."

"And they think Gillian did this? Gillian?" James spluttered and then turned to Bennett. "This sounds crazy! Is it possible to get a propane overdose from some little rinky-dink heater?"

Bennett nodded. "Sure, man. Some of those suckers run off full propane tanks. They can pump out, like, thirty thousand BTUs an hour."

"Speak in English," Lindy commanded. "And why do you even know that?"

"Hey, I camped out a lot as a kid. I was an eagle scout, remember?" Bennett answered testily. "BTU stands for British Thermal Unit. It's the quantity of heat needed to raise one pound of water by one degree Fahrenheit." He scowled at Lindy as they walked. "I know *that* from studying acronyms to prepare for *Jeopardy!*"

"I still don't understand, but I don't care about the scientific definitions. Can you just explain how can a heater kill someone?" Lindy demanded with uncharacteristic impatience.

"The heater eats up oxygen at the same time it produces carbon monoxide." Bennett rubbed his mustache. "That's not good.

Without a source of oxygen, the carbon monoxide can take away your last breath and you'd never know it. It doesn't have any kind of smell. That's why they call that sneaky gas the silent killer. Doesn't happen fast either, so someone must have taped the vents pretty soon after Jimmy went to sleep."

"Wouldn't manufacturers make some kind of safety switch on those heaters if they're that dangerous?" James wondered aloud.

"They did after a bunch of folks had already died from carbon monoxide poisoning." Bennett slowed as they approached Jimmy's camper. "A few years ago, I read an article about accidental deaths caused by those portable heaters in an issue of *Outdoor Life.* If Jimmy had one of those older models, it would've kept right on pumpin' out the bad gas until someone turned it off."

"But Gillian doesn't camp!" Lindy spluttered. "How would *she* know how to use a heater as a weapon? And for crying out loud, what was Jimmy doing with the heater on, anyway? Couldn't he just wear a sweatshirt or use a blanket or something?"

James nudged Bennett. "He was cold yesterday. Remember him asking Hailey for another shirt? And I saw goose bumps on his arms when he came up to the mic to receive his prize. That can't be normal."

"I wish I had some answers, friend, but I don't." Bennett stared gloomily ahead.

A cluster of deputies from the Hudsonville County Sheriff 's Department turned at the sound of Bennett's voice. Lucy stood among them, an unreadable look on her face, but when she saw James, her cornflower-blue eyes betrayed the seriousness of the situation. She slowly raised her hand to wave at her three friends while offering a timid smile, but James saw genuine fear written on her face. Gillian was in real trouble.

Stepping away from her fellow officers, Lucy approached her friends and steered them a few yards farther away from Jimmy's RV.

"They've already removed the body," she told them, her tone sounding detached and official. As she looked at her friends, she rubbed a business card between her fingers until James was certain the ivory card stock would turn to ribbons. "Hailey claims that she had no idea Jimmy's life was in danger. Apparently, she was in charge of keeping an eye on the ribs for today's contest. According to her statement, one or two people from each cooking team must pull an all-nighter on what they call Rib Night." She glanced down at the nearly destroyed business card and stuffed it into her pocket. "Hailey admits to spending the hours between one and three hanging out with the Marrow Men — coming back to check on the cooker from time to time. She then went to catch a few hours of shut-eye in the back of her SUV. She says that lately, Jimmy had been keeping the camper too hot for her to be comfortable, so she slept in the car."

"How does Gillian fit into this scenario?" James asked impatiently.

Lucy shrugged as though she couldn't figure out how best to answer his question. "Hailey woke up at about five thirty and saw Gillian on the camper steps. She thought Jimmy and Gillian might have been messin' around, so she burst into the RV and found Jimmy stone dead on the sofa. She called the cops on her cell and told Gillian to stay put."

"And Gillian listened to her?" Lindy sounded surprised.

Lucy bowed her head, clearly not wanting to make eye contact with her friends. "She didn't say a word, but Hailey says that Gillian was smiling like a deranged clown the whole time they waited for the sheriff and her crew to get here."

Bennett scratched his head. "Smilin'?

And . . . did you say the sheriff is a she?"

"Yes." Lucy glanced over her shoulder. "Here she comes now, and she doesn't look happy."

The conversation among the group of deputies abruptly came to a stop as a petite woman with skin the hue of warm toffee and closely-cropped, dark hair marched toward the supper club members. Her eyes were almond-shaped and sparkled with determination and intelligence.

"Sheriff Jade Jones," she introduced herself, shaking all of their hands with a brief but firm grip. "I'm sorry to have to start your morning off in such an unpleasant manner, but I need to take statements from all of you regarding Gillian O'Malley's interactions with Jimmy Lang."

"There was only *one* interaction!" Lindy spat out. "We didn't even know that she *knew* him until yesterday. And we had no idea what she was talking about when she accused Jimmy of killing her husband." Lindy's eyes flashed. "But I'll tell you one thing I *do* know. Gillian didn't murder anyone. She's a deep believer in karma and in that what-goes-around-comes-around stuff. She doesn't even kill spiders! She *relocates* them to the plants on her front porch. Does that sound like someone capable of an act of cold-blooded violence to you?" After this outburst, Lindy began to cry.

Something that might have been respect for Lindy's loyalty flitted across Sheriff Jones's face for a millisecond. She then shifted her compact, muscular body and gazed into the distance, her expression steely. "We're investigating all angles, ma'am," she said to Lindy. "Miss O'Malley has not been formally charged with a crime, but as of this moment, we're very interested in discovering her history with Mr. Lang."

"So are we!" Lindy retorted and then forced herself to calm down. "Has she said anything yet?"

Sheriff Jones shook her head. "No. She hasn't spoken a word since we found her here this morning."

James eyed the perimeter of crime scene tape fluttering in the morning breeze and muttered, "Jimmy seemed to enjoy rubbing people the wrong way, Sheriff. Just because Gillian was at the scene doesn't mean she was involved." But his words sounded unconvincing, even to his own ears. Did he completely believe in Gillian's innocence or had her bizarre behavior from the day before caused him to doubt her character?

The sheriff stared at him curiously. "And

which people did he rub the wrong way? Mr. Henry, is it?"

When James hesitated in order to gather his thoughts, Lucy jumped in. "The woman who runs the Inn at Fox Hall, for starters. She was pretty irate when she discovered that her *teenage* daughter had fooled around with Jimmy on Thursday night." She pointed at James. "He even saw the evidence on Francesca's neck. That's Eleanor's daughter and Eleanor was pretty livid. Francesca has to maintain a spotless reputation if she wants to become the next Miss Virginia."

"Francesca doesn't seem to give a fig about the upcoming pageant," Lindy added, "but her mother certainly does."

The sheriff tilted her chin at the nearest deputy who immediately produced a pad of paper and began taking notes.

"Mrs. Fiennes isn't the only other possible suspect," James said. "Bennett and I also overheard a heated exchange between Hailey and Jimmy yesterday. I don't know what Hailey's told you about their relationship, but from what we heard, it wasn't what I'd call harmonious. In fact, it seemed downright volatile. Right, Bennett?"

James turned to his friend, but Bennett appeared to be deaf and dumb to anything

197

except the presence of the attractive sheriff. Casting his eyes back and forth between Bennett and Sheriff Jones, James realized that the pair were close in age and were of almost the same height. The comparison ended there, however, for although Jade had a boyish haircut and an air of intensity about her, she possessed a regal beauty that had clearly struck Bennett to the core.

James elbowed Bennett in the ribs, and he was pleased to hear his friend come to his senses and join the conversation. "James speaks the truth, Sheriff." Bennett faced the sheriff. "And let's not forget the dog lady, folks. That crazy woman spit on Jimmy's cooker and called him all sorts of names. She sure looked like she'd have liked to see him sleepin' with the fishes. That was a seriously unhappy woman, yessir." Bennett cleared his throat in embarrassment. "Uh, I mean, ma'am."

Assessing Bennett with calculating eyes, Sheriff Jones addressed the hulking form of the deputy taking notes. "Harding, I'd like this group to be transported to the station immediately. I'd like separate statements from each of them — and I mean down to the tiniest detail — about what they know as fact, have heard as hearsay, or have witnessed with their own eyes in regards to

Jimmy Lang." She pointed at Lindy and Lucy. "I'll take the ladies with me. You can ask the two gentlemen to join you in your car."

"Are we going to be able to speak to Gillian?" Lindy demanded, hands perched on her round hips.

Sheriff Jones considered the question and then nodded at Lucy. "I'll allow you to be present for her questioning, Deputy Hanover. You're an officer of the law as well as Ms. O'Malley's friend. The combination may prove to be fortuitous."

Bennett watched the diminutive woman march toward the parking lot. Every deputy she passed stood a fraction taller as she strode by and several of the men straightened their hats or sucked in stomachs as well. If the sheriff noticed these demonstrations of respect, she gave no indication. "Now, *that's* a woman," Bennett panted. "Holy smokes."

"Get a hold of yourself, Casanova." Lucy gave Bennett an angry pinch. "Gillian needs us. Instead of daydreaming about Jade Jones, use your time in the car to think of precise statements that can get the sheriff's interest away from Gillian. We need to turn a spotlight on other possible suspects until we can start our own investigation." She smiled at James. "You know, that was really clever of you to throw doubt on the theory that Gillian is most likely the killer by mentioning Eleanor and Hailey. I brought up Felicity earlier — that's the dog trainer's name — but I was only able to speak to the sheriff alone for a few minutes."

"What are you going to say to Gillian when you see her?" Lindy asked Lucy and then made a feeble attempt to gather the thick and knotted hair that kept falling into her eyes into a rubber band. When she had completed her adjustments, her hairstyle bore a close resemblance to that of Pebbles from *The Flintstones.* James reflected that Lindy's desire to look like a celebrity had probably not included mimicking a Stone Age cartoon character.

"I don't know, but if I can't scare her into piping up and defending herself, it's going to look really bad for her." Lucy glanced at the sheriff 's back as she issued further orders to the deputies working around Jimmy's RV. "Silence won't win her any points. It makes her look guilty."

As Deputy Harding gestured for James and Bennett to accompany him to his cruiser, James paused in order to grab Lucy's hand. "You can do it, Lucy. You can help Gillian. I know you'll find a way." He gave her fingers a quick squeeze and then released them, relieved to see a look of firm resolve enter Lucy's eyes.

Inside the patrol car, James and Bennett took Lucy's advice to heart. They both quietly concentrated on all of their encounters with Jimmy Lang, each man trying to recreate every moment in which they had been in his presence and remembering each and every reference in which only Jimmy's name had been mentioned. James thought about R. C. Richter's passion over seeing both Hog Fest and the town of Hudsonville meet with success. He decided that R. C.'s displeasure over Jimmy's offensive behavior was worth relaying to Deputy Harding.

Harding was polite but formal. As they arrived at the small brick building that housed the sheriff 's department, he directed James and Bennett to a small conference room and stiffly offered them coffee. Both men readily accepted and then frowned when they tasted the bitter brew.

"You need more sugar?" Harding inquired, wordlessly suggesting that they weren't macho enough to drink the overwhelmingly strong coffee that he himself gulped down as though he were enjoying a glass of chocolate milk.

"Heck yeah, I need more sugar! How

about a dump truck full of it and a gallon of cream, too?" Bennett replied, unfazed by Harding's judgmental stare. "Shoot, man! When the oil in your car runs low, do you use this stuff instead of Quaker State?"

"We use Pennzoil," Harding answered flatly and then gestured at another deputy who had entered the room during Bennett's tirade. "This is Deputy Neely. He'll be taking your statement, Mr. Marshall. Mr. Henry, you'll be staying here with me."

Bennett shot James a thumbs-up and then trudged off behind Deputy Neely, who was so tall and thin that it wouldn't have surprised James to learn that his law enforcement colleagues fondly referred to Neely as Deputy Needle.

"Let's start at the beginning," Harding said, uncapping a pen and settling back in his chair. "When was the first time you became aware of Jimmy Lang's existence?"

"Within a few minutes of arriving in Hudsonville," James answered readily, remembering back to their delicious lunch on the back porch of the inn and how Jimmy had sat down at their table. "I'd say it was a little after one o'clock that Thursday afternoon."

Harding scribbled something on his notebook. "What was your first impression of Mr. Lang?"

James automatically took a sip of his coffee and grimaced. It was still early in the morning and though shock had startled him into wakefulness, he could feel his body crying out for its daily dose of caffeine. Still, he'd have to track down coffee later as the contents of his cup were simply undrinkable. Pushing the foul liquid away, James locked eyes with Harding. "I thought Jimmy Lang was a loud-mouthed pig. He was the kind of guy you might find amusing at first, but within seconds, all you want to do is get away from him." James picked up the plastic stirrer from the table and began to twist it in his hands. "The man was large and crude and, I don't know, I guess I found him repulsive." He pointed at his cup. "Kind of like this coffee."

An hour passed as Harding asked question after question and took careful notes on his pad. Finally, when they had reviewed James's statement several times, Harding recapped his pen and laid it down on the table. Just as his did so, James's stomach gurgled loudly.

"You hungry?" Harding asked James, who nodded honestly in response. "Be right back," the deputy said, and he left the room.

Harding returned a few minutes later carrying a ceramic American flag mug and a paper plate containing three biscuits. James accepted a biscuit gratefully and, even though it was cold and hard, ate it down as though it had just come out of the oven and was oozing rivulets of melting butter.

"This is the coffee we drink on a regular basis." Harding grinned slightly, pointing at the mug. "We only give folks that other stuff before we interrogate them." He grinned. "It kind of sets a tone."

James doctored his coffee with cream and a sprinkle of sugar, not completely trusting Harding, but the hot brew was good. It was smooth and rich, and it brought him some comfort after what already seemed like an endless morning.

"I ran into the sheriff in the kitchen." Harding picked apart a biscuit, took a small bite, and frowned. "These were much better two hours ago. Still, middle-aged bachelors like me will eat just about anything." He brushed crumbs from his hands. "Your friend the deputy isn't having much luck getting Ms. O'Malley to talk."

The last bite of James's biscuit stuck in his mouth. When he tried to swallow, his throat closed up and he inhaled most of the biscuit into his windpipe. Coughing mightily, James gasped for air and finally guzzled his hot coffee in an attempt to move the glutinous mass of biscuit down his throat.

"That's not good," James gasped. When he finally got his breathing under control, he asked, "Do you think the sheriff would let me talk to Gillian?"

Harding rubbed his dimpled chin in thought. "You think you could do better than a trained officer of the law?"

Sensing that Harding wasn't threatened by the possibility that a civilian might be able to provide assistance with their investigation, James nodded. "I do, actually. I think I know exactly what to say to get Gillian to talk."

Harding pushed back his chair and stood. "Then come with me."

James was brought into a stark room containing a table and two metal chairs. A recorder sat on the middle of the table along with a plastic pitcher of water and a stack of paper cups.

"Have a seat," Harding directed and then turned on the recorder and murmured into the speaker. When he was done, he leaned toward James and said, "I'm going to stand off to the side and try to be unobtrusive." At the sound of footsteps outside the door, Harding jumped forward to open it. He ushered Gillian inside and James gave an involuntary cry at his friend's appearance.

He rushed to her and put his arms around her. "Gillian! Are you okay?" He held her while casting an angry glare at Harding over her shoulder. "Why is she wearing this orange jumpsuit?"

Harding, looking slightly abashed, replied, "Her clothes were wet and dirty and she was shivering with cold when we picked her up. We thought she might be more comfortable in this."

James released Gillian and forced a smile for her benefit. "Well, at least it matches your hair."

Gillian kept her green eyes locked on the floor and James remained silent for a moment, simply standing close to her and keeping a loose hold of her hand. "I know you didn't hurt anyone, Gillian," he whispered softly, observing the circles around her eyes. The skin around her nose was bright red, probably a result of catching cold combined with hours of crying. Her chilled fingers trembled within the embrace of his hand.

"That man got to you. I can see that." James gently rubbed Gillian's back. "You thought you were done being sad over something that happened in the past, but you're not. He brought all the memories back to you, didn't he?"

Tears rolled down Gillian's freckled cheeks and she began sniffing. It was the first sound she had made since being brought into the room. James lifted her chin and forced her to look at him. "Don't give in to grief, Gillian. Your friends need you to be strong. Others need you to be able to come home with us. Your employees need you to show up at work on Monday. And Gillian," he felt a prick of guilt about dragging her beloved cat into the conversation, but it couldn't be helped, "what about the Dalai Lama? He couldn't live without you. Who would play bird DVDs for him or fix him plates of organic tuna fish?"

The tears came faster and though Harding held out a pocket-sized packet of tissues, James ignored him. He sensed that he had struck a nerve by mentioning Gillian's tabby, so he pushed on. "You're his mother, Gillian. You can't just give up and rot in jail for a crime you didn't commit. Think of Dalai and tell me where you've been."

Gillian slipped her hand from James's and used the sleeve of her jumpsuit to wipe her face.

"I spent the night with a woman named Felicity," she mumbled, her unused voice coming out in a croak. "She was hired to

207

put on several dog acts at Hog Fest." She sniffled again and this time, James accepted the tissues from Harding and handed them to Gillian. Harding covertly produced his pen and paper, though the recorder was already turned on. "After I saw . . . ," Gillian trailed off, unable to utter the name of the man she despised, so James said it for her.

"Jimmy?"

"Yes. *Him.*" She rubbed her eyes with a tissue and continued in a pained voice. "I just had to get away. I ran to the very end of the campground area and then I got tired. My body is weak. I haven't been doing my yoga lately and I've been sitting around too much after work, meditating and trying to reach a place of Zen." She sank down into one of the two chairs, never once looking in Harding's direction. She fastened her eyes on James as though he were her lifeline. "Anyway, I just ran out of breath by the river where it runs parallel to the campsites."

"Is that where you met up with Felicity?" James prodded carefully.

Gillian touched her bushy hair absently. "She had brought the dogs down to the river as a treat for performing so well. They were running and jumping and barking, and

Felicity was sitting on a big boulder, watching them. She looked so content. She recognized me from the dog show and called to me to sit with her." Gillian balled the tissue in her hands. "I heard her, but it was like someone was shouting my name from a long way away. I just stared at the dogs. I . . . I wanted to jump in the water with them. Get lost with them." She lowered her voice to the faintest whisper. "So I did."

"You jumped into the water?" James watched as Gillian nodded. "And then Felicity took care of you?"

"Yes. What a *giving* soul," Gillian answered. "I felt arms pulling me to the bank and then I was wrapped in a blanket. I remember her voice humming to me and then I slept for a long time. When I woke up, I told her everything. Felicity and I talked long into the night. I . . . we . . . drank, too."

James was surprised. Gillian hardly ever consumed alcohol. "Well, you were pretty distraught."

"I am in agony, James," Gillian replied without any of her usual dramatic flare. "That strawberry wine helped dull the burn, but I only slept for a few hours. At first, I hoped that I'd dreamed the whole thing." She finally gazed at Harding. "But I knew I hadn't. After I woke up, I went to *his* camper. I wanted to know if he was sorry for what he did so many years ago." Her eyes filled with tears again. "He never told me he was sorry. Not once. I wanted to hear the words, so maybe I could think about moving on to a state of forgiveness."

"And did you talk to him?" James asked quickly, before Harding could break the spell by speaking.

Gillian shook her head. "No. I was sitting on the camper steps, working up the courage to knock on the door, when that *awful* woman pushed me away, went inside, and then burst back out of the camper and started yelling at me." She pulled a fresh tissue out of the packet and blew her nose. "I couldn't understand most of what she said because she was shouting in double-time, but I caught on that Jimmy was dead. When I heard that, I couldn't move. It was like getting punched in the stomach."

James eased himself into the chair across from her. "What do you mean?"

"I'm not sorry he's gone to the other side, but *I* didn't send him there." Gillian put her head in her hands. "I wouldn't have wanted him to leave this life until he apologized to me. I needed to know that he felt regret over what he did!"

210

James was almost afraid to speak the words that had formed on his lips, but before he could contain them, they came tumbling out. "You wanted Jimmy to apologize to you for killing your husband?"

Gillian issued the briefest nod but did not look up.

"How did it happen, Gillian? How did Jimmy cause your husband's death?"

Shoulders shaking, Gillian wailed into her hands. "He ran over him! That son of a bitch deliberately ran over my husband."

"With his car?" Harding asked from his corner.

"No." Gillian lifted her head, her green eyes rimmed with red. Sorrow had etched lines in her skin and cast shadows across her face. "Not with a car. With a chicken truck."

Eleven: Spaghetti Bolognese

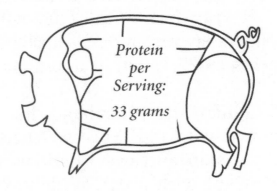

Protein per Serving:

33 grams

An hour after Gillian had been brought to the interview room, she finished her story. The telling of it drained her so completely that afterward, she requested that she be returned to her cell, as she longed for quiet and solitude. Nodding in sympathetic agreement, Deputy Harding handed Gillian off to the officer waiting in the hall and then waved two fingers at James, indicating that he should rise and follow him from the room.

"You guys are going to release her now, right?" James asked Harding eagerly.

Harding shook his head. "She's still a suspect, Mr. Henry. She sure as hell has a motive, so we can't let her go until we've gathered more information."

"But she didn't hurt anyone!" James declared wearily. "She just wanted to confront the man who killed her husband!"

Harding turned the corner at the end of the hall at the same moment Sheriff Jones stepped out of her office. Standing directly in his path, she stared at him inquisitively.

"Ms. O'Malley has given a statement," Harding informed his superior.

Jones was clearly pleased. "Excellent. Let's talk in my office." She turned a pair of tawny eyes on James. "We have your contact numbers, Mr. Henry. Why don't you and your friends go back to the inn and try to relax?"

"No offense, Sheriff," James snarled. "But we can hardly *relax* while Gillian is being held in suspicion for a crime she didn't commit!"

"Understood, Mr. Henry," the sheriff countered calmly. "And we are going to examine every angle, I assure you. My deputies are canvassing the campground area and conducting interviews as we speak. We don't operate under assumptions in this department. We search for evidence and allow the facts to speak the loudest." She placed a kind but firm hand on his arm and steered him toward the lobby. "I will review Ms. O'Malley's statement immediately. In the meantime, I'd like you and your friends to refrain from involving yourselves any further in our investigation. Ms. Hanover has my contact numbers and I've also asked her, as one professional to another, to step aside so that we can gather information during this critical time. As she knows, the first twenty-four hours following a crime of this nature are crucial."

The sheriff only released her hold on James's arm upon reaching the vestibule. At their approach, the supper club members turned distressed faces at him. They looked haggard and uncomfortable as they waited on two of the four wooden benches lining the lobby. Bennett perked up slightly upon seeing the attractive sheriff, but after delivering James to his friends, Sheriff Jones ducked back into the inner hallway without so much as glancing his way.

Without warning, Lucy raced over to James and threw her arms around him, resting her cheek against his shoulder. "You look awful, James. What happened back there?" she murmured into his ear.

James paused for a moment in the circle of her arms, inhaling the fruity scents of her shampoo and enjoying the warmth of her embrace. "I feel like I've been hit by a bus," he said, forcing himself back to reality. He gently pushed her a safe distance away and walked closer to Lindy and Bennett.

"Did you see Gillian?" Lindy sagged against the side of the bench, hugging her purse to her chest in search of solace. She looked at James hopefully.

"She didn't kill Jimmy. That's for sure," he answered and listened to his friends exhale loudly in relief. "But she sure had reason to." Hearing his words echo in the uncarpeted hallway, James gestured at the front door. "Let's find a place where we can talk. I don't want to share her story here."

"The deputy takin' my statement mentioned a place called the Old Hollywood Diner," Bennett said. "He said the décor's kinda cheesy but the food can't be beat."

"I can't believe I could be hungry at a time like this," Lindy moaned. "But I could sure use some comfort food, like a big bowl of macaroni and cheese."

"Or pie," Lucy added. "Warm apple pie. With ice cream on top." She glanced at James. "And big mugs of coffee with loads of half-and-half. Come on guys, we've gotta eat so our bodies can make some energy. Gillian is going to need us to be at our best if we're going to prove her innocence."

"In that case, I'm gettin' the biggest piece of meat they've got," Bennett stated as he helped Lindy up from the bench. "I need somethin' to wash away the taste of that God-awful coffee. No wonder those deputies arrested the wrong person — their brains are bein' turned to mush from drinkin' that sludge." He eyed Lindy's large purse. "You got any gum in that shoulder suitcase?"

The Elvis section of the Old Hollywood Diner was full, so a waitress in a lemon-yellow dress and squeaky white sneakers led them to the Elizabeth Taylor section. Beneath a poster of Liz flashing a predatory smile in her role as Cleopatra, the supper club members perused a menu that was as thick as an anatomy textbook.

"They make everything here," Lindy remarked. "I wonder if that's a good thing."

The waitress returned with glasses of water in amber cups and flipped her pad to the open position. "Y'all wanna hear the specials?" she inquired, chewing slowly on a piece of gum.

James tried to shake the image of the woman morphing into a cow and lazily chewing a long piece of grass against a wooden fence rail. She recited the specials mechanically and then told them to take their time thinking things over as she drifted off to care for other customers.

Bennett was the first to shut his menu. Gazing at the poster above their table, he began to regale his friends with Hollywood trivia. "Did you know that Elizabeth Taylor was born in England? Her parents were art dealers from St. Louis and went over there to open a gallery." He pointed at the poster. "That film is the one where she met hubby number five: Richard Burton. She actually got paid a million clams to star in that movie. That's a lot of dough in today's times, let alone 1963. Won two Oscars as well, but not for playin' Cleopatra."

"I take it your current trivia book is about Hollywood," Lucy said sourly, peering at Bennett over her menu.

Bennett shook his head. "Nope. I'm done brushin' up on that category. And don't go gettin' punchy at me just 'cause you're hungry and worn out."

Lucy murmured an apology as the waitress appeared to take their order.

"How's the Brando Bolognese?" James

217

asked her as his stomach rumbled expectantly.

Their waitress, who wore no nametag on her spotless uniform, shrugged. "Pretty good, I reckon. I don't eat them foreign foods, but *other* folks seem to like it fine." She jotted James's order on her pad. " 'Sides, I don't care for that Brando fella. He couldn't talk right. Sounded like a chokin' billy goat every time he opened his mouth."

Having no idea what a strangling goat might sound like, James nodded his head in agreement. The waitress slapped their ticket on the stainless steel counter separating the eating area from the kitchen and then brought a pitcher of root beer to the table even though no one had ordered soda. "I know y'all wanted tea, but we make it fresh and it's still brewin'," she said by way of explanation. "This here's the best birch beer you'll ever taste, anyhow. It's a house special."

"What *isn't* a house special at this place?" Bennett said and then poured a glass. He took a sip and the caramel-colored foam flecked his mustache. "All right, James. I can't stand it anymore. We got a few minutes 'til Miss Sunshine comes back with our food, so tell us what happened back at the station. How'd you get Gillian to talk and what did the woman say?"

James removed Bennett's tiny recorder from his pocket. "I hope you're not mad, but I've had this with me since it fell out of your pocket in the Bronco and something just told me to press the record button. I think I taped over most of your statistics. I'm really sorry, Bennett."

"It's okay, man. Glad you made such a good call. Now put that thing on the table and let's all listen to what you heard. This not knowin' is drivin' me crazy."

It took a minute or so to rewind the tape, but then James pressed the play button and Gillian's voice fizzled out of the machine's tiny speaker.

"To tell you how Jimmy killed my husband, I've got to go back a few years, to a time I have tried really hard to put out of my mind and out of my heart.

"I married Walden O'Malley when I was twenty. We met while doing volunteer work at the local animal shelter, and we fell in love like a lightning strike. My hometown was so small that the post office and grocery store were in the same building. There was one place to eat, a bank, and two churches. Most folks worked at the local poultry plant, and Walden's family had just moved into town

because his father had gotten a job at the plant. That's why I had never met him until that day at the animal shelter.

"*Walden enrolled in the local community college and was taking agriculture classes. He wanted, more than anything, to own a small farm and raise livestock. We dated for six months and were then married on the courthouse steps. No party, no gifts — just us declaring our love for one another with our landlord as witness. It was perfect.*"

A pause as Gillian accepted a glass of water from Deputy Harding.

"*Walden really loved animals and he couldn't help but ask his father what the conditions were like in the factory. For the birds, that is. His father told him that the conditions for the workers were fair and that was all that mattered. He got really angry and yelled at Walden, telling him to be thankful that they had enough money to pay for his studies, which Walden's father viewed as a waste of precious dollars.*

"*You see, Walden's family had moved from Pennsylvania because mills and factories across the state were closing their doors and turning desperate families out in the cold, with no means of paying for mortgages or car loans or food. Walden knew his father had been lucky to find work, but he still had to* know how the chickens were handled once they were delivered to the factory, so he asked one of the line workers to give him a tour. That's how it all started."

"How what started, ma'am?" Deputy Harding asked gently.

"His . . . interaction with Jimmy Lang. Jimmy was hired as a driver. He picked up the birds from farms all around western Virginia and brought them to the plant. He was truly a cruel soul. He enjoyed bringing the birds to their deaths. And the more they suffered, the more he was entertained."

"But the chicken factory was a processing plant, right?" Harding sounded genuinely perplexed. "That's what they do — process poultry for the rest of us to eat. It's a dirty job, but someone's gotta do it or no one would be eating nice pieces of fried chicken for supper. Does that really make a person bad?"

"It wasn't what they did but how they did it!" Gillian raised her voice in protest. "The birds were stuffed so tight into cages on Jimmy's truck that they couldn't move an inch. Then, Jimmy would unload them with a forklift and dump them on the conveyer belt. He didn't care if some of them fell off or got . . . crushed by machines . . . or died from exposure on the road. He would keep track of *the number of . . . casualties on each load and mark them in a notebook. He and two of the factory workers held a secret bet over who had the highest number of 'accidents' each month.*

"At the time Walden went on that factory tour, we'd only been married for four days. We didn't have any money except for what we both earned working part-time at the grocery store, but Walden promised me a honeymoon week in Philly as soon as we could afford it. He wanted to introduce me to his grandparents and show me the city of his childhood. But he never got the chance."

Silence stretched out on the tape. James noticed their waitress bearing down upon them with a laden tray. She set it on the edge of their Formica-topped table and shoved their glasses of birch beer inward as she rested the weight of the tray partly on the table and partially against her hip. James hit the pause button on the recorder and admired their server as she skillfully handed out hot plates replete with piles of home-cooked food.

Bennett received a plump bacon and Monterey jack burger accompanied by a mountain of French fries and a dish of baked beans. A long platter bearing fried catfish and hush puppies was slid beneath

Lindy's nose, and Lucy was given slices of turkey resting on pillows of mashed potatoes and stuffing. She was also served a small bowl of cranberry sauce and another containing thick, brown gravy. A basket of corn-bread muffins was set in the center of the table for everyone to share.

"Be right back with your Brando, hon," the waitress said, and she squeaked away. Within seconds, she had returned with an oval plate of spaghetti noodles drenched in a thick meat sauce. Along with his pasta, James was served a small basket of garlic bread and a condiment bowl filled with freshly shredded Parmesan.

"Y'all need anything else?" she asked pleasantly as her customers gaped at their plates.

"You got a wheelbarrow?" Bennett looked at her. "We're gonna need one if we eat so much as half of this stuff."

"No one ever leaves the Old Hollywood hungry." She smiled. "Gimme a holler if your drinks start runnin' dry."

After twirling a strand of slippery spaghetti around and around on his fork, James gave up and began to cut the saturated noodles with his knife. He took a bite of pasta and felt some of the tension in his body instantly eased by the taste of the rich meat sauce and the perfectly supple noodles. He sighed in contentment and prepared another forkful.

"I hear you, man," Bennett said, and he held his mammoth burger aloft. "Just what the doctor ordered."

Lindy squeezed a fat piece of lemon over her catfish filet, creating a crooked line of drizzle over the deep brown crust. While Lindy cut into her fish with the side of her fork, Lucy scooped a gelatinous spoonful of cranberry sauce onto a slice of turkey breast. She gestured at the recorder. "Keep going, James," she ordered and then stuffed a large bite of turkey, potatoes, and cranberries into her mouth.

James pushed the play button and Gillian's voice emanated from the speaker.

"Walden got his tour and what he saw scarred *him. I mean, it changed him for good. He came back to the two-room we rented and cried. He just put his face in his hands and let the power of his emotions flow out of his body. Oh, how I loved him for that. But he told me such horrible things that day. Things I'll* never *forget! He said that after the chickens got off the truck, they were hung upside down and dipped into an electrified stunning tank, so they're confused but not unconscious when they're killed. So cruel!*

"And the conditions on the farms were too much to bear! Those chickens spent six weeks crammed into an enclosed structure, standing and sleeping on their own waste. Genetically modified, they grew so fat so fast that tons of them had heart attacks or complete organ failure because of the sheer mass of their bodies.

"If they managed to live the whole six weeks in those conditions, then . . . then Jimmy would come for them. Whether it was pouring rain or ninety-five degrees beneath a sweltering sun, he'd stuff them so tight into their metal cages that they couldn't move a wing. He'd take long lunches at truck stops while the birds endured all kinds of weather. One day, he bragged to his buddies at the plant about how a bunch of boys threw rocks at the chickens and the birds were too dumb to realize they were being pummeled in the face by stones. It's not like they could have moved even if they were frightened or injured!"

Gillian paused again, but obviously only long enough to calm herself.

"Walden was desperate to achieve humane treatment for the poultry, so he started an activist group in our county. You can only imagine how unpopular that made him! The only people who would join were other college students or bored retirees."

225

There was a grunt from Harding.

"After all, the plant employed most of the town. When Walden began picketing outside the plant's front gates, his own father threatened to cut all ties with us. But Walden and his group didn't stop. Workers threw chicken feet and . . . and other body parts at us. They called us traitors and names I'd rather not repeat. We tried to get the press on our side, but the local papers were not sympathetic to our cause. Finally, Walden got a reporter from Washington to come to one of our rallies. This journalist interviewed Jimmy following one of his deliveries, and the story of the chicken's mistreatment got picked up all over the region, but the story was quickly replaced by the news of a missing hiker who happened to be some distant cousin of the governor.

"Nothing changed at the plant or at the farms. The only thing that the publicity did was to make Jimmy Lang furious! He had been portrayed as the malicious cad he was, and his boss heard about Jimmy's monthly bet over the dead chickens. From that point on, Jimmy was told that his pay would be docked for every bird that arrived at the plant dead. Jimmy was furious. The plant had always taken all his birds before — alive or dead. Suddenly, they changed their policy and he wanted revenge. So one day . . ."

Gillian trailed off and fought to compose herself as she neared the most difficult part of her tale.

"Walden always rode his bike to campus. The college was about four miles from where we lived and he rode on the shoulder of a two-lane road that ran parallel to the interstate for about three of those miles. That's where Jimmy spotted him. Jimmy was on his way to drop off some birds, and he had left the interstate to visit a decrepit truck stop that served beer. He was far from sober and had smoked a joint before getting back into his rig."

There was a long pause as Gillian struggled to continue.

Seated at their table in the Old Hollywood Diner, James and his friends had stopped eating and were staring at the recorder as though it were a coiled snake.

"Jimmy swerved that big truck of his and laid on the horn, hoping to scare some sense *into Walden, but once his rig started to skid, he couldn't regain control of the truck and it flipped over, sliding down the highway, pinning Walden beneath its weight . . .*

"The doors to the chicken cages burst open and birds went everywhere. They were strewn all over the road, the embankment, the wildflowers growing alongside the other lane . . .

"The State Police arrived at the scene and took Jimmy away. He was completely uninjured. I went to the courthouse every single day of his trial. He was given fifteen years for vehicular manslaughter under the influence of alcohol and drugs. That's it! Fifteen years in exchange for the malicious act that ended Walden's life."

Another silence. Lindy dabbed at her wet face with her napkin.

"I thought I'd stay and continue Walden's fight against the inhumane treatment of those poor birds, but after the incident, the other activists were too frightened to protest. I became a pariah. Everywhere I went, people seemed to make jokes about chickens crossing the road or fried chickens on the highway. It was awful. I made it through my final exams at college, graduated, and moved away. I've never been back to that town. I've never even visited Walden's grave. I thought I could pretend as though that part of my life never existed. It all happened so long ago. But when I saw Jimmy — laughing and alive, the way Walden should be, I felt like my husband had been killed all over again."

The sound of weeping crept from the recorder.

"But I didn't hurt that man, Deputy Harding. Much as part of me would like to, I didn't. That

wouldn't have honored Walden's memory. He was a pacifist. He was a gentle, giving soul. I wanted an apology from Jimmy. I wanted . . . I needed *to know that he regretted stealing Walden's life away. I needed to know that Jimmy was sorry for shattering every one of our hopes and dreams. But now I'll never know if he regretted what he did. There'll never be closure for me."*

More silence. Finally, the sound of a defeated exhalation.

"I'm tired, James. These memories . . . they make me so sad. May I be alone now, Deputy Harding?"

James turned off the recorder.

"There it is," he sighed. "That's what I heard. That's her story."

His friends were stunned.

"No wonder she wanted to be a vegetarian," Lindy mumbled after a long silence, pushing her plate of half-eaten fish away. Lucy and Bennett followed suit. As they sat, digesting their heavy food and Gillian's tragic narrative, their waitress returned, wearing a look of concern.

"Somethin' wrong with your dinners, folks?"

"No, no," Lucy hastily assured her. "We just wanted to save room for dessert. We've got some serious thinkin' to do and for that,

229

we're gonna need some serious sugar. Apple pie à la mode for everyone. And coffee, please. Lots of coffee."

The waitress nodded and bused their dishes. She wiped their table clean and came back a few minutes later with four plates of apple pie heaped high with vanilla ice cream. She then handed out white coffee mugs and placed a steaming carafe of coffee in the center of the table. She retrieved a dozen individual creamers from her apron pocket and sprinkled them in a loose circle around the carafe.

"I'll check back on you folks in a bit," she said and then bustled off to take the order of a family of six that had seated themselves in the James Dean section.

Lucy dug a small notepad from her purse, uncapped a pen, and gave her friends a penetrating stare. "We've got work to do. We're going to make a list of who we need to interview in order to find Jimmy's *real* killer. I think we should start with Felicity, the dog lady."

Lindy twirled a lock of hair around her index finger. "But Lucy, you're a deputy now. Won't treadin' on the sheriff's territory get you into trouble?"

"This is *Gillian* we're talking about!" Lucy's blue eyes flashed. "I don't care what rules I break, we've gotta find the solution to this mystery before the festival ends!"

"You're right," James quickly agreed. "We've got to get answers from Felicity, Hailey, Eleanor, and anyone else who might have a clue as to what really happened last night." He touched Lucy's hand, and she scribbled intently in her notepad. "But we have to be discreet or we might get sent back to Quincy's Gap."

"And that won't do Gillian a lick of good," Bennett stated.

As the four friends stared at the names on the list, James plowed his fork through the golden crust of the apple pie and scooped a generous bite into his mouth. The apples were so soft they practically dissolved upon contact with his tongue. Sugar, cinnamon, and a hint of nutmeg coated his teeth and he greedily took another bite. He then collected a forkful of the smooth and creamy ice cream and ate it slowly, blissfully, licking every drop from the tines. "This is really good pie," he murmured.

Lucy ignored him and pushed her partially eaten dessert off to the side. Jabbing a finger at the list, she said, "At this point, our suspects are all women."

"Makes sense. It's a mite easier for me to picture a woman climbin' up that skinny metal ladder to that camper roof to tape over the vents," Bennett declared, wiping ice cream from his mustache.

"But a man could do that just as easily," Lindy argued, splashing cream into her coffee.

"Like that pale-skinned guy with the black baseball hat I saw arguing with Jimmy," James said quickly. "This was a serious fight. I think we should keep our eye out for this guy."

"It won't be easy, without the rest of us having seen him and no name to go by, but if he's *that* pasty, he should stick out of the crowd," Lindy said, twirling a coffee stirrer around her finger. "I also don't think we should forget about the barbecue competition."

"You believe someone would murder Jimmy just to be known as the barbecue champion of Hog Fest?" James asked incredulously.

"Not so much for the title as for the contract with Heartland Foods," Lindy replied thoughtfully. "Seems like that kind of offer could change a person's life."

"Good point, Lindy." Lucy scribbled on her notepad. "We need to see which of the other team leaders might be pinched for money. They'd have the most convenient access to Jimmy's camper, after all."

"And didn't that Hailey girl say she had spent a few hours fraternizing with one of the enemy teams?" Bennett pointed his fork at his friends. "In the middle of a competition? Doesn't that strike you as kind of peculiar?"

Everyone nodded in response.

"Maybe Hailey's been lookin' for greener pastures. With Jimmy as my boyfriend, I sure as heck would be." Lindy grunted.

Lucy gestured for the check. "We'll start with Felicity. Hailey will be tied up at the sheriff's department for a while. And James is right, we need to find the guy Jimmy fought with if we can." She glanced at her watch. "When is the barbecue rib contest over, Lindy?"

Lindy dug her folded schedule from her red leather purse and scrutinized it carefully. "It should be done by now. The next food category is Poultry. The judging begins in less than two hours."

"Perfect. We'll just have time to interview Felicity before we start talking to the cooking teams." Lucy looked up as the check was placed in front of her. She slid across the table to Bennett. "What's the damage?"

Bennett eyed the check and performed an instant calculation. "Eleven dollars and thirty-three cents per person." He reached into his wallet and pulled out a ten and two singles. "That includes the tip."

After settling their bill, they climbed back into Lucy's Jeep and drove toward the festival grounds. They waited impatiently at one of the town's intersections as phrases from Gillian's narrative haunted their thoughts. The red light seemed interminable, as car after car passed through the intersection. Finally, a sheriff's department cruiser shot across their path, followed very closely by a car that looked strangely familiar to James.

It can't be, James thought to himself. Panicked, he leaned forward in his seat and peered intently at the moving car, hoping to catch a glimpse of the license plate. He couldn't be certain, but he was relatively sure that it read THESTAR, an abbreviation standing for their hometown paper, the *Shenandoah Star Ledger.*

It appeared that Murphy had ditched her stories on fancy felines and yodeling in order to drive to Hudsonville, and James had the distinct feeling that she hadn't changed her plans solely to spend quality time with him. She must have heard about Jimmy's murder.

"What's up?" Bennett whispered from the

seat next to him. "You look like you saw somethin' strange."

"Oh, nothing unusual for us these days." James ran his hands over his temples. "Just more trouble."

Twelve:
Barbecued
Cornish Hen

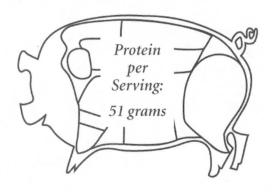

Protein
per
Serving:

51 grams

Felicity was practicing with her dogs on the far end of the campground area. A pair of Jack Russell terriers leapt through a series of hoops in blurs of white fur as they raced one another. At the end of their obstacle course, the dogs barked and smiled, their tongues lolling and their stumpy tails wagging fiercely as Felicity lavished them with praise.

Two border collies began their routine next, dashing through tunnels, climbing steps, and weaving in and out of flexible poles with lightning speed. Felicity encouraged her animals by calling their names and blowing shrill notes on a small silver whistle. As the supper club members walked toward her, James observed that Felicity's dull blonde hair was braided and piled on top of her head and that she wore a baggy, white cotton shirt embroidered at the neck and hem with small flowers. With her long black skirt and mud-covered clogs, Felicity looked more like a Dutch milkmaid than a dog trainer.

"I was wondering if y'all were going to track me down," she said by way of welcome. "The news about Jimmy's death has spread around this place like germs on an airplane. I heard about Gillian, too. I even asked to see her after they were finished questioning me at the station, but they wouldn't allow it." She picked at the end of a coiled leash in agitation. "How is she?"

"Not so great. But at least she had someone to confide in before her arrest, thanks to you." Lindy took both of Felicity's hands in her own. "We are so grateful to you for taking care of Gillian last night. We were all frantic with worry over where she'd gone."

"It was nothing." Felicity waved off the notion that she had done anything special.

"Plus, I made a new friend. That doesn't happen too often at our age, does it?"

One of the border collies trotted over to Bennett and began to energetically sniff at the cuffs of his pants. Bennett shifted his feet and backed away from the curious canine.

"He's harmless," Felicity assured Bennett.

"Everybody says that about their own dogs," Bennett muttered, "but I'm a mailman, lady. I've seen the supposedly *nicest* dogs turn into savage, droolin', postal-carrier-hatin' maniacs in my presence." He eyed the dog fearfully. "This dog's gonna eat me, isn't he?"

"Not Parson. He might lick you to death, but that's it." Felicity laughed and placed her hand on the head of the black and white collie sitting calmly beside her. "And this is Vicar. The terriers are Minister and Clergy. My father was a preacher, as you might have guessed, but he passed away years ago. These guys are my only family now. All four of them."

"Is your show still set for tonight?" Lucy asked.

Felicity nodded. "Yes. Nothing on the schedule's been altered despite this morning's, uh, discovery. That's why we were practicing. Besides, I wanted to get my mind

238

off my trip to the sheriff's. It was very intimidating being questioned by them." She giggled nervously. "I felt guilty even though I haven't done anything wrong."

"Believe me, we've all felt that way before," James said soothingly and Felicity shot him a look of gratitude. "And we can assure you that Gillian's innocent of Jimmy's murder as well."

"I'm sure Felicity made it clear to the authorities that Gillian was too inebriated to have been able to find her way to Jimmy's camper and climb onto the roof," Lucy said, affecting a scolding tone toward James.

Felicity fidgeted with Vicar's collar. "I told them what happened. Plain and simple. We both drank a lot of wine and fell asleep. When I woke up this morning, Gillian was gone." She shrugged in resignation. "I don't think I made a very good alibi for Gillian. She could have left anytime during the night and I wouldn't have been the wiser, I'm afraid."

The supper club members exchanged glum looks. Felicity ruffled the fur on Vicar's neck and sighed. "I'm sorry."

Lucy touched the trainer on the shoulder. "Don't be. All you did was tell the truth."

"Did Jimmy have something against dogs?" James asked abruptly.

Felicity narrowed her eyes for a second and then forced her face to go blank. "I have no idea. Why?"

James's friends shifted their gazes so that none of them were staring at Felicity as he pursued his indelicate line of questioning. "We were standing with him yesterday when you, ah, shouted rather passionately at him." He held out his hands in supplication. "I'm sure you had every reason to be angry at the guy. We'd only talked to him for a few minutes, but it didn't take us long to figure out that he was a louse." He looked to his friends for confirmation. "Right?"

Lindy nodded. "Rude and crude."

"Loud-mouthed jerk," Bennett murmured.

"Don't forget chauvinistic hillbilly," Lucy added.

Felicity studied James and then sat wearily on a folding chair positioned between her tent and a row of roomy dog cages and gestured at a picnic blanket spread open on the ground beside her. "Why don't y'all take a seat and I'll tell you how that demon disguised as a human being caused me to end up here, performing like a circus monkey and sleeping in a tent."

The second the supper club members had gathered on the picnic blanket, both of the

Jack Russells made a beeline for Bennett and, after covering the back of his hand with a frenzy of wet kisses, settled down on either side of his legs and closed their eyes.

"Looks like you've got a pair of bookends," Lindy teased him.

Bennett rolled his eyes in response. "Why me?"

"They must've detected the scent of a fellow carnivore," James remarked and then turned his attention back to Felicity. "So you travel all around with your dogs? Doing shows?"

"That's right. Festival after festival for about eight months of the year. When we're back home in South Carolina, I pick up extra money doing doggie birthday parties and performing for nursing homes and day cares and such." She stroked Vicar's head and the dog blinked his liquid brown eyes at her in adoration. "But this didn't used to be our life. My dogs were competitors and for several years, the best in the Southeast. I used to teach classes at one of Columbus's top kennels, too. That was all before Jimmy came along and ruined that way of life for me."

"What did he do?" Lucy glanced at Parson in alarm. "He didn't hurt the dogs, did he?"

Felicity shook her head. "No, though I

241

wouldn't have put it past the bastard. Two years ago, my camper — this was back when I had a pretty nice one — was parked next to Jimmy's at the Memphis Brews and Barbecue Festival. My dogs were competing in the agility trials and I was also asked to help judge the jumpers event, as my dogs never competed in that category."

"Do the dogs earn pretty good prize money?" Lindy leaned forward, curious.

"It's not bad," Felicity replied evenly. "Top prizes could earn you a thousand dollars here and there as well as food and supplies and stuff like that. We won quite a bit, but I made my money giving lectures and demonstrations. Back then, folks saw me as an expert in the field. My reputation paid my bills." She scowled. "That's how Jimmy got me. He tarnished my reputation to the point where people wouldn't want me to so much as clip their dog's toenails, let alone enroll in my agility training or obedience classes."

"How? He's . . . he was just a tow-truck-driving barbecue cooker." Lucy gave Felicity a look of bewilderment. "How could his opinion matter to anyone in your circle?"

"His opinion mattered when he lied to the head judge at our competition in Memphis. Jimmy claimed that I was giving my dogs illegal substances so they'd have more energy. He said that he removed pills from their food bowls because he was worried they might be dangerous for my animals. Turns out they were illegal steroids — the kind men use to bulk up their muscles! He even claimed to have found the empty pill vial in my garbage!" Felicity slapped her hand on her leg. "As if I would ever put the lives of my dogs in jeopardy. They're my closest friends!"

"But the judges believed him?" Lindy asked, her eyes filled with sympathy.

"Maybe they did and maybe they didn't, but Lord knows they were concerned about having a scandal connected to their event, so they disqualified my dogs, cancelled my lectures and demonstrations, and found another judge to replace me. After that, I was blackballed in the dog world because everyone *assumed* I was guilty. And now," she waved her arm around the campground, "here I am. Barely scratching out a living."

James reached out and stroked Parson's soft fur. The canine winked his eyes in contentment. "But why did Jimmy go after you in the first place?"

"He complained that my dogs barked too much in the early morning when he was try-ing to sleep," Felicity answered and then snorted. "He told me that it was their fault he didn't win his cooking contests that day and if 'my beasts' weren't quiet the next night, he'd teach them or *me* a lesson."

Thinking of how Gillian had described Jimmy's cruelty to the chickens he had delivered to the poultry plant, James believed that Jimmy's threats against Felicity and her dogs were issued in complete seriousness.

"Did you move to a different place in the campground?" Bennett wanted to know.

Felicity sighed and shook her head. "No, I didn't move my camper, and not a day goes by that I don't regret that decision. I was too proud and stubborn to have realized that one man could change my life with a single lie." She shrugged helplessly. "And he taught me a lesson all right."

"Well, I'd like to hurt the guy, but someone's already beat me to it!" Lindy declared and Felicity smiled meekly.

"Like I told the sheriff, it wasn't me. I listened to Gillian's story, drank some wine with her, and fell into a coma in my sleeping bag. When I woke up this morning alone, I was a bit confused, but then I saw the blanket I had lent Gillian folded neatly in a corner of my tent and I knew that she hadn't been a figment of my imagination."

She gazed at her four pets lovingly. "I'm not sorry that Jimmy's dead, believe me, but it wasn't by my hand. If I were sent to jail, then who would take care of my dogs? It may sound silly, but they're my reason for living and I'd never risk their future like that."

Lucy chuckled. "That's not silly at all. Wanna see my babies?" She removed a color photograph from her wallet and unfolded it for Felicity to view. "These are my darlings. Bono, Benatar, and Bon Jovi. I named them after my favorite rock stars."

"Gorgeous!" Felicity exclaimed and showed the photo to Vicar. "Look at these German shepherds, Vic. I bet you guys would have a great time playing together." She handed Lucy the photograph. "Would y'all like to watch our show tonight? We'd be proud to have you in the stands."

"We'll come if we can," Lindy promised, and she got to her feet. "But right now we've got to do everything possible to help Gillian."

"Of course." Felicity slipped a leash around Vicar's neck. "Please let me know if there's anything I can do. After all, she barely knew me and yet she offered me a job. She said she's been thinking of expanding her grooming business into a full-fledged dog obedience school and kennel. Oh, what was the name of her business? The Yuppie Puppy! That's it!" Her eyes grew misty. "She said that I could run the new business with her, as a partner. Just like that, she was giving me that chance to go back to my old way of life. She believed in my talent and integrity."

"That's our Gillian," Bennett stated proudly.

Lucy touched Felicity's shoulder. "But you drew her out of the water, put a blanket around her, and let her unburden herself to you. And *she* was a stranger to you when you did those things out of sheer kindness. You're a good woman, Felicity, and you're now a friend to all of us." Lucy put her hands on her hips in the determined posture James had seen many times on the past. "We're going to straighten this all out, and when Gillian is back with us, we're all going to celebrate together, okay?"

Overwhelmed by emotion, Felicity could only nod in response.

The supper club members said goodbye to Felicity and the dogs and wished them good luck at their show. "We'll keep you in the loop," James promised as they turned away.

"Thank you!" she waved as Vicar barked

in excited accompaniment.

Bennett led the way as the foursome walked through the campground area and regrouped in front of a small lemonade stand.

"I don't think she's our killer," Lindy said in a low voice.

"Me either, but we can't cross Felicity off our list yet. She certainly had both motive and means. And she's camped beside Jimmy before, so she might have known that he used a propane heater." Lucy's eyes scanned the crowd, though her gaze didn't settle on a particular person. "Still, she doesn't strike me as a calculating murderer. We'll just move her name down to the bottom for now. Let's go ahead and question the other barbecue teams next. And don't forget to keep our eyes open for the pale guy James saw arguing with Jimmy. Who knows? He might even be on one of the teams."

"Then we'd better split up," James suggested. "There's not much time left before their next category is due in to the judges."

"Wait a sec." Lucy held up a finger as though to stop her friends from moving forward. "If the other barbecue guys are anything like Jimmy, they're not going to spill their guts to the two of us." Lucy looked at Lindy. "You men might need to break the ice with them."

"You've got a point there. Let's have a gander at the team names again," Bennett said, and the four friends quickly divided the teams between them. Lucy and James paired off and headed toward the cooking area. The first group they planned to talk to was the Adam's Ribbers.

"Better let *me* take the lead with these gals," Lucy said, her eyes sparkling in anticipation of prying information from the four women.

The teammates were all huddled around the grill, clearly engaged in a debate over which sauce to brush on the Cornish hens they had chosen as their entries in the Poultry category.

A plus-sized woman wearing a pink and white striped apron and a white golf visor slapped a pair of tongs against the top of her cooker and shouted, "No more fruit sauces, damn it! They're not working!"

"But it's just a *hint* of orange juice!" a woman dressed in a denim skirt and T-shirt reading *I Love Johnny Depp* argued.

"No. We're goin' with the spicy sauce this time," stated a third woman in a firm but gentle voice. "Thelma's got this sauce just right. It's a winner for sure."

"Men prefer spicy," the fourth team

member, a skinny redhead, declared and then noticed James standing near their grill. "Isn't that right?" she asked him.

"I'm partial to spicy sauces over fruit sauces, yes," he answered truthfully.

The woman in the Johnny Depp T-shirt said, "Hey! You were one of the brisket judges. Now that the contest is over, can you tell us what you thought of the mango sauce we entered in that category?"

"Well, I thought it was a bit too sweet and fruity to complement a piece of red meat." James shrugged. "I'm sorry, ladies. I'm not trying to offend you, but if your friend Thelma's made a spicy sauce, I'd go with that one."

"Would you try it for us?" The Johnny Depp fan gave James and Lucy eager looks. "We're using it on Cornish hens. Would you? Both of you?"

"Sure thing," Lucy quickly agreed.

"I'm Zoe, by the way," the girl said and then handed them each a paper plate bearing a half of a hen. Though still stuffed from their enormous late lunch, James and Lucy took a bite of Cornish hen, chewed thoughtfully, and then took a second bite in order to convince the ladies that their sauce was being carefully assessed.

Lucy set her plate down on the card table

next to the grill. "It's good."

"But not great?" The woman in the striped apron gave Lucy a piercing look and then turned her sharp gaze on James.

"The spices are a bit too subtle for my taste. I think you need a bit more crushed red pepper," he recommended. "But the texture is perfect. It's real thick and savory. As soon as you get the spiciness factor down, I think you'll have the perfect sauce."

Thelma and Zoe beamed while the other Adam's Ribbers thanked James and Lucy. "Can we get you some tea?" one of them asked. Lucy accepted and settled down at their card table, trying to appear as relaxed and casual as possible. James followed her lead.

"So who's the one to beat in the Poultry category?" She directed her question at Zoe.

"The Tenderizers are good at everything." Zoe frowned. "We could beat them in this category, we're sure of it, but only if their team doesn't get any extra help."

"What do you mean?" Lucy gave Zoe a confused look. "Who would lend them a hand at this stage in the game?"

Thelma vigorously sprinkled several ingredients into a large bowl of barbecue sauce. "We heard a rumor that Jimmy Lang's girlfriend was the one who came up with all his secret sauces, rubs, and mops. We also heard that two of the other teams were tryin' to get her recipes from her."

"You'd think they'd let the woman alone!" Zoe snorted in disgust. "Jimmy seemed like a nasty piece of work, but he was still her man. People can be such vultures."

"Did you gals know Jimmy well?" Lucy asked evenly.

"No," they answered simultaneously as they shook their heads.

"We've only been in one other contest with him and that was almost a year ago," Zoe elaborated. "That was our first time cooking competitively, and we were too busy scrambling to get our entries in to pay him much mind."

"Good thing we didn't bother with him," Thelma added with a huff. "I'd have had to smack that boy with the business end of my spatula if he carried on to our faces the way he did at the brisket contest yesterday. What a horse's ass!" She dipped a spoon into the sauce and licked it. Grinning, she winked at James.

"Still, there are men like him all over the place," one of the other women said with a shrug. "You gotta just ignore them and do your own thing, ya know? That's how we all got together. We left jobs run by overbearing, butt-pinching jerk-offs. Now we own our own gourmet food market and do these contests as a hobby." She raised her glass to her friends. "We're havin' a blast and we're gettin' better with every entry."

The women exchanged high fives.

"Sounds like a lot of fun." Lucy finished her tea and smiled at the women. "We'd best be on our way. Good luck to you all in the next contest." She patted the grill lightly. "I think you've got a winner here."

Thelma handed James a handwritten recipe. "Just in case we win, I want you to know what was in the sauce. Keep it hidden 'til the contest is over though."

Surprised by Thelma's generous gift, James blushed and thanked all four women.

"I don't see any motive there," Lucy commented as they headed for the next cook site. "They don't need money and they weren't really affected by Jimmy's death."

When James didn't respond, she turned to look at him and realized that he had stopped walking. "What are you looking at?" she demanded and then fell silent.

Murphy Alistair had appeared from behind one of the RVs and was making her way toward James in quick strides. When she drew close to him, she dropped her briefcase carelessly on the ground and reached up to bring his face toward hers so she could kiss him on the lips.

"Poor you!" she whispered tenderly and held on to his shoulders. "I am so sorry about Gillian! How are you holding up?"

James gently extracted himself from the embrace but Murphy grasped his hand proprietarily. "I'm okay," he responded, keeping his emotions guarded. "How did you find out about what happened?"

"You know I've got contacts all over the Valley. I received an email from a colleague in Charlottesville about Jimmy Lang's death and when I recognized that the murder had taken place in Hudsonville, I called my friend and found out that the victim had been killed here at the festival." Her hazel eyes were filled with concern. "I had to come to see that you were all right."

Unable to stop himself, James asked, "So you're just here for me? Not to write a story about this?"

Murphy released his hand and picked her briefcase off the ground. "Well, I'll cover the story, of course. Our readers would want to know about a fellow town member's involvement in the case."

"Are you referring to Gillian?" James tried to control his rising anger.

"To all of you, actually." Murphy issued a

curt nod of recognition to Lucy.

James took Murphy's arm and pulled her several yards away from Lucy. "Look. You don't know the full picture here. Gillian is innocent and she's going through a lot emotionally right now. Once we get her name cleared and take her back home, she's not going to want to see her name in print in the *Star* or hear people gossiping about her. She's had *fellow* town members hurt her in the past. You need to keep her out of your story."

"I can't leave out pertinent information like that. She's half the story!" Murphy protested. "And people in Quincy's Gap know her and will care deeply about how this whole thing unfolds for her."

"Unfolds!" James spluttered. "She's not a piece of laundry! She's my friend and a damned fine person!" He lowered his voice to a hissed whisper. "I'm warning you, Murphy, leave her name out of your piece."

Murphy was stunned by his ferocity but she recovered quickly. "Why not tell me what's going on in your words, then?"

"You're unbelievable, you know that?" James snarled at her. "You're not here for me at all! I'm secondary to this — the *big* story!" When Murphy didn't deny this, he turned away from her in a fury. "I've got to go. Lucy and I are trying to do some *good* before Gillian has to spend the night in a jail cell."

Grabbing his arm, Murphy pleaded with him. "I could help, too. When I interview people, I might find out information that would throw doubt on Gillian being a serious suspect."

"That would finally put your prying ways to good use, then," James snapped and then relented a fraction. "Let's talk later, okay? I'm short on time."

"And on kindness," Murphy muttered stormily and stomped in the opposite direction.

"Let's tackle the Tenderizers," James growled when he reached Lucy's side. "I'd love to have an excuse to take out my anger at Murphy on some smart-ass, beer-swigging, butt-scratching SOB."

"I love it when you talk tough," Lucy responded, feeling a surge of unexpected happiness.

ADAM'S RIBBERS'
SPICY BARBECUE SAUCE

An all-purpose sauce for use on ribs and steak, chicken, fish, and grilled vegetables.

1 tablespoon minced garlic
1 large onion, chopped
1 1/2 tablespoons olive oil
1 1/4 cups commercial chili sauce
1/3 cup tomato paste
1/4 cup Worcestershire sauce
1/4 cup red wine vinegar
1 1/2 teaspoons hot sauce (Thelma uses Tabasco)
1 tablespoon oregano
1/2 teaspoon crushed red pepper
1 tablespoon lemon juice
1/4 cup honey

Sauté the garlic and onion in olive oil for 5 minutes or until tender. Stir in the remaining ingredients and bring to a boil over medium-high heat. Reduce heat to low and simmer for 30 minutes. Remove from heat and brush on food while grilling. For an even spicier sauce, add more crushed red pepper.

THIRTEEN:
TIE-DYE SNO-CONE

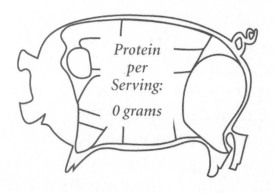

*Protein
per
Serving:

0 grams*

If James and Lucy hadn't been so distracted
by Murphy's sudden appearance, they
might have paid more attention to the
noticeable lack of activity near the Tenderizer's commercial-sized grill. Instead, they
took a cursory glance around and then assumed that the team must be gathered
inside one of the RVs parked nearby.

"This one's the biggest," Lucy said, jerk-
ing her thumb at the RV parked closest to
the grill. She knocked lightly on the door,

waited a moment, and then turned the knob.

As the door swung inward, James caught a glimpse of two horizontal figures on the camper's pullout sofa. He saw a fleshy, tanned thigh, a flash of large, pale breasts, and the round, white plumpness of a man's astonishingly hairy rump. It took both James and Lucy several seconds to realize that the many-limbed creature they were staring at was, in actuality, the entwined bodies of Jimmy's girlfriend Hailey and a man James didn't recognize.

"What the — !" the man shouted as he swiveled his head toward the open door.

Lucy turned around so abruptly that she lost her footing on the camper's step and fell onto James, knocking him flat to the ground. They lay there for a moment, stunned by the fall, and then struggled to separate their entangled arms and legs. In their efforts to detach from one another, they bore a close resemblance to the couple inside the camper, except that James and Lucy were fully dressed.

By the time James stood and brushed loose grass and dirt from his soiled pants, Hailey had appeared at the camper's doorway. Clutching on to the hand of a middle-aged man wearing a pair of faded jeans and an embarrassed grin, Hailey descended the two metal stairs. Her cheeks were spotted with red and her two-toned hair looked like an unraveled ball of yarn.

"Y'all ever heard of knockin'?" she demanded angrily, adjusting her low-cut T-shirt so that it barely covered the lacy cups of her turquoise bra. James couldn't help but ogle the shifting flesh of Hailey's breasts as she fiddled with her gossamer-thin cotton top. Finally, satisfied that the perfect amount of cleavage swelled at the base of her V-neck shirt, Hailey placed both hands beneath the shelf of her bosom and gave her breasts one last shove upward. James watched the two mounds ripple with the motion and then quickly dropped his eyes to his shoes.

"We did knock," Lucy answered once she found her voice. "Sorry. I guess it wasn't loud enough."

"It sure wasn't!" Hailey held up her hand and wiggled a magenta nail at James and Lucy. "And before you go judgin' me, bein' that Jimmy's not even in the ground yet, I want you to know that Bob here is my *real* man. We've been together, well, at a distance-like, for almost a whole year now."

The man stepped forward and held out his hand. "I recall y'all from the brisket judgin'. Damned endive." His face darkened at the memory, but he shrugged it off with a forgiving grin. "Name's Bob Barker. Not the game show host but the contractor with the most. Pleased to meet ya both."

James attempted to comprehend Bob's slogan, but since he couldn't make any sense of it, he simply shook the man's hand.

"I've just asked Hailey to marry me," Bob said, smiling. He removed a black velvet box from his front pants pocket and opened it. "Cost me more than my first truck," he told James and Lucy and wiggled the box in the sunlight so that its rays would illuminate the diamond solitaire. "But my Hailey's worth it."

"It's beautiful," Lucy said, her eyes riveted on the ring.

James glanced at Hailey. Though she gazed at the piece of jewelry with pride, he couldn't help but wonder why the ring was still in its box and not on her finger.

"So why pretend to be with Jimmy if you and Bob have already been together for a year?" Lucy asked Hailey without breaking eye contact with the diamond.

"Well, I didn't know if Bob was really gonna leave his old lady and get divorce papers, but he did. He showed me the papers with all that legal mumbo jumbo last night, after Jimmy fell asleep with that dumb ole heater on. That's why I went ahead and spent the night with him. Bob, I mean. 'Cause I knew it was truly and all over with between Jimmy and me. I was gonna tell Jimmy about Bob and me this morning." She paused and inspected her nails. "But I had some personal business to work out with him first."

Before Lucy could demand what kind of business Hailey had to complete with Jimmy, Bob Barker took a step forward, as if to shield Hailey from further questioning. "I think Hailey's been through enough, don't y'all?" His tone left no room for reply. "She's just gonna help me polish up the mop we're usin' on the Tenderizers' chicken entry and then she's gonna take a nice, long rest."

Hailey frowned. "Don't forget I'm gonna enter this category, too, Bob." She stared at him defiantly. "I told you I was gonna let everyone see who the *real* Pitmaster is. This is *my* chance to shine, and I ain't gonna pass up the chance to be the champion."

Bob seemed prepared to argue, but then his scowl disappeared and he chuckled. "Sure, why not? After this competition, you'll be Mrs. Bob Barker and you'll be one of the Tenderizers." He lowered his voice.

"A behind-the-scenes member, of course, seein' as we *are* a male team." He rubbed Hailey's lower back fondly. "We're gonna win all over the country with you as our secret weapon."

Hailey wasn't pleased. "I don't know that I wanna be any man's secret weapon no more. I'm kinda tired of folks not knowin' that I'm just as good as y'all when it comes to 'cue."

As Bob's eyes roamed around the campsite, he seemed to weigh his options. "Now don't get yourself upset, darlin'," he eventually cooed instead of addressing Hailey's complaint. "Come on back inside and try our chipotle chicken mop and then we can talk some more *in private* about when we're gonna tie the knot."

Hailey glanced at Bob, clearly in no rush to taste the Tenderizers' mop. "You go on. I'll be just a sec. I wanna have a smoke, and I know you don't like the smell of cigarettes inside the camper."

Hesitating again, as though fearful that his future authority as the dominant partner was already being put to the test, Bob scrutinized James and Lucy. He appeared to come to the decision that they posed no threat to his relationship with Hailey. Donning a smile, he shook their hands again and said, "I hope y'all come to see the results of the Poultry category. It's gonna be neck and neck between me and my lovely fiancée here."

After the camper door clicked shut, Hailey walked off toward the edge of the campsite, pulling a pack of Virginia Slims from her pocket. She shook a cigarette loose from the packet but made no attempt to light it.

"That's a heck of a gorgeous ring Bob bought you. Have you accepted his proposal?" Lucy inquired while pretending to casually study the cauliflower-shaped clouds overhead.

"Not yet." Hailey also turned her face skyward, her cigarette dangling limply from her right hand. "I've had some man bossin' me about my whole life. First Daddy, then a druggie boyfriend, then Jimmy. It might be nice just to be on my own for a bit."

"Do you have a job back in Fort Worth?" James asked and immediately realized that he sounded like a chump for implying that Hailey would need something to fulfill her if she didn't marry Bob Barker.

"Not really." Hailey wasn't offended by his question. "I spent most of my time doin' church stuff and cleanin' and cookin' for Jimmy." She flicked her eyes at James. "Now that he's gone, I don't wanna cook and clean for anyone else."

"I don't blame you." James hoped he sounded sympathetic.

Lucy observed Hailey closely. "Did you tell Sheriff Jones about you and Bob?"

"She don't know about the ring, but she knows we were knockin' boots when someone taped the vents shut so as to kill Jimmy. The sheriff lady told me that the tapin' must have happened 'bout midnight. I reckon it takes a long time for that propane stuff to kill someone Jimmy's size." Her eyes misted. " 'Least he died peaceful and had shared his confession with me. We'd had a big tussle earlier that day, about that redhead and why he's been hid—" She cut herself off and stared intently at Lucy. "Why are you askin' so many questions, anyhow?"

"Because the woman under suspicion is not only innocent, but she's a dear friend of ours," Lucy answered tersely. "Did Jimmy tell you anything at all about Gillian?"

"The redhead who said Jimmy killed her man is your friend?" Hailey looked away quickly. "Jimmy just said somethin' about a truck accident. He didn't hurt anybody on purpose though."

"Yes, he did. In fact, that's why Jimmy spent fifteen years in prison," Lucy informed her gently. "He was convicted of vehicular manslaughter, Hailey. Jimmy ran into Gillian's husband with his truck . . . deliberately."

Hailey's face drained of all color and she touched the dove tattoo on her bosom. "Sweet Jesus!" She gazed off into the distance, her eyes narrowed. "That son of a bitch lied to me! He said he was in jail for dealin' drugs."

"Well, Jimmy was high *and* drunk when he drove over Gillian's husband, so there *were* drugs involved, but he wasn't in jail for dealing," Lucy said softly.

Hailey snapped her cigarette in half. "He promised he was givin' me his full confession. His hand was on my Bible! That bastard!" Her pupils grew small with rage. "He lied to me about *so* many things! Why he was in jail, about his *amazin'* cookin' skills, his secret hidin' places for cas—" She suddenly stopped her tirade and issued an insincere chuckle. "I guess I made the right decision to wait for Bob to get divorced. At least he don't lie. He's a gentleman, I'll tell ya. He never even laid a hand on me 'til last night 'cause it wouldn't have been right in the eyes of the Lord."

Ignoring Hailey's list of Bob's finer attributes, Lucy continued her interrogation. "You told the sheriff that Gillian was *inside*

265

your RV when you returned to the vehicle after, ah, spending time with Bob last night. But Gillian *wasn't* inside, was she?" Lucy moved closer to Hailey and stood as tall as possible. She put her hands on her hips and planted her feet shoulder-width apart. Her blue eyes bored into Hailey's. "She was sitting on the camper steps. Isn't that right?"

Hailey looked everywhere but at Lucy. "It was real early, okay? Maybe I got confused about the details."

Lucy's hand shot out like a snake and grabbed Hailey's plump arm. "You'd better get clear on the facts *really* fast. If my friend has to spend the night in jail because you found it *convenient* to say she was inside the camper instead of *outside,* then I am going to hound you for the rest of your time here." Lucy shook Hailey's arm. "Do you understand what I'm saying? I'll be by your side, hanging on you like a leech. I'll be so close to you that we're going to breathe the same air. Get the picture?" Lucy inhaled deeply to emphasize her point. "How do you think *Bob* will enjoy this? Just the three of us, together every second for the rest of this festival?"

Hailey cast James a glance of appeal, but James folded his arms across his chest and tried to look as menacing as possible. It was difficult for him to tear his gaze from Lucy. He wanted to freeze time, to simply stand and drink in the sight of her. With her bright blue eyes ablaze and the sun illuminating her hair and creamy, smooth skin, James couldn't help his heart from swelling with affection as he glanced between her and Hailey, who seemed to have shrunk in size while Lucy seemed colossal, like a goddess in pursuit of the truth.

"All right, all right!" Hailey jerked her arm away. "The redhead was on the steps. Yeah, I remember now. I didn't think they'd haul her in 'cause I said she was inside with Jimmy." She clasped her hands together, her magenta nails flashing in the tired sunlight. "You gotta see where I was comin' from. I've been to jail. I knew they'd take one look at me, see the hillbilly girlfriend with a juvy record, and they'd pin Jimmy's death on me faster than a lightnin' strike."

Lucy gave a small nod but didn't back away. "I can understand you being scared, Hailey. But you don't put someone else's head on the chopping block just to save your own. Will you tell the sheriff what you told me and set things straight?"

When Hailey hesitated, Lucy folded her hands together as though in prayer. "She's a good woman, our Gillian. You've got to do the right thing here."

Hailey focused on Lucy's hands and subconsciously touched the tattoo on the uppermost swell of her left breast. "Yeah, all right. I'll tell 'em." She closed her eyes as she made her promise. "But not now. I've gotta get my barbecued turkey legs to the judges in fifteen minutes. Be a miracle from above if I make it in time. I'll call that sheriff lady once I've got me another blue ribbon."

As Hailey hustled off, her wide hips swaying and her bottom bouncing in another pair of too-tight shorts, Lucy watched the other woman thoughtfully. Within moments, Hailey disappeared between two campers, but Lucy continued to stare into the distance. Blinking, she observed the crowd for a moment and then swung around and grabbed James by the elbow.

"Please tell me you got all that on tape."

James removed the mini recorder from his pocket and hit the rewind button. They heard Hailey's voice going backward in a speedy whine. He waited a few seconds and then played the recording. Hailey's recollection of the actual events of that morning, when she discovered Jimmy's body, was captured clearly.

"She was on the steps," Hailey's voice intoned.

Lucy radiated happiness. "Time to call Sheriff Jones."

Bennett, Lindy, and James treated themselves to sno-cones as Lucy spoke to the sheriff.

"Aren't you going to interview her again?" Lucy asked rather forcefully into the receiver. Listening to the response, she shifted impatiently. "If Hailey didn't tell the truth about Gillian being inside the camper, who knows what *else* she lied about! For all we know, *she* could have killed Jimmy any time that night. Plus, she started to talk about something hidden, and I'm sure the word was *cash.* She also mentioned having *unfinished business* with Jimmy. Why *isn't* Hailey your prime suspect?"

Taking a frosty bite of his sno-cone, James watched as Lucy blushed. "Oh," she answered in a small voice. "I see." Shaking her head, she reiterated her demand that Gillian be released based on the statements she and James had elicited from Hailey and captured on the mini recorder.

"What flavor did you get?" Bennett asked Lindy as Lucy argued in the background.

"Honeydew. You must have the lime. Your lips are all green."

Bennett scrutinized his half-eaten cone of

shaved ice. "I got kiwi but I wish I hadn't. I don't like it too much." He smiled and pointed at James. "Man, take a look at those lips! You've got blue, red, *and* green all over your face. You look like the flag of Azerbaijan."

Seeing the blank looks on his friend's faces, Bennett clarified. "It's a country in southwest Asia. Sound familiar?" He waited. "Guess not. It's between Iran and Russia and borders on the Caspian Sea. Do *any* of those names strike a bell?"

"We're not all trying out for *Jeopardy!* you know." James wiped his mouth with a napkin and then grimaced as he examined the stained paper. "This is what happens when you order a Tie-Dye sno-cone. Mine's got green apple, cherry, and blue raspberry, but I should've just stuck with coconut. There are too many flavors in here."

Removing her wallet from her purse, Lindy returned to the sno-cone stand. A minute later, she thrust a cone into Lucy's hand just as the cell phone snapped shut.

"Oh, thanks." She accepted the cone and took a small bite of the shaved ice. "This is good!" she exclaimed to Lindy.

"Passionfruit. I figured it would match your mood," Lindy said, and she led them all to a nearby park bench.

"Shoot. You'd be blushing too if you heard what Sheriff Jones just told me."

Bennett lowered his sno-cone. "What did she say?"

Lucy smirked. "You're totally smitten with that woman aren't you, Bennett? Maybe *you* should be the one trying to talk some sense into her." She bit off another piece of her treat. "Hailey's, um, activities with Bob give them both a solid alibi. Seems they were kind of, ah, loud, in the back of Bob's camper starting at about eleven thirty. All the other members of the Tenderizers, as well as several of the Thigh and Mighties, heard Hailey praising the biblical prophets at the top of her lungs several times between the hours of midnight and two a.m."

Scratching his head, Bennett creased his brows. "You mean to tell me that in the throes of passion, she yelled out *'Oh Moses! Oh Elijah!'* " When Lucy nodded in affirmation, he chuckled in mirth. "Well, she's original. I'll give her that much."

Lucy clearly didn't share Bennett's humorous view of the situation. "The sheriff *also* pointed out that Gillian still has *no* alibi. Whether she was inside the camper, on its steps, or hiding behind one of its tires, she was still found at the crime scene this morning. That's the bottom line to Sheriff

Jones." Lucy sighed in disappointment. "The sheriff has no immediate plans to release Gillian. We need to find out who's really responsible for Jimmy's death, and soon!" She took a quick bite of her sno-cone and glanced at Lindy. "Did you two have any luck?"

"None. We can rule out the Thigh and Mighties. They're a group of elementary school teachers and this is their first contest. They had no idea who Jimmy was until he took their designated parking/cooking space. They mentioned the matter to Jimmy, who ignored them. They also complained in passing to R. C., but they didn't seem too worked up about the whole issue." She turned to James. "And none of the team members were really pale-skinned or wearing a hat with a tuning fork on it. Sorry."

"The Finger Lickers are not your killer types either," Bennett said. "They're a bunch of dental hygienists who regularly get together to drink beer, barbecue, and avoid their wives and girlfriends. They all thought Jimmy was a hoot and didn't bear him an ounce of ill will." He balled up the paper cone that had once held his shaved ice. "Besides, they're from North Carolina and have only seen Jimmy at two other festivals besides this one."

"Maybe location has something to do with Jimmy's death." James grew pensive. "He was from the Fort Worth area, right?" He directed his question to Bennett, who had an excellent memory when it came to geography. Bennett nodded in assent. "Were any of the other teams from Texas?"

"The Marrow Men are from San Antonio," Lindy said and then handed over the sheet listing the barbecue teams, the names of their members, and their hometowns.

"The Tenderizers are from Kansas and the Adam's Ribbers are all Georgia peaches," James stated, reading from the list. "So only Jimmy, Hailey, and the Marrow Men are from the same state. How far apart are Fort Worth and San Antonio?"

"About two hundred and fifty miles," Bennett answered immediately.

Lucy threw her hands into the air in exasperation. "We're grasping at straws here! Texas is a mighty big state, James, but we need to give the Marrow Men a look-see anyway. Then it's time to go back to the inn and get some answers from Eleanor. She could have snuck down to the campground easily. Keep in mind that she thinks her precious daughter swapped spit and possibly some other bodily fluids with our dead guy."

"That's a charming image." Lindy eyed

her melting sno-cone with distaste and tossed it into the nearest garbage can.

James checked his watch. "They should be announcing the winners of the Poultry category. Let's wrap things up here so we can go back to Fox Hall. I'd really like to take a shower and change out of these pants while you guys are cross-examining Eleanor."

"You might be dirty, my man," Bennett said as he gestured at the mud splatters and grass stains on James's khakis, "but at least you're not wearin' an orange jumpsuit."

"We'll have Gillian back in her own clothes by the time this festival is over," Lucy vowed. "We've solved tough mysteries before, and Gillian's got all four of us working on her behalf." She cocked her head sideways and muttered loud enough for her friends to hear. "Five, if you count the extra help we're getting from an unexpected source."

As Bennett and Lindy stared at her in confusion, James quickened his pace, but he couldn't outwalk the sound of Lucy's words as she grumbled darkly. "That's right, friends. Murphy Alistair, the voice of the *Star,* is here in Hudsonville."

Fourteen:
Tomato,
Mozzarella, and
Basil Salad

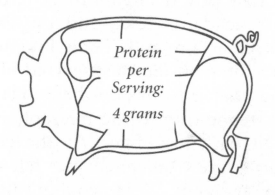

Protein
per
Serving:

4 grams

The barbecue teams were already gathered in front of R. C.'s podium when the supper club members arrived. Having decided to split up in order to better blend in with the rest of the crowd, James meandered around to the outskirts of the audience and fanned his eyes over the throng. It was easy to spot the barbecue teams, as they stood near the front and were once again wearing colorful aprons, shirts, and chef hats.

The Marrow Men, who wore the matching chef hats covered with orange and yellow flames, were holding cans of beer. James stepped close enough to the group of three men that he was able to see that the red foam coolers keeping their beers cold were printed with the text, *Bad to the Bone.* Amused, James also noted that the team members were clearly men who spent a great deal of time outdoors, for the sun had tanned their skin to a light bronze or burned their foreheads, cheeks, and the ends of their noses a faint red. Their fourth team member, the man James suspected of being pale as a phantom, was nowhere in sight.

R. C. stepped up to the microphone and tapped it with his finger. As the crowd's murmuring grew quieter, James felt a pang of sympathy for R. C. He couldn't begin to imagine the stress the poor man must be under. If R. C. had appeared taut and highly strung yesterday, he appeared downright cadaverous today. His clothes seemed to hang from his lanky frame, and his eyes looked dull with fatigue.

James wondered how Jimmy's death would affect the festival as word of the shocking event spread throughout the region. Judging from the knot of people swarmed in front of the podium and the streams of people walking around the fairgrounds, the festival hadn't suffered a depletion of visitors yet.

Of course, it'll take a few more hours for the local press to run inflamed stories about the Hog Fest tragedy, James thought. *But surely the area news channels had begun covering the story within hours of the sheriff's arrival at Jimmy's trailer.*

"I guess rain's worse for this event than a murder," James muttered to himself as a buxom brunette arranged several ribbons and white envelopes on a table near R. C.'s hip.

"Thank you all so much for the most memorable poultry entries we've ever had the pleasure of tasting," R. C. began with a tired grin. "And a special thank you to our judges for their time and expertise."

R. C. inclined his head gratefully to the familiar figures of Mr. and Mrs. Connelly as well as a group of four adults who, based on their similar features and coloring, looked to be related to one another.

R. C. paused and it seemed to James as though the organizer was staring directly at Hailey. Clearing his throat, as though trying to decide what to say next, R. C. blinked and let his eyes fall upon someone else's face. If he had planned to say anything about Jimmy's passing, the moment was now over. Obviously, R. C. had deemed it wiser to pretend as though nothing untoward had happened at Hog Fest.

"And now," his voice rang through the crowd, "without further ado, let's announce our first winner."

Cheers erupted as R. C. awarded the white ribbon and cash prize to the Tenderizers. James spied Bob Barker whistling as his teammate shook hands with R. C. and then waved the third-place ribbon in the air. Hailey stood next to Bob, their hips nearly touching, though she still wore her Pitmasters T-shirt.

Once the member of the Tenderizers departed with his awards, R. C. announced a tie between the Finger Lickers and the Marrow Men for the second-place prize. James couldn't help but smile as a young man with a mouthful of dazzling white teeth bounced up to R. C. to collect the red ribbon and envelope of cash. When he turned back to rejoin his friends, James noticed that his yellow apron was embroidered with a white tooth partially smothered in barbecue sauce. The tooth had been given a smiling face and the text in the bubble above its head read, *Eat 'Cue, Floss, Repeat.*

"I guess those dental hygienists really know how to grill!" a woman to James's left remarked to her friend. "They're mighty cute, too."

The Marrow Men representative appeared from the opposite side of the crowd and James drew in a sharp breath when he stared at the unnaturally pallid skin of the middle-aged man. The man accepted the prizes from R. C.'s hands with mumbled thanks, issued a minimal nod in the direction of his teammates, and then stepped back into the crowd. Heading toward his friends, the man ducked in order to avoid one of Hog Fest's signature pig balloons, and the movement jarred his chef hat loose. James watched with keen interest as the man stooped to retrieve the hat. Instead of replacing it on top of his thinning hair, he pulled a black baseball cap from his back pocket and settled it on his head with the brim facing backward. Once again, James caught a glimpse of the strange symbol that resembled a silver tuning fork.

Glancing around until he had located Lindy, James pushed his way past people sipping homemade lemonade or gnawing on rib bones or barbecued chicken legs until he reached her.

"Lindy!" he exclaimed. "I saw the pasty-skinned guy! He's with the Marrow Men, and he's wearing that hat I told you about.

Can you draw the symbol for me so we can research it more later? Maybe there's a computer at our inn I could use."

Lindy nodded. "Sure. I've got pen and paper in my bag. Where's the guy?"

Keeping his hand at waist level, James pointed to the left. "They're the ones with the flaming chef hats. Except for the guy I saw with Jimmy. His chef hat fell off so he put his baseball cap on. It's black."

"I see him. Good Lord, I've seen fish bellies with more pigment than that guy has. He must work inside all day," Lindy said, and she moved off.

By the time James returned his attention to the podium, R. C. was ready to announce the winner of the Poultry category. James scanned his eyes over the members of the remaining teams as they grew tense with anticipation. A few rows in front of him, Bob Barker placed a proprietary hand on Hailey's shoulders, which she shrugged off in the pretense of having to scratch her lower calf. By the time she straightened, R. C. called a name other than the Pitmasters. In fact, it was the Adam's Ribbers who earned the first-place prize.

Zoe, who had changed out of her Johnny Depp T-shirt in favor of a hot-pink tank top that read, *The Adam's Ribbers: We'll Rub*

Your Butt, squealed all the way to the podium. When she reached the microphone, she pushed it aside, threw her arms around R. C., and kissed him noisily on the cheek. R. C.'s face turned as pink as Zoe's shirt as she pranced back to her teammates in order to exchange high-fives and hugs.

Still blushing, R. C. reminded the audience that the Anything Butt and Beef Rib contests would take place the next day, and he cautioned the crowd not to miss the blueberry pie-eating contest as well.

"We'll announce the name of the Hog Fest Barbecue Champion during tomorrow's closing ceremony, so don't miss it!" he informed the crowd with as much effervescence as he could muster in his state of weariness.

The crowd issued a final cheer and then began to disperse. James happened to find himself walking behind a family preoccupied with tearing apart fluffy pink and blue clouds of cotton candy. When they peeled off from the main throng in search of napkins, James practically stepped on the heels of Bob and Hailey.

"Too bad you didn't win that money, darlin'," James heard Bob say. Rubbing Hailey's back in a gesture of consolation, he sighed. "Now that I've got alimony payments to make, I've got less to spend on us than I was hopin'. Every bit of cash we can get will mean a nicer honeymoon."

Hailey shrugged. "That cash prize was small change. 'Sides, I've got money of my own."

After purchasing two bottles of Budweiser from a nearby vendor, the couple veered in the opposite direction, undoubtedly heading back to the cooking area. James stared after them, noting how Hailey detached herself from Bob's possessive arm.

"Doesn't look like she wants to be Mrs. Bob Barker too badly," James murmured to himself and then wondered why Hailey seemed so unperturbed over not winning the cash prize. She didn't receive a paycheck, so unless she had another source of income, she and Jimmy had survived on his salary as a tow truck driver along with his barbecue contest winnings. "That couldn't exactly have been high living."

As James pondered this riddle, he spied Bennett cresting a slight rise up ahead. Trudging around a clot of slow-moving festivalgoers on their way to the parking lot, James caught up with his friend.

"Lucy and Lindy are checking on R. C.," Bennett said as they walked toward Lucy's Jeep. "Lindy was concerned about the guy's welfare while Lucy wanted to get a read on him. Says he could be a suspect seein' as Jimmy offended people left and right at this fair." He snorted. "She's one dogged deputy, I'll tell ya."

James shook his head. "I don't see the logic in viewing R. C. as a suspect. After all, he wouldn't want any negative publicity for Hog Fest and nothing garners bad press faster than an act of violence." He shielded his eyes from the glare of the afternoon sun. "R. C. must have pulled every string he could to keep the fact that Jimmy's death was actually a murder under wraps, but the story will break soon enough and then the festival's reputation could really suffer."

"Speaking of stories and tall tales and the like, is your girlfriend gonna be one of the media folks giving our man R. C. a series of heart attacks? She does have a nose for drama. But I guess that kind of writin' helps her sell papers, huh?"

Noting the edge of irritation in Bennett's voice, James couldn't help but recall how many articles Murphy had written about his friends and their efforts to shed some extra pounds. She had often revealed far more information than the supper club members would have preferred, and though Murphy tried to redeem herself by touting their crime-solving skills, the personal information she had disclosed about them in print would not easily be forgiven.

"I don't know, Bennett," James admitted. "I had no idea she was even coming here."

"Communication is the key to a successful relationship," Bennett quipped and then grew solemn. "I'd like to *communicate* a few things to Sheriff Jade Jones, yessir."

A few minutes later, Lucy and Lindy returned and the four friends clambered back inside the Jeep. On the way back to the Inn at Fox Hall, James asked Lindy to show Bennett the sketch she had made.

"Does this look familiar to you?" James asked.

Bennett took one look at her drawing and began to chortle. "You really need to watch more sports, my man." He took the picture from Lindy's hands and shook it at James. "This isn't a tuning fork! This is a spur, my friend! As in the San Antonio Spurs? You know, the basketball team?" He narrowed his dark eyes. "Please tell me that you've at least heard of the NBA!"

"Yeah, yeah," James replied irritably. "So I don't watch professional basketball. I didn't think anyone else did either. It's just a bunch of guys with huge egos and inflated salaries tossing a ball around. What am I missing by watching A&E instead?" He pointed at the drawing. "The pale guy is one of the Marrow Men. He was wearing this baseball cap. Did you all notice him when he went up to the podium?"

His friends nodded.

"Hard to miss with that white, white skin," Bennett joked.

"He's the one I saw arguing with Jimmy," James said. "Both men are from Texas and that guy obviously had a bone to pick with 'The Pitmaster.' Jimmy was genuinely affected by this guy's threatening body language and I saw his face after the guy left. Jimmy was scared. I think we need to spend some time with the Marrow Men."

Lindy sighed. "I'm getting tired of smoking grills and barbecued meats. If we've got to come back to do more snooping, then let's have dinner someplace else. Something light, too, like a vegetable plate."

Bennett's lip curled.

"I'm with you," Lucy said as they turned down the tree-lined driveway leading to the inn. "Maybe I can ask Eleanor if I could cook us some omelets or something. I think we could all use a bit of a rest before we get back to work, though I'm going to question Eleanor as soon as we get inside the inn."

"Remind me never to get on your bad

side," Bennett told Lucy.

Lucy parked and the foursome made their way to the front door, walking in fatigued silence. It wasn't until someone spoke his name from a rocker on the porch that James realized Murphy was sitting there, apparently awaiting his return. Bennett and Lindy gave Murphy a polite wave and then stepped inside the inn.

"See you later," Lucy mumbled to James and ignored Murphy completely. She closed the front door behind her and the brass knocker in the shape of a fox head clacked resonantly.

James sank down in the rocker next to Murphy's and closed his eyes.

"Long day?" she asked him in a soft voice.

"Yes, and it's far from over."

Murphy slowly rocked back and forth. "It's really peaceful here. It's probably pretty romantic when it's not so booked up. Might be nice to come here in the winter."

Opening his eyes, James took in the lengthening shadows stretching across the expanse of lawn. "I was out here yesterday morning, too, though it seems like a year ago now. I don't think I can appreciate the beauty of this place while Gillian's in a holding cell."

"Do you want to tell me where you guys

are in your investigation?" Murphy asked casually, but James knew that every cell in her body was squirming in anticipation for information.

"I just want to sit and rest for a bit, okay?"

"I'm not asking you to get details for my story," she said testily. "I have what I need. As a matter of fact, I may have discovered something that you might find helpful."

Refusing to take the bait, James closed his eyes again. "I'm all ears," he mumbled wearily.

"Well, I found out the name of the garage where Jimmy Lang worked," Murphy began. "And I called his boss. The man didn't know Jimmy was dead. Guess Jimmy didn't have any family in those parts and so no one in Waxahachie knows what happened. I didn't find out too much from this Mr. Leggett — just that Jimmy ran his mouth all the time. But he was a responsible worker and the customers seemed to like him all right." She rustled some papers. "What *I* find strange is that Jimmy was able to purchase a recreational vehicle two years ago that cost nearly a hundred grand. He only makes about thirty thousand a year at his job and a few extra thousand in prize money, so how could he afford that camper?"

Murphy waited for James to provide a theory, but he was too tired to think of anything other than the obvious. "He must have taken out a loan."

"That's what I thought until I called the RV dealer!" Murphy exclaimed triumphantly. "Jimmy paid for the whole thing in cash. No financing, nothing. Brought in a duffle bag of greenbacks and drove that monster off the lot. Doesn't that strike you as odd?"

James recalled Hailey's reaction to losing the barbecue contest's cash prize. He opened his eyes and sat up. "Hailey acts like she's got money, too, and she doesn't even have a job. I get the impression she, well, kind of came into some cash after Jimmy died."

Her hazel eyes sparkling, Murphy leaned forward. "What makes you say that?"

"She started talking about how Jimmy had lied to her and how he had these hiding places in the camper. She then started to say the word 'cash,' in regards to what he was hiding, but cut herself off. *And* she's got this boyfriend —"

"Bob Barker."

James nodded, grudgingly impressed with how busy Murphy must have been gleaning information since her arrival. "Yes, Bob

Barker. But she seems to be cooling off toward him as the festival wears on. She told us that she'd like to try living without a man for a while. I wonder if the newfound cash has something to do with her desire to stay single."

"I believe the answer to this whole mystery lies in where all that extra money came from." Murphy smoothed the pages of computer printouts on her lap. "If Jimmy was hiding money in his camper, maybe he meant to buy something on his way to or from Hog Fest."

"Or while he was here," James mused and then jumped out of his chair in excitement. "That's it! When we first met Jimmy here at the inn, he bragged about his ship coming in. Maybe he wasn't talking about landing a contract with Heartland Foods at all! Maybe he had some other kind of deal in the works!"

Murphy smiled. "If you can find out what that deal was, I bet you could find the killer. Perhaps Jimmy screwed someone over and that someone wasn't too happy about it."

James immediately thought of the ghostly-white limbs of the man in the San Antonio Spurs hat.

"I may already have an idea who Jimmy argued with," James boasted and then felt his ego deflate. "But I have no idea what the argument was about."

"You've got time." Murphy placed a reassuring hand on James's arm. "But remember, it's just a lead until you find evidence."

"I know, but it gives me hope." James took her hand in his and squeezed. "Look, I'm sorry I was so short-tempered before."

"It's okay. I was being pretty bitchy myself. I always get that way when I think of you spending time with Lucy. I know she still has feelings for you and you *know* I'm the jealous type."

"You've got nothing to worry about," James answered, but his words didn't feel completely genuine. He had enjoyed investigating with Lucy again, and some of his old feelings for her seemed to be resurfacing, despite his efforts to ignore them.

Gently extracting her hand, Murphy gazed out into the twilight. "Speaking of leads, I went to see Gillian soon after I got to Hudsonville, but she didn't seem to want any visitors."

James swiveled in his seat and stared at Murphy. "Why did you go? To interview her for the *Star*?"

"Of course. I'm a journalist, James," she responded flatly. "She's still the primary suspect."

Trying to not judge Murphy too quickly, James took a moment before he calmly asked, "You already knew her story, so why go?"

Murphy broke eye contact and pretended to examine the potted fern alongside of her. "I wanted to hear her version of the events. I mean, if someone ran down my husband, I might be prone to act on a desire for revenge."

James clenched his fists, anger coursing through him. "Well *Gillian* wouldn't!" He slapped the arm of his chair and Murphy jumped. "I can't believe you! You think she might actually be a murderer! She's my *friend,* Murphy!"

"I know." Murphy's voice was carefully soft. "And like I said, I believe that money is the source of the crime. Still, Gillian *could* be involved and your judgment might be clouded because of your friendship with her. I thought that if I could review Gillian's testimony, then I could check the facts as an *objective* investigator."

"What you mean is that you could determine if she were lying!" James felt like moving his chair away from Murphy's. He had never found her so unattractive as he did at this moment. "And all for some article for our little hometown paper? Is the front page of the *Star* really worth this, Murphy? Because you've put our relationship on the line by questioning Gillian's character." He drew in a breath and squinted his eyes at her. "But I suspect you realized you'd get this reaction before you ever drove down here."

"I'm *not* just writing a *little* article!" Murphy blurted out. "I'm glad we're having this discussion, James. It finally gives me the opportunity to tell you something I've been keeping quiet about for weeks. Right before I met you at the beach for our weekend getaway, I signed a contract with a major publishing house in New York." She looked down at her hands, clearly struggling between wanting to boast of her accomplishment and being concerned that her news should be delivered with caution considering James's already agitated state. "I've been meaning to tell you about this, James, but I wasn't sure how you'd take it. In short, I'm not certain if you can handle having a relationship with someone who might become more of a celebrity than you and the Flab Five."

"You're not writing a book about how we've all blown our health routines by gorging on barbecue and funnel cakes, are you?" he inquired wryly.

"No." Her laugh sounded false. "My book's not about your dieting ups and downs. It's a thriller, actually, and is *loosely* based on how you and your friends have helped solve cri—"

At that moment, the screen door burst open and Francesca leapt onto the porch. Her young, tanned face was set into a smile and she was humming a zippy tune. Seeing James, her smile grew even wider and she tore the headphones of her lime-green iPod from her ears.

"Hi!" She wiggled her long fingers in greeting and stood in front of James. She leaned back against the porch railing and placed the bottom of her bare foot against the slats as though she intended to tarry for a while. "I wanted to say sorry about yesterday morning. That you heard me being so ugly to my mom." Darting a glance at Murphy, she toyed with the headphone wires and gazed at James from beneath her thick lashes. "We've been arguing a lot more lately, which is sad because but she used to be kind of like my best friend."

Francesca dug her hands into the pockets of her skimpy jeans shorts and continued to stare at James. "Anyway," she continued, "I was pretty embarrassed about my behavior."

Sensing that she had suddenly become a

third wheel, Murphy rose and handed James the printouts containing the information she had acquired on Jimmy Lang's finances. "If you will both excuse me," she said and then uttered a relieved laugh, "I think I'll try to rustle up some supper in town."

Francesca waited until Murphy had closed the front door before she asked, "Is she your girlfriend?"

"Uh, yeah," James answered quickly. Desperate to change the subject, he pointed at Francesca's neck. "I see you were able to cover that up pretty well."

Instead of being embarrassed, Francesca looked positively jubilant. "Mom's lucky it's only a hickie and not a tattoo! I'd like to climb to the roof and tell everyone how I feel about my boyfriend!"

Observing Francesca's fidgeting and the dreamy look in her eyes, James began to laugh. "It *wasn't* Jimmy after all! He wasn't the guy you . . . you were messing around with, right?"

Francesca pretended to be horrified. "God, no! I was just pushing Mom's buttons, telling her that mongo lie. Like I said, I was being pretty rotten." She arched a graceful eyebrow at him. "Do you really think I'd let that overblown Cro-Magnon touch me?" She shivered. "Gross!"

"I was having a hard time picturing it, but I did see him, ah, touch you in a familiar way at the festival," James confessed.

Francesca blushed. "And the only reason I didn't smack his face then and there was that Mr. Richter was nearby. My mom is kind of sweet on him, and I didn't want to cause a scene."

James watched as fireflies illuminated the shadowy bushes. Crickets blazed into song, and a chorus of bullfrogs added their sonorous croaking to the evening's cacophony. "Your mom likes R. C., huh? That's cool." James began to lazily rock in his chair. "So are you going to tell her about your boyfriend?"

Pleased that she could talk about her love interest, Francesca settled herself onto the porch swing and pushed it back and forth with the tips of her toes. "He's a year older than me and we didn't hang out in school because he was really involved with academic clubs and all these community service activities." She hugged herself. "That's what I love about him! He has such a *huge* heart! Anyway, he just got back from a mission to Africa and we started hanging out at the Tastee-Freez. He's going to be involved in the county's Head Start program next fall! I totally want to be involved, too," she added with longing. "That's why I don't want to waste time on these pageants. I want to help needy kids."

"Well, I think your guy sounds like a fine young man," James said, feeling that his praise must have sounded rather old-fashioned. "And I bet your mother would be happy to know you've fallen for someone so generous and kind-hearted. It might be nice to tell her about him, so that she doesn't think you were really with Jimmy the other night."

Francesca waved the suggestion away. "Oh, you don't have to worry about that. I left her a note on the refrigerator, like, an hour after our argument. I mean, she might have actually poisoned the man if she really thought I had sex with him." She shivered in distaste and then immediately regretted her behavior. "I'm sorry. I shouldn't speak about him that way now that he's dead. Mr. Richter called and told my mom all about it. I never knew you could die from inhaling too much propane."

"Me either." James was relieved to hear about the note. It meant that Eleanor had no motive to kill Jimmy. He'd hate to think that the mother and gourmet cook might be guilty of murder.

Despite his late afternoon snack, James's

stomach came to life as he pondered Eleanor's culinary skills. It gurgled in demand, loud enough to be heard over and above the sounds of the bugs, frogs, and the creaking rocker.

"Whoa, was that you?" Francesca's eyes grew round and then she giggled. "You must be hungry!"

James tried to camouflage his expansive belly with his arms. "Oh, I don't need anything."

Hopping off the swing, Francesca grabbed James by the hand. "We've got lots of goodies left over from today's tea. Most of the guests were too busy at Hog Fest to eat here and my mom would be unhappy if her food went to waste. She usually gives R. C. late-night snacks, but he's too wiped out to come over tonight."

"Do you think there's enough for my three friends?" he asked sheepishly.

"Of course!" Francesca led James into the kitchen, where the remainder of the supper club had already been installed at the kitchen table while Eleanor chatted and poured glasses of sun tea. Lucy gestured at the note tacked on the fridge and winked at James.

"Francesca told me all about that," he whispered in her ear and tried not to be affected by how pleasant her hair smelled.

"Thank goodness we didn't interrogate Eleanor," Lucy whispered back, "or we might not have been given such a lovely dinner. Here," she ladled a spoonful of tomato and mozzarella salad onto an empty plate. "The fresh basil on this salad is delicious. There's devilled eggs and fresh blueberries, too. This meal is just what we need! All of this protein will give us just the energy required to move ahead in our investigation."

"I hope so," James answered, and he listened as Lindy told Francesca about the ups and downs of being a schoolteacher. Eleanor began rinsing dishes and placing them in the dishwasher, but James could tell that she was interested in what Lindy had to say as well.

Outside the window, the night fell in full force, though the summer darkness was softened by firefly glow. The laughter and companionable conversation resounding within the kitchen allowed James's anger over Murphy's behavior to ebb away. As he stared at the moving reflections of their cozy group in the window, he felt that he was a part of a circle of love and trust that would never let him down.

A few minutes later, Eleanor poured coffee into oversized mugs and placed a napkin-lined basket of warm brownies in the center of the table.

"If only Gillian were here, this would be a perfect night," James spoke his thoughts aloud.

Lucy touched his hand with hers and then selected the largest brownie from the basket and put it on his plate. "Buck up, James. We've made a lot of headway today, and no one's giving up on Gillian. I'm not going back to Quincy's Gap without her."

James gazed at Lucy so tenderly that her cheeks turned pink. "What's that sappy look for?" she teased.

"I'm just appreciating your loyalty," James said. He bit into his brownie. "And that goes for you, too," he gestured at Bennett and Lindy. "You guys are my family and I'd do anything for you. I've never told you before how much you mean to me, so I'm telling you now."

Lindy dabbed at her eyes with her napkin. "Oh, James! Pass me those brownies or I'll cry off the rest of my mascara!"

FIFTEEN:
JIM BEAM
(STRAIGHT UP)

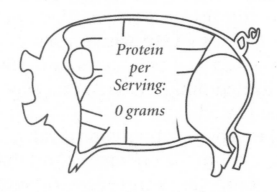

Protein per Serving: 0 grams

James and his friends wobbled through the festival in search of the Marrow Men and their pale-skinned teammate. Eleanor's nourishing dinner coupled with several cups of strong Kona coffee had given them some much-needed energy, but there was something about the multicolored lights, the aggressive movements of the crowd, the thick scent of fried foods, and the constant noise pouring from the loudspeakers that quickly sapped the group's enthusiasm.

"I could never live this life. These people will pack up tomorrow, drive to another town, and get ready to deal with a new crowd. We must all look the same to them after a time," Lindy remarked as she gestured at one of the game vendors.

Beneath a painted sign that read, *Bonzo Bazooka,* a group of listless adults occupied three out of the eight metal swivel stools positioned in front of water guns. James recognized the game. After all, this game, or one just like it, was a fixture at every fair he had ever attended. The point of the game was to determine who could shoot the most concentrated stream of water into the gaping mouth of a demented-looking clown in order to blow up the balloon appearing above the crown of his white head. Whoever could pop the balloon first was the victor.

James had only won the game once as a little boy, but the nightmares he had had the night after the county fair about a monstrous clown spitting a mouthful of brackish water back into his face were hardly worth the plush banana he had won as a prize.

"We need a fourth to play!" a man with a weathered face called out to James as he passed by. "Come on, mister. Win a giant snake for your girlfriend!"

James turned away in embarrassment. Who *was* the giant snake in his relationship after all? Himself or Murphy? True, she had come to Hudsonville to write an article on Jimmy's death, but that was her job and the cause of death *was* unusual. Was he angry with Murphy for seeking the truth about the murder or because she didn't assume, with the same conviction he had, that Gillian was innocent of murder? And what about this book she had written? Before Francesca appeared, James could have sworn that Murphy implied that it was a fictionalized account of the supper club's role as amateur detectives, but why would a publisher be interested in them? They were just ordinary people.

Head down, ruminating over Murphy's book, James paid little attention to where he was walking. As a result, he had a direct collision with a biker carrying a funnel cake in each hand. The funnel cake in his left hand was topped with powdered sugar and fudge sauce, while the cake in his right hand was loaded with a puddle of strawberry jam. Within seconds, James's white polo shirt looked like a canvas upon which a modernist had created a fresh piece of art by zealously splashing the contents of his paint cans onto the blank cloth.

James looked down at his shirt in horror. The biker growled.

"I'm so sorry, I wasn't watching where I was going," James spluttered in apology.

"No shit." The giant of a man took a menacing step toward James. "Ya know, I've been lookin' forward to eatin' those since I hit the road at *five* this mornin'. Now you're *wearin'* 'em instead."

James frantically dug his wallet out of his pants and shoved a twenty into the biker's enormous paw. "Here. Take this to replace your funnel cakes and for . . . for all your trouble. Have a nice evening."

Scurrying away, James's friends had no choice but to follow behind as he plowed through the crowd in the direction of the Marrow Men's cluster of campers. He finally stopped at their cooking area, puffing in exertion and disgusted at his own cowardice.

Bennett, who arrived at the campsite next, slapped James on the back. "My man, there are times when you just gotta cut and run. Back there was one of those times."

Lindy and Lucy hid giggles behind their hands. They observed the cook site — the entire area had a deserted feeling to it, and none of the campers seemed to be occupied. The four friends spread out and rapped on the doors of all the nearby RVs bearing Texas license plates, but no one answered their knocks.

Perplexed, Lindy consulted her schedule and then she began to nod in understanding. "Right after Felicity's dog show, a man called Humphrey the Hypnotist will perform, followed by tonight's main event, a magician called Ivan the Illusionist. Apparently, Ivan travels with a harem of scantily clad assistants. I've seen his poster around the fairgrounds, and if the women are wearing what they've got on in that picture, then that's where the Marrow Men are."

Bennett rubbed his eyes. "What time is it over, 'cause I don't feel like hanging around here much longer. I'm doggone tired."

"I'd say the show will run 'til at least eleven," Lindy said. "There's a fireworks display, too."

Lucy checked her watch. "It's almost nine now." She ran her hands through her hair and sighed. "I feel terrible saying this, but I'd like nothing better than to lie down in my bed back at the inn."

"Well, we can't do much more on Gillian's behalf tonight if we can't interview the Marrow Men," James said, feeling a twinge of guilt. "I vote for bed."

His friends mumbled their agreement and

once again headed toward the parking lot. The campground area was very quiet. Here and there a couple sat quietly talking or parents led sleepy children off to bed, but for the most part, the sound of an announcer's voice murmuring through distant speakers was the only invasive noise.

The hum of several small generators added to the drowsy peacefulness of the night, and James couldn't wait to take off his soiled clothes and his sticky belt (which felt too snug anyway), and step into a strong stream of hot shower water. He believed that even Bennett's rumbling snores would have no effect on the powerful lethargy that had invaded every inch of his body. He couldn't recall a time when he had been so desperate to pull on a pair of pajama bottoms and his favorite William & Mary T-shirt and hit the sack.

As the foursome drew close to Jimmy and Hailey's monstrous RV, they heard a *clank* echo near the front of the vehicle. Instinctively, they all stopped short and exchanged curious looks. Even though they had yet to walk past the camper, they could sense that there were no lights lit near the cooker, but that is where the odd noise had come from.

"Around back," Lucy whispered and pointed at the neighboring camper that could shield them from view as they investigated the source of the sound.

Walking on tiptoes, they crept behind the camper next to Jimmy's and poked their heads around the corner. James experienced a strong feeling of déjà vu from two days previous, when he and Bennett had eavesdropped on the spat between Jimmy and Hailey.

Because a thick cloud layer covered the half-moon, James had trouble distinguishing the shapes arranged alongside of the mammoth RV. Having seen the area during the daytime, he was able to recognize the forms of two folding chairs, a side table, and of course, Jimmy's commercial cooker. A movement near this rectangular black shape caught James's eye, and he nudged Lucy in the side and pointed. Nodding silently, she put her fingers to her lips.

James watched unblinkingly as the person near Jimmy's cooker bent over to retrieve something from a bag at his feet. He assumed that the stranger was a man by his height and build. When the unknown person suddenly fired up a small welding torch, James could see that his assumption had been correct. The light cast from the blue flame illuminated a pale, masculine face, though the eyes remained hidden behind a pair of mirrored sunglasses. After the man adjusted the flame, he applied the torch to an area in the underside of the lid. Jimmy's grill was so large that it actually had two separate cookers, but the man with the torch appeared to only be interested in the right-hand cooker.

"This guy's got a *big* pair of ba— ," Bennett began, but Lindy covered his mouth with her hand.

"What?" Bennett whispered. "He's destroying a dead man's property right out in the open! He's either desperate or crazy."

"What should we do?" Lindy breathed. "Should we stop him or wait and see what he finds?"

"Let's see what he's looking for first," Lucy suggested and the group fell silent again, watching as sparks flew from the around the cooker and disappeared in the surrounding blackness as though instantly snuffed out by dozens of invisible fingers.

"Hey!" a man's voice suddenly shouted from the shadows just beyond the man with the torch. "What the hell do you think you're doing?"

Bob Barker stepped into the illuminated strip of road that led back to the main fairway. He hesitated beneath the light, as though unsure of whether it was a good idea to apprehend a man dressed entirely in black who also happened to be brandishing a welding torch. Turning to the left and then to the right, Bob seemed to be searching for other signs of humanity in the campground.

"He needs to know that he's not alone," James whispered. Without thinking about the matter further, he stepped out from behind the shelter of the camper and waved his arms. "Hey Bob," he said absurdly as the man in black swiveled around to face James and his friends.

Realizing that he was trapped, the prowler threw the welding torch directly at Bob's head. Uttering a surprised squeak, Bob raised his arms to protect his face and the stranger slipped past him and sprinted off into a cover of deeper shadows beyond the campers.

The torch missed Bob by a few inches and landed with a thud in a patch of grass near his feet. When he leaned over to retrieve it, Lucy shouted, "Don't touch that! The murderer's fingerprints are probably on here!"

"Murderer?" Bob looked in the direction where the man in black had disappeared and then moved closer to the welding torch, as though to shield it with his body.

After urgently conferring with Lindy, Lucy

unzipped her large purse, turned it upside down, and unceremoniously dumped its contents into Lindy's. Using a paper napkin, Lucy then picked up the torch and slid it into her bag. The tip of the torch brushed against her hand as she zippered her purse.

"Ow! It's still warm!" She shook her hand back and forth in the air. "That crazy bastard! What was he looking for?"

"Who knows? The grill's black and it's nighttime." Bennett was obviously disappointed. "Hey! Didn't I see a flashlight rolling around in your Jeep?" he asked Lucy.

Lucy nodded, but gave Bob an inquisitive look. "Does Hailey keep one in the camper?"

Bob shook his head. "I've got no clue what's in there. More important, I've got no idea where Hailey's gotten to. I was supposed to meet her at the entrance to the pavilion and we were gonna watch the show together, but she didn't come. She's been actin' right strange all day, so I came here to see if she'd changed her mind about meetin' me." He gestured at the RV. "She said she wasn't gonna sleep in this thing ever again. Said it gave her the creeps to know Jimmy died inside, even if he was a grade-A jackass."

They all glanced at the large vehicle as

though assessing whether it exuded a sinister aura, but it seemed completely innocuous. James stepped up to the door and knocked. As Bob and his friends watched, he turned the knob and pushed it open.

"Hailey?" he called to the still air within. Feeling along the wall, he flipped a light switch and a soft glow emanated from two gleaming brass fixtures hanging from the ceiling above the dining area. The camper was a mess. Pillows from the sofa were scattered on the floor. Their fabric was marked by angry slashes, and white polyester filler oozed through the gaping holes. Cupboard doors had been flung open and their contents strewn everywhere. James sensed that the search of the camper had been conducted with both urgency and rage. He noticed that the searcher had emptied an entire box of Frosted Flakes onto the carpet. Nearby were twin piles of flour and sugar; their torn paper bags thrown carelessly into the sink.

"What do you see, James?" Lucy demanded. "Is Hailey in there?"

"No." James swiveled on the steps. "I think our intruder was in here first, but didn't find what he was looking for. The cushions are all torn, there's food all over the floor, and all the ceiling tiles are smashed. The radio's even been ripped right out of the dashboard. If Hailey walked in on someone doing this, she would have told someone and there'd be cops here by now, I'd think."

"So where is she, then?" Bob asked frantically. "Where's my girl?"

Lindy placed a comforting hand on Bob's shoulder. "I'm sure she's fine. She's probably off looking for you."

James knew Lindy well enough by now to know that she didn't actually subscribe to this belief. The clouds had released a wash of pale moonlight that served to emphasize the fearful look in her round eyes. She gazed up at James as he stood, frozen with foreboding, on the camper steps.

"Time to call Sheriff Jones," James said, directing his comment to Lucy. She nodded solemnly and dug around in Lindy's over-stuffed purse until she found her cell phone. As she spoke in a low, rapid voice, Bennett examined the damaged cooker.

"Can you dig those Jeep keys outta that thing?" Bennett asked Lindy as he pointed at her bag. "I'm afraid if I put my hand in there I may never get it back."

Scowling, Lindy rummaged on the bottom of her purse until her hand closed on Lucy's key chain, which was a polished steel

German shepherd.

"This would make a good weapon in a pinch," Bennett said, taking the key ring. "Be back in two shakes of a shepherd's tail."

"Oh, brother." Lindy sank into one of the folding chairs as Bob began pacing around the cooker.

By the time Lucy had completed her call, Bennett had returned from his short trip to Lucy's car and was breathing hard. After a few minutes, he said, "I gotta have a look in that cooker before the fuzz shows up."

Lucy frowned. "I wouldn't recommend referring to the sheriff that way."

"That fine woman? Wouldn't dream of it. 'Goddess of Justice' suits her best, yessir." Bennett smiled to himself and pointed the beam of the flashlight into the black cavity of the cooker lid. Bennett then partially closed the lid, clearly trying to judge the overall thickness of it.

"There's plenty of room to hide something in here," he stated, tapping on the metal until they could all hear a hollow echo. "Not only that, but the way this thing's designed, the heat wouldn't even get to this chamber. There's no air flow to the whole right side of the cooker and this top part here — where our Man in Black was cuttin' — it's also covered by a thick heat shield, so it wouldn't be affected by the drafts comin' from the left side."

"How do you know how this cooker works?" Lindy asked in amazement.

"I've sneaked peeks at James's history of barbecue book. There's a diagram in there on how air flows through these commercial cookers. Both times we saw Jimmy and Hailey usin' this cooker, they were only grilling on the left side. I bet this whole upper right lid has stayed nice and cool. The dripping pan is clean as a river rock and there isn't a trace of a single wood pellet in here." He angled the flashlight into the crack created by the welding torch. "So if Jimmy didn't use it for cooking, what might he have been storing in here?"

"Bet it's drugs," Bob quickly offered.

Lucy's eyes grew large. "What makes you say that?"

"Jimmy was just too damned jolly. Didn't matter what was wrong in his life, he acted relaxed and chipper to everybody but Hailey. And all that extra flab he's gained over the last few months. He's twice the man he was at the last festival. And his skin looked all bloated and rubbery, ya know? And he was cold when no one else was, but he'd be sweatin' buckets five minutes later. Wasn't normal, if you ask me."

"Mr. Lang had those symptoms because he had an advanced case of hypothyroidism," said a deep voice from behind Bob. Deputy Neely trailed a hand along the sloped hood of Jimmy's trailer and examined the front tire as though he was considering purchasing the vehicle. "This medical condition also accounts for the puffy appearance of his face, sensitivity to cold, hoarseness in the throat, flaky skin, and hair loss. The victim had no traces of medication in his body or in his recreational vehicle and therefore, we assume he was entirely unaware that he suffered from hypothyroidism. He was in the late stages of the illness, in fact."

"Thank you, Deputy." Sheriff Jones appeared beside Neely and shot her subordinate a look that could freeze an avalanche into stagnation. Without a word to anyone else, she opened the door to Jimmy's camper and then went inside. Deputy Neely followed her, looking subdued.

Deputy Harding had also arrived with the sheriff. He issued James a polite nod. James remembered how Harding had made it possible for James to speak with Gillian, and he felt confident enough in the man's capacity for compassion to prod him for information while the sheriff was out of earshot.

"Guess you guys got the medical examiner's results," James stated casually.

Harding muttered, "Yep," took a Maglite from his belt, and began to inspect the cooker.

"We've got the welding torch he used to bust into that grill," Lucy boasted. "You might want to check it for fingerprints."

Harding eyed Lucy expectantly. "Where is it?"

Lucy gave her purse a smug pat while Harding snapped a pair of latex gloves onto his hands. Without saying a word, he reached out for Lucy's bag and after a moment's hesitation she reluctantly passed it to him. Harding placed a pair of sunglasses over his eyes, started the torch, and deftly continued cutting the cooker lid where the man in black had left off.

It was fascinating to watch the white and orange-tinged flame slowly eat through the metal. Harding worked patiently, his hands steady and firm as they guided the torch. Within several minutes, Harding had created a C-shaped panel. Switching off the welding torch, he pushed his sunglasses high onto his forehead and tugged at the separated section of metal. He was only able to lift it up a few inches, but it was enough to allow the light of his flashlight to penetrate into the lid's cavity. Harding grunted and James and his friends couldn't help but gather around the cooker to see what the deputy had discovered.

Harding was too consumed in his task to notice that he had an audience, but when he wriggled a large, plastic-wrapped bundle free from the opening he had made, Lucy gasped and he seemed to suddenly recall that he was being observed.

"Is that marijuana?" Lucy asked him, standing on her tiptoes to get a better look. "Is there more in there?"

Torn between continuing with his search and spending his time dispersing the on-lookers, Harding dropped the bag to his side and bent over the cooker again. He removed bag after bag until a mound of small, plastic-wrapped bundles had been laid out on the grass in a neat line next to his right foot.

"Sheriff!" Harding called out once the cooker had been totally emptied of its secret cache. "I think you'd best take a look out here!"

The sheriff calmly stepped down from the camper and squatted down in the grass in order to examine the bundles. She squeezed them, sniffed them, and turned them over and over as Neely held a flashlight for her.

Finally, she whispered some instructions to Neely and then turned to face an agitated Bob Barker and the supper club members.

"We'll need to take statements about what you witnessed here this evening," the sheriff said briskly. "Did any of you recognize the intruder?"

"I'm pretty sure he was one of the Marrow Men," James spoke up hesitantly. Noting the look of doubt on Harding's face, James continued. "I know it's dark, but the moon was out at one point and when the torch lit up his profile, I was sure it was him. The guy I saw arguing with Jimmy before his death."

Sheriff Jones glanced up at the sky, where lumps of ash-colored clouds formed a barricade over the moon. Only trace amounts of weak light escaped from the cloud cover. "But are you certain it was him?" She turned her penetrating gaze on James. "Would you swear to this man's identity in a court of law?"

James felt doubt assailing him. "Ah . . ." He turned to his friends in search of support, and they gave him brief nods to assure him that they also believed that the intruder was the man who wore the San Antonio Spurs baseball cap. "Yes," James answered with confidence. "I don't know his name, but I could show you who he is."

"It was Mitch Walker," Bob stated firmly. "No doubt about it. And this fellow's right. He's one of the Marrow Men. I looked right into his face, Sheriff. It was Mitch."

Silence followed Bob's statement. The deputies turned their attention to the bundles on the ground, but Sheriff Jones kept her eyes locked on Bob.

Suddenly, Bennett stepped forward and inserted himself between the sheriff and her deputies. He gestured angrily at the cooker. "Do you still think Gillian O'Malley is involved in this? You think a dog groomer from Quincy's Gap is trafficking pot? That she's dealing in illegal drugs with a tow truck driver from Texas who killed her husband?"

Bennett slammed his palm hard against the cooker and everyone jumped, except for the sheriff, who didn't react at all. "This is about drugs and money! Where'd Jimmy get this fancy camper?" Bennett seethed. "Gillian's got nothin' to do with that! Who are these drugs for? Who was Jimmy gonna sell them to? Or did he screw somebody over?" Bennett jabbed his finger into his temple. "*These* are the pertinent questions that have gotta be asked and Gillian's got no answers for you, so give the woman back to us! And

318

I'm not givin' *any* kind of statement until she's free." He slapped the cooker again. "I'm tired! We're *all* tired!" He put his hands on his hips and matched Sheriff Jones's stare.

After a few moments in which James was afraid to release his pent-up breath, Sheriff Jones blinked. "Are you finished?" she asked Bennett, her voice completely calm.

"Just give her back to us," Bennett repeated softly, but with the same level of passion. He let his hand fall back to his side.

"Ms. O'Malley has been free to leave since this afternoon. She has been most co-operative and we had no cause to hold her any longer," the sheriff replied evenly. "However, she fervently requested that I allow her to remain in her cell overnight. She said that she sought a few more hours of solitude." For the first time that evening, kindness softened her eyes and turned up the corners of her full lips. "Now, I don't run a hotel, and I think Ms. O'Malley would appreciate being picked up first thing in the morning as our breakfast isn't exactly on par with the Sunday spread laid out at Fox Hall, but I couldn't say no to such a simple request." Her face grew stony again. "Not all demands are so easily met, Mr. Marshall."

Bennett shifted on his feet. The blaze of intensity was gone from his dark eyes. "I apologize, ma'am. I let my hot head get the better of me. I had no idea that that crazy woman *wanted* to be alone in a cell, but now that you mention it, I can sure see her lighting those little candles and sittin' cross-legged while she *communed with her inner spirit.*"

The sheriff smiled. "She actually said something to that effect. And your apology is accepted. In fact, I think Ms. O'Malley is fortunate to have friends such as yourselves, but now that she is free to go, you should steer well clear of this investigation. I don't expect to see any of you again unless you're fulfilling your judging duties or enjoying the activities of this festival."

"But what about Hailey?" Bob interjected. "She doesn't know anything about this mess either, I'm sure of it. And we've got to find her! Maybe she's been kidnapped or somethin'!"

The sheriff gestured at one of the lawn chairs. "Why don't you have a seat, sir? I'll speak with you in a moment. As for the rest of you, I think you should go on back to the inn and get some sleep. We'll need you to give statements about this evening, but I'm short-staffed at the moment and we've got our hands full here, so they can wait until morning." The sheriff gestured at the bags of drugs and then winked at Bennett with such subtlety that James wasn't even sure he had seen it. In a low, husky voice, she said, "I'll expect *you* bright and early, Mr. Marshall."

Though they had clearly just been dismissed, James thought Bennett might float away with the next breeze. He nodded mutely and practically skipped toward the parking lot.

"Well, we did it, friends!" Lindy clapped her hands. "Gillian will be out tomorrow and we can judge the blueberry pie-eating contest and then get the hell out of this town!"

"No we can't! The case is still unsolved!" Lucy protested. "Hailey could be in danger *or* she could be involved in this whole drug scheme. We have a responsibility to help!"

James climbed into Lucy's Jeep, grateful to be sitting down again. "It's true," he said in agreement. "If we hadn't been snooping around tonight, the drugs could have just disappeared and the sheriff might never have known about them. I know she wants us to butt out, but we may as well keep our eyes and ears open while we're still here."

Lucy beamed at James in the rearview mirror.

"Oh, I guess you're right," Lindy sighed. "Besides, if we don't keep investigating, how else is Bennett going to find a way to hit on Sheriff Jones? Huh, buddy?" She reached around from her position in the passenger seat and poked Bennett on the top of his foot with one of her long fingernails.

Bennett, who had just popped a piece of chewing gum in his mouth, was extremely ticklish anywhere on his feet. When Lindy brushed the skin on the top of his foot, he jumped backward and inhaled the piece of gum. Coughing and spluttering, he wheezed and gasped for air until James became genuinely alarmed.

"Should we pull over?" James inquired worriedly as he pounded on his friend's back.

Bennett shook his head and finally coughed the piece of gum into his hand. "With my skin tone . . . ," he panted, "could be mighty tough to tell if I was turnin' blue, huh?" He balled the piece of spent gum into its empty wrapper. "Lindy, I oughta stick this in your hair instead of putting it in the garbage."

"Sorry." Lindy slunk down in her seat.

"You guys are gettin' punchy," Lucy said,

smiling. "I'd better get you all tucked into bed."

"Amen to that, sister!" Bennett croaked. "It'll just be me and my sweet dreams of Sheriff Jade Jones. She winked at me. Yessir, I think she feels it, too. There's somethin' magnetic brewin' between the two of us." He turned to James. "And you'll be dreamin' of Murphy, unless you're stayin' with her tonight."

"Fox Hall was booked, remember, and I have no idea where she's staying," James mumbled. "And I'm too damned tired to dream. I'm going to fall asleep the second I close my eyes."

"Are you still tossin' and turnin' over there?" Bennett asked in the middle of the night. "You're like a damned kayak goin' through a passel of rapids!"

James pushed his glasses onto his nose and eyed the clock. "Three thirty," he groaned. "Why can't I sleep?"

"Might be that love note you got from Murphy," Bennett suggested grumpily. "Got you all riled up."

James eyed the crumpled missive lying on his own nightstand. "It wasn't exactly a love note. All Murphy wrote was that she had to drive back to Quincy's Gap to make sure that the next edition of the *Star* went out on time and to call if I had any updates on Jimmy's case."

Bennett was silent for a moment. "You're right, that ain't no love letter."

"You might be on target about the riled-up part though, because every time I close my eyes, I start thinking about what Murphy started to admit to me earlier today."

"What's that?" Bennett sat up in bed.

James hesitated. "Uh, she said she wrote a book about us."

"You and me?" Bennett sounded surprised.

"No. All of us. The Flab Five." James squeezed his eyes shut. "And she's already got a publishing deal."

Again, there was silence and then Bennett switched on the lamp. "Say that again." His dark eyes flashed angrily.

"The book's about the supper club members. Something about how we've helped solve murders," James declared hastily. "She said it's not about our dieting or anything."

Bennett rose stiffly from the bed and walked slowly over to the TV cabinet. He opened the small fridge hidden behind one of the lower doors, pulled two bottles from the honor bar, and went into the bathroom. When he returned, he handed James a tumbler filled with an inch of light amber liquid.

Tossing down his drink, Bennett sank down onto his bed. "Go on, man, or you'll never get to sleep."

"What is it? Whiskey?" James sniffed the contents.

"Yessir. Jim Beam." He swung his legs onto the bed and stared up at the ceiling. Neither man spoke for several minutes. Finally, Bennett said, "That's some bomb to drop on a guy in the middle of the night. So Murphy's writing a tell-all book. Man oh man. There's no way I'm gonna get any sleep without a little medicinal aid. You won't either, my friend, trust me."

"It's not a tell-all," James protested weakly, gripping the tumbler loosely. "It's fiction."

"Right." Bennett snorted as he shook his head in disgust. "And no one in Quincy's Gap is gonna know who the black crime-solvin' mailman in Murphy's work of *fiction* is or who the crime-solvin' librarian livin' at home with his hermit daddy is. I can just hear the talk down at Dolly's Diner." He put his arms behind his head and rearranged his pillow, punching it violently into place. "We're not gonna be able to show our faces in town without folks mentionin' your *girl-friend's* book. Whether we like it or not, that book is gonna change our lives."

The sound of the cool air rushing through the vents in the floor followed Bennett's statement, but James didn't know whether he felt more chilled by his friend's words or by the man-made breeze breathing across his body.

"Oh, God." James moaned and then swallowed his drink in three gulps. The whiskey burned on the way down his throat, and a slow and subtle warmth spread through his belly. He felt his clenched hands relax and some of the tension ebb from his knotted shoulders and neck. Scrunching his toes in the thick rug next to his bed, James gazed at his empty tumbler with mournful eyes.

Collecting Bennett's glass, James gestured at the cabinet. "There had better be more where these came from."

SIXTEEN:
CHEDDAR CHEESE
GRITS

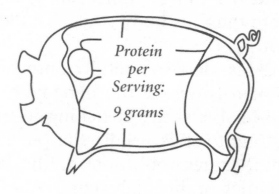

Protein per Serving: 9 grams

When James opened one eye, allowing the other to stay mercifully closed against the bright light infiltrating the room, he sensed that he had slept later than he should. No snores emanated from Bennett's bed, nor was the morning stillness broken by the rush of water through the bathroom pipes. An unnatural quiet permeated the room.

As James put his hand out for his glasses, a sharp pain snapped awake inside his skull and he froze mid-reach. Resting his heavy head back on the pillow, he took stock of his physical state. His head hurt, his limbs felt like lead, his mouth was so dry that he couldn't have spoken a word, and his tongue felt three sizes too large. He desperately wanted water, but sensed that the movement required to walk into the bathroom, turn on the tap, and tilt his mouth under the stream in order to wash away the sour taste and the putrid film coating his teeth was more than his body could handle at the moment.

Easing his glasses carefully onto his face, so as not to provoke the hangover dragon curled over his scalp, clenching like a vise, and waiting to stick needle-sharp claws into his brain, James took note of the litter of small bottles on his nightstand.

"One, two, three, four, five . . . ," he counted. "No wonder I feel like a zombie." He also noticed a yellow Post-it note stuck to the surface of the digital clock. He peeled it off the clock's window, noting that the time was seven after nine.

Sunshine:
When you finally get up, come downstairs for breakfast. I already picked up Gillian and we are all meeting on the back porch. There's coffee and the best

bowl of cheese grits you've ever wrapped your tongue around. I expect your head might hurt a bit right about now, but there's nothing for it but to eat a big pile of eggs followed by an even bigger pile of grits.

-Bennett

"I don't know about food," James addressed the note and then stumbled into the bathroom. He swallowed three Advil and then took a luxuriously long shower. Slowly, doused in a fog of warm water and silence, he felt his headache begin to subside. The thought that Gillian was back at the inn, seated at a table with her friends surrounding her, lightened James's heart tremendously.

"Maybe they'll be so glad to have her back that they won't get too upset about Murphy's book," James said to his reflection as he toweled off the misted mirror. He shaved quickly, wanting to escape from the image he saw in the glass. Unlike the small mirror in his bathroom at home, which focused mainly on the head and shoulder region, this one was large enough to capture the entire upper half of James's body. And before him stood the results of a summer of relaxed attention to good diet and routine exercise.

"You've returned, I see," James stated morosely as he slapped the loose flesh of his round belly. He pivoted sideways, blowing out his stomach so that it became even larger than before. He then sucked in his breath, causing the flesh to tighten and the fat to appear to have miraculously evaporated. Finally exhaling, James rubbed the swell of his paunch one more time and then pulled a polo shirt over his head, relieved to be able to partially disguise the evidence of his weight gain beneath the loose shirt.

By the time he arrived on the back porch, several charming sights assaulted his eyes at once. Directly to his left was the food: fluffy scrambled eggs nestled in a warming tray; crisp, dark brown bacon stacked into neat rows in the neighboring tray; and adjacent to the bacon, a ceramic baking dish containing golden-tinged grits. Next in line was a bowl of plump, cardinal-red strawberries and a platter bearing the remains of what looked like an apricot and cream cheese coffee cake.

James glanced to his right. Francesca was cleaning leaves from the pool in a loose dress with a pattern of large, cheerful sunflowers. The early sunlight created a halo around her flowing hair and her skin seemed effused with an ethereal glow. After every third or fourth scoop of her net, she'd dip one of her bare feet into the pool and wiggle her toes in pleasure.

But James paid little attention to Francesca's beauty, for straight ahead of him, seated between Lindy and Bennett, was the most wonderful vision of all. It was Gillian, dressed in one of her wild, rainbow-striped T-shirts, an armload of tinkling bangles, and a necklace of plastic purple beads. Her hair was its customary bird's nest of orange curls and she had reddened her fair cheeks with rogue and applied smudges of lavender shadow to her eyelids. When she looked at James, she smiled with the inner warmth he had grown accustomed to, but had missed seeing over the past few days. With that smile, James knew that Gillian was her old self again. There was no doubt that she had been wounded by painful memories — that coming face-to-face with the man who had ruined her chance at happiness with her young husband had caused her fresh grief, but James was grateful that the events of the past few days had not altered her permanently. She was Gillian. Spunky, spacey, and spiritual, and she was loved deeply by those gathered around her.

"I heard that you might be feeling a bit

off-center today," Gillian said after James had hugged and kissed her hello. "Ginger tea is simply *magical* at restoring your body's balance after that corporeal vessel's been *flooded* with alcohol." She puffed up a cloud of orange hair. "By Buddha's beautiful belly, *I* could have used some of that restorative brew after drinking Felicity's wine the other night!"

"Have the tea if you want, James, but you have *got* to try some of these grits first." Lucy pointed at the small mound on her plate. "Even if you're not a grits guy, these will warm your body from the inside out."

"I've got enough blubber around my waist to keep me warm," James answered wryly, "but I could use a bit of breakfast if we're going to make it through another day of Hog Fest. I don't think I'd make a very good full-time food judge, Lucy. I'm getting a bit burned out on all this gluttony."

"Too true! I feel like all the pores on my face are clogged by fry oil!" Lindy moaned. "Oh, and don't worry about the pie-eating contest, Gillian." She gave their friend a tender look. "I think you've been through enough this weekend without having to watch grown men wreaking havoc on perfectly good blueberry pies."

"Hey, it won't be all guys divin' into those

pies. Don't you go assuming that eatin' competitions are just for men." Bennett waggled his finger at Lindy. "You're forgettin' about Virginia's own champion eater, The Black Widow. Why, on July fourth, 2005, she ate thirty-seven hot dogs in twelve minutes. And she's a tiny little thing." He held out his arms in a small circle and then pointed at Francesca. "Makes our beauty queen out there cleanin' the pool look like a Sumo wrestler."

"Can you imagine being a buffet-type restaurant owner in The Black Widow's hometown?" James quipped. "Every time she came to visit your establishment you'd know you were losing money! If she can eat thirty-seven hot dogs, imagine what she could do to a breakfast buffet!"

Gillian giggled. "I'm *not* skipping out on the judging. I've missed *so* much time with you already and I'm *fully* prepared to witness a *spectacularly* revolting display of binge-like behavior. In fact, it might do me some good." She gestured at the greedy heap of bacon on James's plate. "I think my time of solitude and *reflection* has prepared me to be more open regarding the food tastes and preferences of my fellow human beings."

"So no more speeches on animal treatment?" Bennett acted stunned. "What on earth would you talk about instead?"

"Of course I'm going to continue to be an advocate for all animals!" Gillian glanced at Bennett with a flash of anger in her eyes and then realized he had been deliberately trying to provoke her. She smiled. "I'm *so* relieved that you are all embracing me with such lack of judgment. After all, I've kept a secret from you, my closest companions, for a long time. I apologize from the very *core* of my being. I just wanted to leave the past in the past, but what *foolishness* to think that I could bury such *intense* memories."

"It was your secret to keep," Lucy said softly. "So there's nothing to forgive."

"But besides me, has anyone else at this table been married?" James asked to lighten the mood.

"No ex-wives in my closet." Bennett refilled his empty coffee cup. "I see *you're* feelin' better." He pointed at the grits on James's plate. "Now scoop some of them down your throat, and you'll be good as gold."

James loaded his heavy spoon with a mouthful of grits and lifted it to his nose, wondering how a gelatinous glob of grains could transform his outlook about spending another day at Hog Fest and put an end to the remnants of his hangover. He inhaled the pleasant scent of baked cheese and then felt the familiar and comforting creaminess of the starch as his lips closed around the spoon.

"They're so light," he breathed in awe and relished the fluffy grits. Lucy was right, they were tinged with warmth and the cozy feeling they created had nothing to do with temperature. In addition to the salty flavors of sharp cheddar and butter, there were hints of Worcestershire and hot sauce. It was just what James needed to perk up his numb mouth.

"Delicious!" he proclaimed to Eleanor as she examined the leavings of the buffet. "You are an excellent cook, Mrs. Fiennes. I'd say that I'm going to waste away when I go back home to Quincy's Gap, but my father's girlfriend is an accomplished food guru such as yourself, so there's no chance of that."

Eleanor looked at James with interest. "A girlfriend? Do you think your father will get remarried?"

"Yes, and I'd be happy for him if he did," James answered. "Milla's a wonderful woman, and I'd love for her to join our family."

Gazing at Francesca, Eleanor gave a satisfied nod. "Francesca idolized her father, but he's been gone for more than ten years now. I'd like to move on, but I worry about how she'll take it. But if I wait too long, I'm afraid that the man I love will give up on me."

"If you're talkin' about your feelings for R. C. Richter, your daughter already knows," Lucy stated matter-of-factly. "And I don't think she minds one bit."

"Really?" Eleanor flushed and clasped her thin hands over her small chest. "Oh, *that's* such a nice thing to hear! He's asked me to be his wife many times, but I keep putting him off."

Gillian rose to refill her tea cup with more hot water and a fresh bag of Mandarin orange tea. "It would seem that you and Francesca are *both* ready for a new phase of life to begin." Gillian lowered her voice. "Lindy tells me that your daughter's greatest hope is to become a teacher. What a *noble* and *significant* profession. Think of how many lives she can touch, of how many young girls she can positively influence! You must be *very* proud?" Gillian emphasized her last point by turning it into a question.

Flummoxed, Eleanor darted glances between Gillian and her daughter. Finally, her eyes lingered on Francesca's beautiful face.

"I should be proud, shouldn't I? Her becoming Miss Virginia was always my dream. But that's the thing. It was *my* dream, not hers. When I was younger, my family didn't have enough extra money for me to compete, but I wanted that crown so badly I used to cry about it at night." Her voice filled with longing. "All this time, I've been pushing and pushing Francesca toward that pageant. She's always done everything I've asked her to until this summer. All along, she's been a good girl — a good person — and I didn't realize how lucky I was to be her friend until I acted so *unlike* a friend."

"Sounds like you've seen the light," Bennett gently mumbled.

"I have." Eleanor dumped the pile of dishes she had been stacking back onto the buffet table. "Thank you for talking to her about teaching," she said to Lindy. "It was my good fortune that R. C. invited all of you to be judges for Hog Fest. You certainly go down in my guest book as some of Fox Hall's most rewarding visitors. Now if you'll excuse me, I'm going to invite my daughter to come inside and tear up her pageant entry."

The supper club members watched expectantly as Eleanor marched to the deep end of the pool. Francesca stood in the middle

337

of the diving board, catching leaves and twigs in her net as she stared dreamily into the water. Though they were too far away to hear Eleanor's words, they were able to see Francesca's mouth break into a heartfelt smile. Her entire being seemed to radiate with light. Tossing the leaf-laden net carelessly onto the ground, she ran and flung her arms around her mother and the two held each other for several moments.

"This is going to be a *splendid* day," Gillian declared and took a noisy slurp of tea.

The blueberry pie-eating competition was scheduled for high noon, so the supper club members took care of business first. They packed their bags, checked out of the inn, and drove to the sheriff's department in order to issue statements about their encounter with Mitch Walker the night before. According to Deputy Harding, both Mitch and Hailey were missing and Bob Barker was beside himself with worry. Three deputies from the neighboring county had been enlisted to help search for the pair, but had yet to find a sign of either one.

Harding had freely offered these juicy tidbits of information to Gillian as she sat on a bench outside the sheriff's building awaiting the return of her friends.

"I'd rather *not* go inside that structure again," she told her friends as they marched up the front steps. "Instead, I shall sit on this bench and try to channel my energy into *seeing* where Hailey might have gone."

Gillian was preoccupied in visualizing her body being made of thousands of particles of light when Harding sat down next to her with a satisfied grunt. He then proceeded to strike a match using the bottom of his shoe, lit his cigarette, and took a grateful drag.

"I heard you found some hidden treasure last night," Gillian said, without looking at Harding. In fact, she kept her eyes completely closed.

"Yeah, sure did," the deputy answered proudly. "A whole mess of tainted pot. Someone planned to make up a bunch of fry sticks and sell them for a big pile of money."

"Fry sticks?" Gillian opened her eyes. "Is that some kind of unhealthy food?"

Harding gave a good-natured chuckle. "No, ma'am. It's a joint, but not made from your run-of-the-mill weed. The marijuana we found in Jimmy Lang's cooker has been dipped in formaldehyde. That kind of pot costs around one hundred bucks an ounce." He cast a sideways glance at Gillian and, seeing the lack of comprehension on her face, held his thumb and index finger an inch apart. "That's about this much."

Gillian frowned. "That's not much product for that amount of money. Is marijuana *that* expensive these days?"

"It's the formaldehyde. It gives you visions," Harding explained. "The kids really like it. And by kids I mean students in high school and college."

"What a shame that they're looking for a phony high when they could achieve a genuine one by some employing simple meditation and breathing techniques." Gillian sighed. "This 'special' pot sounds dangerous," she said with a cough as she waved away the cloud of Harding's cigarette smoke.

Harding nodded. "It is, ma'am. It's like smoking five of these things." He eyed his cigarette with distaste and then took another resigned drag. "The worst part is that the kids who smoke this laced stuff the most seem to overdo it. We've had several college kids hospitalized over the past year 'cause of these fry sticks. Still, they see it as the 'in' drug and, because they're given so much pocket money by their oblivious parents, they can afford to buy enough to keep them supplied for a couple of months."

Gillian was silent for a moment as she

stared into the nearly-empty parking lot. "He really was a bad man," she whispered. "That Jimmy Lang. He was tainted, just like the drugs. I was *truly* prepared to forgive him, but now that you're telling me he planned to sell drugs to teenagers, I can't. He spent his whole life messing up the lives of others."

"We've got no hard proof that Mr. Lang was a dealer," Harding replied testily, though Gillian was aware that his ire wasn't directed at her. "And when we questioned Mr. Walker earlier yesterday, he claimed to have never known Mr. Lang outside of bumping into him at these kinds of festivals, but now that Mr. Walker has disappeared from the fairgrounds, I'm feeling more and more like he's our guy." He sat ramrod-straight on the bench, his shoulders taut with tension. "We've got to find him and get the truth out of him. He was lying to us yesterday, I'm sure of it. Just as I was certain that you were telling us the truth."

"You know, I *strongly* believe in the power of the inner voice." Gillian turned her palms to the sky. "It's the world's way of speaking to us." She cast a subtle glance at the law-man beside her. "*You* seem to have height-ened instincts, Deputy. And how do you know all of these *dreadful details* about these *toxically laced* drugs?"

"Used to live in D.C. It's why I moved here, to get away from that stuff." He shrugged. "Guess you can never really run from all the ugly things in life." He shifted his weight on the bench as though agitated that he had spoken so freely to the woman seated next to him.

Gillian reached out and took Harding's free hand. "No, you can't run, but you *can* refresh your spirit and begin a *new* phase of life."

Though she half-expected tough-guy Harding to scoff at her advice, he seemed to give her words careful consideration. After a few moments of silence, he nodded in agreement and then he gently squeezed her fingers. "I expect you'd know all about that, ma'am. I truly admire how you've handled yourself over the last two days. You're quite a lady." He threw his cigarette onto the ground and coughed nervously. "And a mighty pretty one, too, if you don't mind my saying so."

"Oh, I don't mind," Gillian whispered, blushing as she realized that the kind-faced deputy had yet to release her hand. "I don't mind at all."

The R. C. Richter who handed a stack of

signed waivers to the judges to review was a different man than the one who had appeared in front of yesterday's crowd looking haggard and defeated. This R. C. had a spring to his step, and he whistled as he issued directions to a scruffy teenager wheeling a wagon filled with pies to a line of tables covered in white plastic cloths.

Chairs had been arranged in an orderly row behind the tables and in front of each chair was a bottle of water and a white T-shirt with cobalt lettering that read, *I Turned Blue at Hog Fest.*

Once James had inspected his group of waivers, which had all been signed and dated according to R. C.'s requirements, he noticed a group of teenage boys unloading more pies from the back of a white van. Mrs. Phelps, the baker, hovered nervously nearby, clucking at the boys and pleading with them to be careful. As the young men maneuvered carts of pies to a small tent alongside the row of tables, James frowned at their untidy appearance. Their hair was too long, their pants too baggy, and their soiled shirts were riddled with holes.

"What are you frowning at, James?" Lucy asked as she joined him in staring at the growing number of pies. "Don't you like blueberry pie?"

"Sure. I like all kinds of pie except for rhubarb." He smiled self-effacingly. "I was just being an old fart — wondering why those boys spend good money to look like they're homeless."

"Yeah, I know. That grunge style just won't go away." Lucy tugged at his arm. "But cheer up. Mrs. Phelps has brought all the judges a slice of pie, still warm from the oven. We get to eat while R. C. goes over the rules."

"Again with the rules," James snorted. "He must enjoy what he does. The man's positively beaming today."

"That's because Eleanor told him that she would marry him. She stopped by the festival while we were busy giving our statements. I overheard R. C. telling Mrs. Phelps all about it."

"So everything is looking up for him," James began sarcastically. "Except for the fact that illegal drugs were recovered on festival grounds, the girlfriend of the man murdered here Friday night has gone missing, and a torch-wielding thief is on the loose, things are just peachy for R. C."

"No, not *peach!*" Mrs. Phelps trilled as she appeared in front of a small card table and thrust napkins into the judges' hands. "Local-grown blueberries. The best in the state. Eat up, now!"

James drove his fork through the perfectly-browned crust of the pie and watched as indigo blueberries oozed from beneath the tines.

"This contest is going to be messy." He examined his plate in amusement.

"People love that part of the whole thing. This event's the best free advertisin' a baker can get!" Mrs. Phelps chirped gaily.

"Where do you get all of your extra help?" James asked, suddenly spotting a young man who could easily be the brother of the leather-jacket-wearing teen that had been haunting his library on Friday nights.

"The boys? Oh, they just come out of the woodwork right before Hog Fest," she replied. "It's the same every year. Now, they're not the world's *best* workers, I'll tell ya, and I've gotta pay them right after we're done sellin' pies for some reason that I cannot wrap my mind around, and then they scatter like the four winds 'til next year."

"That boy over there. Is he from Hudsonville?" James pointed at the Martin Trotman look-alike.

"Only one of them lives here, but they all know each other well enough, considerin'." Her brows creased as she struggled to recall the young man's name. "He's got a funny name. What is it? The boys keep teasin' him about it. Oh, it's Trotman! Um, Donny Trotman."

James tried not to allow the surprise to show in his face. Trotman was Martin's last name — he was certain of it. "No offense, Mrs. Phelps, but why are they so eager to get work during Hog Fest? Why is this particular time so important to them?"

She shrugged, still waiting for James to taste her pie. "They tell me it's their annual score. Whatever *that* means. I figure they must be sweet on some of the vendor girls who travel back here every year. Who knows?" She swatted at his shoulder with the edge of her apron. "But they're better eaters than you, honey! Shoot, they'd eat night and day if they had the chance."

"It's called the munchies," James muttered and then took a bite of pie. The sugary blueberries popped in his mouth as he crunched on bits of buttery crust. "Mmmm," he mumbled through closed lips. "Sublime."

Smiling, Mrs. Phelps resumed her role of overseer as the motley group of young men unhurriedly went about their tasks.

While James focused on polishing off his pie, wishing that he had a large cold glass of milk to cut the sweetness of his baked treat,

346

the contestants for the pie-eating competition began to seat themselves at the plastic-covered table. Each man and woman pulled the contest's official T-shirt over his or her own clothes and then made nervous small talk with fellow competitors.

"That's a *fine* piece of pie," Bennett declared as he pushed his blueberry-stained paper plate away. He smiled at James, displaying a row of purple teeth.

"You'd better brush those not-so-pearly whites before you see your sheriff again," James teased as Bennett frantically ran his tongue over his upper teeth.

"Your fangs ain't exactly gleaming white either, my friend," Bennett countered and then looked at his watch. "Uh-oh. Time to stand up and act official. Come on, man. All we gotta do is make sure the contestants don't use their hands to eat their pie and place a new one in front of them once their dish is totally empty. Easy."

James took up his station in front of a pair of newlyweds who got so involved in kissing each other for luck that R. C. had to blow the start whistle twice in order to get their attention. Their demonstration of affection caused them to be several bites behind the remaining eighteen contestants once they finally planted their faces into the center of their pies.

The contestants looked like pigs at the trough, burying their mouths and noses into the deep blue filling and scooping up the crust with their front teeth. At first, James found their slurping and squelching noises comical, but as the first round of pies were consumed and he had to slide two fresh pies beneath the stained and crumb-covered faces of the contestants before him, he began to feel slightly disgusted.

By the time the newlyweds had started on their third pie, half of the contestants had dropped out. James noticed several older men cleaning their faces with moist wipes as they held on to their bloated stomachs. At the very end of the table, right in front of Lindy, a handsome man in his early thirties suddenly dashed away from the table and bent over the closest garbage can, his entire torso heaving as he threw up the two pies he had already consumed.

"You're *so* disqualified!" one of Mrs. Phelps' helpers jeered at the man. Lindy scowled at the impolite boy and then placed a gentle hand on the sick man's back. After he had emptied his stomach, she handed him several napkins and a tall glass of water. Encouraged by her kindness, the man smiled and waved at the crowd. He then wobbled off to an empty seat, his skin still a bit green beneath the faint stain of blueberry.

After this unpleasant incident, James had the unfortunate task of disqualifying the newlywed wife for using her fingers to shovel a particularly slippery bite of pie into her mouth. Frustrated with his own inability to completely empty his pie dish, her husband followed suit a few minutes later, and the lovebirds sat sulkily and watched the remaining three contestants as they made slow headway into their fourth pie.

Once he no longer had an official responsibility, James decided to seize on the opportunity to find out more about the expected "score" the young men had mentioned to Mrs. Phelps. Hoping to appear as though he were merely in search of shade, James sauntered casually to the side of the disheveled young man whose name Mrs. Phelps had recalled as being Donny Trotman.

"You guys sure unloaded a lot of pies," James remarked pleasantly to the boy. "And in this heat." He wiped his brow with a napkin to emphasize the point.

"Yeah. And man, I hope she sells the rest of 'em so we don't have to put any back in the van," he replied in a bored tone. "I'm sick of pies."

"You know," James glanced at him briefly, "I'm not staring at you, but you look just like a kid I know from Quincy's Gap. His name's Martin."

Donny frowned, offended at being referred to as a 'kid.' "Martin's my first cousin. How do *you* know him?" He scrutinized James's creased khakis, spotless glasses, and leather loafers in disdain.

"Oh," James said smugly, forcing his gaze to remain on the pie eaters, "let's just say he and I share the same *hobby*." And then as subtly as possible, James pinched his thumb and index finger together and mimed an inhalation.

"Dude. *All right*." Even Donny's exclamations were tinged with lethargy.

"Know where a guy can score some around here?" James muttered out of the side of his mouth.

Donny paused and then held out his hand. "Yeah, I can tell you how, but you gotta make it worth my while."

Struggling not to show his dislike for Donny or for the sour, pungent odor that arose from the boy's unwashed clothes and skin, James pulled out his wallet, extracted a twenty, and, after folding it in half, placed it on a palm stained with blueberries, flour, and dirt. Thinking that he might actually have consumed a pie created by Donny's filthy hands, James fought down the bile rising in his belly.

"Did you bake any of those?" he asked with dread, gesturing at the dozens of pies for sale.

"Hell, no. I ain't no girl." Donny spit on the ground as a sign of his masculinity. "Listen. If you wanna get hooked up, meet me 'round six at the bleachers where all the big shows are put on. During the closing ceremony, we can get what we came here for and then split."

"Do you always buy from the same . . . contact?" James hoped that his choice of words sounded legitimate. When Donny's face clouded over with annoyance, he knew that he had misspoken.

"Contact?" The boy scowled hard. "What are you, like, a cop? Piss off, man." Donny clumped away.

Suddenly, the crowd's cheers swelled and James saw that R. C. was holding the victor's hand high into the air as he proclaimed a twig of a girl the winner of the pie-eating contest.

"*Where* did you put over eight pounds of pie?" R. C. inquired and then held his cordless microphone below her blue chin.

"I've been stretching my stomach over at the Golden Corral," the young woman announced. "I'm a hostess there."

"But you have no stomach!" R. C. declared.

"Well, two babies have grown in there already, so I know it can stretch," she answered with a charming smile. "And them kids'll sure appreciate this prize money and the gift certificate to the bakery, too. Easiest money I've ever made! I *love* pie!"

"Congratulations to all of our contestants! Don't forget to purchase your own scrumptious blueberry pie and don't leave before the drawing for a brand-new recreational vehicle, which will occur at this evening's closing ceremony!" R. C. called to the crowd. "Sponsored by Richter's RV Sales & Rentals!"

As R. C. continued with a few other announcements, James grabbed Lucy by the arm and pulled her to a semi-private area on the far side of the bakery van.

"I think I've got part of this puzzle figured out, Lucy." He dabbed at his sweating temples with a fresh napkin. "These kids came to Hog Fest specifically to buy the laced pot. They've gotten it here before and have come back for more. They buy as much as they can afford, and then I think *they* resell at least a part of it. In fact, I think this stuff may have gotten into *my* library through the hands of a rising high school senior named Martin Trotman, though I have no way to prove it."

Lucy digested this information. "And these kids think the deal's still on? Even though Jimmy's dead?"

James shook his head. "I don't know who their contact is. Maybe they don't realize that Jimmy's dead or that the Jimmy who died is their seller. Who knows? Maybe Jimmy didn't do the actual selling. You know, I could call the Fitzgerald twins and have them look up which festivals Jimmy and Mitch Walker attended at the same time. If they were partners in this nasty business, then a pattern should be there — something tangible you can show to the sheriff."

"Why me?" Lucy looked taken aback. "*You're* the one figuring this out, James."

He touched her arm. "Any credibility you can get will only help advance your career. If you assist in a drug bust in Hudsonville that has effects in our own county, then you'll be irreplaceable!"

Lucy leaned over and kissed James on the cheek. "You are the greatest guy, James." She patted him on the chest. "You always put other people before yourself. It just makes me want to wrap my arms around you in front of this whole crowd."

Filled with a confusing mixture of happiness and alarm, James was both relieved and disappointed when Gillian bounded over, trailing Deputy Harding in her wake.

"They've found Hailey! She spent some time alone, walking by the river. Like me, she ended up meeting Felicity and the two exchanged stories. Hailey begged for forgiveness for Jimmy's behavior and Felicity *freely* gave it to her! As a result of this *bonding,* Hailey decided to keep going with the competition. She rented her own RV and bought a cheap grill from Wal-Mart. I guess she wanted to enter the final contest with no distractions. If she wins, she still has a chance at being named champion — all on her own!"

"Oh, I hadn't realized that she'd won in other categories," James said.

"Yeah, man. *All* of the ones we weren't at," Bennett informed him.

"And what about Bob?" Lindy asked crossly. "He's been worried sick about her."

"Bob is with her, but Hailey's like a little frightened dove right now," Gillian said, her voice high and light. "She just needs to find a place to roost before she's ready to spread her wings again."

Bennett threw his hands into the air. "You're as loony as ever, woman! Still, I can see why Hailey might not be in a hurry to strap herself to another man. Shoot, her last one wasn't exactly the kind to bring home to mama."

"Deputy Harding tells me that Bob and Hailey are talking through the concerns Hailey feels about the future of their relationship," Gillian stated knowledgeably. "He wisely gave them some breathing room to do so. I'm *certain* that they're reconnecting right now and that Bob is willing to treat Hailey as his *equal*." She beamed at Harding. "I think that was *very* thoughtful of you, Deputy."

Harding looked uncomfortable. "Well, now we've got to redouble our efforts to track down Mr. Walker. And by 'we,' " he eyed the supper club members sternly, "I mean the sheriff's department."

James elbowed Lucy in the side. "Go on, tell him," he hissed.

"Tell me what?" Harding's eyes sharpened with interest.

"If you haven't found Mitch Walker by the closing ceremony," Lucy announced importantly, "I think you can expect him to show up there."

Fox Hall's Cheese Grits

6 cups water
1 1/2 cups quick-cooking grits
3/4 cup margarine or butter
1 pound extra-sharp cheddar cheese, grated
2 teaspoons seasoning salt
1 tablespoon Worcestershire sauce
1/2 teaspoon Tabasco sauce (more or less to taste)
2 teaspoons salt
3 eggs, well beaten
paprika for garnish (optional)

Preheat oven to 350 degrees. Lightly grease a 9 × 13-inch baking dish. In a medium saucepan, bring the water to a boil. Stir in the grits. Reduce heat to low. Cover and cook 5 to 6 minutes, stirring occasionally. Mix in the butter or margarine, cheese, seasoning salt, Worcestershire sauce, Tabasco sauce, and salt. Continue cooking for 5 minutes, or until the cheese is melted. Remove from heat, cool slightly, and fold in the eggs. Pour into the prepared baking dish. Bake 1 hour in the preheated oven, or until the top is lightly browned.

Seventeen:
Chilled
Watermelon Wedge

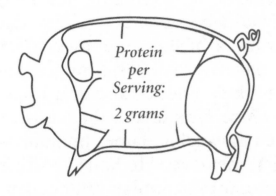

Protein per Serving:

2 grams

While Lucy conferred privately with Deputy Harding, James found a pleasant seat in the shade of a large maple tree and dialed the home number of the Fitzgerald twins. Francis and Scott lived in a garage that had been converted into an apartment by an entrepreneurial widow. At first, the arrangement had come with the stipulation that the boys would need to help old Mrs. Lamb with her yard work, but before long, the brothers had not only taken over the landscaping chores, but also chopped wood and completed all necessary repairs around her house. In return, she cooked them several bountiful dinners each week. Over time, they had become a makeshift family.

James glanced at his watch. It was a few minutes to two. The large midday meal typically served after church services would have been consumed and the dishes soaking in the sink, so it was highly possible that the twins would be outside — busy trimming Mrs. Lamb's bushes or mowing her lawn. James dialed, crossed his fingers, and listened as their phone rang and rang. When Scott's voice announced that he and Francis were unavailable, James hung up without leaving a message. He called information, got Mrs. Lamb's number, and called her.

"Hello?" an ancient, raspy voice answered. James could hear the whine of a motor in the background.

"Mrs. Lamb!" James shouted. "This is James Henry. I'm looking for Scott or Francis. It's kind of important."

"Who is this?" she croaked suspiciously.

"James Henry. I'm their boss — Scott and Francis's! At the library! It's important that I speak to one of them!" he shouted. "Are they there?"

"Henry? Oh, you're Jackson's boy. I

haven't seen that handsome devil in a mighty long time." She issued a licentious cackle. "Now stop hollerin' at me, child! I may be old as the hills, but I've still got two good ears attached to this white head!" She coughed. "Francis is on the mower, but Scott is just finishin' up with the weedin'. He'll be in directly for some tea."

There was a clunk as though Mrs. Lamb had set the receiver on a hard surface.

"Hello?" James called into empty space. He waited, listening to a series of rattles and clanks in the room where Mrs. Lamb had left the phone off the hook. After three full minutes, a door opened and closed and two voices began to speak. James was sure that the male voice belonged to Scott, but if so, why wasn't he picking up the phone?

"Scott!" James yelled into his cell phone. *"SCOTT!"*

"Hello?" Scott said in surprise.

James blew out his breath in annoyance. "Didn't Mrs. Lamb tell you I was on the phone?" he asked crossly.

"No, Professor. Sorry." He added with a whisper, "Her memory is a bit off these days."

"I'd say," James mumbled. "She called my father a handsome devil. Listen, Scott. I need a favor. I don't have access to a computer here, and I could use some long-distance help." James gave a brief account of Jimmy's death, the discovery of the laced marijuana, and his suspicions about Mitch Walker.

"You should write a book about all of the things that have happened to you since you moved back to Quincy's Gap!" Scott exclaimed. "You've *got* to lead the most exciting life of any librarian in this country!"

Naturally, Scott's words brought to mind Murphy's book deal. James struggled not to take his anger out on the boisterous young man. "Can you find out if Jimmy and Mitch have crossed paths at one of these festivals and call me right away with the info? It's kind of urgent."

"Sure, Professor. These lightning-fast fingers are at your disposal. Francis and I will get you what you need. Let me go boot up the laptop."

After Scott hung up, James leaned against the stout tree trunk and wondered what to do about Murphy. He felt so betrayed that she had written about him and his friends, and then sold the book without telling him what she was up to until the ink on the contract was good and dry. He thought of all of the evenings he had left her apartment so that she could write, and there she had been, adding colorful fabrications to characters and events based on his real life. And now her book was going to be printed, without him having read a word of its contents. How would she portray him? How would she describe him physically? Would she reveal to the world childhood stories or intimate details he had shared with her after making love?

Imagining segments of his life captured in Murphy's book for all to read and judge, James balled his hands into fists. With the rough bark pressing against his back, he sat as still as a stone, realizing that it had been a long time since he had felt such white-hot anger toward another person.

His cell phone, which was settled in a patch of scraggly grass growing between two tree roots, began to buzz. Because it was set on vibrate and it was resting on uneven ground, it looked like a black beetle as it wiggled and slid down the curve of one of the roots until James scooped it up.

"Professor?" Scott said. "Your theory is dead on. Mitch Walker and the Marrow Men have been at every single festival or cook-off event that Jimmy Lang and the Pitmasters have attended over the last three years. The only difference in their schedules is that the Pitmasters entered contests in three extra festivals this year. But together, they've been to . . ." He trailed off as he counted. "Fifteen events in total. There's no way that Mitch guy can claim not to know Jimmy."

"True. But he can claim to know nothing about the drugs." James ran his hands through his sweaty hair. "Time's running out, Scott. I've got to find a way to link these two together as drug traffickers or the sheriff down here won't have enough evidence to hold Mitch — that is, if they can even find him."

"I thought you said there might be a drug deal tonight."

"But that's a big maybe. The drugs have been seized and though the kids who want to buy some don't know that yet, Mitch certainly does. If he shows, it'll only be to tell the kids where to meet him in the future." James paused. "The next festival's in North Carolina in two weeks, so he might just tell them to come down there to complete the deal, but it's a pretty big chance to take."

Scott hesitated. "That does sound risky. *I* wouldn't take that chance."

"But he just lost a lot of money when the authorities discovered that stash of drugs. He might be desperate to make it up." James said, playing devil's advocate. "Also, I think Jimmy's been dealing solo this past year and may have cut Mitch out of his half of the earnings. Jimmy bought a big camper and seems to have hidden chunks of cash somewhere in that RV."

"But if Jimmy and Mitch were partners and Jimmy had the drugs in his cooker, what was Mitch's role?" Scott questioned. "How did he earn his share of the profits?"

James grew quiet, thinking. Then he sat up with a jerk, his tailbone digging into a sharp root. "What if Mitch's cooker is outfitted with a false chamber, too? Maybe *that's* why he's hiding! Maybe he still wants to sell his share and then get out of here. I'll have to ask the deputies if they checked out his grill."

"That's a thought, but I've got another wrench to throw at you, Professor." Scott had a smile in his voice.

"Great," James grunted. "What's that?"

"Well, if the pot's laced with formaldehyde, where's it coming from? You can't just buy that stuff at CVS."

James stared at the grass in front of him blankly. "I have no idea."

"Listen, Professor. Francis and I will Google this guy and see what we can dig up. But if you've only got a few hours left 'til everyone goes home, maybe you'd better find out as much as you can about this Mitch Walker."

"Thanks, Scott. I knew I could count on you guys to help."

"And Professor. Be careful. It sounds like this man has a lot to lose. You know what they say about cornered animals . . ."

"They're twice as dangerous." James nodded to himself and thanked the young man once again.

The rest of the supper club members found James beneath his tree a few minutes later, still deep in thought. He had a paper napkin on his leg and had written some notes on it using a pen he had borrowed from Mrs. Phelps. Lucy waited until he had finished writing, and then squatted in front of him, the sun highlighting her caramel-colored hair as it streamed through the canopy of emerald maple leaves.

"They're going to have one of the deputies from Russell County go undercover. He's barely twenty-two and if he wears some false tattoos, a baseball cap, and carries a skateboard, they're hoping he can get close enough to the other kids to see what happens at the closing ceremony."

"This is kind of scary *and* exciting!" Lindy

shivered with anticipation. "And here I thought we'd be spending the weekend leisurely strolling through Hog Fest and overeating."

"Well, we've got the overeating part down." Bennett patted his thick waist.

Gillian clasped her hands together. "Oh, I *do* hope these young people will get the help they need. Addiction just steals away *precious* spiritual energy and the body's ability to remain balanced!"

Bennett arched his eyebrows and then turned to James. "What are you doin' over here anyway?" He gestured at the napkin. "Writin' poetry?"

James pointed at the napkin. "Actually, I've been thinking about Mitch's cooker."

Lucy's eyes widened as she instantly caught on to James's line of thinking. "That *he* might have been transporting drugs, too?"

"Oh, that would be *terrible!*" Gillian screeched. "We need to stop those *tainted* drugs from getting into the hands of those caught between childhood and adulthood."

Bennett offered James a hand. "Get up, big boy. We've got to get over to the Marrow Men's cook site. And Lucy, if we find anything significant there, I'm gonna hog all the credit. If I don't get Sheriff Jones to agree to go out to dinner with me before we leave Hudsonville, then I won't be able to concentrate on a single danged trivia question ever again!"

"The credit's all yours, Bennett," Lucy replied. "But she's a pretty sharp lady. I bet she's had one of her deputies check the other cookers. If not, then you can call her yourself and announce your brilliant discovery."

Once again, the group set off for the cooking area of the festival grounds. James felt as though he had walked the same path a dozen times already and was looking forward to bidding farewell to the crowds, the sticky heat, and the ever-present smell of food.

As soon as the supper club members approached the Marrow Men's cluster of grills, they quickly became aware that it was going to be difficult to draw out information from the barbecue cooks.

Three men bustled around two large grills. Neither of the cookers were the commercial-sized grills that Jimmy possessed and the Marrow Men seemed to have reached a crucial moment in their preparation. James found it challenging to pay any attention to their equipment once he noticed that the pieces of meat the Marrow Men were placing on the grill racks came from a Ziploc bag inside a cooler. The chunks had a pink hue resembling lamb, but James didn't think he recognized the type of raw meat at all.

Apparently, Deputy Neely, who stood behind the shoulder of one of the Marrow Men, was also fascinated by the unidentified hunks of meat. He put his hands on his slim hips, bent over the grill, and casually asked, "So, none of y'all have seen Mitch all day?"

The man retrieving the meat from the cooler frowned. "Look, we told you already. We haven't seen Mitch and he didn't travel with his own grill. He always used ours. He told us that he had a boring office job pushing papers, and that's all he ever said about his work. We were grilling buddies, dude. That's it. We hung out a few times a year and tried to win some contests." He gestured at his companions. "We like beer, women, and meat. We don't talk about much else. That's the whole point of gettin' together — to have fun and forget about our lives for a little bit."

Neely scrutinized the remaining three Marrow Men as though weighing the truth of these words, but they met his gaze unblinkingly. After a few uncomfortable seconds, two of them resumed brushing sauce over the meat on the grill while the third forced pieces of the cubed meat onto bamboo skewers.

"Is that lamb or veal or somethin'?" Neely inquired, unable to quell his curiosity.

"It's goat," one of the men answered curtly and then noticed James and his friends staring. "You wanna ask us questions, too?"

James shook his head and Gillian took a few steps backward, obviously uninterested in getting a closer look at the Marrow Men's preparations. "Um," James stammered. "We just wanted to see what folks were cooking for the Anything Butt category. I can't say that I've ever had goat before. How are you going to prepare it?"

"Gotta use mesquite wood chips, for starters," the Marrow Man replied. "Then we season the meat with salt, pepper, and garlic. We're going to use a curry yogurt sauce to give it a bit of an Indian flavor. It's real good. Lots of folks turn their noses up at goat, but it's a real nice meat if you don't overcook it."

"Do you know if anyone else is cooking goat?" Lucy inquired as she eyed the Marrow Men's cooler.

"Don't think so," the man replied as he deftly turned the skewers. "One of the teams is usin' venison, and I think the Tenderizers are usin' scallops. The Adam's Ribbers are goin' with rabbit, and Jimmy's girl claims to be usin' coon, but I think that's just big talk to draw attention to her, just like her old man used to do."

James and his friends exchanged looks of disgust.

"Did Hailey and Mitch know each other?" James couldn't stop himself from asking.

"Not that I ever knew. Sure never saw 'em talk to each other. Now can ya'll give us some breathin' room?" The Marrow Man threw irritated looks at Neely and the supper club members. "We're tryin' to win a contest here."

"Absolutely. Sorry," Lindy answered. "And good luck to you and your team."

As they moved away from the fragrant smell of the roasting goat, Bennett said, "You're not gonna like me sayin' this, Gillian, but I'm feelin' peckish all of a sudden."

"Oh, Bennett." She rolled her eyes. "I cannot believe your appetite can be so *active* in this setting."

"Well, I need a snack and that's that," Bennett replied tersely. "It doesn't have to be meat, but nothin's gonna be open in town on a Sunday, so I think we're stuck with fair food."

"I can't take anything fried, stuck on a stick, or covered in powdered sugar!" Lucy declared.

"Hey! I saw a place by the community center that sold chilled watermelon wedges," Lindy suggested. "Since it's gotten so hot again today, it might be nice to have something naturally sweet."

Everyone agreed on a snack of watermelon slices, and Lindy led her friends through the milling crowds to a small stand with a red, white, and green-striped awning. After each of them paid for two thick slices of watermelon and collected a handful of napkins, the five friends decided to sit on the grass away from the throng of people.

"So, I guess the sheriff's department isn't exactly inept," James said and then bit off the tip of his first piece of watermelon.

"No one thought they were," Lucy replied defensively. "We just don't *know* what they've investigated, and they don't feel like sharing information with me anymore. I think the discovery of the drugs changed things. Now they've got a murder *and* illegal drug dealing going on, and the clock is really ticking for them."

"Have the Fitzgerald twins gotten back to you yet?" Bennett asked James.

"Oh!" James exclaimed, reaching for his phone. "I turned it off out of habit. They could have called and I wouldn't have known."

They all listened with watermelon slices held in the air as James's phone chirped into life. The black text appearing on the silvery screen indicated that he had one new message waiting. James set the complicated phone to its speaker option, placed it on the ground, and waved at his friends to scoot closer.

"You figured out how to get that on speaker mode?" Gillian was impressed. "I'm lucky if I can answer a call with mine. These machines are *so* complex."

"Don't credit me," James answered. "The twins showed me how to use all the features I thought I'd need. I'm hopeless with most technical gadgets. Here we go." He pressed several buttons and Francis's energetic voice emitted from the phone.

"Professor? Scott and I think we discovered something that you might find pretty interesting. We did a Google search on Mitch Walker from San Antonio, Texas. There were a couple of them, but we were able to narrow them down by cross-referencing the info we learned about Mitch by visiting a bunch of barbecue festival websites. Still, there's not much on cyberspace about this guy. It's not like he's got his own website or anything."

There was a pause, and James rolled his eyes and said, "Those two have a flair for the dramatic."

Francis finally continued. "We think Jimmy was partnered with Mitch Walker in regards to the laced marijuana. See, Mitch works for Sunset Gardens in San Antonio. That's a mortuary, Professor. Mitch was listed on their website's staff page as an assistant mortician. You see what that means, Professor? If Mitch works at a funeral home, then he's got access to formaldehyde."

"Bingo! You've got your bad guy number two!" Scott shouted with exuberance as he grabbed the phone from his brother. "Now all you've got to do is figure out where they bought the pot. Unless Jimmy had a giant greenhouse or a big piece of land, they bought it somewhere cheap, like Mexico."

"How do you know Mexico has cheap pot?" Francis demanded in the background and Scott answered his brother, completely forgetting that he was leaving a message on his boss's phone. "I researched it, bro. I went to a bunch of government sites and checked out filed newspaper stories and recent DEA busts . . . oh, sorry, Professor.

That's all we've got on Mitch. Call us if you need more info. We're ready and waiting to —" At that point, the time allotment given for individual messages on James's phone expired and Scott was cut off.

James closed his phone and held it in his palm.

"I think Mitch is Jimmy's partner *and* his killer," Lucy declared. "James, when you saw the two of them arguing that first night it must have been over the drugs."

"I agree," James said. "Jimmy has gone to several festivals without Mitch this year. He was able to buy that big RV and squirrel some extra cash away. I think he's been stiffing Mitch and Mitch decided to get his revenge by poisoning Jimmy with the propane. Then, he planned to take all of the drugs for himself, but we interrupted him."

"And if there's cash *inside* the camper, he couldn't search for it the night he killed Jimmy because Gillian was sitting on the camper steps. Gillian, your being there also kept Mitch from getting into the cooker," Lucy stated. "And who else but a partner in crime would know the drugs were hidden in that secret compartment?"

"Well, if the drugs *did* come from Mexico," Lindy began and then paused to delicately remove a black seed from the tip of her tongue, "that's probably where Mitch is by now."

Gillian closed her eyes and shook her head. "No, he's close. I *truly* sense that he didn't leave. I think he's too angry."

"But that's crazy, woman!" Bennett practically dropped his slice. "The law from two counties is after that pasty-skinned fool. Why would he still be here?"

"He's got too much to lose," Lucy answered, her eyes distant. "I've got a strong hunch that Gillian's right, though I'm not sure what his plan is."

"But the drugs have been seized," James mused aloud. "So what does he stand to gain by taking this huge risk?" He rubbed his finger on the smooth, green rind in his hand. "I doubt he'd risk prison just to tell a bunch of kids to meet him in North Carolina in a few weeks."

"For a hundred bucks an ounce, he just might," Bennett said.

The group fell silent. They finished eating their watermelon and tried to clean their sticky hands with their napkins, but bits of paper clung stubbornly to their fingertips. Lindy sifted through her bag and came out with a package of wet wipes.

Accepting a towelette, Bennett grinned. "I guess there's somethin' to be said for overpacking."

"It's called being prepared," Lindy snapped and then puffed out her cheeks. "Sorry, I didn't mean to bite your head off. It's just that I don't like the way things are ending up. We've always stumbled upon the answers in time, but I'm worried that the bad guy is going to get away. We only have a few hours left."

Lucy stood, collected all the garbage, and walked off to a nearby trash can. When she returned, she didn't sit back down. Instead, she paced around her circle of friends as though engaged in a game of duck, duck, goose. "We need more evidence linking Jimmy and Mitch to the drugs." She stopped and looked at James. "Do you think there's anything to the Fitzgeralds' idea about Mexico? I mean, San Antonio isn't that far from there."

James shrugged. "Those boys are pretty smart, but even if the pot came from south of the border, we can't ask Hailey if Jimmy liked to take international road trips. She's in the middle of the Anything Butt judging."

"I doubt Big Jimmy would have told her anyway," Bennett added. "She seemed to be in the dark about his sideline business."

"Wait a minute!" James slapped himself in

the forehead. "Murphy left me a bunch of papers and one of them had the name and home phone number of Jimmy's boss. Maybe he could tell us more about what Jimmy did with his free time."

"Why would this guy bother telling you anything?" Lindy was dubious.

James put his hand out and patted the ground next to him. Perplexed, Lucy sat down. "Because. He thinks he's going to be in Murphy's next book and if I pretend to be her assistant, he'll tell me anything I want to know."

"She's writing books?" Gillian seemed impressed. "What kind of books?"

James looked at Bennett in appeal. His friend held out his hands and said, "It's all you, man. Better get it over with."

"Um. She's written a thriller. Or maybe two, I don't know." He shifted nervously. "The thing is that they're loosely based on, um, they're about . . ." He trailed off, his mouth going dry. He swallowed hard and spluttered, "Murphy's books are based on us."

James wanted to call Jimmy's boss immediately, but his phone battery had run low and the reception on Lucy's was less than ideal. Therefore, James asked the receptionist at the community center for the use of an office and permission to make a long-distance phone call. After getting the okay from R. C. via walkie-talkie, the woman showed them into a small office and told them to make themselves comfortable.

As James settled onto the swivel chair behind the tidy wooden desk, he noticed that only Bennett would make eye contact with him. All three of his female friends were still grappling with the news that their lives were about to become works of fiction. So far, their initial reaction seemed to be that of mistrust. This was unsurprising, as Murphy hadn't always painted them in the rosiest of colors in her past articles.

James dialed the Texas number, and when a man with a deep, raspy voice answered the phone, he asked, "Is this Mr. Leggett?"

"Depends who's callin'," the man replied.

"I'm Murphy Alistair's assistant. I'm calling because Ms. Alistair requires a bit more information for the exciting new book she's writing. I apologize for phoning you at home and on a Sunday, but the chapter she's writing about Jimmy Lang . . . and you, of course, is *very* important," he added hastily and tried to ignore the fact that the looks he was currently receiving from his friends contained enough acid to burn holes right through his body.

"Well, sure thang. Anything to help that nice writer lady."

James set the phone to speaker mode.

"I'm going to put you on speaker, Mr. Leggett. That way I can take notes for Ms. Alistair," James lied glibly. "What we're trying to figure out today is what Jimmy liked to do in his free time. For example, we'd like to know who his friends were. Do you happen to recall Jimmy having a friend in San Antonio?"

"Yep. Some fella he met at a bar-b-cue fair a few years back." Mr. Leggett gave a dry laugh. "At first I thought Jimmy was sweet on some gal down in San Anton', 'cause he drove there quite a bit, but then he told me he was startin' a side business with some fella there. Don't know what they was up to, but Jimmy must've been doin' just fine with it. He bought that big ole trailer with the money he made. Shoot, that camper thang's so big my whole family could fit in there, and there's nine of us Leggetts."

"How do you know that Jimmy's new business paid for that? Hailey believes Jimmy's aunt left him an inheritance."

"Pffah!" Mr. Leggett guffawed. "What aunt? Jimmy's been a ward of the state since he first opened his eyes. He ain't got no family, and none of his foster families would go leavin' him a pile of money. They ain't got none themselves."

"I guess he could have taken out a loan," James persisted, hoping to glean more information from Jimmy's boss.

His ploy worked. "Look, I *know* the fella that sold Jimmy his camper. He said Jimmy walked in with a grocery sack full of greenbacks and drove that camper off the lot an hour later, neat as you please. Jimmy told *me* that he wasn't gonna work for me no more after his trip to Virginia, so it's a good thang I took him on his word and put an ad in the paper. I got me a new boy startin' Monday. Can drive the tow truck and help me with these confounded computers. Not a bad deal."

James felt a momentary pang of sympathy for Jimmy Lang. He had no family to speak of, his girlfriend had a new man, and his boss had a replacement driver ready and waiting to take over Jimmy's job.

Would anyone even miss Jimmy? To be so easily forgotten except by those trying to solve the mystery of one's murder doesn't make a pleasant epitaph, James thought morosely.

"You still there?" Mr. Leggett asked anxiously from Waxahachie, Texas.

"Yes, sir. I was just gathering my thoughts." James glanced briefly at Lucy, but she was intently studying her fingernails and frowning in concentration. Finally, she looked up and whispered, "Mexico."

"Ah, back to Jimmy's hobbies and such, did he travel anywhere besides to cook-offs?" James asked in a businesslike tone. "How about out of the country?"

"If you count Mexico as bein' another country, then yeah," Jimmy's boss answered immediately. "Sometimes you can't tell the difference between Texas and Mexico, but Jimmy went there. Always brought me a bottle of Patrón tequila, too. I'm gonna miss those freebies."

"Did he happen to drive his cooker down with him?" James asked timidly, knowing what an odd question it was.

"Funny thing, that, but he did. I figured ole Jimmy was givin' those Mexicans a few lessons in exchange for booze or other kinds of favors." Mr. Leggett chuckled.

"He liked tequila that much?" James shared in the joke.

"Jimmy liked to drink everything, eat everything, smoke everything, and talk to every cute girl he saw. And he talked big. Shoot, he lived *big*. That's why he and Texas made such a purty pair."

James asked, "And Hailey? Did she live big, too?"

"Nah. She's a churchgoer and Jimmy's little shadow. Ain't got nothin' going on of her own, that girl. She's gonna be lost without Big Jim," Mr. Leggett stated confidently.

Noting the frowns on Lindy's and Lucy's faces, James replied, "Oh, I wouldn't be too sure about that, Mr. Leggett. I've got to type up these notes now, so thank you for your time."

"Hey!" Jimmy's boss quickly shouted, before James could hang up. "You think this book's gonna be in Wal-Mart?"

James shook his head and took the phone off speaker mode. "I don't know, sir, but I'm sure Ms. Alistair will mail you an autographed copy or two."

"Hot dog! I'm gonna be famous!" Mr. Leggett hollered in farewell.

James replaced the receiver and remained silent. Mr. Leggett's reaction to Murphy's publishing success was quite the opposite of James's friends.

"Well, you might not have been lying to the poor man, James," Lucy said acidly. "Murphy may be busy as a little beaver gathering material for a book on the Hog Fest murder."

Gillian touched Lucy's hand. "Let's cleanse our minds of this subject and place our focus on a woman who may need our help. Think of Hailey now."

Lindy nodded. "You're right, Gillian. Sorry to sound like Dr. Seuss, but if she found Jimmy's stash of cash, Mitch may go after her."

"She's not going to miss the announcement of the Hog Fest Barbecue Champion," Bennett chimed in. "So she's bound to be at the closing ceremony."

James checked his watch. "We've got two hours until then. Let's track her down and stay by her side. That way, nothing can happen to her."

In full agreement, the group trotted off to the camper Hailey had rented from R. C. The door was ajar, so James pulled it all the way open and called out Hailey's name. After stepping inside, he immediately backed out and turned to face his friends.

"I'm having some serious déjà vu. Hailey's camper has been trashed." He jerked his head toward the door. "Gillian, I'm afraid you were right. Mitch Walker is still here and he's really pissed off."

EIGHTEEN:
COLD GREEN TEA

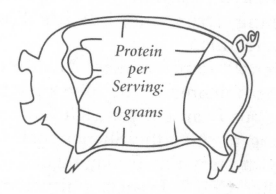

Protein per Serving:

0 grams

As the rest of the supper club members debated over whether to contact the sheriff regarding the state of Hailey's trailer, James decided to place another call to the Fitzgerald brothers. He had plugged his phone into a wall outlet while at the community center and, while it was nowhere near fully charged, he believed he had enough juice for a short call. This time, he dialed the twins in their apartment instead of using Mrs. Lamb's home number.

Francis answered immediately. "Do you need us to do more computer forensics, Professor?" he asked James eagerly.

"Not exactly. I just wanted to know the full name of the ringleader of that teen group coming to our library on Fridays. I know his first name's Martin, but I wanted to double-check the last name."

Francis murmured something to Scott. "Just wanted to ask Scott before I told you something erroneous, but it's Trotman. Martin Trotman."

"Gotcha!" James smiled. "I don't know what the outcome of the Hog Fest mystery will be, but I can tell you right now that we are going to solve the Shenandoah County Library mystery this Friday night."

"Really? Cool." Francis whispered something to Scott. "In that case, can we let Mrs. Waxman have the night off? Scott and I want to be there when this all goes down."

"Absolutely, boys. I can't think of anyone I'd rather have by my side when we put a stop to their little business."

"Are you going to tell us what it is?" Francis was breathless with curiosity.

"When I get back," James answered. "I'm not trying to hold out, but catching them in the act is going to take some planning, and I don't want to go into it until we can meet to discuss strategy. However, I was wondering if you guys have one of those little cameras that you can mount in some unobtrusive location and watch the feed on a computer screen?"

"We do, actually. We tried to talk Mrs. Lamb into letting us set up a security system for her, but she said if anyone breaks in she'll crack them on the head with her iron, so we just use the camera as a web cam now. It's a piece of cake to hook up."

"Bring all that stuff to work tomorrow, will you? I've got a special assignment for you and Scott. Technical stuff."

"Awesome! Sounds like a Special Ops mission. You can count on us, Professor!"

James gazed at the blinking symbol indicating his phone's dwindling battery life and stuffed the soon-to-be-useless gadget into his pocket. It would have to remain in its dormant state until he hooked it up to the car charger in the Bronco. As James watched his friends talk, he couldn't help but notice the bulges in both Bennett's back pockets, and assumed his friend was carrying his wallet and his minirecorder.

"I'm not even gonna ask why you're checkin' out my behind," Bennett said. He jerked his thumb toward Hailey's camper. "We're off to visit Bob Barker — see if he and his fiancée are killin' time before the announcement of the Hog Fest champion. If she's not with him, I'm gonna place a personal call to that fine, fine Sheriff Jones."

Bob Barker's camper was only minutes away. The contractor was inside fussing over his graying hair and had the door propped open. Singing along with Sinatra, Bob met the supper club members at the door with a smile. With one hand still slimed with hair gel, he took a final swipe over his hair, slicking the strands into place on the sides and forcing the front into stiff, upright rows.

"Almost time to hear who's the champ of 'cue." Bob grinned as he shaped his hair. "Doesn't matter to me, though. I've got my Hailey and she's the *real* prize. If you folks are lookin' for her, she's primpin' for the closing ceremony. Did y'all know she won the Anything Butt category? She's got a shot at winnin' the whole shebang!"

"She won? With barbecued raccoon?" Lindy asked in repulsed shock.

Bob laughed. "Oh, the rumors that go around during cook-offs! You must've been talkin' to one of those Marrow Men. They've been steamed up that a woman might steal that Heartland Foods contract from them since they found out Hailey was the real talent behind the Pitmasters."

Noting the look of pride on Bob's face, James assumed that he and Hailey had reached an understanding over establishing equality in their relationship. "What was her entry?" he asked.

"Believe it or not," Bob answered while rinsing his hand in the small sink behind him, "she made barbecued Spam. Some of the other competitors argued that it was an illegal entry, but Mr. Richter said it was a-okay for the Anything Butt category." He dried his hands on a checkered dishcloth and then folded it neatly and placed it on the tiny countertop. "We came in second with my salmon specialty. Don't know what those Marrow Men were thinkin' makin' goat with yogurt sauce. Came out way too runny."

Lucy stepped forward and touched Bob briefly on the shoulder. "Are you sure Hailey's back at her camper? The new one she rented?"

Bob nodded. "The rented one, yeah. She'd never go back into the old one. She said she took what she needed from inside and gave the cops the keys. It's all locked up. No one can get in except for them. Why are you asking anyhow?"

"We just came from Hailey's RV and she's not there," Lucy began to explain when Gillian interjected.

"Someone has been in her camper, obviously looking for something." Gillian reached forward, pushing Lucy out of the way, and grasped Bob's shoulders. "Now, focus on my face, Bob, and take a deep breath in. Right now. Deep breath in. With me. Her camper's been ransacked, Bob, and there's no sign of Hailey."

Stunned, Bob did as Gillian instructed, but then he shook her off and began pacing up and down the narrow aisle of the camper. "Not again! Look, will someone tell me what is going on here? If you're not Jimmy's killer," he pointed at Gillian, "and I'm not and Hailey's not, then is it Mitch? Over the drugs in Jimmy's grill? And is he now after my girl?" He stopped pacing, his face tight with anger. "Tell me! Has he got her? She could be out there, needin' me, and I don't know where! Someone tell me what the *hell* is happenin'!"

"Mr. Barker, Hailey may be in danger," Lucy answered in a calm, flat voice. "She might be in possession of money that Mitch Walker believes belongs to him. Mitch was Jimmy's partner in this drug business, but it appears that Jimmy may have kept more than his share of the profits."

"There's a motive for murder — wrapped

up all nice and pretty!" Lindy added with dramatic flair.

"Well, I've got to find her!" Bob tried to elbow James and Bennett aside. "He can have the cash! He can have whatever he wants as long as my Hailey doesn't get hurt!"

Gillian grabbed Bob's arm. "Wait! We must pause and *concentrate* on where she could be. There is too much ground to cover to just run off in all directions. Please, let's all sit for a moment and *think*."

Bob cracked his knuckles one by one in agitation, but followed Gillian's advice.

"First things first," Lucy stated in her deputy voice as she squeezed onto the sofa in between James and Bennett. "Bennett, you need to call the sheriff and go wait for her at Hailey's rented RV." She checked her watch. "One of us needs to be at the closing ceremony, in case Mitch shows up there. We know which kids to keep an eye on, even better than the deputies do. Now, I know there will plenty of police presence there, but anything can happen."

"I'll go," Lindy volunteered. "No one can read a high schooler like I can."

"Why do you think Mitch will be at the ceremony?" Bob looked confused. "Isn't everybody huntin' him?"

"Yes," James nodded, "but he may try to pass a brief message on to some of his buyers."

"Okay, you guys get going." Lucy continued to command her troops. She pushed her cell phone into Bennett's hand and he and Lindy left Bob's camper. With Bennett gone, James was able to spread out by a few inches on the scratchy sofa.

Gillian, who had settled herself in the camper's passenger seat, began to hum quietly. Bob, James, and Lucy exchanged perplexed glances.

"What's that loopy lady doin'?" Bob demanded. "We should get moving!"

Lucy held up a finger. "Just give her a minute. Sometimes she comes up with the craziest ideas that end up making perfect sense."

They were quiet for several seconds, listening to the rhythmic sounds of Gillian's humming, which seemed to have mutated into some kind of musical chant. Suddenly, she opened her eyes and swiveled around in the seat. "The Spam!"

"What?" the other three said in unison.

"Felicity had some in her tent. She said it's a convenient way for her to get protein when she's on the road." Gillian rose from her seat. "She told me she knows a dozen different ways of cooking it, and one is more delicious than the next! Don't you see?" Her face was aglow with excitement. "Hailey was with Felicity only yesterday. Remember? She and Felicity talked and then Hailey went out to rent her own RV from R. C.'s company. Felicity must have told Hailey how to barbecue Spam!"

"So you think Hailey's seeking refuge with Felicity right now?" James asked.

"Yes." Gillian closed her eyes again. "Felicity has such a kind soul, such an open and *nurturing* spirit — someone like Hailey would be absolutely *drawn* to Felicity, especially when looking for a safe harbor."

"Lead the way, Gillian," Lucy said. "I think you're onto something."

James thought of the agility with which Mitch Walker had handled the welding torch. "Ah, shouldn't we take a weapon of some sort?"

Lucy shrugged. "The method Mitch used to kill Jimmy was pretty cowardly, so I don't think he's packing a gun. Besides, there are four of us. I think we can take him, James."

Feeling a tad emasculated by Lucy's confidence, James was relieved and grateful to note that Bob had armed himself with a grilling fork. "It's real sharp," he whispered to James as they jumped out of the camper and turned toward the river.

By the time they reached Felicity's tent, announcements were being made through loudspeakers in the distance that the moment had arrived for the public to make their way to their seats in order to enjoy the final event of Hog Fest. The closing ceremony was set to begin in thirty minutes.

Felicity's tent was empty but, unlike Hailey's camper, it was completely tidy. In fact, it looked as though Felicity had packed most of her belongings and stowed them in her old Suburban in preparation to leave. All four of her dogs were locked in their cages and were barking with such animation that Lucy gave them her full attention.

"These guys aren't just greeting us," she said seriously, "I think they're upset." She squatted down next to the pen bearing Vicar's name and tried to calm him, but he would not cease his frantic barking.

"Is something wrong, Vicar?" Lucy asked the collie while Bob rolled his eyes in disbelief. "Where's your mama?" At the word *mama,* Vicar's barking became frenzied and he repeatedly pawed at the door to his cage. Lucy ducked inside Felicity's tent and re-emerged with a gauzy lavender scarf she had seen wrapped around Felicity's waist the first time they had noticed her as she passed by Jimmy at his cooker. Forcing the scarf through the bars of the cage, Lucy pressed it against Vicar's nose.

"Show me Mama!" she commanded and then began to undo the cage lock.

"What are you doing?" Bob asked in alarm.

Ignoring him, Lucy swung back the door and repeated "Show me Mama!" in a stern and commanding voice.

Vicar seemed to understand completely, for though he immediately dashed from his cage and darted into the nearby woods, he reappeared again a few seconds later, tail wagging, tongue lolling, and eyes wild as he waited for the slow humans to catch up to him.

"He's probably on the scent of some possum," Bob remarked caustically. "We're wastin' time!"

"Then go your own way! I'm following Vicar!" Lucy snapped as she raced after the dog.

Gillian pushed James in the back. "Go after her! I'm going to get some help. I sense a *threatening* presence in those woods."

James nodded and took off after Lucy and Vicar, but quickly found it a challenge to keep up with the pair. Even Bob, who seemed to be in better shape than James, dropped behind as he tried to decide whether to continue following Lucy and Vicar or search elsewhere on his own. Darting a glance over his shoulder, as though uncertain whether Hailey was back in the more populated areas or somewhere in the shadowy woods before him, Bob plunged ahead of James, shouting at Lucy to wait.

The blood in James's body pumped rapidly as he trotted around narrow Loblolly pines and ducked under dead tree limbs and thin, whiplike branches. Needles and twigs crunched beneath his feet, which grew heavier as the pursuit progressed. Soon, the two humans and the tireless dog were completely gone from view.

Defeated by their stamina and speed, James leaned against an ancient oak and struggled to bring the beating of his swollen heart under control. He bent over at the waist, panting much like one of Felicity's canines, and tried to listen for Vicar's bark, but he could hear nothing over the clamor of his own breathing.

James tried not to think about how much he would like a drink of water, but they had veered away from the stream several minutes ago, and he got the sense they had traveled at least a mile away from the outskirts of the campground. There was no one around, and he had no idea where he was.

Plodding forward again, James thought he heard the sound of barking along with a woman's shout. He picked up his pace as best he could, but the underbrush had grown noticeably denser, and his face and bare arms were already criss-crossed with dozens of narrow, red slashes.

Here, deeper in the forest, the pines had woven their needles so tightly together that they had effectively blocked out most of the late afternoon sun. James felt as though night were descending, that time was playing tricks with him as he barreled ahead into an even thicker copse of trees. Picking his way over a fallen trunk, marred with a wide, black scar that only lightning could have produced, James distinctly heard a woman's cry coming from another group of trees off to his left.

Within seconds, he was able to see several figures grouped together in a small clearing. He slowed his approach, sensing that stealth might be more effective than charging into the midst of a potentially volatile situation.

Peering around the stringy trunk of a pine, James was first able to catch a glimpse of Hailey and Felicity. The two women had been forced to a sitting position with their backs pressed against a tree. Someone had used duct tape to wrap their torsos so that they were not only attached to the tree, but to one another. The tape also covered the mouths of both seated figures, and the filtered sunlight created little flashes of silver each time one of the women moved her head.

"Is that the same tape you used to cover up Jimmy's vents?" Lucy's voice shook with anger.

"I just meant to teach him a lesson," Mitch Walker replied in a slightly nasal tone. "For screwing me over. But no one's going to miss that fat bastard. I don't see why you're poking your nose into this mess anyway. It's none of your concern."

"Forget about me. *You've* got bigger problems than me. After all, you're going to have a tough time running your 'business' alone. How are you going to get the pot from Mexico now?" Lucy persisted, and James wondered if she was stalling in hopes of receiving help from an unexpected source. Was she waiting for him to come to the rescue? Daring to take in the full scene, James moved his entire face from the shelter of the tree. He saw Bob and Lucy standing side by side, their bodies rigid with anxiety. Mitch stood between his two captives and the pair of intruders. James was dismayed to see the glint of metal in Mitch's right hand. He held on to a large carving knife, the kind used in horror films. In those movies, the blade was always slick with blood, but so far, Mitch's was shiny and clean.

James exhaled in relief and then noticed Vicar's limp body splayed on the ground. Fighting back the impulse to yell out his rage over the condition of Felicity's loyal companion, James tore his eyes away from the inert animal.

The sound of Mitch's high laughter startled James and caused him to duck behind the trunk again. "*I* was the one with the contacts in Mexico, and now that I have my little nest egg back," he pointed his knife at Hailey, "thanks to *her,* I can get out of here. And I'd like to do that right now, so get yourselves down by that tree and sit like Hailey and her doggie friend and no one will get hurt."

"You're not going to be able to run, Mitch," Lucy said without budging. "The sheriff knows everything — about the drugs, Jimmy's murder, the extra cash. If you didn't mean to kill Jimmy, then you'll face a reduced sentence. But if you hurt someone else, it's gonna mean a whole lot of prison time for you, Mitch, and I don't think you'll fare so well in prison. You're too skinny to fend off the bigger guys."

"Shut up!" Mitch shouted. "And get down against that tree! If I've gotta tell you again, I'm going to put my blade into this dog's neck! Got it?"

Felicity issued a muffled yelp and writhed against her tree. James took the chance to begin an agonizingly slow tread toward the place where Mitch planned to secure Lucy and Bob with a fresh roll of duct tape.

"How much cash did you get, Mitch?" Lucy taunted him even as she obeyed his directions and slid to the ground, her back against the scratchy surface of a pine trunk. "A few thousand?"

Mitch gestured at the pink knapsack near his feet. "About ten grand. That's enough to buy me a new identity, which is all I need to get back in business. Unlike Jimmy, I didn't spend all my profits on some fancy camper. I've got money stashed in a safe place. I just need to collect it and then I'm gonna be just fine."

"Why did you partner with Jimmy at all?" Lucy demanded as Mitch dragged Vicar by his collar to where Lucy and Bob were seated, the knife poised over his furry neck. "If you had the connections in Mexico and the formaldehyde, why did you even need him?"

"You met Jimmy," Mitch answered emotionlessly and put the knife between his legs so he could pry up the edge of the duct tape. "He had a way with people. Knew how to talk to them. He could sell our stuff for top dollar to all kinds of folks, though it was mostly kids who bought it." Mitch snorted and James halted two trees away, afraid that the sounds of his footfalls would be heard if he got any closer. It was already miraculous that he had been able to get this close, and he knew that the thick layer of pine needles had been his saving grace.

"Me? I'm not a big talker," Mitch continued and James heard the sound of tape ripping. "But to keep the money rollin' in, I'll learn to be one." He edged closer to Lucy and, despite the risk of being seen, James peered around the trunk in order to figure out when to make his move. He knew that he had to distract Mitch before Lucy and Bob were rendered immobile, or all would be lost.

"One last question," Lucy began, but Mitch shook his head.

"No more questions. I've had just about enough blabbing from you, girlie." He slapped a strip of tape over Lucy's mouth with one hand while keeping the point of the knife pressed against her neck. He smiled in satisfaction, but his smile disappeared as Bob shifted his weight on the other side of the tree.

"Don't be a hero, Bobby," Mitch growled as he prepared a strip for Bob's mouth. "You move an inch and I will sink this into her jugular." He pressed the knife against Lucy's skin. Lucy issued an involuntary whimper and Bob froze. "All you've gotta do is be still and then I'll be gone," Mitch snarled. "It that so hard to understand?"

Mitch pushed a piece of tape over Bob's mouth and then, holding the knife close to Lucy's throat again, stuck the end of the tape on her chest and prepared to wind it around her body until he reached Bob's chest. James waited. He could feel the pulse at his neck thumping in a fear-induced frenzy as every one of his muscles tensed in preparation to leap forward. He had to time his move perfectly or Lucy could get hurt.

It was necessary for Mitch to remove the knife blade from Lucy's neck and move it to Bob's as he wound the tape across Bob's torso. James allowed Mitch to complete his half circle around Bob's body, but as he passed behind the tree and the knife was held momentarily in the air, suspended for a second until it would return to its threatening position near Lucy's throat, James took action.

He burst from behind his cover and took two giant strides, crackling leaves and sticks beneath his feet. Mitch hesitated and began to turn toward the sound. His eyes met James's and he began to raise the knife against this latest threat. Ignoring the blade, James leapt forward, his arms outstretched, prepared to knock into Mitch's left side, thus avoiding the knife and pushing the other man off balance. But Mitch was too quick and had foreseen James's plan. Pivoting his body in order to avoid the full force of his opponent's weight, Mitch lifted the knife arm higher, so that he would be poised to strike at his attacker once James was in range.

Time seemed to stop. The small handful of seconds it took for the two men to react to one another was enough of a window for Bob to reach behind his right hip and grasp the handle of the meat fork. Tucked into his shorts, the weapon had been hidden from view and Bob had only withdrawn the tool from beneath his waistband before seating himself against the tree trunk.

With an upward thrust of his muscular arm, Bob plunged the twin twines into Mitch's right side. Mitch's shoulder instantly crumpled. He dropped the carving knife at the same moment James collided with his left side. Both men grunted and fell.

James rolled on his hip and quickly got to his feet, bracing for retaliation, but Mitch was still struggling to raise himself to his knees. Doubled over, he held the wooden handle of the fork embedded in the flesh between two ribs and stared at the bruised and bloodied tissue surrounding the area where the fork tines had disappeared into his side.

"Don't pull it out," James whispered urgently. "You'll bleed more."

Mitch didn't respond, but his hands slid down his stomach and flopped like dead weights onto the ground. He leaned toward his left side and began to cough. He seemed surprised that his spittle was red. Mitch stared fixedly at the spattered leaves and pine needles as a thin line of blood trickled down his chin and stained the collar of his shirt.

As Mitch fought for breath, Bob ripped the tape from his mouth, grabbed the carving knife, and raced to free Hailey and Felicity. Lucy came to James's side.

"Are you hurt?" She put her hands on his face, searching his eyes.

"No," James answered quickly. "Are you okay?"

"Yes," she whispered, darting a glance at Mitch. "We have to get help."

Nodding, James pulled off his shirt, wadded it into a loose circle, and pressed it around the fork in Mitch's side. "He's having trouble breathing. I'll stay with him. You guys go."

James heard Felicity wail as she knelt over Vicar's prone form. "My baby!" she cried.

"He's all right," Lucy assured her loudly. "Mitch punched him and knocked him out, but he's going to be fine. I promise!" She stood. "I gave my cell phone to Bennett. You guys have got to get back to the festival and get help." Lucy pointed at Felicity. "Call the sheriff first, and then ask for paramedics. The county will have someone on call to help Vicar, too. Hurry!" she shouted firmly. "Go! Follow the river and go!"

"I know the way back," Felicity stated, brushing dirt from her skirt. She cast a miserable glance at Vicar. "I'll send help."

"You aren't coming?" Bob asked as he stooped to retrieve Hailey's pink knapsack. Hailey held onto his free arm and buried her face in his shoulder, weeping silently.

"No. Now hurry!" Lucy turned away from

the foursome as they began to briskly walk back in the direction they had come. Bob spoke gently and coaxingly to Hailey, urging her forward and promising her that all her troubles were over, until James and Lucy could no longer hear them.

"I could have handled this alone," James scolded Lucy as he listened to Mitch's raspy breathing.

Lucy smiled. "I have no doubt about that. The way you shot out from behind that tree . . ." She inclined her head toward the pine. "You looked so fierce! I knew, no matter what happened, you were out there and you weren't going to let anything bad happen to those innocent people."

"Or to you," James whispered softly, but Lucy heard him.

They sat in silence, alternating between watching Mitch and looking at one another. A dozen thoughts competed in James's head, and he longed to sort out what he wanted to say, but he didn't know where to begin.

Lucy touched his hand. "I miss you, James," she said. "I miss 'us.'"

That's exactly what I feel, James thought, but before he could speak a single word of agreement, explain how betrayed he felt by Murphy's book, or confess how skittish he felt about trusting his heart again, Deputy Harding appeared behind Lucy.

Without speaking to James or Lucy, he turned back to Gillian and grinned. "Thank you, Ms. O'Malley. Your instincts have been as sharp as a spear. Now, it's best you walk back to that fallen tree trunk. There's no need for you to view this scene, ma'am."

As soon as Gillian moved off, Harding turned back to Mitch. The deputy's grin evaporated like morning mist and he didn't bother with courtesies. Giving James a stern look that garnered no argument, Harding knelt beside Mitch. "If you'd step away, Mr. Henry and Ms. Hanover, I believe we've got it from here."

Lucy began to splutter in such loud indignation that James feared he'd have to replace her duct tape before she said anything she'd regret. However, Harding was too busy barking codes into his radio to pay her any mind.

"Is he dead?" Gillian asked with trepidation from her seat on the stump.

"Mitch? Not yet," Lucy answered. "Sounds like he's got a busted lung. Guess it's up to the medical folks now."

Handing each of her friends a glass bottle of chilled green tea from her hemp purse, Gillian sighed. "I'm glad he has a chance to live. There's been enough death at this festival. Memories of it and the real thing. I'd rather focus on life."

James and Lucy joined her on the fallen tree and drank deeply from their tea bottles. The friends grew reflective over the ups and downs of their long weekend in Hudsonville.

"I am very proud to be your friend," Gillian said, breaking the silence. Her eyes shone with tears. "You saved the day."

"It was mostly Bob's doing, to be honest," James stated and then listened as Harding received a burst of information over his radio. "Without really thinking things through, we just worked together to help one another."

Gillian sighed in contentment. "*That* is *exactly* how we should live *every* moment of our lives. Perhaps I was meant to come to this event in order to remember that lesson." She smiled as Harding came toward her, and she wiped the tears from her cheeks and unconsciously began to fluff her hair. "And to learn some new ones."

Nineteen:
High-Protein
Smoothie

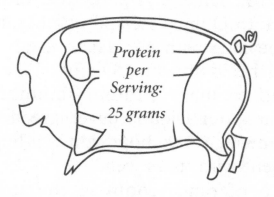

Protein per Serving:

25 grams

On Monday morning, James once again found himself seated at a table across from Deputy Harding. It was five past nine and the rest of supper club members had just completed signing what they all hoped would be their final statements for the Hudsonville County Sheriff's Department. However, Sheriff Jones reminded them several times that some or all of them would likely be called to testify in court, should Mitch Walker refuse to fully confess to his crimes.

"How is he doing?" James asked the deputy once he had added his signature to the typewritten statement and stood.

Harding shrugged. "He isn't feeling too great, but he's going to be fit enough to have to answer a mess of questions in a day or two."

Sheriff Jones waited for James and Harding in the hallway. "I know you all have to get back to Quincy's Gap," she began, "but after speaking with Ms. Hanover about her goal to build muscle, Deputy Neely was inspired to make protein smoothies for everyone. Your friends have agreed to our refreshments, so we hope you will linger for a moment with us as well."

The conference room in the sheriff's department felt packed to capacity. Not only were Lindy, Bennett, Lucy, and Gillian standing inside the room holding Styrofoam tumblers, but Bob Barker, Hailey, and Felicity were there as well. Scattered here and there, in their brown and khaki uniforms, were men and women from the department, sipping smoothies or helping to bring refills in from the kitchen. As soon as James entered the crowded room, Lucy put a cup in his hands.

"It's a berry smoothie," she explained.

"Deputy Neely is interested in trying the protein diet I've been following." She frowned. "Not that I've stuck to it over the last few days, but I'm going back on, starting today."

James took a hesitant sip of thick, pink liquid. It tasted like creamy sherbet. "This is too tasty to be healthy. What's in it?"

"Fresh blueberries, bananas, strawberries, raspberry-flavored frozen yogurt, whey protein, and some fruit juice," Lucy answered. "Even though Eleanor let us stay an extra night at Fox Hall, I knew we were going to have an early start today, so I thought it would be nice to wake up and have a good source of energy."

James dropped into a seat next to Gillian, who was sliding a raffle ticket across the table to Felicity. "This is for you, my dear."

Felicity looked surprised. "What is it?"

Lindy swooped over from where she was arranging a tray of smoothies and grabbed the ticket. "Gillian! *You* have the winning ticket?" She waved the stub in her right hand. "This is for a brand new RV from R. C.'s company! That's so cool!"

Gillian shook her head. "It's my *partner's* new camper." She gazed fondly at Felicity. "You're going to need this when you take the Yuppie Puppy obedience classes on the road. I've already been in touch with two other grooming facilities, and they'd like you to run training classes for their clients as well. I can't have one of my employees sleeping out of a tent. How would that make me look?" She fluffed her hair and shot a flirtatious look at Harding. "Not that I don't *personally* revel in nights spent beneath the moon, with the open air breathing across my *naked* skin, but you've got to regain your professional footing. This is a start on that journey."

Felicity stared at the raffle ticket, which Lindy had placed reverently in front of the dog trainer's folded hands. "Gillian. This is much too generous."

"You and I were meant to meet this weekend," Gillian told Felicity, her voice trembling with emotion. "Because of your kindness, you sheltered two lost and frightened women. Your destiny came full circle when you aided the girlfriend of the man who tried to ruin you. Now, karma and I shall join together to show you that you are worthy of great success and happiness." She dabbed at her moist eyes with a tissue. "Besides, I can't *wait to* see the Yuppie Puppy's logo painted on that camper. There's *nothing* more thrilling for me than to venture into new entrepreneurial territory. And don't worry about R. C.; I've already called to tell him that you possess the winning ticket."

"Thank you, Gillian," Felicity whispered gratefully. "I can't wait to relocate to Quincy's Gap. From all that you've told me, it must be a charming town."

"You got that right!" Bennett declared. "And we've got the best diner in the Valley," he added. "Dolly's. We're talking *real* homemade cookin'. Dolly's serves a meatloaf so tender that you wanna cry, with a side of mashed potatoes so smooth you'd think they were mixed with cream from heaven, and a pile of butter beans that pop in your mouth with a shout of hallelujah! If you like that kind of grub, then you'll be glad you moved."

Sheriff Jones strode over to Bennett's side. "Did you say Dolly's Diner?"

"Yes, ma'am, I did."

"I ate there a few years ago when I was passing through Quincy's Gap, and I can still remember that establishment's homemade pecan pie." The lovely lawwoman rolled her eyes at the memory. "What I wouldn't give to have some of Dolly's coffee and pie."

"Well, when all this mess is straightened out, I'd sure love to invite you to be my guest for pie and coffee." Bennett shifted nervously. "And maybe some dinner before dessert?"

Allowing herself a small smile, the sheriff nodded. "I'd enjoy that, Mr. Marshall."

"There's one condition, though," Bennett added with a nervous cough.

The sheriff looked intrigued. "A condition? What might that be?"

"I might need you to quiz me on some trivia durin' our date. See, I'm takin' the test to be a contestant on *Jeopardy!* and I've only got two weeks left to prepare. Every wakin' moment has got to be filled with facts and statistics." He cleared his throat. "Is that a complete turnoff, uh, Ms. Jones?" He said her name with a breathless whisper.

Her smile grew larger. "Oh, quite the opposite, Mr. Marshall. Quite the opposite." Trailing a finger seductively across his chest, the sheriff left the room.

Bennett sank into the nearest chair. "I do believe that woman just set me on fire."

Giggling, Lindy handed him another smoothie. "That is *exactly* how I feel every time I see my Luis." She checked her watch. "I can't wait to get back home and tell him all about our adventures!"

At that moment, two gentlemen dressed in light gray suits entered the room. They shook hands with the deputies and made their way toward Hailey, who was leaning against one of the back walls as Bob shared his barbecued salmon grilling techniques with Harding.

Instinctively, James and his friends grew silent. With the exception of Gillian, who hadn't been on Fox Hall's back porch the day the rest of them had met Jimmy Lang, the supper club members all recognized the businessmen as the representatives for Heartland Foods. Even though they had been wearing polo shirts and khakis during lunch that day, the small heart pins attached to their suits easily identified them. They had worn those same pins on their shirt collars as they dined at Fox Hall.

"Uh, Ms. Lang?" the first man asked as he approached Hailey.

"My name's Hailey Mellon. Jimmy and I never got hitched, so you don't have to lay his name on me, thank you."

The man stuck out his hand. "My name's Dan Bicknell, and I'm here to congratulate you on winning the title of Hog Fest Barbecue Champion."

Hailey, who was modestly dressed for the first time since James had met her — in a white, scoop-neck T-shirt that covered her ample cleavage and a long, blue skirt of crinkled cotton — smiled at the two men. "You must've nearly fell over when you realized that y'all were gonna have to offer that contract to a woman."

"And a fine looking woman at that," the second man said, trying to sound as though he hadn't been floored by the announcement that the winner was female.

"Just don't look her over too closely," Bob pretended to protest. "This is my future wife you're talkin' to here."

James noticed that Hailey was wearing her engagement ring. In fact, she raised her left hand and proudly wiggled the piece of jewelry so that the light caused it to twinkle like dozens of tiny mirrors.

The two men from Heartland Foods exchanged relieved looks. "Ms. Mellon? This might seem like an unusual question, but will you be taking your husband's name when you get married?"

Hailey shrugged. "Hadn't thought about it, but since I've never had a man offer his name to me before, I think I sure will become Mrs. Bob Barker." She smiled adoringly at Bob. "I've never had a man do all the things you've done for me, darlin'."

Mr. Bicknell grinned at the pair. "Seeing as how you two are going to be starting a new life together, how do you feel about being the *joint* faces of Heartland Foods barbecue line?"

"Kind of like the First Couple of Barbecue," the second added quickly, his eyes shining with excitement. "I can almost see the labels on our sauces and rubs. Both of you, wearing denim overalls and standing in front of a cooker with a slab of glistening ribs grilling over a low flame."

Hailey grabbed Bob's hand. "I'd love it. We gonna do everythin' as a team from now on. And I'm not going back to Texas — not ever — so you can reach me usin' Bob's number from now on."

"Don't you have things there you want?" Bob seemed surprised by Hailey's proclamation.

"Nope. The 'partment lease runs out this month, and all I care about is my gran's quilt and my photo albums. The landlady will send 'em to me if I let her sell all our junk. She's a good soul."

Bob shrugged and then licked his lips greedily. "What about Jimmy's new RV?"

Hailey waved him off. "I've already gotten rid of that. Now, I know you liked that big, fancy camper, Bob, but that thang gives me the creeps. Jimmy *died* in there, 'member?" She stroked her fiancé's shoulder. "We got a world of riches, baby. We got the cash prize from the contest, this here contract, and each other. We've got everythin' I'd ever dreamed of."

Confused by the exchange between Hailey and Bob, Mr. Bicknell turned to Harding. "We've got a flight to catch, Deputy. Do you think we could speak to these folks in private before we go? We've got contracts and such for them to see," he added as though the legal paperwork was something distasteful. "Do you have a room we could use?"

"Sure thing. Follow me, everyone."

As Hailey passed by James, she hugged him briefly and whispered an emotional thank-you in his ear. "Bob couldn't have saved me without your help. You're the hero that was backin' up my hero." She pressed something into James's hand. "A sweet lil' orange-haired birdie told me you might spread some good with this. I sure hope so. Bless you, James Henry."

Hailey then proceeded to hug, kiss, and bless the rest of the supper club members. In a much more reserved fashion, Bob shook everyone's hands, promised that they'd all be invited to his and Hailey's wedding next spring, and then followed Mr. Bicknell and his partner from the room.

James finished the last slurp of his

smoothie and dropped his cup in the trash. He unfolded the thin, pink piece of paper crumpled in his left hand. It was the title to Jimmy's trailer, which had been registered in both Jimmy and Hailey's name. Using a round, bubbly script, Hailey had signed it over to the Shenandoah County Public Library. On the line identifying the sale price, Hailey had carefully penned "charitable donation."

Speechless, James gaped and stared at Gillian's orange hair. Finally, he bent over and waved the title under her nose. "Do you . . . ? How did you . . . ?"

Gillian smiled indulgently at him. "Hailey didn't want to have anything to do with Jimmy's camper. She was looking for a quick and easy solution to be rid of it and the idea to donate it to the library just *blossomed* in my mind out of nowhere. If you were able to get a hold of someone who does custom work on recreational vehicles, such as Richter's RV Sales & Rentals, then you could *transform* the camper into something much more beneficial . . ." She trailed off and allowed James to picture her meaning.

"As in a bookmobile," James breathed, overawed at his sudden good fortune. "Yes!" His mind raced with excitement. "I could use the donations we've received for a new vehicle toward making the necessary alterations. That means we'll only have to rely on Wendell's old school bus until R. C. can work some magic on our new bookmobile."

"Precisely." Gillian sighed in contentment. "You see, James. There are no coincidences. We were all meant to meet these particular fellow beings and to walk away *changed* by our interaction with them. Everything that happened here was predestined." She gestured theatrically at the ceiling. "It was *all* written in the stars."

James looked back at the title in his hands. "I guess wishing on those twinkling balls of gas really does pay off." He then touched his friend on the arm. "Thank you, Gillian. Hundreds of patrons will benefit because of what you suggested to Hailey. You saved our bookmobile program. It's practically the heart and soul of our library."

Gillian shook her head. "No, James. *You're* the heart and soul of that library. And all of Quincy's Gap knows it."

Flushed with embarrassment, James tucked the title into his pocket. He checked his watch, his visions filled with the upcoming transformation of Jimmy's luxurious RV into the most cutting-edge bookmobile in all of western Virginia. James interrupted Bennett's conversation with Deputy Neely about the upcoming Virginia Tech football season by saying, "It's time to hit the road, Bennett. I'm ready to go home."

The Fitzgerald twins knew that their boss wouldn't make it into work until close to lunchtime, and they had trouble going about their tasks with their usual amount of fervor due to their curiosity over exactly how the unpleasant events in Hudsonville had turned out. When James had phoned them at home to say that he would be late and that they would have to open the library, he had sounded elated. However, their boss had claimed that he was in too much of a hurry to explain the source of his good mood or provide more details about his plan to catch Martin Trotman engaging in illicit activities within the hallowed halls (or restroom) of the Shenandoah County Library.

Francis was the first to spot James's old white Bronco pulling into the parking lot. James breezed in, clutching a Polaroid facedown in one hand and the battered briefcase from his days as a professor at William & Mary in the other.

"Gentlemen." His face was beaming. "Gather 'round."

"What's that a photo of, Professor?" Scott

pointed at the Polaroid.

James flipped the picture upright and the twins gazed at an enormous recreational vehicle. "I come bearing excellent news. This is Hailey, our new bookmobile."

"Whoa!" Francis leaned over the photo until his heavy glasses slid down his nose. "How did you manage this, Professor?"

"It was donated to our library," James answered. "I'll tell you the whole story later. Right now, let's get down to brass tacks over how we're going to coerce our teenage criminal into confession. Show me your surveillance gadgets."

Scott rubbed his hands together and elbowed his brother at the same time. "Bro, don't we have the coolest job?"

Several hours later, once James had finally turned off the lights and locked the library's front door, he slid into his Bronco and headed for Main Street.

"You must be as tired as me, old girl," he said, affectionately rubbing the worn leather of the steering wheel, "But we've got one more thing to do before we go home."

As James climbed the stairs to Murphy's second-floor apartment, he felt a growing sadness at the realization that he was probably ascending to her door for the last time.

He thought about how many summer evenings he had practically leapt up the stairs, taking them two at a time, in his eagerness to see his girlfriend. Today, he trudged up each one and even his knock was tinged with regret. As though sensing who stood on her front mat, Murphy took several moments to respond to his knock.

She opened the door slowly, a halfhearted smile of greeting on her face. "I thought I might see you tonight," she said in a heavy voice. "At least you've come to tell me in person. I hate being dumped over the phone." When James didn't speak, she stared at him for a few moments, perhaps hoping that he would argue the reason for his visit, and gestured for him to come inside. "Would you like some wine?" she asked.

"No, thank you." James looked around at the neat, familiar living room. He had always felt comfortable in Murphy's home. He liked her sense of orderliness and how she had decorated each room using neutral tones. Her beiges and creamy coffee colors were highlighted with bright splashes of the primary hues in the pillows, table runner, and still-life paintings she bought from local artists.

Looking over her place, James suddenly

became aware that he didn't want to go back to living in his boyhood bedroom. He'd like a place of his own, where he could listen to music without hearing his father's blistering commentary on every song, where he could choose what show to watch on television, and where he could entertain his friends without clearing it with Jackson first.

Murphy had disappeared during James's musing. She now returned from the doorway of her spare bedroom, which also served as a home office, with a shopping bag in one hand and a rectangular box in the other. She dropped the bag by her feet and held the box out to him, as though it was a valuable offering.

"This is the book. The first one, that is," she added sheepishly. "You can read it if you like."

James kept his hands down at his sides. "It's too late for that, Murphy."

Murphy placed the box on a table, tears forming in her eyes. "I'm sorry. I guess I wanted it all. The paper, the book, and you. But it didn't work out how I hoped it would."

"It could have." James felt anger stirring but fought to quell it. This was not the time to assign blame. They had moved beyond that point now. "You should have trusted me, Murphy. We never stood a chance once you told me about the book. You should have explained what you were doing before you signed a contract."

"I should have?" Murphy was doubtful. "Are you telling me that you would have supported my work, knowing that I was writing about you and your friends?"

James shrugged. "I don't know. Maybe I would have read some and protested about certain things. Maybe I would have begged you not to submit the manuscript for publication. I don't know what I would have done, and now we'll never know, because you didn't trust me. Without trust, there's no point in us being together."

Murphy fell silent and then reluctantly nodded. "I know." She picked up the shopping bag and handed it to him. "This is just some stuff you kept around here. I almost stole your *Best Country Duets* CD," she teased morosely. "But I can get my own copy."

Digging the CD out of the bag, James set it on the coffee table. "It's yours."

"So . . . are you going to talk to me anymore?" Murphy asked after a brief hesitation. "I mean, I don't want you to say the *we can be friends* line, but are we going to be civil? Friend*ly,* at least?"

"Of course. We're Southerners, remember?" James joked and then took a step toward her and gave her a tender kiss on the cheek. "There are no hard feelings, Murphy. I still want you to succeed in all you do. I don't know how I'm going to feel about that book when it's released, but I'll deal with that when the time comes. That's the best I can offer right now."

"Fair enough." Murphy squeezed his hand and walked him to the door. Part of him longed to wipe away the twin tears racing down her chin, but he let them fall undisturbed. "Good night, James Henry," Murphy whispered and then closed her door.

James sat in his Bronco for a moment, grieving the loss of the happiness he had felt with Murphy Alistair. He stared up at her building, at her bedroom window, and at the sheer, white curtains that billowed in the breeze like a pair of tethered ghosts. When the light came on in the room, James started his engine and drove into the night.

Twenty:
Celebratory
Tiramisu

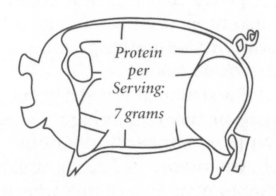

Protein per Serving: 7 grams

By Friday afternoon, James and the Fitzgerald brothers did their best to appear as though the evening shift at the Shenandoah County Library was business as usual. Scott and Francis had outdone themselves in regard to wiring the men's restroom with a tiny camera. Scott, who wired the camera to a computer set up in the custodial closet, was now manning the "control center," and Francis was shelving books. The twins had played rock, paper, scissors to determine who had to sit in the lightless closet on surveillance duty and who got to replace stray books. Francis, who had his paper cut by Scott's scissors twice in a row, lost with grace.

The regular crowd of high school seniors had returned, including nerdy Harris and Martin's short-skirted female assistant, but along with these two regulars, James noticed that there were half a dozen college-aged kids he had never seen before and a few additional twenty-somethings milling about the magazine section.

Harris had stationed himself at one of the computers in the Technology Corner and was trying to appear innocuous. James watched with interest as Francis walked over to the young man and calmly whispered to him behind his shoulder. Harris's eyes snapped open in alarm, and then he gathered his things and stood, briefly shaking Francis's hand on his way out. When Francis turned to James and issued a contrite shrug, James sent him a thumbs-up, letting the twin know that he heartily approved of giving Harris a chance at a clean slate. After all, both the Fitzgerald brothers and their boss knew what it was like to be a bookish and shy high school boy desperate to be accepted by the popular crowd.

Sometimes we act really dumb in the search for acceptance, James thought. And though he wasn't looking to punish the wayward teens, James wanted them to learn a lesson they'd never forget so that they'd stop using illegal and potentially dangerous drugs.

It didn't take long for the noise level inside the library to rise to the point where the older patrons began to cast searching looks in James's direction. Mrs. Waxman, who refused to take the evening off and miss all the excitement, made a cursory sweep through the magazine section, frowning and shushing as she breezed by. The teens quieted momentarily and then resumed their raucous banter with renewed vigor as the elderly librarian returned to the information desk.

Finally, when James feared that Martin was truly going to spend the evening absorbed in the library's September issue of *Bon Appétit,* Martin whispered into the ear of the giggling blonde seated beside him and sauntered off to the lobby. This was the point at which James would know whether his guess as to Martin's destination was correct. The young man could linger in the lobby, or he could turn, as James supposed, and enter the men's restroom. Nodding briefly to Francis, James pretended to busy himself on the computer at the circulation desk, but all he did was scroll up and down Yahoo!'s home page while his heart thumped loudly in his chest. Seconds later, one of the college students also left the magazine area, and James waited impatiently, reading the weekend's forecast several times over. It looked like much-needed rain was on its way.

At last, Scott emerged from the janitor's closet and slipped behind the circulation desk. "I saw the deal, Professor. Martin handed that other kid a snack-sized plastic baggie and the guy gave him some money. Martin pocketed the money and then made a mark on a piece of paper. Looks like he's got several people waiting to buy from him tonight."

"Could you tell what was in the baggie?" James whispered.

Scott shook his head. "Not exactly. The film quality's too grainy, and it was kind of small. I couldn't even see how much money Martin took in."

"My beloved library is being ill-used." James scowled. "That's one young man who could get mighty sick off those drugs if it's the same laced stuff Donny Trotman hoped to buy from Jimmy Lang. Time for part two of the plan. Alert Francis and Mrs.

Waxman."

Scott walked purposely toward Francis and handed him a book to be reshelved. The book was *Old Yeller,* and it was code that part two was taking place. Francis then handed Mrs. Waxman a copy of *Spot Goes to School* to be returned to the children's section. Mrs. Waxman issued a satisfied smile and bustled off. James watched his devoted employees as he dialed Lucy's cell phone number. She answered immediately and promised to come right over.

It was at that moment that James saw the college student who had been Martin's first customer return to the magazine section. He elbowed one of his buddies, took the magazine from his hands, and sank into the upholstered chair his friend had vacated. He looked quite pleased with himself.

"Hurry, Lucy," James muttered as Martin's second customer headed for the bathroom.

Scott lingered for a few minutes at the Tech Corner and then disappeared into the closet again. James abandoned the circulation desk and dashed into his office, just in time to see Lucy's sheriff's cruiser pull into the parking lot. Something about the sight of her in uniform, opening the rear door so that all three of her monstrously large German shepherds could exit the car, flooded James with relief. Lucy said she knew exactly how to handle the situation at the library, and James had complete faith in her.

Lucy led her dogs straight into the library, bypassing the restrooms, and met James at the circulation desk. They exchanged casual small talk and James did his best not to try to gauge the reaction of the cluster of students in the magazine section who were now sharing a space with a member of the local law enforcement and her enormous canines.

"These guys have been out on patrol and are super thirsty," Lucy said, her voice well above a whisper as she gestured at Bono, Benatar, and Bon Jovi. "Do you have a bowl or something I can use for water?"

"Sure thing," James gave his scripted answer. "In the custodial closet out in the lobby. You can fill the bowl up in the rest-room. I'll show you."

"Thanks," Lucy said, and she turned away, the dogs trailing her with bright, eager eyes and open mouths. All three of them seemed to be smiling in anticipation, their pink tongues hanging over a row of pointy teeth.

Lucy paused for a minute at the open door of the closet, but it was long enough to her to witness the exchange between Martin and his second customer. Unfortunately, one of the dogs saw something exciting out the front door and issued a single, resounding bark. On Scott's computer screen, the two young men looked at one another in apprehension. The customer hastened to exit the restroom while Martin retreated into a stall. His friend gestured for him to hurry and they both left the bathroom, coming to an abrupt halt before the black muzzles of three snarling hounds.

"Hello, gentleman." Lucy raised her eyebrows and allowed her dogs a few additional inches of leash.

The college student looked terrified, but Martin did his best to maintain his customary look of nonchalance.

"Do you smell something?" Lucy asked her dogs and they barked in a unified response. Lucy narrowed her eyes at the two boys standing before her. "You wouldn't be carrying anything my K-9 officers would be interested in, now would you?"

The college student paled but remained silent.

"Like a bone?" Martin scoffed.

Lucy gave the dogs even more slack. The college student inched backward toward the restroom. "N-no," he whimpered, his eyes

431

never leaving the three sets of flashing white teeth aimed directly at his crotch.

"Let's just see about that, shall we?" Lucy released one of the dogs completely from its tether. "Seek, Bono, seek."

The shepherd with the blackest coat made a beeline for the college student. After sniffing up and down the legs of his pants one time, the young man shrieked like a little girl assaulted by a spider and then plunged his hands into his hooded sweatshirt, which bore the Greek letters of a fraternity, and tossed the plastic baggie he had acquired from Martin onto the ground. "Here! Get him away from me! Get him away!"

Lucy took a step forward and reclaimed Bono. She made no move toward the package on the floor. "You," she ordered the college student. "Go back and sit with your friends. Tell them no one is free to leave without my say-so."

As the shaken young man scuttled back into the library, Martin shoved his hands into the pockets of his leather jacket. "You can search me, lady. I'm clean."

Ignoring him, Lucy opened the restroom door and gestured for Martin to follow her inside. She then held her finger out to James, indicating that he should remain in the lobby.

James immediately jerked open the door to the janitor's closet so that he could see what Lucy planned to do, but was surprised to see that Scott's computer screen was filled with snow. "What happened?" he asked anxiously.

"Ms. Hanover told Martin to pull the camera out of the ceiling." Scott replied in shock. "What is she doing in there?"

"I can't imagine," James answered and began to pace around the lobby.

He didn't have long to wait for Lucy, however, for she re-emerged from the bathroom just in time to greet Deputy Glenn as he strode through the front door. "The goods are under the ceiling tile above the second toilet," she told him. "Martin's inside. He'll show you."

Donning his sternest expression, Glenn brushed by Lucy and stormed into the bathroom. A minute later, he led Martin out. James noticed that the teen was handcuffed and seemed close to tears. His head was bowed and his tread was so reluctant that Glenn had to practically drag him from the lobby to the front door.

"What did you say to Martin in there?" James asked Lucy once Glenn and his captive were outside.

"All I did was have him rip down the

camera," Lucy said with a smirk. "Then, I told him there were no witnesses and my dogs were very, very hungry. He told me he's been selling pot and fake IDs all summer and that his cousin Donny was his supplier. He also told me that there's very little real pot left in those bags because Donny was unable to provide him with a fresh supply. Apparently, Martin's mixed traces of pot with tea leaves, tobacco from the inside of cigarettes, and some of his own Ritalin." She shook her head. "What an idiot! Good thing we got the stuff before anyone actually smoked it. They could have gotten really sick!"

She stroked the heads of her dogs. "Listen, I'm gonna speak to the rest of the kids in there," she said. "But at the end of my little lecture, I'm gonna let them go. We've got nothing on them, except for the two who paid Martin, and we can only question them if Martin gives us their names." She turned to Scott and put a hand on his shoulder. "You did a fine job with this setup, Scott. You and your brother are mighty talented. You tell Francis I said so, will you?"

Scott's cheeks flushed with pleasure. As he watched Lucy enter the main room of the library, he cast a sideways glance at his boss. "She's so cool, Professor."

James watched his friend march toward the magazine section. "I've always thought so."

Just before the library closed for the evening, an unusual thing happened. Jackson Henry called his son at work for the first time since James had become the head librarian.

"Can you stay outta the house for a bit longer tonight?" Jackson asked in as nice as tone as he could muster.

"Sure, Pop," James replied, perplexed. He couldn't keep himself from asking, "How come?"

"Just find something to do!" Jackson roared and hung up.

Wondering what had made his father so agitated, James called Bennett and asked if he'd like to be quizzed.

"Only if we can do it over some cold beers," Bennett answered. "Jade is comin' for dinner tomorrow and I'm having a mess of trouble concentratin' on European History when all I wanna do is dream about her sittin' across the table from me."

"Don't worry," James assured him. "I'll pick up a six-pack on my way over."

James spent the following two hours asking Bennett a barrage of questions using a trivia website Bennett routinely turned to in preparation for the *Jeopardy!* tryouts, which would be taking place the next week. After finishing his second beer and the website's segment on migrating birds, James decided to make his way home before he was tempted into opening another beer.

Driving through the quiet streets of Quincy's Gap, James rolled the window down and stuck his arm into the cool, summer night air. There was the scent of change in the breezes that blew inside the Bronco and circulated around James's face. He detected the expectant aroma of one season taking over while another faded into the past. The thought of autumn inspired James. When the Sunday paper arrived, he would begin looking for a small house to rent. Someplace close to work, but with a yard where he could plant a small garden and hang up some birdhouses. Perhaps he would plant an apple tree. Maybe he would adopt a pet.

James was so busy conjuring images of his future home that he almost walked right past the painting propped on the kitchen table. However, he stopped short as he realized that the two candle tapers burning were the only source of light in the room and that the dinner dishes were still piled in the sink.

The flickering light illuminated the small painting that James readily recognized as being one of his father's creations. Like the other paintings Jackson had completed over the summer months, this one also featured hands as its subject. On the left side of the painting was a woman's hand. It was petite and soft, and there was a slight dusting of flour over the first and second knuckles. James recognized the gold charm bracelet that Milla always wore dangling from the wrist. The hand reached out, as though to take something offered by the second hand.

The hand on the right side of the painting was turned palm upward. In the center of the palm, which was wrinkled and criss-crossed with a multitude of lines engraved in the flesh through the course of a long life, was a wedding band. At the bottom of the canvas where Jackson normally signed his name, were the words, *Will You?*

Jackson had asked Milla to marry him using this painting.

James put his hand over his heart, over-whelmed at the tenderness expressed in the painting. As he sat down at the kitchen table, staring at his father's finest work, he noticed that a piece of cake, a clean fork, a folded napkin, and a small note had been left on the table for him to find.

Dear James,

There's barbecued brisket leftovers in the fridge if you're hunry. I was inspired by your trip to Hog Fest and I do believe that I could hold my own in any BBQ contest with this recipe. You don't even need a grill to make it! I think your father proposed just so I'd cook that brisket for him again! I saved a piece of our tiramisu dessert for you. Seems it turned into an engagement cake, for I said "yes" to your daddy, of course. My heart is filled with delight over being asked to join this family. See you in the morning, my dear.

Love,
Milla

Though James wasn't hungry, he took several bites of the dessert in honor of his father's engagement to the lovely Milla. He swallowed the sweet, creamy cake and gazed at the painting. Then, after blowing out the candles, he went back outside. Jackson and Milla deserved privacy on a night such as this, so James returned to the Bronco and retrieved his cell phone, wondering whom to call in hopes of borrowing a spare bed and perhaps a toothbrush.

He pressed one of his speed-dial numbers,

expecting to hear Bennett's voice pick up, but Lucy answered his call instead.

"Hello, James," she said. She sounded surprised, but pleasantly so.

"I'm sorry to call so late," he said. "But I need a favor."

"Anything for you," Lucy replied without waiting for him to explain the situation. "But you already know that, James."

MILLA'S AMAZING
OVEN-BARBECUED BRISKET

1 (3- to 4-pound) beef brisket
1 teaspoon garlic powder
1 teaspoon onion salt
1 teaspoon celery salt
1/4 cup apple juice
2 tablespoons Worcestershire sauce
1/2 teaspoon liquid smoke
Dry rub (Milla uses *Emeril's Original Essence* spice or *Napa Valley Spicy American Barbecue Rub,* but use any kind you like)
1/2 cup store-bought barbecue sauce of your choice (Milla uses *KC Masterpiece — Original)*

Trim the fat from the brisket. Mix the garlic powder, onion salt, celery salt, apple juice, Worcestershire sauce, and liquid smoke in a small bowl. Using a flavor/marinade injector, inject the liquid mixture into the brisket (at an angle works best). You won't use it all, so discard the rest. Sprinkle the rub generously on the meat and pat it into the surface. Brush on the barbecue sauce (Milla just spreads it around with her fingers) and wrap the meat in heavy-duty aluminum foil. Place it in a roasting pan and chill for 8 hours. Bake in a preheated 300-degree oven for 5 hours or until a meat thermometer reads 190 degrees. Let stand for 5 to 10 minutes and then cut the brisket on a slant (against the grain) into thin slices. Serve with a small bowl of warmed barbecue sauce on the side.

ACKNOWLEDGMENTS

The author would like to thank Holly, Mary, and Anne for donating their time and wisdom in order to make the Flab Five better; Karl Anderson, Barbara Moore, and the Midnight Ink team; Jessica Faust at Book-Ends; Mark and Travis of the Short Pump Midas for explaining large engine mechanics; the fine folks at the Short Pump Panera (my café office); Kathy Watson of the Victoria Public Library, Virginia, for sharing interesting stories about things she's witnessed in her career as librarian; my Cozy Chicks friends (Diana Killian, Karen MacInerney, Michele Scott, Maggie Sefton, Heather Webber, and Kate Collins); Lelia Taylor of Creatures 'n Crooks Bookshoppe for hand-selling the supper club books; my family for living with someone whose mind is elsewhere half the time; and you, dear reader, for befriending the Flab Five and spending a few hours with them. I'm in your debt.

ABOUT THE AUTHOR

J. B. Stanley has a BA in English from Franklin & Marshall College, an MA in English Literature from West Chester University, and an MLIS from North Carolina Central University. She taught sixth grade language arts in Cary, North Carolina, for the majority of her eight-year teaching career. Raised an antique lover by her grandparents and parents, Stanley also worked part-time in an auction gallery. An eBay junkie and food lover, Stanley now lives in Richmond, Virginia, with her husband, two young children, and three cats. Visit her website at www.jbstanley.com.